About the Author

John Clegg was born in Crosby, Isle of Man in January 1948.
His family moved to Ludlow Shropshire mid 1950. He
attended Ludlow Grammar school and later went on to obtain
an honours degree, reading Humanities at Surrey University.
After a spell with Kodak, he succumbed to the wish of
becoming self-employed and moved to north Lancashire. It
was here he was introduced to Peter Hayes, father of Paul,
sometimes known as Mr. Morecambe and thus began his
antique dealing career, the majority of it spent back in
Ludlow, selling largely, period furniture to the trade. After
thirty years, even though by now, having got the hang of it, he
sold his shop and bought a house in Istria, Croatia, where he
now spends much of his time.

Dedication

The marvellous Mrs. Bodenham, who taught at East Hamlet junior school, Ludlow, Shropshire and encouraged me to write stories and the equally marvellous Fred Reaves, who taught at Ludlow Grammar school and helped fire my passion for history.

John Clegg

THE TELLER

AUSTIN MACAULEY PUBLISHERS™

LONDON • CAMBRIDGE • NEW YORK • SHARJAH

A CIP catalogue record for this title is available from the British Library.

ISBN 9781398408746 (Paperback)
ISBN 9781398408753 (ePub e-book)

www.austinmacauley.com

First Published 2021
Austin Macauley Publishers Ltd ™
1 Canada Square, Canary Wharf
London
E14 5AA
+44 (0)20 7038 8212
+44 (0)20 3515 0352

Acknowledgements

Thanks due to Austin Macauley Publishers.
Also thanks to the internet, for Google Maps and endless details regarding flora and fauna etc.
A mention and also thanks to Nathan Madera, production coordinator at Austin Macauley, who patiently made my last minute, small but necessary, amendments.

Part 1

Chapter One

The fire in the centre of the hall had become a huge fearsome blaze with flames like leaping spirits crackling sparks aloft to die in the smoke as its glowing heart amid the circle of bronzed faces cast monster shadows of those at the back of the Great Hall standing and feeling for more favourable places to sit. Faces and dark places flickered to life at random, before being plunged back into gloom as the fire seemed to take on a life of its own.

Apart from scraps left for the men to pick over, the main feasting was done. There was beer of course, but no longer supplied by willowy figures swaying through the throng topping up horn beakers from the jug. This was now an all-male gathering, free to help themselves from the vat, but even in this warrior world there were limits. Respect was demanded by the upper echelon, was avidly sought by all as a life mission and so pity the man who faltered or fell down drunk before all the night's proceedings had been completed. To gain respect here was a long tough process and to lose it, all too easy.

There had been exhibitions of sword play, which even though only mock battles could become over heated and draw blood, trials of strength, arm wrestling to decide whether last year's champion was still, 'The Ox!' and music from flute, reedpipes and drum to which the prettiest maidens in their finest attire, enjoying the hunger in men's eyes, had danced to in practiced unison. Once these had flitted from the hall like a long colourful ribbon there had been a short drama based around a recent comic entanglement and the butt of their joke had had no choice other than to take it in good part by joining in the roars of laughter. He received a few slaps on the back, proving he still belonged, part of the tribe, respect not quite in tatters and gradually the noise simmered down as they settled to await the storyteller.

He walked in with robe flowing and mounted what had been specially provided out of respect for his status, a small wooden platform. He went to sit down, but hesitated, picking up the stool as if searching for a possible treacherous hole in the floor or loose leg. Accompanying a narrowing of eyes, he held out a forefinger as if to say, 'I've heard all about you people.' A huge cheer went up.

His hair was grey, worn loosely tied in a casual manner, but with two thin plaits left dangling to frame a look of distinction life had chiseled on his face. A silver linked choker glinted warmly from his neck and the elaborate coloured stitching adorning front-edges and cuffs of his robe, set him aside from other men. He was allowed this artistic touch without his manhood being brought into question, as it added to the sense of theatre. From within one of the generous cuffs, a blackthorn wand appeared, being held and waved slowly, to gain full attention. My Lord. *He bowed to the chieftain.* Gentlemen, thank you all for inviting me here this evening to humbly tell my tale. I hope it raises a little mirth and holds enough interest not to have me tossed into the water trough as I'm told, happened to a previous Teller who didn't quite come up to the mark. *The roar of appreciation must have been heard way down in the valley. He raised his wand again.* Now I'm not here to tell you tales of the dragon, heroes that can fly, heroes that can beat an army single handed, have all limbs severed and yet by magic be restored for battle next day. No. I'm here to tell you deeds of your forefathers, stories of your heritage, of real people who lived right here in this your territory, before the knowledge came. In fact the story tells exactly how the knowledge came. I will tell it as it has been handed down through the generations and at times repeat the very words of Erdikun himself, as if he were here like a vision right before your eyes. *He held out the wand again and with head raised implored,* Bring me magic. The magic of words. Grant me the magic of words to paint pictures in the minds of these good people.

The tale starts with three homesteads, down in the very same valley to the east of where we now sit. Where present day hamlets and villages stand, yes there were houses, but nothing like the density of population we witness today, meaning there was not the same intense rivalry between tribes and communities for land and the bounty held therein. Not the same degree of political wrangling and bloodshed. That is not to say they didn't know how to take care of themselves, as will be evident as the tale unfolds. Houses and villages were protected from wolves, four and two legged, (*the Teller pause for cheer of appreciation*) by wooden palisades, but nothing like the elaborate deterrents and mighty showpieces of power we construct in present times. (*He gave a smile in the direction of the chieftain*) Also their tools and weapons, although fashioned from bronze and stone did not make them any less of a thinking, creative and at times courageous people than we have here in this hall tonight.

"Flint? Stone? You mean cavers!!" *came a youth's cry of derision from the back.*

If Erdikun could be here this moment he'd make you swallow those words. Consider yourself lucky he isn't! And now I think about it......did it never cross your mind that our lord and master of all he surveys, right here in this hall tonight, is directly descended, if but in a distant way, from these people of legend?

This reminder of what should have been obvious, brought a collective gasp. Senior advisors turned, hoping to spot the culprit and it wasn't hard to imagine wide-eyed alarm on a face drained of colour as it sank low as physically possible into a pair of hands in the dark. How could he have been so stupid as to indirectly insult the chieftain himself?

Trying to lighten the mood somewhat the Teller said, Just remember - manners, young man! They don't cost anything. *Order restored, with arms held out wide, he said loftily,* Picture the scene; a funeral pyre befitting a queen on that final voyage to the land of her ancestors, the fatted ox roasting, wailing sadness of the pipes, every type of food prepared and ready for the whole community there in attendance to pay their last respects. Midst it all stands Erdikun, tall, proud, last of his generation almost in a dream, lost in the memories of his sister and their humble beginnings; the battles to survive winter; the small houses that formed their simple community; the years in virtual servitude to the warlord up in his lofty camp where we now sit.

The Teller bowed again and said quietly and directly. I relate this with utmost respect, My Lord. *Those worthies, sitting alongside the chieftain, craned forward and on witnessing a wry smile slowly creeping, sat back with a sigh of relief.*

Erdikun's grandfather, Tollan, had chosen, what proved to be an ideal location to settle. It was beside a ford across a pretty stream, well within the shelter of main camp. He'd wondered why the location hadn't been taken before, until the clearing of tangled growth and saplings showed that in a way it had. He came across post remnants and a hearth long gone cold, evidence of earlier occupation. The people, having exhausted the surrounding land had moved on. The fact that apple and plum trees grew so conveniently nearby was further evidence and stands of holly guarding against the evil ones, either side of the main approach down which the north wind blew, confirmed his suspicions. Basic human nature doesn't really change and just as would happen today, curiosity got the better of the locals who wandered along to watch Tollan's endeavors and offer advice, whether sought after or not. The man was a paragon of diplomacy, however and in his slightly strange accent, simply thanked them for their warnings of poor soil and carried on regardless. He became to be known as a man of flint. Not in the sense of a razor, although having said that, no-one dared cross him, for he was solid, unyielding like a rock. His powers of endurance were legendary and he was also known as a man of thrift. It was said out of earshot that if pushed to it, he would go to the trouble of skinning moles with no more than a sharpened dog bone, rather than part with good bronze for a winter coat.

Locals who had advised against setting up home in that particular location and who had made it their business to be just happening by as harvest time approached, managed to hide their dismay at the sight. Rather than looking feeble, the crop, though modest was more luxuriant than anything they had ever produced. They were not informed that the contents of the middens, ancient and new, had been the reason for the miracle and had felt even more downcast when their pleas regarding retribution for the obvious collusion between Tollan and the evil ones - what else could explain such an abundant harvest? - had been rebuffed out of hand by the powers up on this hill. That's not to say the latter didn't keep an eye on him. All they could glean, however, was that he'd wandered into the eastern regions with just the clothes he stood up in and had been given work and food by a family living in the shadow of that grand summit where, he that now lords over all, we revere his name and yours my Lord, had his capital. It later came to light that his prodigious work rate made him an ideal candidate for what was referred to as 'good breeding' and so his new family had not been averse to a love match between him and their eldest daughter, Vana, especially as no dowry had been required.

They were not so enthusiastic, however, when hearing of their plans to venture west, but Vana, a clever, spirited girl,

15

was not at all daunted by the coming venture into the unknown. She had in fact looked forward to it, visibly glowing at her good fortune. Not only had this powerful man wandered in from out of nowhere to melt under her feminine charms, but had been rendered slightly malleable, owing to his urgent need to become fluent in her language. All the tribes could converse by sign language, but as you know it has its limitations and hardly satisfies minds hungry to share hopes and visions. One can hardly experience that glow of satisfaction, that sense of coming alive, with basic hunter-warrior sign language.

Those in power, looking down from here in their aerie began to take even greater interest in the settlers, on them becoming the first to daub paint on their hut walls, starting what can only be called a new fashion across the valley. Information then filtered up that the stream they had settled beside, had had part of its flow diverted to run down a freshly hewn channel, not only for irrigation, but for the nurturing of fish in a newly dug pond.

An invitation was offered in the form of an armed escort and Tollan was marched up to the Great Hall. Here he charmed them with his unassuming manner and actually came away with a regular order for fish, smoked or fresh, provided a tenth part was offered in gratitude for the granting of such a generous royal warrant. The same imposition had been put on his harvest. As with all the harvests of the community in fact. He stood patiently listening, while yet again it was explained, the tithe was for the good of all, feeding not only the brave warrior elite that protected the people and kept the savages at bay, but the holy men, who by use of their mysterious knowledge, harnessed the power of the spirits for the good of all. It was in fact his patriotic duty, not only to the tribe, but to those in power, who having had such onerous duties thrust upon them, were merely extracting the tithe to do what was considered best for all. The tithe had started as a voluntary contribution and was still referred to as such, even though all volunteers now had no choice. Same as with the expectation to lay down one's life, if need be, in defence of tribal land, plus adherence to the edict stating, all young males should become proficient with spear, sling and arrow. The latter two requirements of course laid the basic foundations for what is expected today. Admiration of Tollan's enterprise and demeanor under scrutiny had led the chieftain, a fair-minded ruler, to act on impulse and provided he remained the main beneficiary, granted the man guardianship over the nearby Black and Offering Pools, functioning as what would be termed today, a fish bailiff. Tollan was wise enough to ensure any side deals were kept to a minimum and were not done with those residing close to home. What had been granted could just as easily be taken away.

By the time Erdikun, known simply as Erdi, was growing up, the settlement on the river bank had swollen to the massive three homesteads as mentioned earlier. You laugh, but as I said, folk back then were thinner on the ground. His father, Penda had a sister, Morga who in defiance of local tradition, when marrying a local man, Dowid, persuaded him to come and join her family, rather than the accepted custom of her leaving to live with his. I'm not losing you am I? Penda and his sister Morga, despite having been born right there in the community, still hadn't completely thrown off the suspicions and mutterings about them not being true locals and so Morga had had no qualms as regards flying in the face of local time-honoured ways. Dowid liked their free-spirited attitude and healthy disregard for stifling convention and having a slightly rebellious side to his nature, jumped at the chance. He slotted into managing the fish and eel enterprise as he seemed to have a flair for it. They had four children that lived, but suffice to say for simplicity, their oldest boy, Dowin, nicknamed, Yanker was the bosom pal of Erdi. They were inseparable when growing up.

The third house was occupied by a young couple, Dommed and Inga, who attracted by the community's zest and enterprise had requested to join them. Penda and old Tollan had spent quite some time talking to them, bearing in mind so much hinged on everyone getting along and on judging them to be a potential credit, welcomed them to set up home. By tradition all families pitched in to help with both this and the clearing of fresh land. They had five children that lived, the eldest being Talia, quite a pretty girl, same age and close friend of Vanya.

Erdi had a younger brother Mardikun, known to his family as Mardi and of course there was also, his little sister Vanya. Erdi's mother, Mara, dark and slender had a genial untroubled look about her, but if her eyes happened to narrow with a piercing look of scrutiny, then beware, as her words could hit their target like the sting of a whip.

Erdi and Yanker from the outset took an interest in their fathers' duties and did their best to emulate them. They learnt to hunt, fish and farm, knowledge necessary for when supporting families of their own. Vanya and Talia, when playing with dolls, reproduced in their fantasies what their mothers did as a daily round and from an early age learnt to forage, bash tight bundles of clothing with a rock in the stream to wash them and then had brimmed with pride on finding they could do as their mothers managed daily, return home with a water pot carefully balanced on high without spilling a drop. On that first occasion, grandma Vana had welcomed her granddaughter at the enclosure gate with arms open wide and a smile on her face, almost as if it had been a rite of passage. So these good people weren't that much different from today really and their roundhouses were virtually the same, even down to the fact, some had storerooms and work spaces attached. They felt no need for defensive earthen walls and ditches, a simple palisade surrounding homes and stores, sufficing, plus beyond there was usually a stockade with a small roofed area to keep the animals in at night and whenever the snow lay heavy.

Erdi and Yanker took to their tasks avidly, proud to be classed as men, little realizing at the time, they would eventually be expected to strengthen their families' standing, by way of an approved marriage.

Yes, you've guessed it, there could be problems ahead. Erdi carried the spirit of granddad Tollan in his veins and was likely to prove troublesome come the day. His brother Mardi was different altogether. He could play for hours with the toy horse and cart Tollan had made him, completely oblivious to others in the room. Quiet as he was, however, he did have a strange tendency, sometimes blurting out observations so unexpected, they could stop a conversation dead. In fact in certain company, he could be an absolute liability. He had been only tiny when he'd shouted out, "Pooo muck!" recoiling from what one could only imagine was accidental seepage, as a neighbour's wife's rear end had loomed large to settle itself beside him. This had brought instant, if rather suppressed laughter, from his Uncle Dowid, Yanker and Erdi. Grandma Vana had ducked away from view, eyes brimming, but Penda and Mara had been non too pleased with their young lad and the woman in question hadn't seen the funny side either.

Erdi would talk quietly to his little brother in the shadows at night, fascinated to learn how his mind worked. Some of the odd ways he looked at life could have him rolling around in agony laughing. Mardi would smile weakly not understanding what had been so funny. He often asked Erdi to tell him stories, especially those about Zak and Big Hendi the giant. He never tired of them. Erdi loved his brother for just being who he was and was forever fearful he might be picked on, bullied for being different. He also loved his exciting little package of a sister, but was scared lest the malignant spirits, being jealous of her energy and passion, took the chance to harm her in some way. He didn't ever say, but he would channel his efforts for the chance to acquire scraps of bronze, no matter how tiny, to offer to Earth Mother up where the magic spring sparkled out clear sweet water. He prayed for the safety of his family, but most of all for Mardi and Vanya.

So their houses were roughly the same as yours, they ate virtually the same food and each house even had its own quare fella. Just like now they couldn't say the word - *he mouthed Brownie* - for fear of upsetting him. He would generally guard the home, but say the wrong thing and he could sour the milk, ransack the place in the night or even leave for good. I know some say they don't exist, but I don't share that point of view. Tell me. How can you drop something right by your foot and it end up way over by the door, hidden under something unless there was - *he whispered* - a Brownie at work?

So you might be thinking that their way of life was almost the same as now. Largely it was, but for one big difference, the might of **bronze**. Everyone needed it, but its arrival and magical conversion from rocks to metal was completely controlled and no-one could avail themselves of it other than by dealing with the chieftain sitting right here where we sit today. *He bowed yet again to the headman and paused. Seeing the hint of a smile from the old warrior's narrowing eyes, he continued.* Anyone caught trading with a bronze runner would have his belongings confiscated and home torched, before being forced to witness the smuggler being strung up at the border as a warning to others. Bronze meant power and with the resources of tin and copper becoming more and more sought after, the value of the metal soared to unsustainable heights.

More will be revealed as the tale unfolds, but beware feeling smug at their apparent naivety, as history can have a nasty habit of repeating itself. People can be lulled into the trap of thinking things go on forever, but of course they never do.

Before I return to Erdikun, in his sorrow at losing his sister Vanya; before I return to the scene of her funeral all those years ago up on this very hill, let me explain something. They of course spoke differently to you and I and they had some

20

pretty strange superstitions. Of course they did. But when I say their words, real or imagined, I'll not attempt to convey them in what would only sound like a stilted tone. This would portray them as archaic. They weren't. So when I attribute words and phrases to them they couldn't possibly have known back then, please be tolerant and allow some artistic license. I want to convey the fact your ancestors were vibrant and inventive, the best being equal in intelligence to anyone here and the worst - *he threw his voice to the back of the hall* - just as stupid! *There was a huge cheer and dull drumming of feet on the rush-strewn hard earth floor.*

I will take you back to the scene of Erdi aged and alone with his thoughts on the passing of Vanya. He'd had no stomach for the food on offer. Strange so much at such a sad occasion. Yet the people had kindly turned up to pay their last respects and couldn't be sent home without sustenance. Moreover, Vanya would now be entering the spirit world, welcomed by her ancestors and the feast not only celebrated the miracle of this transition, but symbolised life continuing back here in the real world. For all that, Erdi still couldn't bring himself to eat. He slipped away to the ramparts overlooking the valley and called out into the night.

At this point The Teller produced a strange object from beneath his robe. Speaking through it, his words took on a sepulchral tone and seemed to resound, as if actually coming from the back of the hall, rather from where he sat. The slight ruffling amongst his audience showed an involuntary betrayal of unease.

"Vanya, you will never be forgotten. You will live on. Live on through your descendants. Live on in the tales to be told down through time."

He could hold them back no longer, as he turned and forced himself to return to the dimming glow of the pyre, tears at last welled up in old Erdi's eyes. A few friends and family

21

welcomed and led him into the Great Hall. As if in a trance, he let himself be moved about in the bustle of well-wishers and sympathisers. They all spoke his language, but not in the way those who had shared his experience of the old times had done. Who could he turn to now, to enable his spirit to come alive? They had all gone. Traveled on to the land of the ancestors. He was the lone survivor of the legend he had lived through. What did these people around him know of the age of bronze? They meant well, but didn't really understand his deep yearning to talk once again with kindred spirits. To share stories with those that had lived through the time before the knowledge had come. Only later, once the peripheral guests had left, did he feel the numbness lifting and strength returning, providing the will to once again face the seemingly stupid, insignificant details that made up daily life. He at last took some food and the beer helped mellow his mood. He even laughed at some of the memories, tales of his sister whose inner spirit had never really aged. A few younger family members pleaded with him to mount the dais. People still flocked to hear his stories. Erdikun, although reluctant, allowed himself to be ushered and applauded up into the light glowing from the hearth.

With his voice slightly altered to mimic that of an aged man, the Teller continued: "My first significant memory of my sister Vanya was when she lay in her cradle. As you know, most at that early age simply lie there sleeping or wailing. I remember creeping forward to examine her cot. It was hanging from the rafters and through the wickerwork, I saw a pair of huge brown eyes, staring at me as if we'd met before somewhere. She tried to crane her little head as if expecting, even at that age, to be able to peer over the side, not looking like a bewildered first-time arrival, but more like the inquisitive spirit of one just recently returned.

She wasn't in wet-rags for long, kicking them off as if in a dash to be growing up. She would stagger around from one support to another in an effort to follow her granddad Tollan.

She adored him. The feeling was mutual and seemed to give the old man a new lease of life. Then in seemingly no time at all she was running around everywhere, tanned from head to toe, needing to be caught when the need arose, to get her into clothes. I can still hear that throaty laugh on finally being captured. She always seemed to be making things, inventing games that others begged to join in. In fact she was a natural leader without ever wishing to appear like it. She hadn't even wanted to be the Spring Queen. On arrival, up at the Feasting Site on the Dwy river, all the young girls changed into their best attire, their princess costumes, but Vanya having reluctantly donned hers, went missing. We looked everywhere. Finally, it was Dowid I think who spotted her. She was pulled out from beneath one of the stalls where she'd tucked herself and struggling all the way was led and shoved into line with the others. She gave a grumpy look of resignation, then beamed a smile and won. We paid our respects with a bronze offering later, lest willful demons thought we might be gloating. You can't be too careful!"

So Erdikun related more tales from the life of his sister and these and others were handed down to me. He kept his eulogy fairly brief as he could feel his voice starting to crack with emotion. He finally asked them to raise their drinking horns and then had to turn away, feeling the need to be on his own again. He retreated with his memories into the shadows.

The Teller continued with the tale well into the night, but finally, with the fire no more than a deep red glow, he announced he would return to relate more of the story the following evening.

Chapter Two

Next morning was clear and fresh. Warm enough, however, for just simple linen shirt and leggings to suffice. The loose-fitting clothes suited the Teller's mood. It was good to feel free from his theatrical duties as he strolled through the camp, exchanging greetings with those he met. People were going about their business and children were playing. A young man approached in a most obsequious fashion and handed him a gift of warm apple cake. He requested forgiveness and the Teller gladly gave absolution, realising him to be the youth who had interrupted him the night before. He wandered over to the camp's main entrance. It led down to the base of the hill protected on either side by tall, sturdy wooden palisades and at top and bottom by gates. The expanse of ditches and defences surrounding the fort were enough to deter all but the foolhardy. To the east lay a wooded ridge and turning he could just make out the dim outline of hills that held the lofty encampment of those known back in time as Gatekeepers of the South. He finished eating his gift and was on the point of continuing the circuit when a group of youths ran towards him. "Tell us a story," they begged him. "Tell us about Erdi." They clamoured in a ring, surrounding him. His heart sank and he did his best to resist, being fatigued from the previous night's exertions, but in the end capitulated and perched himself on the fighting step of the fortress wall while they seated themselves in an eager group below. He explained the main characters and then said,

Now where shall I start? I know. I'll take you way back to when Erdi was beginning to explore his locality. He was still just a boy. It had been a dream of his to climb that far ridge. The one behind me now. He yearned to see what lay beyond. He knew there were numerous lakes, for that was where his grandfather Tollan had trapped fish to add stock to their local pools, but apart from that and the fact the people talked a bit funny - *The boys laughed and said that they still did.* - the world beyond the ridge was a mystery. Erdi and his cousin Yanker had both finished the day's grind of producing flour from the quern and were now at a loose end. Suddenly, as if from out of nowhere, an exciting plan materialised. They would set off on a little journey of discovery to see what lay beyond that enigmatic east ridge. Even at this early age Erdi had become noted for his accuracy with slingshot and they both carried their trusty staves everywhere and so were well equipped to face danger. They slipped away unseen and headed along the well-worn path winding through the trees. This petered out into what was no more than an animal trail and the sun had started its dip to the west by the time they reached a tiny brook that marked a personal boundary. The winding ooze of water, never more than a chuckling brook even in winter, was of no great significance other than the fact that beyond it, lay the great unknown. They had never ventured further than this before. Penda and Dowid had told their sons that beyond this point lay danger. They had never specified exactly what type of danger, but had given strict instructions not to take so much as one step beyond that seeping trickle, hardly audible just beyond their toes. The boys stared long and hard at forbidden territory. It looked much the same as where they were standing. They continued peering into the trees and shrubs ahead expecting to see at least some clue as to what might lurk, but hard as they looked, they received not the slightest hint. Maybe there were monsters, dragons or giants as in stories related to frighten and quell children's natural tendencies to wander. Maybe tendrils

25

would entangle and drag them, bound as food for the green forest spirits to devour. They looked at each other and back at the woodland ahead, appearing no different to that they'd just scrambled through and concluded, 'Monsters? Surely not. Why not just go a little way and find out?'

Exchanging a look for confidence they decided to take that first decisive step. They could always jump straight back again if something awful suddenly reared up in front of them. As nothing of the sort did, they simply shrugged and continued.

The going became steeper and any hint of a path dwindled to nothing. Briars tripped and lacerated ankles and calves. Long spiny tendrils seemed determined to grab at their clothing. In places trees had grown into such tangled thickets, they had no choice other than to backtrack and try and seek a way round. They stopped at intervals, exhausted and took the precaution of remembering certain features to avoid becoming lost. They'd been warned of the lost boys, those that had wandered off never to be seen again. Erdi said they'd just top the ridge and make that their goal for the day.

Something stirring in the darkness beyond the gnarled greening trunks stopped them dead. They peered into the gloom, hearts beating, but it was just deer ghosting through a dusty half-light. They were encouraged by the sight of brighter, possibly less entangled ground ahead and ripping the last of the clinging branches and briars from their clothing, fell with relief from the willful twists and snarls that had seemed so intent on imprisoning them. A drumming of hooves shook the ground and they froze as if spell cast. It was just wild ponies they'd disturbed. Then their hearts leapt as a hare sprang from underfoot to bound away ears erect. Growing apprehension brought on wild imaginings, illusions, jangling the nerves in a growing sense of panic. Yet still they were drawn on.

Their spirits rose. Beneath more widely spaced trees, open ground beckoned. Ever watchful, one hand tight-clenching the stave, the other poised on the verge of signalling, '**stop**,' they dared edge their way forward, constantly checking behind, dwarfed by ancient living columns supporting the green canopy. There was bracken, knee high grass and the occasional slippery rotting branch, but at least the going had become easier. Prodding the ground ahead for snakes, they continued, curiosity drawing them yet further onwards. They couldn't stop now, for they had spotted something strange up ahead.

A shaft of sunlight lit a myriad of butterflies and quivering shades of green in what appeared to be a magic circle deep in the forest. They ducked from sight on spotting a figure emerging from the shadows beyond. Holding her gown clear of the grass as she walked, the woman suddenly stopped as something caught her attention. Their vantage point seemed stifling, airless, yet out in the open her hair billowed, its aubern glow highlighted by the sun. Curiosity getting the better, they crept closer. What was a woman doing up here alone? They watched fascinated. She appeared to be foraging, looking as much at home as any of the forest animals. Ominously her search led in their direction. Something had caught her eye. She crept a few steps, then bent and scooped whatever it was from amongst the ferns. Like all children through time, they had been taught not to talk to strangers and so the boys watched and waited.

Almost as if catching a slight hint of their scent, she suddenly looked up and peered in their direction. They recognized the face of a woman they'd seen before, but only vaguely knew. With it being obvious she had now actually seen them, they stepped from cover and joined her in the glade, not only warmed by the sun, but now by her smile. This lingered, hardening slightly as she scrutinized. She had rounded features which the weather had bronzed to blend perfectly with the rowanberry glow of her cheeks. A white blouse was just visible beyond the thin red trim, edging her light grey gown. Her dark eyes, shining as bright as bedewed bramble berries, watched them intently. Was she unraveling their very thoughts? When she did finally speak, it was actually quite disarming, "You look like two lost souls up here in the woods."

Erdi doing his best, in vain alas, to sound older than his years, tried explaining they were in fact not lost, but exploring. These happened to be the first words said to the lady who was to have such an influence on their lives. When she pointed out the possible dangers, Yanker countered, "With great respect, dear lady, if it's that dangerous, then why are you up here alone?"

She laughed and said with a wave of an arm. "This is my home. I live here. The animals are my friends and the forest is my provider."

Erdi wondered why the breeze seemed to blow on her alone. Her gown wafted gently as she approached to reveal the contents of her basket.

"Just leaves," Yanker muttered to Erdi.

She overheard. "Agreed, but not just any leaves." Picking out a sprig, "These have healing powers, when pressed in a wet mash and bandaged over a wound." A beech tree was indicated to show their origin. A different clump was extracted from the basket. "These are called 'heal-bone.'" She rooted deeper and chuckled, "Here are some you ought to know." They were dandelion leaves, 'Wet the bed,' "And the magic of these others is…. look." They were held up for them to see the detail. "If these are boiled it brings forth a certain juice. A juice that gives strength." She clenched an arm and gave a wink." *The Teller acting the part, brought laughter from his young audience.*

Erdi then asked, "What about bad weather? How do you survive in the winter?"

"Oh you mean, where do I lay my head at night? I have a house deep down and hidden in the woods. You might think I'm in danger, but there's a magic circle cast around it. That suffices to keep me safe."

The Teller could alter his voice so they knew who was saying what in the story.

"What sort of magic circle?" *It was Erdi talking.*

They were both were beginning to feel uncomfortable, as if her beauty might suddenly dissolve to reveal a hideous witch lurking within. Well you can't blame them, *said the Teller.* I bet you boys know of places you daren't walk. Places where an old crone might cast her spell on you.

This was no old crone, however. She had a kind face, but even so, Erdi and Yanker remained on guard. Out in the open, they thought her magic couldn't be that potent, but if inside a building, then there'd be no telling the power of it. She said, "I can take you to the circle if you like. You won't see anything of course, but you might feel its energy. Do you want to see where I disappear to? You'll need to look very carefully mind you." She gave Erdi's hand a friendly touch, "Smoke from the fire should give a clue."

He looked back at her stunned. A strange cool draught had accompanied the approach of her fingers.

"Look you've cut yourself," she said gently brushing his forehead and on feeling the same mysterious wafting of air, he recoiled slightly.

"Don't be frightened," she said smiling, "Even the wolves are my friends. They come for the bones. Not to the house of course." She laughed as if glad of the company. "They won't dare enter the circle. The deer will. I have to chase them off the few things I manage to grow. But not the wolves. Come, you might just feel the power of the circle, but you won't see it." She rambled on a little, as to be expected from a woman living up there alone, "It's entirely invisible. Do you want to see my house, warm under the ground?"

Pulling away slightly, they both gave a shake of head. She laughed. "Don't look so terrified. I didn't cast the circle for the likes of you. It's there to keep all bad things out."

29

"I saw you pick something up just now," said Erdi.

"Oh this. One of my little friends." She carefully parted leaves in her basket and the face of a toad stared up at them. That did it. They were off. The ridge top could wait for another day. They ran down a path not caring where it led and didn't stop running until back on level ground. Both doubled up, gulping for air, stared at one another, hearts pounding, too out of breath to talk. A glance at the sun and horizon told them roughly where they had ended up and on spotting familiar landmarks, they were able to find their way, with great relief, back within sight of home.

So the two brave warriors had returned without mishap and trying to sound nonchalant Erdi asked, "Mother?"

Something about his tone made her brace herself. Like most mothers she seemed able to read a young son's mind. "Yes?" she said.

"You remember telling us about a woman who lives up in the woods?"

She couldn't, but asked him to continue.

"Who is she?"

"I hope you haven't been up there without telling us!"

Mara could see he was lying. "That's just Elsa. She's harmless enough. PENDA!" Her husband was summoned and after dark mutterings between them, he took Erdi aside demanding to be told the whole story. Tollan, appearing from the work room, stood and listened. Penda, having reached for the hazel rod, was about to administer suitable corporal punishment when his father intervened, staying his arm.

"Let me deal with it. Come with me Erdi." When out in the light he said, "Go and fetch your cousin." He led them beyond the compound, sat himself before the two contrite young explorers and gave them a man to man talk as to why they shouldn't wander off without telling anyone. It actually made more of an impression than a damn good thrashing.

Later Erdi was told more of Elsa and her strange gifts. His mother said, people racked with pain, hardly able to walk let alone work, had over the years sent out pleas for her help. Just by jerking shoulder and back in a certain way had left them, relieved of a little payment, usually food or bronze, and of a massive back pain. Elsa had cured countless ailing hands, feet and limbs, had quelled fevers and had wrenched many a stiff neck to transform beleaguered looks of pain into those of wonder and relief. She could somehow interpret the wildest dreams and sometimes, could even predict outcomes from them. She had a knowledge of plants and fungi that kept her in all the things her woodlands couldn't produce like, lentils, wheat and barley.

"How by magic?" Erdi asked.

The Teller enquired, Do you boys know the answer? *They all shook their heads.*

She had a knowledge of natures' secrets. The locals, although regarding her as a bit wild and eccentric, had no actual fear of her. In fact, she was considered to be the genuine Seer, rather than the man some referred to as the 'bone rattler' up in the camp. It was born in her system. She had something you couldn't teach. Somehow she knew what helped an aching wound, an aching head and even an aching heart. A few of the right leaves could bring her a whole basket of peas, bread, or what have you, traded up in the market.

Anyway, I'll hand you back to Mara herself, talking to Erdi about the mysterious Elsa.

His voice became a rendering of Mara's and those watching almost felt they were young Erdi looking up and listening.

"Elsa inherited her strange powers from her mother. She's probably the closest thing we have to Earth Mother in human form. Nobody knows who her father was. Some say he was a pixie." *The Teller clamped a hand to mouth, saying,* "Don't you breathe a word I said that, Erdi! It was wrong of me. Stop laughing! Really. Please we shouldn't. She's got more of a gift in one of her little fingers than that bone rattler up at the camp has in his whole body. He tried to have Elsa's poor mother taken in for 'a little examination' was how they'd put it. The people here take most of what's put upon them, but they weren't having that! She'd done too much good for them. His lordship could see the Seer had stirred up unneeded trouble and to everyone's relief, she was released. Don't you go repeating what I've just told you, Erdi! Especially not the pixie and bone rattler bits. Certain folk take great pleasure in spreading what could be construed as damaging information about others."

So you see boys, *said the Teller, noticing his audience had swelled slightly in numbers,* nothing much has changed.

They looked back at him stunned by the way he delivered the tale, almost like a one man play. He continued in Erdi's voice, "I thought most of the people were our friends,"

"Some, but others are at their most dangerous when smiling. Even a good neighbour can turn traitor when their own skin's threatened."

"But that seems incredible!"

"That son, I'm afraid," *the Teller eased down from his perch and ruffling a young boy's head, said,* "is life!"

So boys, they'd learnt their lesson. The next opportunity Erdi and Yanker had, they asked permission from their parents and headed off towards the elusive east ridge. Using another thing learnt from their first attempt, they circled the base of the hill to find the path they'd hurtled down in such a state of panic the time before. On this trip, however, there was no sign of the magic circle nor of that strange lady, Elsa. They looked, but found that just like love, certain things stumbled upon by happy chance often elude when actually in search of them. With finally reaching the crest and looking south towards the ghostly blue hills almost lost in the clouds, came the revelation of how small their own world was and how vast was the great unknown lying out there. Staring, feeling lost in the enormity of it, Erdi's face took on a look of wonder, as a strange premonition crept over him.

Chapter Three

The Teller noticed some girls had joined his audience. He welcomed them and said they were just in time to hear a little bit about Vanya. He explained briefly who Vanya and the rest of the characters were and then asked all to take note that time had moved on about four years or so.

Now when Vanya was still but a tiny mite, having said that, even at such a tender age, you could already perceive the little woman starting to shine out of her, she and Talia happened to be playing outside with their dolls. These were simple things with painted faces, carved from wood, available from the Fire Feast winter market. Their mothers had made tiny clothes to fit, but Vanya now decided the game required more realism, with the little mothers and baby dolls needing a home of their own. Her father, Penda watched with amusement as she enrolled Erdi and Yanker to cut and trim branches for leaning against the apple tree to provide support for elder branches fresh into leaf. They were from the resurgent shrub he'd been trying to eradicate. The boys did this cheerfully, taking instructions from the confident little lady who made it seem like fun and in all fairness, it wasn't a bad effort. He had been quite taken aback at the way Vanya, still not that articulate, had managed to organise it all. She and Talia crawled inside to play in their new secret world and the two boys, their usefulness now over, were dismissed with the explanation there wasn't enough room for them all.

Penda had learnt from that resilient elder. Generally, it was revered as a miracle tree. Its blossom could be made into a refreshing drink, or as with the fruit, wine, the berries also providing jam and vinegar; its bark and leaves were used as dye and medicine, plus the latter warded off evil, when hung in a doorway and its timber, by virtue of being easily hollowed, provided the perfect material for whistles and pipes, but this particular elder was in the wrong place. There were others growing nearby and so loss of the shrub wasn't viewed as a tragedy. Its persistent nature, sprouting thicker every time he hacked it back, gave him the idea of taking the tops out of apple and plum trees. As new growth sprouted, they too thickened, providing greater shade and fruited not only in greater abundance, but at a more convenient height. Then looking at the lean-to play house, another idea struck him. He checked on the tally board recording the passing year and his suspicion was confirmed, Vanya's birthday was almost due. He discussed his idea with Dommed, Talia's father and a few days later Erdi and Yanker were instructed to take the two young ladies to their nearest neighbours to stay for a night. These had been more than glad to help and were looking forward to having the two girls as guests. The boys were told not to linger, but to come back and help.

The family concerned weren't the brightest, but decent enough folk. Their son Brone who Yanker had nicknamed Blade was a bit of a dullard but his company was endured largely on account of his sister Donda making up for lack of brains, with the burgeoning shape of her body, plus the fact at times she didn't really mind their healthy interest in it.

"Shall we take Blade a bag of gravel?" Yanker asked with a grin. *The Teller again played out the scene using different voices for each character.*

"No don't push it too far." Erdi enjoyed a bit of a joke, but didn't relish tackling Blade if riled. He was two years their senior and a bit handy with his fists to say the least. The joke had started when he'd asked them both if they knew why

35

stones needed clearing annually from the fields? One patch was particularly troublesome. So many stones had been extracted over the years there'd almost been enough to form an enclosure.

Without pause for thought, Yanker told him, "You've got one of those special fields, Brone."

"Of course we have." Brone puffed himself up as usual and then confided, "Our dad says we've got the best of the land in these parts. But why's this field different? Every year we find yet more stones have popped up like giant mushrooms. We clear them, then the next year up come more."

"Surely you know."

The answer was a blank look.

"Lucky field, Brone. Certain fields are lucky and actually grow stones. Best time for picking 'em is after a good," his clenched fist for emphasis caused Brone to back off slightly, "sharp frost! Just like it's best to pick rowan berries after the first frosts, it's best to go a-stone picking early spring after the last frosts. If you're really lucky the field will grow enough to build a wall to keep out all the rooting pigs and what have you." With an arm embracing his solid friend, he said in confidence, "Don't go letting on I told you this, but if you bury small stones just after the harvest, they'll come up nice big and handy in the spring and you can finish off that wall of yours. It's no good replanting those you've already cleared. Too mature. You need nice fresh young 'uns. 'Seeding stones,' is what we call 'em. About this big." His hands cupped, slightly apart, indicated the size. "And don't go shoving them in just anywhere. They'll only work in the lucky field."

"You mean like those stones from the river. Our dad says we got the best river stones round here. Nice and flat. We've lugged them up in the past to line the floors of the grain pits. We only take the best mind you. There's always more after every flood. They seem to gather there on that bend we get the skimmers from. I could carry a few loads up here for our dad's field."

"You've got it Brone. Carry up the best. Just the very best. Next spring you'll be rolling out some belters for that wall of yours. You're a blade you are. A proper blade! Those stones will be perfect."

Brone became quite animated. "Carry them up here…..?" and watching Yanker nodding encouragement said with enthusiasm "Bury them. Bury them right up in our dad's field?"

"That's it, Blade. Not too deep mind. About a hand's depth. And be sure to plant 'em early."

"Our dad says…."

"Enough of the dad stuff, Blade. Don't you go telling your dad a thing about this. Keep it a surprise."

"Blade? Why d'you keep calling me Blade?"

"Well what's a blade like?"

"Meant to be sharp."

"Meant to be sharp." He slapped him on the back. "Exactly! There's your answer."

Brone's look darkened, but the inclination to deliver a sharp slap in reply, dissolved on seeing Yanker's grin broadening and with a smile slowly spreading in accompaniment, he drew himself up to full height, the proud young owner of a new special name. From then on, that special name, Blade, just seemed to stick.

Yanker had asked him later that year how the stone planting had gone? Blade told him he'd carried out his instructions, "And our dad didn't spot me doing it."

"That's it. Just keep it between us. Don't go, 'our dadding' about any of this."

"No Dowin I won't." Sorry to be confusing, but Dowin's nickname Yanker came a little later. Blade was entirely the reason for it, but never knew it. Having said that, he did get a bit of an inkling a few years down the line as you'll get to hear later in the story.

I might as well tell you now how it happened. It was like this. A fishing trip was organized the following spring in the pool scoured out by winter floods up at Blade's, just upstream from that stony beach he'd referred to. They'd done their best to get Donda interested, but she'd had one of her moods on, not helped by smelly breath and an angry looking boil on the side of her nose.

"Fine as sunshine one day," Yanker had mused, "Black as thunder the next. That's girls for you." They'd sorted out the pick and shovel from Pa Blade's hut, but were stopped in their tracks by the booming "Where d'ya think you're going with those?" He was a big man with a big voice.

Erdi explained the fishing notion and the need to dig out worms from the midden.

"Just you mind how you go with that shovel!" he warned. It was an ox-blade. "You break it? You replace it!"

Unlike you today with your iron implements, there was nothing available like it back then. Bronze was too valuable to make a shovel out of. A knife, a scythe, a shaving blade, an axehead, yes, but not the humblest of outdoor tools. They made do with an antler pick and shoulder blade shovel. Any animal's shoulder blade could of course be put to use, but the ox-blade was huge and held a kind of magic. We're talking top of the range here boys. As now, oxen were revered not only for their strength, but also for the fact they were probably the deciding factor whether you were going to make it through the winter or not. How else would heavy ploughing get done? The larger horses, same as you have today, had made an appearance, but were not available to humble farming folk. So just as now, barren sheep and fattened swine were butchered and salted down to last the winter. Oxen, however, were better kept alive as long as possible -- working, breeding and revered. Consequently, if you broke your last ox blade shovel there could be quite a wait for the next. This one sported a long wooden handle.

Now it just so happened that shortly after excavations had begun on the midden, Blade came out in a sweat and doubled up in pain he'd wheezed, "Bad guts!".

Now I hope you don't mind this next bit ladies, *said the Teller,* but I'll have to relate it on account of it being true.

Erdi said, "Nip behind that bush there, Blade," He'd instantly realised the cause of Blade's distress, having got wind of the problem earlier.

Yanker gave Erdi a nudge and when Blade had got himself round the shrub to shuffle himself into a suitable posture, the shovel was stealthily offered under the foliage ready to receive. No wonder he'd suffered such discomfort! Out wormed a seemingly endless steaming mound to be proud of. Deserved a flag planting in it. The shovel was quietly yanked back and its cargo hidden in the midden. No point wasting it.

Blade tidied himself up a bit and turned to inspect and admire. He gasped, looked around puzzled, peered inside his gusset, moved aside to see if he was standing in it, then stood there scratching his head. He appeared from around the bush and said almost in a whisper to his two friends, who could hardly keep their faces straight, "It's the strangest thing."

"What is Blade?"

"I've just done a whopper back there, but it's gone! Can't find it."

Joining him as if in search, Yanker suddenly chimed, "You know the answer don't you, Blade?"

"No. What?"

"You Blade my friend have done one of those specials."

"Well of course. Our dad says -----" He paused. "Special yes, but in what way do you mean special?"

"I've heard tell of such things, Blade. It's those little people. They've got a nose for those specials. Once they're on the scent they're in like a flash! Before you can turn round the little devils have made off with it."

"Whatever for?"

"To make a Brownie, of course!"

Erdi, still in pretence of searching for the lost manure, clutched his sides simply aching from suppressed laughter.

Yet Yanker had the ability to remain composed in a way that seemed remarkable, for lowering his voice and looking around as if fearing an eaves dropper, he'd asked, "How's that stone growin' goin', Blader?"

"Well alright I suppose." said Blade. "But our dad says the worst of them seems to be over now. They appeared after the frosts, just like you predicted and I don't want to seem ungrateful here, but they were in fact a bit of a disappointment. We took them to the side, out of the way before the ploughing, but there were nowhere near enough to finish that wall."

"I'm genuinely sad to hear that, Blade. But be patient, planted stones tend to turn up in the end. They'll turn up alright, you can be sure of that."

Following Erdi's retelling of the story, the nickname Yanker stuck like pine resin. The fishing trip by the way? It ended with them taking turns on the sturdy honeysuckle rope tied to an overhanging branch and swinging themselves with whoops and splashes into the freezing cold pool.

So taking you back to what I was relating earlier: it was a little later in the Spring of that same year when Erdi and Yanker happened to be on that mission of delivering the young girls, Vanya and Talia, up to Blade's place to stay for the night. They lived in hope of Donda being in the mood for a little suggestive banter, but it wasn't Donda who first appeared, but Blade.

The Teller spoke in the voice now recognized to be Yanker's, "Not looking your sharpest today Blader. What's the matter?"

His father had been in a filthy mood after ploughing up flat river stones in the small walled field and had asked how they'd got there.

"Didn't tell him, did you?"

"Course not. It was bad enough I had to clear them up, let alone getting a thrashing for putting them there."

Yanker put a consoling arm around him. "Didn't work then. Strange that. Usually does."

"Well, you did tell him they'd be certain to turn up." Erdi said cheerfully. Yanker flashed him a grimace and continued, "Tell him the Brownies put them there."

"No. Our dad says, you only find Brownies in houses, not doing other stuff out in the fields."

They all walked on up to the house and the girls were dropped off as arranged. Refreshed by a drink of Ma Blade's elderflower juice, they had started to wend their way back down the path, when the unexpected sighting of Donda stopped them in their tracks and sent pulses racing. It's not that she was a raving beauty, but you have to remember they were just young lads and she didn't have much competition. It seemed strange she should just happen to be there for no apparent reason, other than for drawing a circle in the dust with a toe. Erdi asked what she was doing? She'd just laughed and said, "Wouldn't you like to know."

The two lads wandered on slowly as possible, hoping to prolong the time in her company. Once beyond view of the palisade they experienced that strange nerve tingling feeling that surges through youths, when realising they are at last alone with the object of their fantasies and maybe, just maybe that mysterious creature, visibly advanced towards womanhood, might at last be in the mood for the sort of banter they had in mind. When, however, instinct warned her she was being drawn a little too far along where their suggestive talk was leading, she sneered, "Don't know why I'm even bothering with you two! Bet you young whelps don't even know where babies **come** from!" Erdi was just about to assert that he certainly did when a jab from Yanker silenced him.

"No we don't Donda. We were hoping you could tell us." His long blond hair, fine features and blue eyes widening with his smile of innocence, gave him quite a disarming, angelic look.

He had seemingly saved the day as Donda relenting, took a deep breath and said, "WELL! You're not going to believe it, BUT…." She started what they hoped would lead to her using her own generous assets as practical examples, but as their gentle coaxing went from, "Tell us," eventually on to, "Show us,"-------- with innate feminine instinct on full alert, she turned on her heel with, "You must be joking! Whelps!" and thwarted they watched the object of their boyhood fantasies disappear back up the path with head in the air.

"They take some understanding," said Yanker scratching his head. "Look at her! Even those swinging hips seem to be laughing at us. She's not even bright! It's like girls get to have a bit of a practice of how to deal with men before they're even born."

Back at home the work had been going on apace and as they hadn't gone to the same trouble as they would have had the house been for living in, the miniature version of a round house was completed by the following morning. No suggestion of a hearth of course.

Vanya and Talia were sent for and just before reaching home, were blindfolded. When these were removed, both just stared at the little house in astonishment. They approached cautiously in disbelief. Penda said, "It **is** for you, you know. It's your birthday. Have a look inside." Mara had spread reeds within and both their dolls lay awaiting. Of course, they loved it, played in it daily, chores and weather permitting and even wanted to live in it, but as it lay just beyond the palisade their wish wasn't granted. Locals came to look and spoke in terms of surprise and admiration, but in their huddles later, shared the view that Penda's little community must have gone quite mad. Strange therefore, that not long after, a few followed their example, creating playhouses for village children and were openly quite proud, as if having dreamt up the notion themselves.

Chapter Four

The Teller looked at the eager faces staring up at him and said, Now I need to tell you a bit about Mardi. I see we have a few more in the audience. *He again sketched out details for the newcomers.* One day, Mara, who I explained was Erdi's mother, stopped him mid-stride by asking, "Have you forgotten you've a brother? He must feel left out with you dashing off exploring with your cousin at every opportunity. Mardi worries me. It's not right to be so self-absorbed every day. He needs to have some fun. Why can't you take him with you sometimes?"

Erdi said he would, but envisaged it curtailing their escapades somewhat. He remembered how his brother had done his best to follow them when just an infant. They had teased him, climbing a tree leaving him stranded below. He yearned to be big like them laughing and joking up in the branches. Later when seeing the sadness on his little brother's face, Erdi enfolding him with a comforting arm, led him, explaining it was quite way, but at the end of the walk there would be a special moment. The path led to a portion of the stream they often played in and Mardi arrived proudly riding on his brother's shoulders. On a lazy bend there was a shallow pool, scene of numerous games and beside it stood an ancient willow, its draped branches gently moving in the flow. The daring angle of the trunk, which age had riven like the inside of a boat, made it particularly easy to climb, thus its name, the Easy Tree. Erdi holding his brother's hand, led him carefully up to where years of coppicing had left the perfect secret space to sit and dream, hidden in the branches, as the waters and wildlife carried on regardless below. Once there, Mardi was told he was now special. He had climbed his first tree. The young lad's eyes had widened in disbelief at now being considered 'big' like his brother and cousin and he'd absolutely glowed with happiness. He asked Erdi, could they always come back? Always return to the Easy Tree. "Promise? Even when we're grown up?" Erdi gave his solemn promise.

Doing his mother's bidding he now went looking for him, but having no success, asked Vanya where he might be. She told him, "He often likes to sit alone in my playhouse." Sure enough there he was on his own in the gloom.

"What are you doing sitting in here in the dark, Mardi?"

"Watching the sun, Erdi."

This was worrying. "But there's no sun in here, Mardi." He crawled in and put an arm round him.

"There look." He pointed to a patch of light on the floor. "I watch it move."

"Mardi I'm going with Yanker to pick watercress. There should be some down in the slow stream by now. Why don't you come with us?"

"What if it's not true, Erdi?"

"What's not true?"

"Sun going down in the sea getting colder and colder."

"But Mardi, people have seen it."

"But our sun goes down behind the hills. There can't be a different sun for everyone. I know the sun gets cooler and cooler so we get the shorter freezy days. Do our gifts to those spirits actually work? All that sacrifice before every winter feast?"

"Dear me, Mardi. This is serious stuff you're worrying yourself about. Paying our respects to a miracle that happens every year seems to work. Don't you enjoy the Fire Feasts? They're good fun. Everyone's happy. The new sun begins its progression back along the horizon heating the days up.

Everyone goes away with a feeling of hope. Warmer days are on the way."

"Yes I know what happens. The new sun comes up way over on Hill of the Eagle and goes back towards winter, sinking beyond the Skreela hills, but what if it did it anyway?"

"Mardi be careful! That's dangerous!"

"But I've been watching it Erdi. I think it does."

"But that would mean we're making those sacrifices for nothing. I often make a wish myself. Only giving up tiny scraps, but it seems to work."

"But we all toil so hard just to live Erdi, without throwing what bit we've got left into the water."

"I know, father says we work harder to gain less and less. Ten baskets of fish used to get us one rond, now it's twenty."

"Why don't we just hide the sacrificial bolts and ronds, say nothing and see what happens?" They sat in silence for a while. Sounds of the women talking and laughing drifted up from the stream, meaning it was wash day. From over by the sty, energetic squeals and grunting indicated feeding time. "But I believe in those spirits, Mardi," Erdi said at last.

"There can still be spirits. But the sun might not need them."

"How else do you explain what happens?"

"Something inside me says there's an answer. I get these feelings. They scare me sometimes."

"Don't you dare say a word about any of this, Mardi. It's dangerous. Come on let's go and hunt watercress. It doesn't move very fast."

Mardi smiled.

"We can have it with bread later. Doesn't taste of much does it, until a good chew brings out that lovely burning flavour. Come on Mardi," he coaxed. "It worries me thinking of you sitting alone in the dark."

"Erdi? Tell me the Zak story again."

"Which one, there's lots."

"The last one. Zak and Big Hendi. Where he shoots Big Hendi's hair off."

"Will you come with us if I do?"

Mardi nodded.

"Are you sitting comfortably?" His young brother nodded again, wriggling in anticipation.

The Teller looked down and asked, And are **you** all sitting comfortably? Then I'll begin.

"Many years ago, Mardi, there was a giant in our valley called Big Hendi. He was built like a mountain and so strong he could pull up trees and brandishing one as if as light as a sword, could scare off an army of the bravest warriors. The Lord of the Hill and all his men could do nothing about it when Hendi took it in mind to go on the rampage. He'd stomp up there at night, step over the walls as if not there, shake their houses until teeth rattled and blow in through doorways sending ash and dangerous sparks everywhere. He stole their sheep to eat and they could do nothing but ask the spirits for help. They were wasting their time, however, for the spirits thought the people up on the hill were vain and greedy and refused to help.

Now the king had a beautiful daughter and promised that whoever stopped Big Hendi scaring folk and munching their sheep could have her hand in marriage. Even the bravest of the brave were too frightened to help. All except one young man. He was fairly new to the area, went by the name of Zak and had proved himself to be the best with the slingshot in the whole valley."

"Like you, Erdi." Mardi loved and admired his big brother.

"It was a rare thing, Mardi, even though Zak was not one of the lord's chosen warriors, he was authorised to wear a sword. The concession had been awarded by another chieftain out of gratitude for the valiant services rendered to him and his people. This rankled with the lord up on the hill, but having made enquiries, the news came back, Zak had every right to bear such arms, which in these circumstances also conferred on him the romantic notion that he could even be some sort of prince.

So when Zak announced he would do battle with the giant, the lord on the hill was more than a little pleased thinking, that would surely be the end of him and the ticklish problem of a foreign upstart wandering around armed with a weapon he had not personally authorised. Everyone else of course thought Zak was mad and not long for this world. But Zak wasn't stupid. Oh no. First he realised he needed to go in search of information---- find out more about Hendi, such as where he lived. He trudged all the way up to the house of the Earth Mother."

Mardi said with enthusiasm, "We've got an Earth Mother Erdi! You told me about her."

"No this one's different and lived up in the far-off hills where the big river starts. Some people said she was born way back at the time of the great flood. Anyway, she liked Zak and admired his bravery. She said she would ask the help of the little people, but warned him they would only lend a hand if he proved he was not a vain man like those living in the big fort up on the hill. Zak made his way up to their magic pool where it was said they often danced at night. He had a dagger. A beautiful dagger. It was one of the most important things in his life. He was about to throw the dagger into the pool as a sacrifice to the spirits and the little people when an idea struck him. He took a rock and broke the knife so that it was useless, proving that even though he valued this above most things, he was willing to smash it and offer it into their watery realm to show his humility and respect for their nether world. The spirits were impressed by this sacrifice and decided to help Zak. They sent out the little people who found where Hendi lived. They sneaked up and spied on him. Then they reported back to Earth Mother. They'd found out Big Hendi's secret. They had watched him in his cave woefully holding a clump of hair that had parted company with his head. "I'm losing my strength!" his roar making the hills shake. Hendi's strength was in his hair. Without it he would go all big and floppy." Mardi laughed and even though he knew the story, couldn't wait for the next bit.

"Earth Mother told Zak how to find the giant's cave and said he would know he was getting close as the trees would be bigger than normal and even some of the animals might appear to be a bit on the large side.

Zak took three pieces of flint and napped them that sharp and flat you could almost see through them. He went along the river that led up to the cave where the little people had told Earth Mother, Big Hendi lived. Sure enough the trees were bigger than normal, the deer were massive and Zak marveled at the size of a frog hunched down by the stream. It was the biggest frog he'd ever seen in his life. There had to be something in the water.

He watched and waited. He waited three days, living off hefty trout and massive bunches of juicy watercress. At last, on feeling the ground trembling, he knew his patience had been rewarded. It was big Hendi approaching. Rocks fell out of the cliffs and trees quivered as he drew closer. Zak took his sling and the three sharp stones and walking out into the open, planted himself on the path in front of Big Hendi, to shout, "Not so fast, Big Hendi!"

He looked so small that the giant had to stoop to see him properly and with his adversary being so puny, Hendi put hands on hips, threw back his head and roared with laughter. "HA! HA! HA!" Laughter so loud all the birds took to the air in fright and deer ran into tree trunks. The only thing not to take fright was the giant frog, who seeing things were getting interesting, shuffled up behind the giant hoping to get a better view.

"You have to stop your sheep snatching!" shouted Zak.

Hendi laughed, until silenced by one of Zak's stones that zinged through the air cutting one side of his hair clean off. It fell to the ground and lay there like a small hay stack. Hendi was mighty angered, but his attempt to reach down and snatch up Zak, was stopped by the second stone, that hummed, rotating, shooting the other side of his hair off. Another step and the third rendered him completely bald apart from hair at the back that dropped off in shock, completely covering the frog. At the sight of the very last vestige of his strength making a break for it, hopping towards the stream, the big bald giant broke down in tears. Zak almost felt sorry for him as he cried white ravines through the dirt on his face. Zak told him he would ask the lord up on the hill if Big Hendi could be forgiven, but he'd have to start being a good giant. He could do things like clearing the forest to give the people more farmland. Once he'd grown his hair back of course. In payment, Hendi would be given food. The grateful people up on the hill would leave it in the valley for him. Hendi wiped his eyes. They shone blue when he smiled. He nodded with enthusiasm at Zak's idea and Zak walked back down along the river and up the hill to the mighty lord to tell him what had happened, hoping to claim the hand of his daughter."

With this Erdi started to crawl out of Vanya's playhouse. "What happened next? Don't go! What happened next?"

"Yes what happens next?" *was called from the gathering sitting below the Teller.* Well --- *said the Teller*--- Erdi said to his brother, "You know what happens next."

"I know but I still like hearing it," wailed Mardi.

"I'll tell you a bit later. Come on. We'll go and find Yanker."

Mara returning from the stream with a huge basket of washing balanced on her head, paused and watched them go. She breathed a sigh of relief at the sight of Erdi with Mardi under his wing so to speak.

Later that evening Erdi spoke with his father about what he and Mardi had discussed earlier: the onerous expectation on the people to make significant sacrifices to hidden forces that supposedly had such a control over their lives. They talked out in the large open patch beyond the palisade so no spirits of tree or stream could overhear. They certainly didn't discuss such dangerous notions in the house where the Brownie could be listening. Erdi said it was obvious that the sun and water gave them life, but what if?" He whispered, "What if it's all just natural and would carry on happening whether we offered the bronze in sacrifice or not?"

Penda's face had a craggy, wise look about it that didn't seem that handsome on first meeting. The strength of the man in mind and limb added a magic ingredient, however, so that an allure began to radiate, making you wonder why you'd not seen how handsome he really was on first encounter. Chin stroking, he said at last, "A few of us have been thinking the same way. Nothing we say here should ever be repeated by the way. Swear to me." Erdi gave his word and Penda continued. "It's like many things. It is not as simple as it first appears. Firstly, if a few of us withdrew support, not sacrificing bronze, we'd be branded as traitors to the rest. They'd be stirred up into a mood of hate for having to carry our burden. Secondly there are plenty who'd like to see us turned off this golden piece of land so they could grab it. They wouldn't care if what we said was right or wrong as long as they could benefit from our families' destruction. And thirdly too many people rely on the structure of power that the miracle of the metal supports. There's his little army supposedly there for our protection, then the poor trapped fools who work his fields feeling their future is guaranteed, but in reality, receiving only just enough to stay alive, then there's his so-called Seer plus minions and finally, in a lesser way there's us and others like us who have improved our lot thanks to the fact we're rewarded for what we supply up there. I suppose it all started well enough, but people now resent the excesses especially now the eldest prince is approaching manhood. What the royal highness wants the royal highness gets, but it's our toil and sweat that's paying for it."

"But we could get together, turn the lot of them out and start again."

"I know, but it's too dangerous. Speak to the wrong person, a betrayer and they could have you turned off your land before next sunrise. Or strung up like a bronze runner. It would need something really massive to change things. I've puzzled about it long and hard, but I can't think for the life of me what it could be."

Erdi promised yet again not to say anything. "Not even", said Penda "if someone tries to lure you with the bait of supposedly having the same viewpoint." He wasn't even to mention it jokingly to those his own age. And certainly not to the likes of Brone.

"Perhaps we could get Big Hendi to help us."

His father, looking down with a wry smile said, "Yes. It would take something as momentous."

The next day he and Mardi went bird nesting. Erdi had done his chores. He'd ground the wheat, lugged water in leather buckets dangling from the poplar yoke, rather than the way the women carried it and he'd fed the pigs. Having told Penda his plan, the rest of the day was his. Poor Yanker was stuck for the day, weeding one of the patches that had become infested.

Nesting as you know lads is one of the bounties of spring and will continue as long as you leave enough eggs to hatch for the following year. The early part of the season was over and eggs they'd left would have already hatched. Today, pigeons were in their sights. Not the eggs, but the squabs, to be carried back for fattening. Their journey took them north near swampy ground, the source of one of the local streams.

It wasn't far, but far enough to relate the end of the Big Hendi story. "Now then where were we?" Erdi asked.

"Zak had shot Hendi's hair off and was going back to marry the princess," said Mardi eagerly.

"Oh yes, now I remember. Zak climbed the hill towards the fortress gates and a soldier spotting him from the ramparts called down in amazement to people below shouting, "Zak's alive! What's more, he's at this very moment walking up to the main gate."

They all rushed to greet him, but on seeing his look of determination, parted to let him through. They were full of questions, but what he had to say was for one man only. He was received inside the Grand Hall where the lord and his officers waited in their coveted places around the hearth. He told the Lord of the Hill how he'd subdued the giant and the deal that had been agreed. He apologized for not having asked his lordship's permission prior to negotiating the deal, but had been in fear of Big Hendi's hair starting to stubble up again, putting him in a difficult frame of mind. As it was, Big Hendi had given his word and could turn out to be a huge asset rather than the giant problem he was at present. "So now, My Lord" said Zak, "Would it be in order please, for me to meet the princess?"

"Not so fast," said the lord. "How do we know he will keep his word?" Zak was told to wait until Hendi's hair restoration gave sufficient strength for him to clear a patch of forest for farming. No tree clearing, no princess.

So Zak waited, but was allowed to take food daily to Hendi. They would at least sacrifice that much to show they were honouring their side of the bargain.

Following the next full moon, it was announced Big Hendi was ready to start work. The people came from far and wide to watch and were amazed as he ripped out trees as if they were mere weeds. He cleared as much in a day as the lot of them could have managed in months. Also there was a bonus, a mountain of timber ready to be chopped into firewood. So naturally, Zak expected to meet his princess at last. The lord, however, said he still wasn't entirely convinced the giant had changed his ways and would give the matter serious consideration once having inspected the results of the second day's toil. After the third day and still no glimpse of the princess, Zak began to think he and Big Hendi had been tricked. He told the giant to put his feet up for a bit and he walked all the way back up into the hills to ask the advice of Earth Mother.

Listening to his story, she said he needed to make the princess fall in love with him. That way she would implore her father to let her marry Zak. Zak asked how this could possibly be achieved with him not even allowed to meet her? She looked long and hard into the steam rising from her magic cauldron and a message came to her in the form of a vision. The princess would fall in love if she saw a picture of him.

'Well that's simple then,' thought Zak with a touch of irony. There was not one solitary person in those parts even remotely gifted enough to paint a likeness of a face. He knew the Seer was a fair hand at turning out the odd animal sketch prior to a hunt, but it was pretty basic stuff, just symbolic really. Even on a good day his effort of painting a face was hardly likely to render a princess smitten. And anyway, the Seer was never going to attempt a rendition of Zak's face on account of him being in thrall to the lord himself. Furthermore, he had yet to meet Her Royal Highness let alone stun her with a portrait.

When he walked back up the hill to the palace he was grabbed by the guards and marched in to explain to their lord why Big Hendi hadn't shown up for work that day. Zak said the giant was now his friend and wasn't clearing more forest if his lordship couldn't keep his side of the bargain. The lord gave a shrug and said it didn't really matter as Hendi had already cleared just about enough for them to manage. Zak of course was furious and marched out of the hall knowing he and Big Hendi had been tricked.

Outside the main door a girl's voice whispered from the shadows. She was one of the royal handmaidens and having heard all that had gone on, was willing to try and help. Zak explained he needed to somehow meet her mistress, but didn't know how. She told him she would persuade her highness to take one of her favourite walks the next morning along the river bank. Zak was extremely grateful and thanked the girl, but it still left the problem of the portrait. He thought long and hard into the night and suddenly like a flash the answer came to him.

Next morning the weather was fine and the princess and her ladies-in-waiting started to amble along the river bank, chattering and laughing. It rang out like the music you'd imagine from sunlit icicles. They stopped at the most beautiful spot on a bend in the river where a willow draped its branches like a woman grieving. The princess looked into the deep pool and gasped, holding her hands to her face. She had seen Zak's reflection in the water and as Earth Mother had predicted, had fallen instantly in love. Looking up into the tree, she asked Zak who he was. He climbed down, bowed and introduced himself. She was completely smitten and couldn't wait to hurry back to ask her father to arrange the marriage.

The old rascal wasn't at all pleased, however. A mere youth who had wandered in from foreign parts had outmaneuvered him! He told his daughter, "NO!" She screamed and stamped her feet so hard and fast it gave her ear ache, but he wouldn't change his mind. Worse than that he had a wooden tower built and locked the princess in a small room at the top. She could come back down if she promised to forget Zak forever.

"How did she get up there?" asked Mardi.

"What?"

"How did she get up there?"

He'd never asked this sort of question before, but Erdi supposed it was a sign he was growing up.

"Oh they made the longest wooden ladder any one had ever seen, but took it away and hid it once the princess was safely locked away out of Zak's reach."

"So what did she eat?"

Erdi paused to think. "Every morning the ladder was put back so one of her faithful handmaidens could climb up with food and drink and take away anything the royal highness didn't need."

"Like poos and stuff?"

"Mardi it's a fairy story. You don't have to worry about things like poos and stuff. And don't forget she's a princess."

"But we all got to do it."

"Yes I know, but it's not necessary to go into that sort of detail."

"Thing is, I know she's a princess Erdi, but it would still get pretty stinky up there with all that poos and stuff."

"Alright!" said Erdi with a sigh. "Each morning one of the princesses' faithful handmaidens would climb the ladder to take her food and water and come back down carefully carrying a pot full of poos and stuff. Happy now?"

Mardi just gave a throaty chuckle.

"Zak got to hear of the princesses' plight and came up with a plan to rescue her. He walked back up to the Lord's Grand Hall to ask for the princesses' freedom. The Lord of course laughed in his face. Zak put up with this humiliation, because, "Ha-ha," that was not what he'd really come for. He needed a good look at that tower. Outside, he gazed up to where his love was imprisoned and saw a tiny window no bigger than one of her slippers, inserted to let in a chink of light. He then spotted the handmaiden bringing the morning's food. Luckily it was the same lady in waiting who had helped before. He managed to quickly whisper his plan before the guards shouted and manhandled him away. They made a great show of marching him to the main gate and jeered as they shoved him into his first steps back down the hill.

Now---- next day a cart load of clean washing was being taken up to the fortress. There was no natural water supply up on the hill so they didn't dare waste what they had on mere washing and Zak had bribed the driver of the cart to smuggle him into the fort. Once inside he saw his chance and slipped out of the back of the cart and hid himself behind the wood stack near the main hall. With him he had his trusty sling, a length of strong thin twine and an equally long length of rope. In the night when all but the guards were asleep, he crept from his hiding place and managed to reach the foot of the tower unseen. Having tied his twine to a rock, he took careful aim with his sling and sent the stone zinging on high. It fled through the tiny window like a home-winging bird. Success at the very first try. Following the instructions handed on from Zak, the princess pulled up the twine and on the end of the twine was the rope. She tied the rope to a stool she'd been allowed as the only concession to comfort in her prison. Zak pulled on the rope and the stool jammed hard in the tiny window. Praying to the spirits, he climbed. The door had a bar across which he carefully slid to one side. He pulled on the door, his heart pounding. It creaked open and the two lovers stared at one another. Zak, with all his heart, wanted to sweep her into his arms. The princess was shaking with fear and excitement. She smiled at her prince, safe in the knowledge she was able to receive him into her small place of confinement without fear of it smelling the slightest bit stinky ----- Mardi.

Descent was difficult, but with Zak's help she lowered herself down the rope. They crept to the palisade and up on to the walkway. Zak quietly eased himself over the fencing and reaching up, lowered his princess safely to ground. They escaped into the woods and over the hills to live happily ever after.

"What about Big Hendi?" Mardi liked the next bit.

Hendi? He'd been getting more and more angry at the way the Lord had broken his word. So angry that steam had started to come out of his nose and ears. The very next day he walked up the hill to the fort, kicked the gates open and pulling up the prison tower, smashed the Grand Hall to pieces with it. Slapping his huge hands together with satisfaction, he marched back down the hill and off into the woods never to be seen again.

"Good job the princess wasn't still inside," said Mardi. "Big Hendi showed 'em!" he added punching a palm with his fist.

The Teller leant down towards his applauding audience and put a finger to his lips. "Hush Mardi! I can hear something!"

He now told the tale more rapidly. Erdi pulled his brother off the path and they ducked for cover in amongst the trees. The dull thudding of hooves grew louder and two horses at full gallop thundered past. The riders were crouched low, whipping their mounts in an intensity that was alarming, capes billowing out behind. They rode at such speed it had been hard to pick out details, other than their swords and shields confirming them to be armed warriors, either fleeing or pursuing. The two brothers crept out on to the path and then began to run back the way they'd come. Erdi paused where a gap in the foliage offered a view into a small valley. Across the far side a mounted warrior waited, leather shield on arm. Suddenly, looking behind, he whipped his horse and frantically dug his heels in. The startled beast bolted from cover and two riders sped from the trees in pursuit at full gallop. The lone rider, taking advantage of a solitary oak, wheeled in the lee of its mighty trunk, separating his two attackers. His sword flashed, and the leading pursuer, frantically attempting to rein in and offer arms, steepled back obviously wounded. Somehow, he managed to retain his seat and slumping forward, clung on. His comrade, hauling in his mount, which although screaming at being forced to rear and turn to face the lone rider, still sprang forward to attack. With shields raised, reins between teeth and swords flashing, they clashed and thrashed at each other with unbelievable ferocity, out on the open ground. There was a repeated ring of metal and dull thudding of swords biting leather. Then, no longer able to continue the manic intensity, the two broke off the action and the pair that had ridden with such intent earlier, left the small valley at hardly a canter. One had blood leaking through his fingers from a shoulder gash and the other looked barely able to remain mounted. It had all happened so quickly.

Erdi and Mardi were scared white and shaking. Fear swirled in a way that made it hard to think. They continued along the trail bent low, sprinting from one patch of cover to the next. Once feeling they had gone a safe distance, they relaxed into a more normal stride. Their path descended gradually to level out on the more open ground,

"Who were they?" Mardi whispered.

"I don't know, but keep quiet there's still one of them ahead of us somewhere." They rounded a corner, stopped dead and slinked back from view. Erdi peered from cover. He could see a battle horse ahead of them grazing, but there was no sign of the rider. He looked again scanning the open ground, petrified the warrior might suddenly materialise as if out of the earth itself. They waited, hearts pounding, but still saw no sign of the man. The horse moved away and then broke into a trot, a feathered lance bouncing from where it was still strapped to its side. Still they waited. Erdi told his brother to stay in cover while he climbed into the fork of a nearby tree. Scanning what seemed a strangely peaceful clearing, he finally spotted the body. The warrior's brown clothing had acted as camouflage. He wasn't lying in wait, but prone, on his side, head drawn back, offering throat to the sky as if frozen in pain. Erdi climbed down and they crept from cover. The man wouldn't be faking injury. it wouldn't make sense. They stood, watched and waited, but there was no movement. Emboldened by the thought the warrior might need help, Erdi edged closer.

"Erdi! Erdi!"

An annoyed flap of an arm stopped Mardi's hissed call of panic. There was a huge dark patch shining moist on the man's tunic and blood oozed from a corner of his mouth. A gentle shake on his arm brought no response. He was surely dead. No sign of a pulse proved it.

"Is he dead?" whispered Mardi.

"Brave man. He fought off two of them."

"Look at that dagger!" He was obviously a man of rank. The wooden hilt had silver ringed decoration. His undershirt had colourful needlework embroidery around the collar and adorning the ends of his dark tresses were a number of small tubular bronze rings. Their gaze returned repeatedly to the dagger, but they couldn't rob a dead man. Erdi noticed the man's sword scabbard was empty. "He's lost his sword. We'll look for it. He won't need it now."

They searched the ground back towards the scene of battle and were on the verge of giving up when Mardi spotted it glinting in the grass. It was beautifully wrought with hilt decorated in spirals. Erdi picked it up. It was finely balanced. They returned to the body and both stood and saluted the stricken warrior and Erdi, giving thanks to him and the spirits for the sword, gently closed the brave man's eyes.

"We can't keep it," Hissed Mardi. Even he knew the penalty for carrying a sword without authorisation.

"Hush! Let me think." An instinct told him it was vital in some way, but his reasoning was scrambled. Finally he said, "We'll conceal it in the squab bag and then hide it near home."

"We can't Erdi. It's dangerous!"

"If we hide it well enough, no-one will find it. They'll think his attackers took it. It's not like we robbed a dead man. The sword was nowhere near the body. When all this has been forgotten we can conceal it within easy reach, closer to home. I'm certain we'll need it someday."

Using grass, Erdi wiped the blood off the weapon and wrapped it in the squab bag. With legs still shaking, they walked home. Their prize was tightly swaddled and concealed under a trailing root of a forest giant. An oak standing like an ancient sentinel watching the generations come and go.

They described what they'd seen to their father, but didn't mention the sword. He'd have been absolutely incensed and would have made them hand it in. Erdi did ask if he should go back and retrieve their bag, a thing too valuable to seemingly mislay, but Penda told him not to go near the place and not to mention a word of what they'd seen, just what Erdi had hoped he'd say. So the little nesting venture had turned into a nightmare. Nothing more was said to anyone and they waited for news to filter through.

The story came back, the warrior was of royal blood and his killers were five, not two, marauders from the north. He had single handedly withstood the incursion from the band of raiders intent on pillage and destruction. Strange the brothers had never seen the warrior before, on fairly regular visits up to the fort and even stranger, the pointless encounter they had witnessed had been turned into an epic. Soon it would probably be retold as one against an army of ten, but they could hardly afford to reveal the truth.

When feeling the topic had at last died down, they received a nasty jolt. A young warrior, looking hardly old enough to be mounted and armed, toured the settlements and outlying homes. Even though only of the most junior rank he already bore that superior air typical of the soldiering class. He'd been sent to enquire into the serious matter of a missing sword. The shield of the hero had been recovered near the battleground and interred with his ashes, but there had been no sign of the sword --- a weapon of huge value. The penalty for an un-enlisted man possessing such a weapon was stressed, which was a sickening reminder when coming from one not much older than themselves and there the brothers hoped the matter would rest.

Erdi worried about his brother's troubled sleep, however, for the intensity and ferocity with which the rivals had slashed at one another was obviously still haunting his mind. He was certainly not soldiering material and the more Erdi thought about it, decided, neither was he.

He couldn't make sense of it. Why had two warriors apparently from the north been galloping, as if the devils were after them, from the south? How was the man lying in wait, himself surprised in attack from behind? Why had any of them courted needless death? It all made sense when told as an epic tale, but not in the strange reality he had witnessed. No, soldiering was definitely not for him. So it was even stranger, what eventually happened.

Chapter Five

An annual problem all faced was of course surviving winter. But also, before the miracle peas and vetch ripened, there was another short food gap in the year. After the first burst of spring with fresh hawthorn leaves, dandelion, nettle, endive and dock there was little in the way of a palatable vegetables available other than watercress and lamb's leaf, unless you persisted eating that just mentioned as it became tough and bitter. Penda thought a solution could maybe be found in pigeon squabs. Not vegetables admittedly, but certainly nourishment. The play house had given him the notion. If he built a small, simple nesting house, captured pigeons, roosting and breeding offspring, would treat it as home. They seemed to lay eggs throughout the year and so would provide, not only these, but their chicks ready for fattening. They had kept pigeons for years as they were the only means of long-range communication. The women always took a caged bird with them when out foraging. Its return home from their previously disclosed destination, meant trouble and their men could be quickly be on the scene. So early one morning, Erdi and Yanker were excused duties and sent into the woods. 'It's squab hunting again,' thought Erdi, slightly concerned, when considering what had happened on the previous occasion.

Their search took them to the southern end of the eastern ridge, Erdi not bothering to explain why he had no wish to look north that day. The ring of battle persisted in his mind, coming out of nowhere in the occasional flashback. Pigeon nests, if you can call them that, are easy to spot, but of course not all contained what they were looking for. They had two baskets apiece and hoped to return with at least 12 birds. Their endeavors took them into the afternoon and heading yet further south, they entered Scratch country. Scratch was a shortened form of the man's nickname. He didn't farm land, but relied on raising pigs for a living. Penda traded produce for Scratch's piglets every spring. It was easier than housing a boar, a potential killer and easier than taking a sow to be covered each year. Scratch was reputed to have been handsome in his youth which was hard to imagine looking at him in middle age. His wife, they say, had had a lucky escape, dying in child birth and she was survived by her only child, quiet Luda. Nobody had ever heard Luda laugh. Not that there was much to laugh about surrounded by pigs and having a shambling mess of a father who seemed constantly intent on scratching and rooting in his nether regions and even worse, up around the back of them, thus the name.

They could smell Scratch's domain before sighting it and its sea of mud beyond. Smoke idling its way from the thatch of his roundhouse gave it the look of a massive smouldering bonfire. Grass and some sort of slimy green culture had been left to flourish and in places the thatch had slumped that badly, it hid the wattle walls.

The boys were startled by the sound of a voice raging, "Come here you sow!" followed by a wailing, "No father! Please no!" They laid down their baskets and crept forward, keeping out of sight of the dog that had worn a mud circle around the post it was tied to. Daub, in places, had cracked and dropped off the neglected wattle walls, providing chinks they could peer through into the gloom.

Scratch was visible, a mound slumped by the fire and then they saw Luda approaching, looking terrified.

"You know what to do, sow!"

Even at that distance, they could see she was shaking, but couldn't make out exactly what she had lent forward to do, or why her face was averted with such distaste. He grabbed the

63

back of her neck forcing her down. Recoiling with tears streaming, Luda gasped, "But it smells!"

The resounding slap across her face, even made the two onlookers jump and Yanker pulled away from the wall almost gagging up vomit.

"Whose there? Get from me sow there's someone outside!"

The boys ran to retrieve their baskets and fled the scene with the dog screeching hysterically at the end of its tether and Scratch roaring like a bull behind them. "Come back here!! I know who you are!!"

'There's something about going squabbing that seems to turn the spirits against me,' Erdi thought as he ran. Back home they hunted out Penda to tell him what they'd witnessed and a council of war followed.

Penda, Dowid and Dommed, having been told by their wives "It is obvious someone has to act," discussed the options. Luda couldn't be left to endure that monstrous existence. It was finally agreed, the girl would be offered a new home. If she was willing to leave her father, they would look after her. It seemed callous of them, considering the scale of the girl's misery, but the problem of who would bear the eventual burden of her dowry wasn't going to melt away, it had to be discussed. They finally agreed to share it. Then there was also the small matter of next spring's supply of piglets. Where would they come from? They decided they'd just have to breed their own and marched off, heading towards Scratch country, the two boys along with them.

He knew of course why they'd come and stood in his doorway, with a weak smile of welcome. When his pleas of, "Look I can explain" and "What d'you expect? I'm a man stuck out here without a wife," fell on deaf ears, he grabbed the axe he'd concealed in the doorway and bawled, "Get off my property!!"

"Stand aside. We've come to talk to your daughter," Penda replied.

The dog was barking manically and repeatedly running full pelt at them, somersaulting backwards each time as if seriously intent on self-strangulation.

"Clear off! It's none of your business!" Scratch yelled above the racket. "What goes on here has nothing to do with you!"

"We're making it our business," said Penda. "Shut that dog up!" he marched over and raised his staff. The brute slunk away growling and slid under its lair of wooden planking rendering itself invisible, but for hatred still glinting.

"Where is Luda? Is she inside?" He called, "Luda!"

But for the sound of pigs rooting and grunting, there was silence. It had turned into a beautiful evening and suddenly a blackbird, as if aloof to the machinations below, mocked them with a melodious solo.

"Luda!" he called again.

"Leave her be. It's obvious she wants nothing to do with you!"

"Stand aside we're going in!"

Scratch raised his axe and came at them. The swing of it was caught by Penda's stave, Dowid jabbed his staff into Scratch's vast belly and Dommed bloodied his skull. Cowering within, Luda would have been petrified on hearing sounds of male brutality and the dog's renewed screaming and barking. They found her white and shrinking deep into the gloom. Out in the sunlight, she stood arms tightly clasped and was bowed as if ashamed, the violent shaking of her body, sufficient to make bells tinkle. She had a purple swelling shining below one eye and tears had streaked brown smears on her face. Penda's, raising of stick, was enough to shut the hound up again and he quietly put their offer to her. Luda glanced nervously at the men, silent, grim-faced and armed with staves, then down at her father, still a pathetic heap by the door.

"Don't leave me Luda," he pleaded.

Her bloodshot eyes flitted nervously and she began chewing at the corner of her lower lip as if intending to eat it. Erdi wouldn't have admitted it, but he was starting to have misgivings about what they were taking on.

Penda said softly, "It's your choice, Luda. We won't take you against your will."

"Don't leave your poor father." Such a small wailing voice rising from a thing so gross.

As she looked down at him again, you could almost hear her brain churning, then suddenly, without warning, Luda dashed inside to re-emerge clutching a rag doll, looking as if one hug away from falling to bits. As they left, Scratch pulling himself up yelled. "Don't think you'll get away from me! I'll fetch you back! You sow!! And don't expect any more pigs from me. Child robbers!!"

Penda turned and shouted above the cacophony of barking, "I wouldn't have another pig from you if you **gave** me the thing!!"

When back in the warm comforts of home, the women took over in a great caring fuss and flurry. They cleaned her up, replaced her rags with what they could spare and she sat meekly by the hearth, a red bow in her hair, sipping at a bowl of the day's pottage. She looked transformed, but still had the doll remnants on her lap. They hadn't dared wash the thing for fear of it disintegrating. The moment she was relieved of the empty bowl, she clutched it to her. making for a sad sight in the arms of a girl past the age of puberty.

Vanya crept over, sat and put a comforting arm around her.

They all agreed not to divulge the real reason for Luda now living with them, but somehow, as always, the news leaked out. Scratch still traded his meat up at the fort, but was now shunned by most. There were of course those few who simply viewed the episode and his loss of clients as an opportunity to drive him to a harder bargain.

There's also no accounting for what goes on in some people's minds. For instance, Erdi and Yanker had made a delivery of thatching reeds up to Blade's home one evening, hitching up Blackie the pony for the task. Donda was out somewhere with her mother, but Pa Blade made them welcome. There's often a price to be paid for hospitality, however, with him of course, wanting to know all about Luda. The boys just kept things simple and told him, she seemed to like living with them, was a good worker, that sort of thing. They managed to get away, but were followed by Blade. He walked along with them, nudging and asking to know more.

"What's she like?"

"We've just told your father, weren't you listening?"

"No I mean really. What's she like. You know."

"Quiet, but gets on with things."

He said with a swelling of his chest, "Our dad says," and emphasizing with quick backwards and forwards motions of half clasped fingers in front of his crutch, "we could do with a bit of that up here."

Yanker stopped to face him. "Your dad seems to know an awful lot Blade. Do you think your dad would know the whereabouts of a good man handy at fixing teeth?"

"Our dad? Oh yes, I would expect so."

"That's good, 'cos if he ever says that within my hearing, he's going to need one!" His staff was offered up in emphasis.

A day or so later, Mara said to her husband, "Penda? You remember you said the name Scratch was short for something? What is it?"

"Scratch and sniff," said Penda carrying on with what he was doing.

"Oh my MOTHER!! That is disGUSting!"

"Well you did ask."

A little voice chimed up at the Teller, "What was that nasty man doing to poor Luda?"

Oh he was just being a pig. A big nasty pig. But Erdi and Yanker rescued her didn't they?

"YES!!" *Came the united chorus.*

"Is Luda alright now?" *enquired another young girl.*

67

Well I don't know. Shall we find out? "Yesss!!" *came the chorus again.*

Chapter Six

One day Vanya came bouncing in, full of excitement, with a bunch of bluebells for her mother. Mara thanked her, but demanded to know where she had been.

"I've seen something," she swung her arms over her head in an arc and did a little jump as she said, "Hewg!"

"What? An eagle?"

"No hewger than that!"

"Vanya! Where have you been?"

"Only by the stream."

"No you weren't," said Erdi getting his hand slapped by his mother as he broke off a section of bread from where it lay on the stone baking slab. "I've just come back from there. I looked all over the place for you."

"Well I was not by the bit you were looking at. By another bit."

"Look I've warned you about wandering off on your own! How many more times.....? But her mother's flow was stopped by the question, "Mama, what does a bear look like?"

Erdi stopped chewing.

Mara said, "You can't have seen a bear, treasure, there aren't any left round here."

"They're huge," said Erdi, "thick brown hair, walk along on all fours, have a nose like a dog's but bigger. Much bigger. Bigger than that on a horse. They're taller than a man when they stand up."

"That's it!" She clapped her hands excitedly, "I'm seen a bear!"

"It was probably a horse. They come out of the forest to drink. Sometimes things can trick you if you only get a glimpse of them."

"It didn't trick me." She stood hands on hips. "I saw all of him and the him was a bear! A big brown BEAR!"

"And what was Mr. Bear doing?" Mara asked, humouring her.

"He was walking along. Then he stopped and looked at me. Then he started walking again. I saw him on the green bit along the river. He was simply hewg. Come with me Erdi I'll show you."

Mara, now grim faced looked at her son, gave a slight sideways flick of her head towards the door and Erdi taking Vanya's hand, did as instructed. He always carried his slingshot, but this time also armed himself with his father's spear.

They walked upstream, along the far bank and wondering how much further his little sister would be leading him, Erdi said, "Vanya, this is getting ridiculous. You can't have walked all this way. We'll soon be up at Blade's place!"

"I think we're getting close, Erdi. He was just around this corner I think," she said peering.

They fully rounded the bend and Erdi stood stunned. A bear was in the water ahead of them. It gamboled forward, scooped with a paw and the silver flash of a fish leaping from its grasp brought an almost perplexed look as if it was asking while scanning the water. "Where's fishy gone?" Then there was a loud splashing as it turned and galumphed upstream in chase. Erdi, eyes not leaving the massive creature, backed carefully away holding on to his sister.

"That's the most amazing thing," he muttered to himself.

"Told you I'm seen a bear," she whispered, not at all troubled.

"We're getting away from here!" He pulled her arm and they hurried back downriver.

"But, Erdi," Her voice sounded jerky as she tried to keep up, "I want to show you something else as well."

"You can show me another day. It's too dangerous to stay round here."

"But it's not here. I saw it up that other one."

"What other one?"

"The kinny one. You know. We jumped it earlier."

A little further on she said, "Look there it is." The kinny one turned out to be a silvery glint between weeds as water seeped along a tree lined ditch towards the river. Animals following the river had created a path down into it and out the other side.

She ran a few steps, almost slipping and beckoned him down with an urgent wave. Erdi had been constantly checking back over his shoulder, each time expecting to see a huge shape with a rippling brown coat, rumbling close upon them.

"It's just along here, Erdi." Vanya pointed up the brook. "I found it before the bear came."

"Not today Vanya it's too dangerous. We'll come another day. And are you saying you followed that bear?"

"It's not far Erdi." Ignoring the question and looking at him, head slightly atilt, in that manner some girls seem to be born with, she asked sweetly, "Please Erdi?" Having his arm tugged, he followed and not far up from the main river, they came to a flat open area beneath oaks just coming into leaf. The ground was a vast carpet of bluebells. Their whereabouts was of course known to Erdi, but this year the air itself seemed to shimmer blue.

"Lovely," said Erdi, "but can we go back now?"

"No not these. I don't mean these. Look over the other side."

He looked across the brook and saw, waving in the breeze, lit by a patch of sunlight, a vigorous looking spread of nettles.

"Can we have them Erdi? We could come back and move them. They'd be all ours. We wouldn't have to go searching for nettles anymore."

"Full credit to you, Vanya, that's the finest bunch of nettles I've seen in many a day, but it doesn't quite match up to seeing the bear."

"But they could be ours, Erdi! Can we come back and move them?"

"It's not quite as simple as that, Vanya. You can't just move them. They're not sheep. First we'd have to cut them, then dig up the roots, carry them home, dig up a patch and re-plant the roots for new nettles to grow."

She frowned and with her big brown eyes studying him, her mind wrestled with the logic, 'What's sheep got to do with it? Course they're not sheep, they're nettles! Why do boys have to make simple things so complicated?'

He hurried her back home, the house now full of faces silently emitting the same question. There was obviously astonishment that it really was true, there was a bear roaming the area and they all rushed, the men fully armed, racing each other, over the ford and up river to take a look. But as is usually the way with life, it wasn't there anymore.

After a bit of coaxing, Vanya eventually got her way and shortly after the day, forever remembered as, 'The day Vanya saw the bear,' - and also had her wings severely clipped by the way - the cart and Blackie were hitched to go nettle gathering. Erdi and Yanker crossed the stream by way of the stepping stones, Mardi took the cart reins while Vanya, Talia and Luda clung on in the back, screeching and laughing as they rumbled and rocked through the ford.

Yanker muttered, "Erdi, I just saw Luda laugh."

"Don't say anything, but did you notice? The old rag doll's not there anymore."

They had borrowed the sickle, an implement as important to them all as a sword was to a soldier and they had rags to bandage hands against stings. They threw themselves into the task with relish, with the patch being completely cropped and their bounty heaped up on the grass by the cart. Dock leaves were rubbed ruefully on the painful rashes left by the seeming willful nettle strikes. Then using antler picks, the roots were prised up and pulled like yellow entrails from the surprisingly loose soil, which contained old animal bones along with fragments of pot and charred wood. Lingering remnants would start another patch. The roots were loaded aboard, followed by the stinging cargo and they set off for home with a feeling of triumph and tingling fingers.

Using pick and shovel the boys worked on a patch they'd been allocated, deemed too rough for normal cultivation. They were on the point of mixing in midden contents when a stern voice said, "You're not wasting that on nettles! They'll manage by themselves. And didn't you think to prepare the patch before you all went a'nettle hunting?" They were boys. They would learn, but he marveled at the fact his tiny daughter, Vanya had been the inspiration behind the whole affair.

The roots were dug in, then watered and the girls stripped the nettles, the leaves being put aside for brewing and the stalks left to soak in the stream ready for splitting when soft. The pith would be teasled and spun to make fine fabric. Luda glowed like it was the best day of her life. She even shared in the laughter when Mara, brandishing her besom broom shouted, "Out you lot! You're not coming in here with **those** filthy shoes!"

Chapter Seven

Sometime later at one of those regular male community meetings, the subject of pigs was discussed. Although they all admired the way Luda had blossomed since first being adopted, circumstances surrounding her now being part of their happy band, left them with the ticklish problem of where to get the next year's pork supply from. Their own pigs were being fattened for the annual Fire Feast and to see them through winter, leaving none for breeding the following spring. Various ideas were discussed, but they settled on trapping a few of their own. It couldn't be that difficult.

A clearing was selected on the evidence of recent pig rooting and osiers were cut from willows. They thrived in the marshy valley bottom to the south. These were carted to the construction site and straight slender trees were chopped, cut to length and their trunks split using wooden wedges. The right type of tree didn't do anything so convenient as grow alongside the other straight slender trees and so the whole enterprise, including digging post holes ran into three days hard work. The wattle enclosure was fitted with a small trapdoor. It opened one way only and was just big enough for juvenile pigs to enter. They had no wish to capture an adult boar or sow, for fear of being ripped to bits trying to deal with them. Grain they could hardly spare was laid in a trail leading to the pile left within as the main bait. The plan was, the pigs would nose their way in and the trap door would allow entry, but not escape, so the men could then simply roll up with a wicker cage on the cart and collect their prize.

Yanker went out to investigate early the following morning and ran back with the exciting news, the trap had worked. There were five young pigs just waiting for them. They accompanied the cart in a mood of high expectation. Blackie was tethered downwind of the clearing, out of sight and sound, so not to cause alarm and with hardly a rumble or squeak, the cart was quietly manhandled alongside the pen. It stood ready to receive the young captives to be dropped into the cage. They all crept on tip toe and five faces cautiously peered over the fence to witness their quarry in a state of oblivion, grunting and munching.

Penda, feeling it was his job to act as catcher, eased his way in. They were at most, about two moons old and so theoretically, it shouldn't have been a problem to grab a back leg and dangle the squealers up to Dowid waiting on the cart. Of course, Penda had handled pigs before, but as he carefully lowered himself inside the pen, these particular pigs caught their first sight of humanity. All looked up. Snorted!! Then hurtled round from wall to wall in a dizzy, mad panic. Penda was repeatedly at risk of having his legs knocked from under him. It wasn't so much a matter of catching them, as dodging them. Then like a pack of dogs, they ran full tilt at the fence, scrambled up it and out over the top, back into the forest.

"Well! I'll kick my arse to the river!!" said Yanker's dad, truly shocked.

Penda, too prosaic to imagine such a thing sailing through the air and sploshing near an unsuspecting angler, said as he stared around at emptiness, "Admittedly, that could have gone better than it did."

They decided a higher fence was required and set to work extending the existing one. The bait was laid once more and four young pigs, still with minds intent on food, followed their noses and ended in the same trap they'd so athletically sprung themselves from the day before. The party returned with a ladder and nets and this time managed to 'come home with the bacon', two at a time. The sty to receive them had of course been altered to suit in view of the previous lesson learnt and stood like an example, simple but effective, of what gives some men the edge over their surroundings.

Chapter Eight

The Teller paused. So you see. *He bent down to address the little ones sitting at the front,* Luda is really happy in her new home, living with those good people. You'll hear more about her later. But now I would like you younger ones to run off and play for a bit. Go and play while I tell the next part of the story. I don't want your parents angry with me, saying I've frightened you."

They moaned, but did as asked. The Teller said to those remaining, The next little chapter isn't actually frightening, but I didn't think they'd quite understand.

One day Yanker and Erdi were out inspecting the hare traps they'd set and returning empty handed, their conversation, as often happened, turned to food. They were growing boys and constantly starving hungry. It was quite common for their stomachs to literally ache from the lack of something solid. Erdi had mulled over the knowledge that beaver had been at work in the stream above where Blade lived and turning to Yanker he said, "Crayfish!" Beaver would have dammed the stream causing a pool to swell out behind.

"What d'you mean crayfish?"

"I bet there'll be crayfish in the beaver pool. That one we heard about up above Blade's place. We'll make some fish traps," said Erdi

Yanker was all for it. "Oh! I can almost taste them now. There'll be crayfish, eels, Donda swimming naked and all sorts up there." He started to break into a run.

"What about Blade's dad?"

Yanker stopped. "What about him?"

Erdi laughed. "Don't tell me you've forgotten you threatened to rearrange his teeth?"

He for once looked lost for an answer. Then his face brightened, "Come on. I'll think of something. He might be twice our size, but he's not exactly quick on his feet. Look upon it as a challenge."

Erdi shook his head in disbelief at his cousin's ever bright optimism. He always preferred a well-planned approach to things himself, not having Yanker's ready wit to get himself out of trouble.

They cut and trimmed straight willow branches. These were tied tight at one end and flared out at the other to form a funnel shape which was interwoven with osiers. There was no shortage of materials in the locality. A stubby tapering funnel of the same construction was made to fit into the open end of the larger one and there was a hole in its narrow end to allow fish to enter. They made six of these and found six pine cones to wedge the bait into. A small fish was netted from their keeping pond and they were ready. It was late in the day, but if they hurried, they could lay the traps ready for night feeders and still be back to attend to their duties before dusk. They told Grandma Vana that they were off upstream to fish and asked her to pass on the message.

With fish traps strapped to their backs they hurried away from the compound. The shout of, "What about your chores?" fell on deaf ears and they were gone, with thoughts of food and a voluptuous young wench in mind.

"What are you two doing up here?" demanded Blade on their arrival. "Our dad wants a word with you, Yanker!"

"We thought you might be in need of some company, Blader. We've made a trip specially. Thought you might like to join us fishing."

"Fishing? Where? Invite me to fish our own fish? You've got a cheek! You're not putting those traps in **our** pool! Our dad says what's in that pool is ours."

78

"Nobody owns the river, Blade." reasoned Erdi, "but that's not the pool we're heading for. We're going higher up."

"Our dad says, what's upstream is ours!"

'Well, they have got possessive,' thought Erdi, remembering how different things had been on a previous occasion.

Yanker chipped in, "I think you'll find there's plenty who'd be willing to disagree with that, Blader."

"Where is your father anyway." Erdi asked thinking it best to tackle a potential problem head on.

"Out on the trail of deer that came nosing round. Lucky for you he's not back yet."

"Oh that's a shame," Yanker taunted. "That is a shame."

"You're in for it when he gets back!"

They called out of courtesy to say hello to Ma Blade. Donda was home and although curious as to why they had appeared from out of nowhere, tried to disguise her interest with an arm stretch and yawn, "You're always up to something, aren't you, Erdi?"

Her sudden unexpected focus on him in particular, struck like a tiny dart. He hadn't wanted the flush of colour to creep up his neck, but was completely at its mercy and lowered his head hoping she hadn't noticed.

"What you gone red for, Erdi?"

Now he could actually hear the blood pumping through his temples and the throbbing heat of his face could have warmed a pair of hands on a frosty morning.

Ma Blade, big and comfy looking, bustled to his rescue ordering Donda to go and fetch water.

The boys thanked Ma Blade for the scrap of bread with apple jam she'd given them and walked outside to witness Donda, chest out, walking imperiously, one foot precisely in front of the other and an arm raised to steady the water pot balanced on her head. "So you boys are back tomorrow then?" she called, carefully turning, in order to make full eye contact with Erdi.

"Yes. Make sure you're up bright and early, You wouldn't want to miss us." Yanker quipped back.

'Why is it he never goes red?' thought Erdi.

On continuing upstream with their fish traps, Yanker said, "Well! I've never seen her quite like that before. She seemed different."

"In more ways than one," Erdi added.

"Perhaps we could persuade her to take a dip with us. We could promise not to look." he said grinning and eyes glinting through open fingers.

"Enough," said Erdi. "You know if you imagine it, it never happens."

They heard a loud slap on water followed by splashes as they approached the beaver dam. Beyond was a wonderful sight. The stream had swollen into a huge pool that once settled, reflected a clear replica of blue sky and white puffy clouds. The breeze occasionally riffled the picture that, when eventually reset, showed the clouds had moved slightly. Iridescent dragon flies whirred across on oblique missions close to the surface and busied themselves amongst reeds growing beneath the steep far-side bank. In the near shallows, swirled a mat of green fronds, recently inundated. They cut their fish bait into small pieces and forced the flesh into the open pine cones. These were put into the traps that were weighted with stone and lobbed into the pool. The ends of the twine to haul them back in were tied to short wooden pegs and evidence of their whereabouts camouflaged. They didn't want their good friend Blade stealing the catch.

They ran back home, avoiding Blade's house with its likely threat of confrontation and on arrival, launched into their tasks with an enthusiasm that was commendable. Even though the light was fading and mothers and children had wandered out to enjoy the sunset, they didn't pause, lugging wood for the fire, filling the water troughs and were hard at the quern, grinding wheat, when Penda wandered over. He'd seen them leave earlier, had taken notice of their hurried return, their

80

unusual zeal and asked breezily, "So, been off on a little fishing trip then?"

They told him what they'd done and intended to do, hoping he wouldn't put a stop to an early morning departure by dreaming up some urgent task needing doing.

"Why did you take the traps all the way up there? You know how stupid and awkward he's got lately when people use the stream beyond his place. What's wrong with our bit? You could have saved yourselves a walk."

Yanker looking up, grinned enthusiastically, "I don't think it's ever been trapped before. Could be teeming with stuff."

"Anyway he doesn't own the river," said Erdi. "Nobody does."

"I know, but there's no point stirring things up. We're trying to dream up a system right now, as it happens. One that's fair to everyone." He was just turning to leave when he asked, "By the way, Erdi, how's that little madam, Donda?"

Erdi could feel his colour rising again.

"It would be a sensible idea I think, if you share the catch with them tomorrow. That's if there is one. Oh, and another thing, take Vanya with you. We have to be careful. I don't like her habit of wandering off."

Erdi's flush of embarrassment was immediately quenched.

They left at dawn the next morning hoping to slip past Blade's house before Pa Blade was up and with any luck he'd be out working when they called in later to share the catch.

Vanya was an energetic little soul, but couldn't match their pace and so slowed them somewhat. Blade was up and waiting for them on the path.

"Our dad wants a word with you Yanker!"

"Splendid, lead the way," his words hiding the instant stab of terror. There was nothing stopping Pa Blade giving him the thrashing of his life.

"They're here dad!" called Blade, with a note of triumph as they entered the house.

Pa Blade was on his feet in an instant and advanced at a pace surprising for such a slow thinking man. "Outside you two!"

Yanker deftly side stepped the attempt to drag him to the door and dodged behind a roof support-post to shield himself from further efforts. "Would this be about comments said regarding Luda?" he asked loud enough for all to hear. "Poor little frightened Luda? We can just as easily discuss those remarks in here."

"I'll punch the living lights out of you," growled Pa Blade trying to reach around the post and snatch him. "I'll use your guts for slinging shot!"

"Don't you hurt my Yanky!" scolded Vanya on the verge of tears, rushing to protect him with her tiny body.

"Stop, all of you!" Shouted Ma Blade. "What sort of comments?" She had been as appalled as anyone regarding Luda's plight. She'd even donated a dress Donda had grown out of.

"Well go on, tell her," insisted Yanker emboldened now he'd stood and faced the threat of a good beating.

"What sort of comments?" Her fresh demand brought silence. A silence so long and sticky, it made it possible to hear the faint call of a cuckoo.

"Nothing. Forget it. I've got work to do." He brushed past them, stomping out into the yard followed by Blade calling, "Daaaad?"

She turned to Erdi for the answer, but he just smiled and said, "Nothing that important. Best forgotten." Her husband's fear of having unsavoury details revealed was Yanker's only insurance against the future threat of a good beating.

The cousin's, looking up on hearing the light tread of footsteps, received a jolt at the sight of Donda, darkening the doorway. It altered the whole mood. "What's going on?" she asked slightly breathless. "I heard voices." She had on a long woolen skirt and noticing how the tight bodice above, struggled to constrain, the cousins stood gazing, just willing her to sneeze.

On being told it was just a small misunderstanding she gave a frown of disbelief and sailed on past into her small allocated section of the house.

"What are you doing now?" Demanded Ma Blade. "I need that barley spreading. There could be rain later."

"Just changing. It's too hot in this. I could go up to the pool with them later." She poked her head from behind the screen from where she'd been busying herself, "Would you like that Vanya?"

"The boys might not want you there," called Ma Blade.

"Oh we don't mind," they said in unison.

'Screen,' in fact was a generous term for something that barely hid her disrobing and the young men could feel their pulses quicken and throats go dry. There was a strange stirring of the lower body as if an overall mild bout of shaking could be imminent. The sight of breast-feeding women was an almost daily occurrence and not of the slightest interest, but this, the odd glimpse of a girl glowing with womanhood and obviously pleased with how nature had so recently favoured her, was totally different.

Yanker, realising they'd been caught looking, brightly asked Ma Blade, "Would you like us to do anything? Something to help while we wait for Donda?"

Her narrowing of eyes confirmed, she'd seen them alright, "Yes. Now you mention it, it would be a help if you shelled those peas for me."

Donda swept past and her mother demanded, "You're not going out like **that** are you?"

"Why not? It's too hot in that other stuff."

"Well I hope you've got something on underneath it."

"I like to feel the breeeeze," she said theatrically, with backward sweep of arm.

"You'll get more than the breeze up there, my girl, if you're not careful!" Strangely, the look she exchanged with

Erdi had a slight hint of mirth. The woman then called out to the disappearing figure, "You mind they're not looking down on you. They love nothing better than to punish the vain and brazen!" Although such words of warning were familiar wisdom, the way they were said suggested a vicarious pleasure derived from her daughter's behaviour. She then bent down and said to Vanya, "You can stay in here and help Aunty. I've a nice little job for you."

Her term, aunty, of course implied closeness, rather than connection by blood. It was hard to imagine this kindly bundle of maternity bursting into anger at the slightest provocation, but she certainly could. Vanya looked excited at the prospect of helping with grown-up women's work.

Yanker carried the peas up to a level area and Erdi struggled behind with the basket of damp barley to be dried in the sun for malting. They helped lay the cloth and weight it down, then both lounged on the bank below where Donda, with her back to them, began spreading the seeds. She didn't crouch at her work as most women would have done, but stood legs apart making it easier to bend from waist down, going to great pains, almost over-elaborating in fact, giving gentle sweeps of the hand to evenly spread the barley. The boys could hear an indistinct tune being hummed as they edged a little lower down the bank.

After a while she turned and demanded, "Are you two looking at me?"

"Difficult not to," said Yanker, "Seeing as how you're right in front of us."

"You know what I mean! A certain part of me!"

"Of course not Donda. What a hurtful thing to say!"

"Yes you were. I could feel your eyes burning into me! Look you've shelled none of those peas!" She crouched on the lip of the bank directly above them, rocked, but by ever so gently, by parting her legs, regained balance. Erdi could feel a strange tingling pulsing through his system and was at a complete loss when through a menacing smile she asked, "So!

84

What is it you both find so fascinating?" She jabbed each with an enquiring finger, "**Eh? Eh**?" The curves of her body pulsated and in doing so, seemed to gradually swell.

Yanker, chirpy as ever, "Well remember you asked, did we know where babies came from?"

She gave a tolerant nod.

"Erdi and me have been wondering. Haven't we Erdi?"

Erdi's mind was in numbed confusion. Donda, glowing with femininity, looked transformed and had become something beyond anything he felt he could confidently handle.

"Wondering what exactly?" Even she sounded breathless.

"Well Donda," he said pointing, "It doesn't seem possible. Do they really come from in there?"

Parted lips now glistened and with a slight tilt of head, Erdi was asked with a smile, "Well what do you think?" It was obvious of course, they were bound to know, having seen pigs, lambs and calves born, but she was as excited by this game as they were. Erdi was flattered but confused. Why was she favouring him when Yanker was the main instigator?

Yanker pointed "D'you really mean a whole baby comes from inside there?" His trembling finger was within a hair's breadth when they heard the serious little voice from behind, "What are you doing?"

Not even Donda had seen Vanya's approach. She sprang to her feet, gave the front of her skirt a vigorous swipe to smooth it and saying "Get away from me you dirty dogs!" marched off.

"What were you doing with Donda?"

"Nothing," said Yanker. Then having gathered his wits said, "Well what happened was ----It was like this. We saw a mouse run up Donda's skirt. It frightened her and we were trying to chase it out."

"A mousy. Can I see it?"

"No, Vanya it's gone now. Don't say anything will you? Donda's mummy hates mice and it'll upset her. Come on let's finish these peas and then we'll go and find some fish."

The traps had been spectacularly successful, with crayfish, two eels and a trout having been caught.

They took the crayfish home and left the rest of the catch as a placating gift. All the way back they impressed on Vanya not to mention the Donda incident.

"Now are you sure you understand?" asked Erdi.

Vanya, lips seriously pressed together, vigorously nodded her head.

"Now are you really sure?"

Same response.

They had hardly got through the door when Vanya blurted, "Erdi and Yanker been a dirty dog with Donda!"

Mara looked at them shocked and Yanker's father, Dowid who had just taken a gulp of beer paused, eyes bulging.

"Them was looking at her mousy!"

Beer burst from Dowid's mouth. He had to go outside almost choking with laughter.

Penda also laughed when told later, but then thought it best to have a word. While he applauded their healthy interest in the mysteries of life, he warned that one mistake in early years could trap them for the rest of their days. Donda's looks were alluring now, there was no doubt, but looks can fade, feminine curves can turn to fat and she wasn't the brightest of girls. A native cunning maybe, but not bright. Did they really want Brone and his father as future family? Just to drive the message home, he put them on watch, taking turns day and night, on duty, ready to report the instant the heavily pregnant cow under the shelter, started to calve.

The Teller paused here and said it would be a good idea if they all took a little food as the sun was now high in the sky. The boys in his audience had groaned with slight disappointment at Vanya's interruption of Erdi and Yanker's attempted exploration into the realms of procreation, but all had laughed out loud at her summary of the little episode.

"Will you tell us more this afternoon?" *came the plea.*
We'll see.

Requesting calm, using a gentle downward motion of both palms, the clamour ceased. He paused as if seriously mulling over the idea, Well alright. We'll all meet here a little later.

Pointing high to the south, "We'll meet after another full span of the sun."

Part 2

Chapter Nine

The Teller began to make his way back to the main hall. Gaps between houses on prominent central ground, offered views of the far western hills. Their misty blue outline still held a slightly ominous feel as they would have done in Erdi's time when the wild Skreela swept down from their lofty fastnesses into the valley to trade, or to do worse if the notion took them. He politely refused offers of food and drink as he wended his way, for sustenance had been pre-arranged and his absence would have been taken as an unforgivable insult. He carried out his profession with an air of nonchalance, but the pressures were ever present. His lighthearted style of delivery disguised this and went against convention, but he wasn't one for grandiloquence and privately felt scorn at the pomposity of some of his contemporaries. His style had brought him popularity, but he never forgot, levity could be construed as disrespect and he was certain there were those who would gladly point this out, conspiring to have him brought low.

When he returned to the East Gate, an audience awaited, swollen in numbers. Mothers now accompanied their younger children. They were given a brief introduction to the main characters and running explanations where relevant. Those won't trouble us here.

So, *said the Teller.* We come to that time of year when there is abundance, but those long rose-gold shadows and sound of swallows excitedly gathering before departure to their mysterious destination south, brought an urgency to the people as they knew winter would soon be upon them. The wheat, barley, peas and lentils had been harvested; hay racks and barn were full; pelts had been flint-scraped and cured; apples gathered for the cider, jam and vinegar; fish and game smoked or dried; beechnuts and acorns gathered; hazelnuts and mushrooms picked and the first frosts were awaited.

Penda found himself intrigued by something. He had become aware that at every meal when meat was on offer, Vanya secreted a small portion and later slipped from the compound thinking she had not been noticed. As her absences were short, he hadn't felt the need to reproach her - she had obviously learnt from the bear encounter - but he was still fascinated to know what the little miss was up to this time. When asked she simply replied, 'it was a present for Minchy.'

"And who exactly is Minchy?" This got him nowhere as Minchy apparently was just a friend. He at first simply shrugged, thinking it might just be a name for a spirit friend, children sometimes have. At least she didn't insist on Minchy having a place reserved next to her each mealtime. Then remembering the bear incident, he decided he had better follow to see who this Minchy was. He hadn't needed to go far into the woods to witness to his horror Vanya, with a fully grown wildcat winding itself around her legs. The thing was at least knee high to her. It must have been the same length from whiskers to end of dark banded tail as his daughter was tall. She reached out and placed the small portion of meat for it to eat. It crouched and began to gnaw until hearing, "VANYA!!" at which it turned, gave a savage face-wide hiss and bounded off into the undergrowth.

"You frightened her! She hasn't been here for days and now you've frightened her!"

"Come here Vanya, don't you realise how dangerous they are?"

"Minchy's not dangerous. She's my friend."

"Vanya, wildcats are friends to no-one. They might look cuddly, but they can never be tamed. They belong out here in the forest. No matter what kindness you offer, a wildcat will always remain wild. They kill our lambs. One bite, dead! If it bites you, it's like poison."

"Minchy isn't poison. She's not a snake."

"I know she isn't but they can still be deadly. I heard of a man who almost died having been bitten by one of them. Not a huge wound, just two fang marks on his hand. In the end, if they hadn't have cut his arm off, the spread of poison would have killed him. I can't believe this wild thing comes so close to you."

"She makes a funny rattling noise when she's happy. But she won't let me touch her. If I try she runs off. Well I did once when she curled up next to me in the playhouse."

"What?"

"She sleeps in there sometimes. That's how I met her."

"How do you know it's a she?"

"She just is. Minchy is Minchy."

Penda realized she needed another serious talking to. He and Mara drove home the point as best they could and even Erdi joined in, commenting wryly, "You'll be bringing home wolves next."

So there the matter rested. Or so they thought.

Work continued in preparation for winter. The weir had been repaired and it would soon be time to lay fish traps for salmon lured up the water channel. The grain pit had long ago, been filled and sealed. The boys helped their fathers chop, gather and stack wood. The green timber was left neatly piled between staves to dry and the trimmed dead wood loaded on to the trailer to be added to that already put by, under cover in the compound for the coming cold. Beech leaves and any oak chippings from their lumber activities were collected for smoking the meat. As they busied themselves gathering the hazel nuts, beechnuts and acorns Yanker commented, "We're like a bunch of those nut hoarders! They seem to know we're too busy to take a shot at them." The squirrels he referred to, often a tasty addition to the family pot, scurried everywhere, bounding across open ground and swirling like furry red ribbons up tree trunks, competing with them in the annual battle for survival.

In the three family homes, as with every autumn, little spare room remained, but sight of the season's bounty in columned basket stacks, gave a feeling of comfort -- security. The houses had had a springtime repair, but all was checked again for the coming rain, frosts and snow. The thought of winter raging outside and everyone huddled safely together with enough food, drink and warmth almost felt like something to look forward to.

Erdi told Vanya the roof of her playhouse also needed some attention. In truth it hardly needed his efforts. What he actually did was secrete the sword they had found into its thatch. He didn't mention this to Mardi. It wouldn't have been wise, dredging up bad memories to plague his brother's sleep and what he didn't know couldn't harm him.

After the first frosts, rowan berries, rosehips, bullace plums and sloes were gathered and processed in a seemingly never-ending bustle as they all prepared to settle in as if for hibernation. Soon would come the time for the spirits of pig and barren sheep to be shown the peoples' respect, before giving themselves up for the pot, salting and smokehouse. The first really severe frosts signaled that that time was upon them and families visited one another to help with slaughtering, fat rendering, sausage making, cleaning the offal and joining in a feast day held outdoors around the roaring fire. By tradition they ate and drank into the night. The Fire Feast pig still awaited its fate, but as regards those animals predeceasing it, the meat was not usually eaten immediately, but cured to last the community through to spring. What was actually feasted on was blood sausage and delicious dumplings; tripe boiled until tender to be chopped into strips and added to stew; chitterlings, fried until crispy and eaten with a pinch of salt;

seasoned pork scratchings left from fat rendered to lard, which in turn was used for the searing and basting of meat through the ensuing year.

Just as now, the frost spirit was welcomed. They even gave him a name, the same as he is known by today. He brought flavour to the winter fruit and was treated as a harbinger of good fortune for the following year, ensuring healthier crops, fewer flies and other pests. 'Put on extra clothing, slap your hands together and get on with it,' was their cheery attitude. You can almost imagine their breath visible in the cold morning air as they went about their chores. That spiky frost sprite of course made their lives a good deal harder, but they were hardy people and knew he was basically their friend.

Vital at this time of year of course was salt and Penda's little community had been blessed by a stroke of good fortune regarding this. The trade was strictly controlled by the tribal chieftain, as was the importing of copper and tin to smelt bronze. There came a trader from the north, however, by the name of Egrik, who for some reason, on one of his annual tours, had struck up an understanding with Penda. He traded salted fish from the sea. This kept through winter and if soaked overnight in fresh water before cooking, tasted as fresh as any recently caught. The flavour was different, however and a treat they looked forward to on a cold winter's night. Not only was it the basic ingredient of a succulent stew, but could also be pounded into a delicious white creamy paste. He traded, what in fact looked like unappetizing rigid grey sticks, for dried venison and he was one of their secret outlets for smoked eel and other cured fish. They were one of the first on his calling list and he always kept enough stock back to fulfill the order placed the previous year. Any slight imbalance in a deal was recorded on a tally board and a personal mark scratched so all could be equaled out, more or less, on the next trip. Why did he favour them? He just shrugged and said he liked them. Just one of those things. The floor of his cart was held in place by wooden pegs, but four could be twisted loose to allow a single board to be lifted from what was in fact a false bottom. Below was a secret chamber holding the bags of salt. In the presence of Penda alone these were taken out and hidden. This cargo was of course highly risky and to compensate for that risk he was paid in pick of the year's best hides. The day was treated like a small celebration and news was avidly exchanged: tin from the south was becoming scarcer; the tribes from beyond the sea were bringing in hunting dogs as big as ponies; slaves could be appearing for sale at next year's spring fair; a bronze runner had been hung up by the North River, he'd seen the body. He put in a request for what was needed next trip, which included venison and strangely, baskets and fish traps.

"Why? Can't they make their own up there? Is there some sort of willow blight?" asked Penda.

"No. Not really. They stack well and are light to carry atop the load. Just thought they might trade well."

Penda laughed. "There's something you're not telling me."

"Well things like that compensate for the hit."

"What do you mean, hit?"

"The amount they rob, for the privilege of trading here. Tax -- hit," he shrugged. "It's just a term us wayfarers use."

"I still think you're hiding something."

"Well I know we're friends, Penda, but it wouldn't do to tell you everything now would it?"

Penda smiled and more beer was poured.

So this friend Egrik, known to them as Grik the Fish, gave them the edge. Deer and boar, beyond their immediate needs, could be hunted and with the extra salt preserved and hung ready, either for trading or for their own consumption when the worst of winter made hunting an act of desperation and misery.

The few skins traded brought twice the return of any similar transaction negotiated up at the fort, but it was still vital to procure their normal quota of salt from his lordship. Not to do so would alert those in power to the fact they were almost certainly dealing in contraband and their activities would attract even more scrutiny than they already did. The smuggled salt came from the sea and up until that point, not even the mightiest had had the temerity to tax that. The salt normally used in the valley came from the mines located somewhere in the flat lands two day's hard travel away below the spine of hills, to the north east. It could be obtained in block or crushed form provided the high asking price was met. The chieftain controlling the mines, exacted his price, as did their chieftain in turn. In theory any could bid for the salt at the autumn fair, the catch being, it was traded as one lot and no single person other than their lord and master had the wherewithal to trade for it. Once in his possession he could squeeze whatever price he thought fit.

The daily demands up at the fort were quite enormous. There was no ready wood or water nearby and so this had to be continuously hauled there. The lord, his family, his retinue, his small army, his seer plus acolytes all had to be fed. Horses and other animals had to be fed. They needed everyday tools and utensils, leather, rope, baskets, napped flint and special woods for arrows, spears, yokes, needles and axe handles. Medicinal plants, floor rushes, beeswax, tallow, wool, horn and luxuries such as honey and fine fabric were all taken there on a regular basis. The list seemed endless. They were kept in the manner to which they had become accustomed, on account of the fact that without them, their loyal subjects would supposedly fall prey to all those ferocious tribes living beyond their borders. All this was paid for with bronze. At the autumn fair the salt was in turn paid for with the lord's bronze. He recouped this and of course more when trading it on to the other tribes and his people. So in fact the price the salt traded for in any particular year, within their territory, set the ultimate value of bronze. Not the other way round. This of course was as long as salt and cheaper bronze from beyond the lord's control didn't find its way in to undercut the value. Thus the severity of punishment for any caught salt or bronze running. You could fashion ingots of the metal into tools, thus enhancing usefulness or trade value, but if caught with large quantities of its constituents, copper and tin, you could lose everything. The art of bronze smelting was a closely guarded process and only allowed within this very fortress, under the watchful eye of his lordship. Anyone caught dabbling in the secret alchemy required for its making, could not only lose their livestock, house and land, but life itself. Which in fact was what their salt-fish supplier risked with every trip. Penda didn't know exactly how the man avoided a rigorous search. Maybe with being such a regular and paying the trade duty on his goods each trip, they just waved him through. He suspected he sailed his wares down the North River, the Dwy, which south of the Feasting Site, came curving in from the west, from out of the Skreela hills. That was where he guessed Grik re-united with his cart, left there from the previous trip, before heading into their territory from the north west. As virtually all their salt came from the north-east, no-one would be looking for it arriving from the opposite direction. Somehow he even managed to circumvent Gwal, a defended toll on the Dwy, meaning his salt arrived tariff free and so for a little hard work, ingenuity and incredible courage he was rewarded with the pick of Penda's furs and pelts.

The Teller lent down towards his audience. Sorry to burden you with all that. I can see some of you getting a bit twitchy. Still you were lucky. You had an abbreviated version compared to last night. You see without knowing that sort of detail it would be hard to understand the daily lives back then. It's quite fascinating really. *The Teller pushing his sleeves back, leant forward again the better to confide with them.* The fact is, as the value of the revered metal increased the less of it the folk needed to procure the salt, but of course the catch being, they were required to trade inflated amounts of their own goods to obtain the bronze in the first place. It actually got far more complicated than that---- Oh I'm sorry, *he said.* I know. All that detail's enough to send you walleyed. Still, that's got that sort of stuff out of the way.

Now back to Erdi and his family. No before that. Stupid of me. Must tell you this bit and it's not more trading detail. I promise. It seems that Egrik, also known as Grik the Fish might have had another reason for his circuitous route into their territory. Penda had heard a whisper of certain female involvement. He had gently probed regarding this, but initially, his friend had simply brushed the subject aside. When pressed further, however, Grik, with a resigned look had said, "Well as you know Penda, I'm a traveling man."

"**And**?"

"Well you know."

"No I don't. Tell me."

"Well," he explained with a sigh, "I must admit -----" As he paused, Penda caught the glint of a smile in his sideways look, "There are a few places I can go if I want my clothing interfered with."

The Teller's little gathering burst out laughing. These were innocent times.

Once Grik had gone on his way, Penda went up to Mara, who was in full flow discussing the baffling intricacies of women's matters with Morga her sister-in-law and with them both staring at his untimely interruption, he said, "Mara? Do you know what? I think Grik could be a bit of a ladies' man."

Both continued to stare--- looked at each other--- then Mara said, "Never!! You'll be telling me he trades fish next!" This, plus their chortling merriment at his expense, left Penda feeling a little wounded. He was known for his strength and determination, but he did sometimes envy his wife's ease of perception, her understanding of life's little subtleties. He'd noticed Erdi had a touch of the same. Something that enabled him to steer a course, seemingly without effort, between impulse and logic.

So, back to what I was saying. All winter's urgent needs had been tended to, domestically that is, meaning the men were now free to go hunting. They had three dogs in their compound. All three were watchdogs, but one, Harka the smallest, was especially gifted at tracking game. He'd not been fed the day before, nor that morning, so was rather keen for the chase. The hunting party was made up of the three fathers, Penda, Dommed, Dowid, plus the sons Erdi and Yanker armed with arrow and spear. Erdi had his sling and salvo pouch, but doubted it would be much use in the tangle of the forest. Penda also had an axe strapped to his back.

Erdi had hardly been able to sleep the night before. These hunting trips were a highlight of the year and for the first time he and Yanker were part of the team rather than merely, interested followers. What they were doing was exciting, dangerous, but necessary for the sake of the three families. He'd checked his weapons at least three times before finally attempting to sleep and was up before first light to join the hunched figures moving towards the remnants of the fire. They chewed thoughtfully on the bread left there. Mardi appeared from the shadows. He had been asked to offer up a plea to the spirits. Even though yet still young, it was felt the job somehow became him. With his voice now deepened and jaw hardened on the cusp of manhood, something strange had started to emanate. He was the natural choice.

He offered up the deer antlers and with eyes closed made a low guttural sound. All around the fire closed their eyes in concentration and Erdi felt a shiver go through him. The same was done when the white skull of the boar was raised. Having thus shown their respects and prayed for spiritual help they rose from the fire and left like shadows. Penda ruffled Mardi's tousled hair, as yet uncombed so early in the day. His son looking up, said, "I was hoping to feel the spirit of the deer today. I didn't. I just had an emptiness. The boar's spirit was strong, but why does this come through me? I don't know what's happening. It worries me. I'd much rather be like Erdi and Yanker. Please take care of them."

Penda looking down at the sadness in his son's eyes, gently clasped his shoulders, "Maybe you can come with us next year."

They left for the forest, cladding the northern edge of the ridge to the east, with Harka whimpering and straining at the leash. Erdi was full of hope and expectation. He and Yanker had stumbled across countless deer, pony and boar on their explorations, as always happens when not adequately armed to take advantage, but now it seemed as if the forest was empty. His slingshot had sent up feathers and dropped one, then a second rock dove at their feet, but to return with just these would leave them open to ridicule. The women loved nothing better than to occasionally wound the pride of their men folk. With the sun now high, all the eagerness and energy of the morning had been sapped and what had seemed like an adventure now felt like extremely hard work. Their small food pouch was emptied and they slaked thirsts and refreshed their faces from a cool trickle of water that wound its way down through soggy moss and brown autumn leaves. Harka ravenously swallowed his food whole.

After mutual commiserations regarding their bad luck, all knocked knuckles on the nearest oak to prevent spirits therein from hearing as they discussed their next move. A change of direction was decided on, heading south along the edge of the ridge. Almost immediately, things took a turn for the better. Harka was on to something. His tail went up, his nose snuffled vigorously around one particular patch and then he was off leading them through the tangle. The pace was rapid and care was needed not to whip the person following with the branch just pushed past. The scent led them on across the ridge and although there was no visible hint of their quarry, Erdi had a premonition this would lead to the culmination of their day's efforts. At the sight of Harka standing, ears pricked and a front leg poised, they all halted, straining to see what they'd been tracking. Just ahead, in a clump of stunted oaks, something very large was rustling. It was probably eating acorns and was probably boar or sow. The spoor of the creature wafting on the breeze gave confirmation. Below them was fairly open woodland. They communicated by sign now. The three men eased their way downhill using cover of shrubs and trees while the youths crept up the slope to drive their quarry towards the ambush. Even Harka was silent, no longer panting. He had been trained well. Avoiding twigs underfoot and carefully parting branches to silently return them to rest as they passed, Erdi and Yanker stealthily edged into position. All depended on them outflanking, gaining the higher ground for the drive. After that it was down to the accuracy of the men lying in wait---------- until the wind shifted.

The massive boar caught scent of those below and growling as it gathered speed, hurtled from cover towards the youths. With both parting to get a shot at its flanks, Yanker tripped and sprawled headlong. The enraged beast veered in his direction with the clear intention of ripping him to pieces. Erdi, now thankful for years of practice, deftly loaded his sling and the stone he sent whirling was accurate and blinding, bringing an absolute cacophony of screams echoing through the forest. His shot had stopped the boar long enough for Yanker to regain his feet and for Harka to run in, springing from side-to-side barking and goading. Suddenly there was an uproar------- growls, shrieks and barks and the poor dog was first ripped and then tossed into bushes where it lay plaintively whimpering like an injured child. His bravery had given enough time for the cousins to tackle the bristling monster, driving spears in from either side. The men arrived on the scene, tearing through the undergrowth and Penda, wielding the back of his axe, clubbed the writhing boar to death. Poor Harka was ripped beyond repair. Penda's eyes glistened, on the edge of tears as he gathered up his faithful hound from where it hung trapped in branches. When laid softly in the grass, Harka licked his master's hand, before closing his eyes for the final time.

The men stood in silence, revering the departed spirit of Harka and giving prayers of thanks to the spirits that had offered up their prize. A stout pole was cut and trimmed and four were needed to bear the weight of their trophy, edging their way through the forest towards home. Harka's corpse was wrapped in a cape and hoisted on to Yanker's back. They arrived back in triumph, but immediate mention of sad loss of their dog was avoided, his body having been left in the fork of a tree on the edge of the forest.

There would normally have been great feasting after such a hunt, but when the tale of brave Harka was finally told, celebrations were muted. Later his hide was cured, teeth made into a necklace and flesh boiled from the bones. This meat was hidden in stew and consumed without the young ones being any the wiser and Harka's bones were given a burial as if he'd been one of their children.

Chapter Ten

As the autumn progressed the men all turned their hands to crafting items for their own use and for trading. Baskets and fish traps were woven from willow; skewers made from spindle wood; clothes-pegs from split ash bound with willow bark; rope fashioned from lime bark; glue made from birch bark; tool handles shaped from beech; boat paddles made from light aspen; ox yokes from hornbeam and bucket yokes from poplar. The women largely concentrated on weaving cloth on the loom and knitting woolen garments. They all talked, laughed or sang as they worked and sometimes Erdi was asked to relate one of his stories. When the weather permitted the younger children played outside. Why, do little girls so often scream when they play? *The Teller asked with a smile.*

The adults heard the usual boy, girl taunts and tried to calm things when the latter rushed in to complain the boys had ruined their skipping just when they'd mastered using two ropes at once. Then they'd run roughshod through their mother-baby game while playing Skreelas and warriors. The boys countered with, "Well they're always ruining our target practice on that lumpy patch you said was ours! Why do they have to keep dragging those horse-head sticks grinding up dust, up and down and round about on our bit?"

The women eyed one another. The unexpected reminder of that first strange innocent tingling, experienced years before, had them momentarily silenced. Mara finally said, "Go back outside, the lot of you and play nicely!"

One woman in the Teller's audience frowned disapprovingly, another suddenly found a strap on her footwear required adjusting and a third stared at him straight faced, but with a wicked smile shining from her eyes. Returning her look, he gave a sigh of resignation and continued.

Luda had become one of the family and now being properly fed had grown into quite a strapping girl. When she worked, her fingers were a blur and when she played the boys had to watch their step as she was alarmingly strong and a match for any of them. Erdi had taught her to fire slingshot and had been amazed at how quickly she had mastered it. Now you might have noticed, *said the Teller,* when it comes to stone throwing most girls seem to have the wrong body action as if their arms are somehow joined differently to their shoulders compared to those of boys and their flapped efforts tend to make male onlookers laugh. But when Luda first let fly in one of their competitions, throwing stones across what they called the Black Pool, they watched in silence as her stone didn't splash like their's had done, but thudded into the far bank. Even Yanker had been temporarily dumb-struck, before at last managing to mutter what sounded like, "Muscles like hissing bullwhips."

Luda hadn't realized it, but by taking up women's work in her new life with such enthusiasm, she was rewarding their kindness tenfold and apart from the odd tendency to slink away to a quiet spot to be alone, seemed to have recovered from the horror of her former existence. The men did wonder, however, what her marital chances might be. She was a bit of an odd package.

It was she who raised the alarm regarding eel theft. Very little went to waste in their community and that which could not be eaten was fed the pigs or if really disgusting, dropped into the keeping pond to fatten the eels. She'd spotted two of the neighbour's boys energetically spearing into the pool as if having been invited to do so. Penda had been back near home under the ox cart at the time, readying it for the trip to the Fire Feast. He and Dowid had split aspen into planks and were busy repairing the vehicle's floor. They both ran over at the sound of Luda's cry and Erdi, burdened for the day with sheep minding duties, leapt at the opportunity to join them all at the pool. Penda had the wriggling youths by the scruff of the neck and was threatening to cut their thumbs off. The youngest lad was crying and had wet himself in fright.

Erdi arrived just in time to catch, "Come here I'll do you first. You'll never hold a spear again!" It was time to intervene. And quickly! His father's quivering bicep was hard as flint when first grasped, but gradually Erdi felt its tautness slacken as he persuaded him that perhaps a quiet word between them might be in order. His uncle guarded the two culprits while Luda stood arms folded looking menacing. The thieves stood heads hung, a pitiful sight and at their feet, still slowly looping and squirming, lay the thing that could change their lives forever, an impaled dying eel. Erdi reasoned that the boys had probably been encouraged to steal by their father, a man who had always caused him inexplicable unease. Wouldn't it be best to lay the blame at his door? It would surely make more sense than taking immediate retribution, disfiguring his sons. To do so would not only start a lifelong feud, but could also bring them unwanted trouble from on high, for seriously handicapping two potential defenders of the realm. Penda now saw reason.

The boy's hands, thumbs still intact, were tied in front of them, the dead eel was hung dangling from the neck of the eldest as a mark of shame and they were marched back to their home down by the slow stream. The warning given by the barking dog, brought their father to the door and motioning it to its kennel, he welcomed them with an obsequious posture and slimy smile of innocence. This told Erdi everything. If he'd have been escorted home in such a fashion his father

106

would have been furious. Penda slapped the eel down at the man's feet and demanded, "Your sons are thieves! What d'you know about this?"

The man gave a helpless shrug, "What d'you expect? They're just boys. It's a boy's prank. Like stealing a few apples."

"Apples? Prank? Those eels are part of my livelihood as well you know."

"I'm sorry." With that same infuriating shrug and open palmed gesture of helplessness, he chided, "Calm down. It's just one eel."

At this Penda snatched him, almost leaving his head behind, lifting him clear off the ground. Wrenching him close he snarled into his startled face, "Pity the thief who gets caught first time! You're lucky I didn't cut their thumbs off!"

He shoved the man away in disgust. Erdi, watching him straighten his collar and upper clothing, sensed the same danger you'd feel if attempting to handle an injured weasel. That was until Penda, still far from finished, roared at him. It was that loud the man visibly flinched and raised an arm as if warding off a gale, "If I catch them anywhere near my property again, you know the consequences!" The eel spear was thrown to ground and bone prongs stamped on and smashed. He added, "You pathetic excuse for a man!" With a sweep of his arm and head shake of incredulity he continued, "Here you live in perfect eel country yet you send your boys to steal mine!" Looking down at the dead fish he said "Hope the thing chokes you!"

With that they marched off leaving behind a void of silence. Even the man's dog, on daring to leave its kennel, had a worried eye and tail between its legs.

Back home there was talk of little else. How the thieves had come within a blade edge of having their thumbs severed. How terrified their father had looked when suddenly parting company with the ground. Had Penda been right regarding the man's guilt? Of course!

107

"I don't know what it is?" said Dowid, "He's a nice bloke but nobody likes him,"

Even though they all now knew every last scrap of detail, they still relished going over it again. Then yet again. All except Mardi. Having listened initially, he'd drifted into a world of his own. Erdi felt a glow of love flow over him and an idea flashed in his head. He had a quick word with Yanker and then with their parents.

After the evening meal, to which all had been invited, Penda asked Mardi to stand. Never one to seek prominence, he wore a puzzled look as hesitatingly, he rose to his feet. Everybody. I mean everybody cheered as Penda hung the boar tusk pendant around his neck.

"But they belong to Erdi and Yanker. They're theirs. Bravery."

"They've decided to give them to you Mardi," said Mara softly.

"They can't. They won them. They won the highest honour."

"You brought us the boar's spirit," explained Erdi. "They belong to you now."

Mardi gazed around as if worried it might all be a trick. He blinked and in his stunned look of disbelief there was the glint of a tear.

In the darkness his grandma Vana hid the fact, she really was crying.

The year was ageing like a snake skin ready to be cast off, the old sun had become weaker and weaker, trees stood bleak and barren and days and nights were now colder. Then Stench the charcoal burner came calling.

Penda went out to meet him with bread and cider. Mara wouldn't have him in the house. She knew he couldn't help being constantly dirty, but why did he have to smell so bad? There were streams in the forest. He could wash. She fanned the air in front of her nose, "The stink of him would startle a starving dog off a pile of rotten guts!" It wasn't like her to talk like this, "But really! The smell of the man would drive anyone to extremes."

"You've left it late, haven't you?" Penda called out. "We've no real need right now, Stench. Not until the spring fair." With face averted, he handed the bread towards the man's quivering fingers.

"Thank you, Penda. We can surely do a bit of a deal."

"But you know we've no need for charcoal now until after the spring trade."

Stench stopped chewing and gulped the mouthful whole before looking up towards the region of Penda's forehead to gabble, "Well t'won't eat nothing. You can store it 'til then." He had the unfortunate habit of wanting to talk as close as possible to the listener's face without actually looking them in the eye.

Penda backed off trying not to breath in. "We've got nowhere to put it, Stench" he said, as quickly as possible through gritted teeth.

Stench, oblivious to the effect he was having, advanced a step for every one Penda took backwards, "Shove it in the byre. The cows won't mind."

"Nobody trades away their food this time of year. You know that, Stench. We need the food ourselves." His name had been used for that long the owner had long lost any notion of being offended by it.

"Look, Penda! I'll do you a good deal."

Normally the two massive panniers of charcoal on his pony would trade for two baskets of peas or something equivalent.

"But we really don't need it right now, Stench. Try someone else," was said quickly, all in one breath from behind a shielding hand. The smell of the man was making him cough and his eyes water.

"I was counting on you, Penda."

"Back-off, Stench! I'm starting to feel sick," he croaked.

"I'll do the whole load for one basket of peas."

"I'm sorry Stench, Mara would never forgive me."

"I didn't want to do this, but now I'm begging you, Penda."

The man looked truly desperate. The top of his jerkin was wet from his trembling attempts to drink the cider.

"Look Stench, I can't let you have peas but I can do you some flour. Well not flour as such, Mara would kill me. Wheat grain. You'll have to grind your own."

A red smile of relief spread across the ingrained black of his face.

"What exactly are you doing?" demanded Mara.

"It's only one small basket and we've got plenty this year."

"Penda! Have you taken complete leave of your senses?"

"Just one basket, Mara! And I've traded it for his whole load of charcoal."

"I'll remind you of that when we're snowed in and running out of food!"

"The man's starving, Mara. I can't see a man starve."

The charcoal was loaded into the byre. "I'll never forget this Penda. You've just saved my life. I'll collect the panniers about bluebell time."

"Save the thanks, Stench. No get away! I don't want a hug!" Penda pushing him off and almost at a run, gained the safety of the house, retching from the smell lingering in his nostrils. Mara didn't speak to her husband for two whole days. When she finally did, on hearing of Stench's intended springtime basket collection, she scolded, "Well, keep him away from those bluebells. One whiff would flatten the lot of them!"

Now with the daylight time shrinking to only half that of high summer they started to plan for the Fire Feast. With three families and only two carts, food, bedding and other requirements needed careful sorting to provide everything they needed without cramming the two vehicles to excess. Fodder was put aside for Blackie the pony and Garrow the ox. Harness was checked, axles greased and skin canopies repaired. There was an overall feeling of excitement. Then the Seer arrived.

Silence greeted the ominous figure clad from head to foot in a long grey hooded robe. His three minions followed, heads held high, looking that disdainful it made fingers itch from the desire to slap them. The branches of mistletoe they carried, had been stripped of their poisonous berries.

Mara forced a smile of greeting as they entered. They couldn't be denied, they were too powerful, so it was best to endure and be done with them as quickly as possible. She eyed the blackthorn staff of rank, the boar's tusk necklace and hoped the Seer hadn't noticed her covering Mardi's recent award by flicking a cloth over where it hung from a post.

The menfolk entered, followed by their families and all stood in silence. Morga, Penda's sister and Inga, Dommed's wife quieted their babes in arms. Food and drink was offered their visitors and as the Seer raised his arms to offer thanks and blessings, the cuffs of his robe dropped to reveal a faded jumble of fabulous beasts amid swirling patterns tattooed on his pale wrinkled skin. Turning to all he said, "Thank you for this warm welcome. As you know, very soon we will be giving thanks to the spirits for this bountiful year and making generous offerings for the next. Each year seems tougher and tougher and yet despite the unusual late flood of rain, the crops have been gathered. Your grain has thankfully ripened despite strangely cool days. We give thanks to our strength that has helped overcome these hardships and above all we give thanks to the spirits that have kindly smiled upon us."

He stared round at the circle standing in what he took to be reverential silence. The dust he threw dust in the fire went, 'Wooomf!!' in a cloud of smoke and although they all knew it was coming, it never failed to surprise.

He lowered his voice, "But what of the future? It cannot be taken for granted. I am weary. Yes my people, I am weary." He wiped his brow with the back of a hand. "I commune with the spirits, but they are ever more demanding. They drain me of strength. Help me my people. They demand ever more offerings."

111

The Seer crouched, staring about wildly and almost dancing with each step, went from one to the next beseeching wide eyed, "Will you help? Will you help?" As the boar's tusks rattled on his collar, his watching minions wore sickening looks of adoration.

All in his congregation gave a nod of assent as he passed, then watched slightly worried as with one leg raised mid-stride, he stopped, searching this way then that, resembling a predatory bird sensing prey. A loud gasp resounded, for as if pulled by an invisible force, he suddenly jerked sideways to pour all his intensity on to Mardi. "Will you help, young man?"

Mardi stood boldly, arms behind, causing those who knew the signs to hold their breath. An arm jerked forward and he thrust a barren pig's thighbone within a whisker of the Seer's face.

Looking puzzled by the sight of them all, a hand to mouth, staring at him aghast, he felt it best to explain and in a matter-of-fact tone said, "Bone for the bone man.".

"The **what**?" With eyes flashing anger, the Seer pulled himself upright to imperiously demand, "What is the matter with that imbecile?"

Mara rushed over and held her son close. "Forgive him. Please forgive him. He knows not what he says."

"He means no harm," added Penda. "Please don't take offence. He's a good lad, but just says the oddest things at times."

Gradually the Seer was placated. Everyone fussed about him. He couldn't be allowed to leave bearing a grudge and having retribution in mind. They were almost reduced to pleading, before he finally deigned to shake off the insult and lay out his star and moon woven blanket to collect their bronze offerings. His acolytes gave out the branches of mistletoe. These would be hung above doorways to welcome in the spirits from the cold and to ward off witches. Early the next year, six days on from the Fire Feast, the dried leaves would be brewed into an efficacious elixir to aid fertility.

When he and his retinue had gone and were safely out of earshot, there was a collective sigh of relief. Penda silently blowing out air from puffed cheeks said, "Mardi, Mardi, Mardi. You'll get us all hung."

Then the laughter started.

As the day of the Fire Feast approached, Erdi, Yanker and Mardi took great pride in bringing home holly and ivy to be hung in the houses. It symbolized renewal, but for them it was just something they always did at that time of year and meant the big day was almost upon them.

First, however, came the Day of Offering. All the boy in question hadwore their best clothes and joined others assembled at the Offering Pool. The lord and his lady arrived, not walking, but driven there in the royal wagon, bronze mounts polished and gleaming. They emerged from the fur-lined interior, his lordship needing help as they stepped down on to the rush woven matting. Regaining composure, he waited godlike as courtiers furnished him with helmet, shield and sheet-bronze torque, the latter garlanding his neck, to glint shimmering patterns. All the female interest was drawn to the young lady's noble face and attire. The beauty of her large dark eyes was made all the more striking by their contrast to the ivory and rose tones of her complexion and almost hidden, glowing between soft brown tresses, were fine annular earrings of burnished gold. Around slender neck hung an amber and turquoise, bead necklace, the weave of her tight woolen cap held gems of worth untold; an intricate brooch clasped front fur-cape edges and as raised skirt swished, parting pleats revealed embroidered fabric and slung low on her hips, glinted a girdle of gold.

The proud chieftain smiling, offered his right arm and together along the rush strewn trail they approached the lakeshore. His body was ensconced deep inside a bearskin coat and the tall bronze, boar-tusked helmet gave hint of his

113

progress for those viewing from the edge of the throng. A sudden breeze gusting off the lake to swirl his coat open, revealed a magnificent sword and mace of office hanging from a bronze studded belt and on his free arm gleamed the splendid circular, ceremonial bronze shield.

Behind came his Seer, wearing not only his boar tusk necklace, but also full liturgical white cape hemmed, weighty, with yet more tusks. He had the blackthorn staff of office in one hand and a gold sickle in the other. With hands clasped and eyes lowered as if in silent prayer, his acolytes followed. Behind them walked a handmaiden cradling the royal baby, followed by the lord's advisers and bringing up the rear with a collective air of arrogance and detachment came the warriors armed with sword and spear, their number including the two princes, begot from the old queen.

The people strained to see the ceremony. They raised their eyes to the sky as staff and sickle were thrice offered up. All knelt as the spirits were beseeched. Those helping launch the skin boats, aided the holy men to sway aboard and handed the bags of bronze to be offered to the spirits. In the deepest section of the pool, black over by sheltering willows, where wreaths of grey mist still hung, the incantation rang out followed by the low throaty response on shore as one by one the pieces of cargo splashed out dark ripples on entering the water.

"They could be dropping rocks for all we know," Yanker muttered, receiving an elbow jab of reprimand from Morga, his mother.

Time of the Fire Feast was fast approaching, *said the Teller to his ring of listeners.* Even the pig was invited and on being dispatched to the next world, its spirit was given mighty thanks. Nothing was wasted and all was packed and put ready for the journey.

At last, departure day arrived. Grandparents, Tollan and Vana, who remained to take care of home and livestock, stood in the gateway to wave them off and wish them well.

Garrow the ox, with water steaming off him, was driven to trundle on ahead while Blackie was put to the task of making two trips to deliver all dry-shod over the ford. The stream, as was usual this time of year, was swollen and its freezing cold waters would have made the long trek one of misery had they not clung to the carts as they groaned under their loads to the far bank.

Nearing the dark outline of the fort, the well-defined trail north was taken and they passed fellow pilgrims on foot bowed under their burdens. All looked up from their struggles, smiled and gave cheery greetings. Light from the east gradually transformed the dark mass of nearby trees into individual trunks and gaunt glistening branches. but there was no hint of warmth left in the old dying sun.

They caught up and joined the convoy of carts heading for the Feasting Site up on the Dwy River. Progress was dictated by the slowest and so was barely at walking pace, but none minded, not least the children who could play near forest edge then run and catch up, to excitedly relate to their families, what they'd done and what they'd seen. A troop of warriors, however, shouting for clearance and cantering past brought wry comments along the lines of, 'At this rate we'll be lucky to get to the spring fair in time, let alone the winter one.'

Well into the morning they arrived at the first halt. A hamlet lay beside a large pool in a clearing and the travelers stopped to rest and water their beasts of burden. Mara cut up the cooked tripe and served it cold in three large wooden bowls. Salt and cider vinegar was added and bread for all lay spread ready on a cloth. They were starving and tucked in with relish.

The day was clear now and although still chilly, all gave thanks for it not being wet. Well into the afternoon, the trail dipped precipitously into a section made challenging by a small stream, Nant Crag, that over years had deeply eroded it. Compared to major rivers this barrier looked insignificant, but it in fact marked the northern edge of their territory. Beyond it lay foreign land, the flatlands ruled by the Salt King, as he was referred to locally. The banks were soft and muddy and the way across had not been made any easier by the passage of previous carts. All helped heave as horses and oxen, steam rising off them, strained through the mire and slipped in muddy gouges attempting to find footing up the far bank. Once gaining dry ground families returned to the ooze to help those yet to cross. Thus friendships were forged. Many took a welcome pause once safe on the north bank, gathering strength for the final section, leading to their destination. Their loads were given nothing more than a cursory glance by Charge the tallyman. Banter was exchanged. No-one really went to the Fire Feast to trade and so his presence was just a token of the lord's authority. He'd been called Charge for that long, no-one could remember his real name. He, or another like him, would be back there in the spring to tally their loads in earnest for the tithe gathered at the end of fair. The officials were moved around, so not to become too familiar with regular users of routes in and out of the territory. Charge was just as likely to be found out west where Penda suspected his friend Grik the Fish entered, or east in view of the distant high hills ranged along the horizon, or south on the river crossings. "The job gets me about," was how Charge cheerfully put it. His manner wasn't typical. The fact that tallymen were generally reviled for what they did tended to make them clannish, set apart from normal society. They didn't mix and no-one encouraged them to.

There was a growing sense of anticipation as the afternoon wore on and although stomachs once more, felt hollow with hunger, a renewed energy fired, for they were approaching the river. Then as the chill of early evening mist descended, from the lip of the ridge they finally espied its curve, like a massive grey serpent winding in the flatlands below.

The light was fast fading, but through the dusk, distant twinkling of Feasting Site campfires, told them they were almost there.

Families greeted as they entered and they were offered a space by those keen to renew friendships, struck up at previous gatherings. They had brought enough dry wood for the first night's fire and embers from the clay fire carrier were blown and soon brought it crackling to life. Pot-boiler stones were put deep in the embers to heat. Dumplings to be later served with bread were placed to bake on the family hearthstone, transported there in a slot beneath Blackie's cart, but first chitterlings were fried. They had been pre-cooked and so were soon brown and ready to serve with bread and salted scratchings. There was the usual cry of, "Can I have the burnt crispy bits?" from the children and the aroma now wafting from the campsite gave hint of the feasting to follow. Some slept on dried hay bedding under the cart awnings and some beneath the carts themselves on hides spread over springy ground-strewn branches. When at last under blankets, a final shiver of relief brought laughter as they snuggled together for warmth.

Everyone was up before first light. They assembled at the sighting stones, where Seers from all three tribes waited in full regalia. None of the holy men had slept, having huddled the night long in shuffling clusters offering up mysterious chants and incantations, grasping the last available opportunity to beseech the spirits for safe delivery of the new sun. The tribal chieftains, their families and honored dignitaries sat silhouetted upon their wooden platform, a people set apart. The eastern sky lightened from black to murky grey and eyes strained for first sight of the new sun. They were blessed. Arms were raised to greet that all-important first glint. All except the nobles, that is, who simply stood in acknowledgement. The alignment of its light from tip of the Crown Stone to the top of the lower Kneel Stone confirmed it to be the new sun. Throughout the assembly, each turned to hug a neighbour, giving greetings and well wishes, relieved and joyful at having been safely delivered into the new year. Music was struck up and the fires were prodded back into life.

Men and boys went deep into the forest to gather wood to keep the fires bright for the coming festivities. Each year they needed to travel further and further or pay locals in bronze for that stacked up and dried in readiness.

Now the Fire Feast pigs were roasted and best beer drunk. There was singing, dancing, storytelling, but no fighting. Even the wild Skreela knew, violence within what was in fact a shrine, would be met with instant expulsion. The Feasting Site belonged to the people and was ruled over by no king. Armed warriors remained camped beyond the simple wooden enclosure, confined to three distinct tribal areas to avoid clashes, entry to the hallowed ground only allowed if unarmed.

Excited children running around everywhere, exploring and chasing, found a welcome at each campfire. Vanya a few years before had complained to Erdi with a frown, that one of the boys had given her unwanted attention. "Him keep piling at me," she'd said.

Erdi told her that smiling boys were a thing she would probably have to get used to. The boy in question had been a young Skreela prince and it seemed, even with the passing of time, he'd still not lost interest.

Luda glowed in almost trance-like awe taking in all about her. This being her first Fire Feast, she began to wonder if she was still on this earth or in fact in heaven.

Erdi renewed his contact with two brothers from the lofty citadel to the east. Their fortress girded a high cliff top and their lord and master controlled the salt trade. Difficulties in translation were aided by universal sign language. Mardi, having found a soul mate in the more thoughtful younger brother, joined them and the two seemed to share an understanding even through interludes of non-communication.

Yanker went from camp to camp, laughing and joking, treating people as if he'd known them all his life. Some looked as if they'd gladly take him home with them.

Blade skulked around beyond the palisade, watching the soldiers and Donda had been spotted over by the trees, being courted and teased by a number of warriors from the eastern tribe. Revelling in the attention, to the point of looking quite breathless and starry eyed, she completely ignored Erdi and Yanker .

Penda went in search of Vanya, gone missing once again and found her beyond the compound watching the Skreela boys. They were wheeling and thundering round on their nimble ponies, long hair blowing in the wind. A rider would gallop full tilt and without pause swing down to pluck a wooden dart from ground to sling it winging towards a straw target, before pulling his pony round to avoid skidding beyond the line of elimination. Vanya was mesmerized.

Looking up at her father, she complained, "They're speaking language." She'd obviously tried to communicate and had failed. "I want to speak language."

As he led her back to the family she asked, "Can I have a horse?"

With her already being hard to keep track of, Penda sensed disaster. "I'll let you ride Blackie," he said.

Vanya pictured Blackie, the time she'd seen him slowly - painfully slowly - hauling a load of fresh cut grass that had been that massive it had hidden the cart, giving the impression he'd been dragging Penda astride a complete haystack. "I mean a fast arrow horse."

Penda smiled "They're not arrow horses, Vanya. They're ponies from the Skreela mountains."

She pondered this for a while and said, "But can I have one?"

"We'll see."

So, *said the Teller,* Vanya wanted a horse. But as we know horses are either hard to catch or expensive to come by and Penda was not a rich man. He had hoped that the traditional gifting of presents to all the children at that time of year would have taken her mind off it. But no. He could see she was smitten. Anyway, let's progress towards the Spring of that new year.

Chapter Eleven

With the previous year having been quite a battle, close won against such inclement weather, talk at the elder's meeting centred around discussion of problems and possible improvements of method. A major problem, being loss of crops to foraging animals. The small plots they'd planted had been denuded around their edges having been grazed by deer at night. Telltale hoof prints gave irrefutable evidence. Straw effigies in old clothes scared them off during the day, but for some strange reason, not at night. The animals could seemingly lope effortlessly over any barrier constructed and so there seemed no solution other than to reduce their numbers. Of course, the aim was not to completely wipe out a useful meat supply, but if just young bucks were targeted it could strike two flies with one hit, so to speak, leaving the remainder of the deer to carry on breeding as normal. Even though the thrill of stalking and chase was a thing prevalent in most men's blood it was considered in this instance, too time consuming. It was reasoned, deer needed water to drink and as their tracks often led to the Black Pool, this would be where they'd concentrate their efforts.

First bait had to be laid and so a block of rock salt was placed near the water's edge and then having seen evidence of deer's hoof prints and salt licking they thought the time ripe, to sacrifice sleep and lay in wait for their quarry. The skin boat was taken down from where stored, hung from rafters of the cow byre and after having checked it for leaks, was taken up to the pool in readiness.

Mardi was again asked to commune with the spirits and beseech them to bless the coming hunt with good fortune.

In the cool mists of morning the men, including Erdi and Yanker crept into their positions for ambush. A hind and two young does approached nervously and only when satisfied no danger lurked, melted through a patch of deep bronze fern to reappear at the water's edge. Tongues energetically flicked at the salt block. Taking care not to drench his fellow hunters, Penda's shake of branch was all it took to frighten them off. It was chilly waiting by the cold water and hands were blown on and rubbed to maintain circulation. At last, a lone buck wandered into the glade. It paused and sniffed the air. The predators watched in the morning's silence hardly daring to breathe. Drawn by the salt-lick it ventured hesitantly towards the lake. It stood as if sensing danger, but at last unable to resist, bent to lick the bait.

Shouting and waving the hunters ran forward. The buck's head jerked erect in fright. A frantic attempt to escape along the shoreline was blocked, first one way, then the other, leaving no choice other than taking to the water. Dowid, Erdi and Yanker were soon afloat and in pursuit. The struggling animal eyed them fearfully as they paddled, skimming lightly to quickly overtake and a paddle slapped on water, sent the confused creature, straining every sinew, back towards the shore. As it approached the shallows, Penda calling out thanks to the spirits, ran into the water and clubbed it dead. The carcass was hauled ashore and lashed to a pole for the return home.

One spring morning Mara was sitting beside the hearth stirring the contents of a bowl for first meal of the day, but on eying Vanya's approach and sensing something was amiss, put it aside and made her lap ready. She lifted her daughter, enfolded her in her arms and asked what was the matter?

Vanya, large brown eyes magnified by imminent tears said, "I had a dream. A big bear dream. It was HUGE!" (she could now say the word properly) "The bear was in here. It looked at you, it sniffed at me. I could feel its breath. It sniffed everyone, but nobody woke. Then it went over again to Mardi and Mardi sat up and looked at the bear. The bear stared down at him. It frightened me, mama. 'Don't!' I shouted, but Mardi didn't listen. He reached up and put his arms around the bear's neck and was gone. Mardi was gone, mama."

"What, the bear ate Mardi?"

"No, mama!" A big tear slowly rolled down Vanya's cheek. "Mardi was now the bear!"

Later, after everyone had been fed, Mara touching Penda on the arm, beckoned him out of general earshot. She told him of Vanya's dream and they both stood in silence trying to interpret its portent. Penda finally said that they had best consult Elsa. Mara was relieved. She had hoped the dream would be taken seriously. Penda would seek out Elsa up at the next market. He and Dowid not only supplied smoked eel and fresh fish to the lord, but now, having taken a regular pitch, traded their growing bounty of venison there. Plus of course, they still occasionally baited the boar trap they had gone to such trouble to construct and became known for their speciality of dried hams. The small tariff for the privilege was easily outweighed by the extra amount traded. In fact, you could almost say, sold. Bronze was becoming a recognized currency, rather than merely a collection of useful objects or bars of metal that could be rendered into such.

Penda, with not managing to meet Elsa as hoped, left word that her services were required. One evening she called out, "Penda? Mara?" warning of her approach and stood waiting silhouetted in the doorway. Strange thing, the dogs hadn't barked. Mara, trying to hide slight apprehension, welcomed Elsa to sit by the fire. Soon all those in the community became aware, 'Elsa's here' and assembled wondering what to expect. Mara sketched out the details of what had happened, then Elsa asked to speak to Vanya and Mardi alone.

"She's an awful long time talking to Mardi," Mara said to her husband, who quieted her with, "Leave her be. She knows what she's doing."

The mysterious lady, didn't deliver her verdict in the manner of the Seer, full of self-importance and authority, but more in the manner of a humble medicine woman.

She took Penda and Mara to one side and said she wasn't quite certain regarding the dream, but was willing to share her instinctive feelings on the matter. "First though, before I start, would it be possible for us to discuss this alone?"

Penda gestured to the gathering and they all filed outside.

"You seem to have a very special boy here. I think I detect something burgeoning. I sense a power within that will grow as he grows."

"What Mardi? Quiet Mardi?"

"I know it seems hard to believe now," she said turning to Mara, "but whether it seems credible or not, I think the power is in him. Have either of you, way back in your family history, heard mention of a similar visitation?"

They both shook their heads. "It's strange isn't it. No-one knows how it gets into a person or where in fact it comes from. It can be inherited of course, that's why I asked, but in other cases it just seems to arrive out of nowhere. A gift from the spirits. If I'm right Mardi is showing signs of having this great gift, but you must be careful."

"What's in him exactly?" Mara's voice rose with concern.

"Maybe a similar power to that which flowed through my father. I was just a young girl when they came for him. He smiled and told us not to worry. It was just a mistake. He would soon be back, but we never saw him again. You must be careful. I think Mardi has a similar power to see things, understand things that others can't. As I said, it's too early to say for sure, but I trust the feeling I'm getting. You have to be careful who he talks to. There are those, the ones controlling the people, who are terrified by genuine Seers, those that receive visions of the truth. It goes beyond and against

124

everything they preach. They will try to ridicule him, turn the people against him ---- or worse. They will do everything they can to prevent the true knowledge getting out."

"You say the true knowledge," said Penda. "I don't understand."

"Well in actual fact, I don't fully. All I know is, I believe in the spirits around me, those that provide for me, but I'm content with my beliefs without feeling a need to make a public show of it. Also I don't feel the need to bribe them with pieces of bronze. Respect them, yes, but not bribe them. I believe the cycles of sun, moon and tides are being controlled by something incredibly powerful, some strange force, but I don't believe it has anything to do with offerings of bronze. True Seers can predict the strange occasional darkening of sun and moon. Don't ask me how they do it, but they can. Maybe the ability to do this feels completely unremarkable to them, just like being able to whistle. I partly understand how they might feel in view of what I instinctively know and others don't. People wonder at how I sense things and as if by magic know things, but for me it just feels normal. As a small girl I thought everyone felt as I did and understood everything I understood. It was only as I grew older, I realized I was different and had something abnormal deep inside me. I didn't have to learn it, it just came naturally. And what I didn't know, the answers just seemed to come to me from out of nowhere, like I was breathing it all in. Mardi and I had quite a long talk as you know. I realised as he spoke, there are feelings inside him similar to those I had when growing up. And as I said, you must be careful who he talks to. I have never spoken as freely as this to anyone before." Elsa's eyes sparkled and she seemed breathless, "What I sense in Mardi gives us a sort of bond. Yes that's it. What's in him has given us a common bond."

"You said, 'worse' earlier. 'Turn the people against him, or worse.'"

"I'm sorry, Mara. I didn't intend to frighten you. Just warn you. It wasn't a prediction."

Mara felt a shudder, for as Elsa had said this, a brief look of puzzlement had clouded her face.

"But you haven't mentioned the dream. What about the dream? Vanya dreamt of the bear. Then the bear became Mardi." Mara wanted to hear something more definite, not just talk of vague feelings and instinct. This was her boy they were talking about.

"Dreams as you know," said Elsa, "can evaporate like mist in the morning sun, until all you have is a dim memory of them. But in this case the dream is strong and I think it refers to the power."

"You THINK?" Mara was getting impatient now.

"I can only interpret my feelings. I can't give you hard and fast answers. The bear is a symbol of power and in the dream, Mardi becomes the power. With this and the feelings I sensed when talking to him, I think Mardi will have powers beyond mine, something similar to those my father had."

"It's your doing!" spat Mara at her husband. She took the boar's tusk necklace down from where it still hung from the wooden upright and shook it in Penda's face. "I warned you, you were playing with forces you didn't understand!"

Penda explained to Elsa the hunting tale and how they'd asked Mardi to summon up the spirit of the animal and how they'd rewarded him with the boar's tusk trophy.

"Ah! So you understand what I'm talking about. To do what you did means you must have had a slight sense of this power way before the dream." She quieted Mara explaining softly, "By asking Mardi to do what he did wasn't like opening a door, letting unstoppable forces escape. The power was already there inside Mardi. All they did was channel it." She turned to Penda, "I'm glad you told me this. It confirms everything I've felt."

"Was your father a Seer?" Penda felt compelled to ask this even though frightened to hear the answer.

"Yes he was." She looked directly into Penda's eyes with the admission, but Mara sensed Elsa's heart and soul were as distant as her voice had just sounded.

Back with them once more she continued, "Your family has been blessed, but you have to guard Mardi carefully."

Mara held her arm as she rose to leave, "You say those in power will be terrified by the knowledge of a Seer. But His Lordship has his own Seer."

Elsa simply replied by raising an eyebrow in a look that said, 'Really?'

As she left the stunned couple, it suddenly dawned on Penda, he'd not offered any reward for her services and he followed her outside. Even her reply was rather unsettling, for she wanted nothing, only to be kept informed. She added that if they required her help again, they only had to call on her or failing that, leave a message and she would be there as quickly circumstances allowed. She placed a reassuring hand on his. Watching her leave, he wore a stunned expression, for he hadn't imagined it, accompanying her touch had been a cool gentle breeze.

With Elsa now gone the rest of the family reappeared bustling through the doorway. Of course, they were concerned, but worthy expressions barely masked their eagerness to hear all the juicy details regarding the strange woman and her visit.

"What did she say? What happened. What did she say?"

"Oh some nonsense about boars and bears," said Penda. "She's a crazy woman from the woods. We should have had more sense than to ask her." Having their interest so instantly quashed, they drifted back to their duties but the way Erdi eyed him from the shadows, Penda knew, his eldest son hadn't swallowed what he'd said.

Chapter Twelve

Spring at last began to bring a little warmth and also a surprise to all the youths living in the immediate vicinity of the fortress. They were ordered to report for duty and prove their proficiency in the use of bow, spear and sling. It was an obligation for all men to practice and maintain certain standards and if not met, their families could incur a serious fine. Erdi and Yanker talked about this sudden random check and both came to the same conclusion, there was more to this edict than met the eye. As only the youths were being summoned it could in fact be a recruitment drive. It could be the opening of a process that led to the best being channeled into the warrior class. Neither liked the look of this opening, sensing it led, not in fact to a desirable opportunity, but into a trap and so decided, when asked to show their skills, to do just enough, but no more. Enough to pass the test, but not enough to have them drafted into the force now led by the eldest of the crown princes. At the conclusion of this weapons test, they suspected, the most proficient youths would be expected to volunteer and failing that would probably be put under pressure to do so, but if that also failed, the lord himself had the power to put it to them, that in reality they didn't actually have a choice in the matter. So Erdi and Yanker thought it wise not to look like soldiering material. *The Teller paused and addressing the eldest youths in his audience said,* For you living here in and around the fort it's different. Most of you grow up expecting to be trained as warriors, but back in Erdi's time there wasn't the same need. As I said at the beginning of the saga, there was not the same population density, so not the same territorial rivalry, not the same constant threat of tribal clashes. Yes they stole each other's cattle, but more in a stylised game rather than outright warfare. Back in those far off times the chieftain was not expected to show his might by the building of vast ringed fortresses and in general, life was not fraught with such danger that the people felt the need to live in them. Yes, there were hints that a power race was looming, but Erdi and Yanker had no wish to be part of it. Their attitude was also massively influenced by the fact they had no respect at all for Crown Prince Gardarm, the man who would be giving them orders. A young man who could lead them into reckless ventures merely to further his own glory. They referred to him as Crown Prince Smarm. Or just Smarm for short.

None of their family envisaged them leading strictly regulated lives as soldiers and knew they were certainly not the sort to take endless orders. It was thought better all round if they stayed on the farm. Agreed, the seasons and need to feed the family totally dictated the pattern of all their lives as would military life, but somehow it didn't really feel like it. A cage only feels like a cage when the door is locked. The boy's parents were glad the independent spirit of old Tollan was still alive and well, flowing through the boy's veins. They admired the fact that a basic instinct had made them wary of the recent call to arms and agreed it could be a potential trap. Therefore, none were interested in watching the proceedings and had faith in the boy's ability to sail through the tests and quickly return home. They did wish them good luck, but no more than that.

So bracing against a chill east wind on the morning of that fateful day, Erdi and Yanker in working clothes topped by comfy lived-in coats, ambled up for duty at the weaponry test in quite a laconic manner, which didn't go unnoticed, for it contrasted markedly with the youthful enthusiasm of most of their smartly turned out contemporaries. With it being a long flat section below the fort, ideal for archery, the competition area was called the Arrow Field. A huge multitude had assembled to watch the proceedings and eagerly jostled for best positions on the vantage point of the lower section of the fort's embankment.

At conclusion of the archery session, Blade swaggered, chest out, having for the first time ever, scored higher than Erdi and Yanker and he was keen to let everyone know. "Our dad says, I'm the best shot here."

Spears as you know are launched in these parts with the aid of a wooden spear-thrower that sends them sailing far beyond any effort undertaken by arm alone. Yanker feigning ineptitude, brought much laughter, as he got into a fumbling mess trying to use it. Then seeing him trip over his spear and noticing the thunderous black looks it brought from Gardarm, they were doubled up. Finally, the sergeant at arms, intervened, preparing him and the spear for the run and launch position. His look of trepidation brought more laughter, followed by a gasp of disbelief, when sauntering up, he sent his effort to land quivering, dead-centre of the straw target. His look of incredulity and theatrical bow brought a cheer and more laughter. Crown Prince Gardarm looking down from his perch, a lofty viewing platform cut into the bank, was far from amused, in fact clearly fuming. He became quite animated as he discussed the affrontery with his officers, but Yanker was so clearly enjoying himself, he was oblivious to the trouble he was brewing. It took Erdi to point out the danger, urging him to keep a lower profile and so for the final two shots required, he simply ran up and sent his javelin to gain a proficient score, but no more. The crowd still cheered, however. He'd started something he couldn't stop and Crown Prince Smarm, the Lord's representative of authority for the day, was taking it personally.

The central target for sling shot was a peg, but if an effort sailed between two outer pegs it was marked as sufficiently proficient. Now you wouldn't say Erdi was a legend, but

Smarm had certainly heard of his prowess and so took a keen interest in his efforts. Erdi did as planned, enough and no more and Blade was almost dancing now, having once hit centre peg, thus outscoring him. Yanker also did enough and no more and as others surrounded the sergeant at arms eager to put their names forward for warrior selection, Blade being one of the most vociferous, the two prepared to leave.

The crown prince, looking down with a face like he'd just been scalded, muttered an instruction. The officer relayed this to a man at arms who ran and blocked the cousins' path with his spear. On looking round, hearts sank as the pair could see on high, the beckoning finger of the prince.

They stood on the slope, a respectful distance below the vaunted man and heard him sneer, "Don't think I don't know what your game is. Do you think me stupid?"

Both realized it was not the time for a truthful answer.

"I have vested in me, the power to have you both drafted into service!" This wasn't quite true as that power really resided in the hands of his father, a hard, but fair and genial leader, but 'twas not a time to be splitting hairs.

"What you've done here is a disgrace!"

"With due respect Your Highness," said Erdi, "we both showed sufficient accuracy to pass the tests set us."

"But I know you're both capable of more and I need to recruit the **best!**" His rod of office slapped his leggings in emphasis. "The chance to join my warriors, the force that defends the people, my band of brothers should be looked upon as an **hon**our, (slap) not something to be a**void**ed.(slap) Your whole attitude was an insult. And as for that farce with the spear......"

"Everybody has an off day," said Yanker hopefully. Then added quickly, "Your Highness."

"**Off day**? Consider yourselves lucky I haven't made an example of you. Had you both **WHIPPED**!(slap)" That final swipe actually stung which didn't help his mood any.

They both waited, hoping they looked suitably chastened, expecting this to be the end of the matter. They had done their duty, passed the test and were now quite keen to return home. Alas, it was not to be.

The prince raised his arms for attention and all below fell silent.

He called out, "Erdigan has challenged me. **Me,** the crown prince, to a competition at the slingshot. I will humbly rise to this challenge, hoping the spirits favour me. As I don't profess to be up to Erdikun's standard I hope to have their help and your support." (He was in fact a crack shot. He'd bested all those in the fort and gloried in the chance to show his prowess to the people) "If Erdikun wins, he and his cousin are free to return to their farm. But if by favour of the spirits, I triumph, they will both, by having the sheer temerity to offer this challenge, be drafted into my fighting force."

As you can imagine, this was followed by a significant outbreak of murmuring. Those who knew Erdi thought it out of character for him to do anything so rash. Those that didn't, only had to look at the differences in age and stature. The prince was almost into manhood compared with Erdi, who looked young for his age as if hardly yet needing to trouble a shaving blade. The prince, trained and fine-fed for soldiery since the age he could straddle a horse, had a girth that simply dwarfed the young man. The challenge didn't make sense. Gardarm stood proud and aloof, taking the mutterings he heard to be a sign of burgeoning support from loyal subjects. Unfortunately, those massed below had actually come to the conclusion that for a simple lad off a smallholding to challenge the might of Crown Prince Gardarm just didn't seem plausible. But who were they to say?

Erdi had no choice but to quell his anger at the injustice, return to the Arrow Field and prepare himself as best he could for the challenge. Yanker looking white with worry, muttered to all in earshot, that the prince had fabricated the whole story. He also tried, as best as he could under the circumstances, to advise Erdi and give him moral support. "Forget the fact he's a lying slug. Forget the possible consequences. Just concentrate on each shot. Forget his years of military training -------- Bum-dirt!! Shouldn't have said that. Forget I said that, Erdi," he pleaded.

"Bum-holes and blast it! Sorry cousin. Pressure must be getting to me. I trust you Erdi. Stay focused on that peg and do what you're good at. I have faith in you cousin. You can beat him."

As with the earlier competition, baked clay shot was used rather than stones. Each had three efforts, the tension building with every shot and both managed three hits. Their accuracy had stunned the crowd, into gasps of amazement and purring sounds of admiration. The sergeant at arms watched each shot to judge fair strike or miss. The clay ball had only to nick the peg not actually knock it over.

For the next round, this was moved further down the field. Smarm oozing confidence, scored a hit with his first shot, the 'Click' bringing polite applause from the crowd. He wore a sickening self-satisfied look as he eyed Erdi, still quite a young man remember, stepping up to the line. When his effort merely nicked the peg, Prince Smarm ordered a miss to be registered, but in fairness, the sergeant overruled him. He pointed out the mark the missile had left and the decision stood. The prince's next shot hit the peg solidly once more and he turned to bask in polite applause. There was a groan when Erdi missed. It was close, but in fact a miss. All depended on the prince's next effort. A hit now meant an unassailable lead and an army life for the boys. A loud sigh of relief was heard as it sailed a whisker too high over the target. With a petulant look of annoyance, he slapped where he had been standing with his sling. Then glowering, he repeatedly took out his anger on the small patch of turf as if it alone had been the cause of his failure. Now it was up to Erdi. He tried closing his mind to his opponent's antics and to the fact the future course of his life depended on the next few moments.

He swung repeatedly, concentrating, shutting all from his thoughts other than the peg in the distance. Releasing the shot, he shaded his eyes to watch its flight. Those in the crowd curved their bodies slightly, as if doing so would steer the small projectile to its target. As the clear click of contact was heard a cheer rang out.

Yanker gave him a hug and a friendly punch on the arm. But then watched aghast as the peg was moved yet further, to an almost impossible distance, for the next round. It was beyond the range they normally practiced. They felt no need for this sort of long-range accuracy when hunting. It made more sense to use guile, to stalk their prey as close as possible before letting fly. To shoot from such a distance would be foolish, detrimental, having more chance of scaring the quarry rather than bringing it down. Eying the smug smirk on the prince's face, Erdi realized he was now in difficulty, for it was obvious Gardarm regularly practiced these long shots.

Yanker tried not to show his concern. "I've got faith in you cousin. Go out there and beat the smarmy, greasy lump!"

A few nearby overhearing, turned to one another, hands smothering a laugh, saying things like, "My word!"

They drew for first shot and the prince won. He gave a little clench of celebration, anticipating victory. Pressure always mounted on the one shooting second. Smarm went through the theatrics of raising his arms to beseech spiritual help and sent his shot winging. A long silence then, '**click**.' The cousins had never heard a sound so sickening.

Erdi approached the firing line. His heart was pounding. Yanker felt that tense, his knuckles were white and fingernails almost drew blood from his palms. Even though not personally taking part, his legs were visibly shaking and so he wondered, 'what must Erdi's be like?'

Erdi swung and taking careful aim at the distant target sent his shot only to hear, "Miss!" called out by the sergeant at arms. Yanker, fearing the worst, thought although Erdi's effort had been valiant, it was surely now all over. He muttered, "Time to get the coats. Time to report for duty," and began to mentally prepare himself for the inevitable.

Smarm strode to the line. His stone pinged off the very top of the target splitting it slightly and on hearing slight applause, gave an exaggerated bow.

Erdi looked up to the sky praying for inspiration, gritted his teeth and walked slowly to the line. He stared long and hard at the peg. He swung repeatedly, almost trancelike, taking careful aim and watched his effort sail into the distance. He knew it was close. The crowd knew it was close. But how close? The sergeant raised an arm and shouted "**Hit!**" which brought a mighty cheer, but all quickly simmered down, on realising the shot had only brought a reprieve.

Before taking his position for the final shot, the prince went into an angry discussion with his officers, who with the contest not being their idea, looked understandably bemused.

"You're getting to him Erdi. You can do it," muttered Yanker.

There was no appeal to the spirits, no swagger, Smarm was angry. He would show the upstart. One more hit and he couldn't be beaten. He swung his effort with venom and watched in disbelief as it thudded beyond the peg. A clear miss. 'How could this be happening to him?'

Erdi knowing, that yet again, their futures depended on his next attempt, tried to force this from mind and in fact, looked quite calm, although inside was feeling anything but. His shot knocked the peg backwards. The crowd roared. Yanker hugged him, lifting him off the ground, but it still wasn't over.

The peg was moved yet again. It was now at the very limit of slingshot range and in view of this the competition became sudden death.

Whether the prince was affected by the muted applause he'd received or whether his anger had been detrimental to performance, it was hard to tell. Perhaps he'd never faced pressure like this before. Anyhow, the outcome was, he'd started talking to himself. "You're up against a peasant. He's a nobody. A skinny youth who I bet can't even reach the peg let alone hit it. Now come on!" He stamped a foot. "Remember who you are! Pull yourself together!" The outcome, however, was a miss. He'd actually missed by quite a wide margin sending the umpiring sergeant ducking for cover, which the crowd thought hilarious. The prince, standing glaring, anger throbbing, shook his head in disbelief. He dared not look anyone in the eye, for his own glistened with tears of rage.

Yanker gave yet more encouragement. "You've got him now. Look at him he's beaten. You can do it Erdi!" He in fact could hardly dare look. Whatever the outcome he felt a glow of pride and admiration for the way Erdi, although looking so miss-matched and alone out there, showed no sign of nerves. He showed true courage. The crowd had also come to appreciate this, marvelling at the transformation that had taken place right before their eyes. The once proud prince now seemed like a spoilt, bullying juvenile and Erdi stood there like a man.

He took a careful sighting and swinging his sling, ran light of foot, up to the line, to launch his effort with all the power he could summon. The crowd held its breath, watching the ark of the small projectile. Away in the distance awaited the peg. As if by magic it suddenly jerked backwards. There was a roar. People jigged around and hugged each other. Yanker refused to believe it until the arm of the sergeant signaled a direct hit. Only then did he raise his arms to the sky and shout, "THANK YOU!!" The spirits had favoured them.

The prince marched off, his face twitching with such anger, a glare from his eyes could have set tinder alight. Consoling approaches from his officers were pushed away.

"Ahh he's crying," said Yanker. "Couldn't have happened to a nicer bloke."

The prince obviously heard the eruption of laughter, making the lonely walk back to his horse, all the longer.

The throng, well not Blade and his family I have to add, clamoured to congratulate Erdi, but he just gave each a bashful thank you as he threaded through to where Yanker awaited. They donned their coats, fitting like old friends and still shaking from the pressure, left the Arrow Field to the sounds of "ERDI, ERDI!!" ringing out. They felt a wave of relief wash over them, but celebrations were muted by knowledge of the fact, they had made a very serious enemy. They half expected the thunder of hooves. A troop of soldiers. The order to immediately return for a whipping.

Penda listened to their tale and with eyebrows raised, shook his head in disbelief. What was it about them that had managed to turn such a seemingly simple task into an epic?

"Neither of you go near the fortress for a while. That man is dangerous at best of times. Wounded there's no telling what he might dream up."

He gave his son a hug. "And as for **you**!" He gave Yanker a friendly cuff under the chin.

Chapter Thirteen

One sunny spring morning one of the Forest Folk arrived. They were called this simply because that was where they lived. They grew a few crops, but mainly survived by hunting and gathering. The young man had a basket full of dried mushrooms on offer, plus some strange shiny red blobs that didn't look particularly appetizing. He marveled at the uncommon sight of bluebells waving in the breeze outside the main roundhouse.

He asked Mara who'd had the notion to plant them? She managed to understand the man even though he had the thick accent and strange word formation of Forest Folk when trying to communicate in their tribal language. Mara, nodding to slender figure of Vanya, disappearing through the compound opening said, "That little madam there."

Vanya had left the compound to take a look at her playhouse, for guilty at having neglected it of late, she had felt the sudden compulsion. With the recent warmer weather, she and Talia had been drawn to more outdoor activities, joining in the boy's games, playing with them down by the stream. One of the pastimes, other than trying to splash one another with well-aimed stones, had involved finding as many ways as possible to cross the flow without getting feet wet. There was the weir with its stepping stones, various shoals to leap on to, but also trees to climb. They'd edge along overhanging branches until able to jump dry shod on to the far bank.

Vanya approaching the playhouse, peered into the darkness. She froze in the doorway, turned and ran as fast as she could back to her mother. Mara was given no proper explanation, but being dragged by the arm with such insistence, she followed her daughter to have a look. Out of interest, the forest dweller wandered after them. Vanya put a finger to lips and they all crept to peer in through the low doorway. Against the far wall lying on its side, fully spread out was a wildcat. It gave a threatening silent gesture of a hiss, but didn't move. A litter of kittens was feeding along its belly.

"Don't frighten her," whispered Vanya. They all withdrew to a safe distance. Mara and the visitor were momentarily lost for words.

"It's Minchy," said Vanya excitedly. "Minchy's come back."

"Your father won't be pleased," said Mara. "Those things take our lambs."

The young man shook his head in disbelief. "As you know I live in forest and I've never heard of such thing. Normally wildcats won't come near settlement. You rarely atually see them. One hint of human and they gone. But to atually have kitten right here virtual mong you, it's unbeevable. Wait 'til I tell back home."

"I told you Minchy was a girl," said Vanya.

The stranger looked up at seeing a dark-haired youth approaching. He had an easy walk, a nonchalant air, was rangy in build and when closer, the man realised he had quite a handsome face.

"Erdi. Erdi," Vanya called. "Minchy's back and she's got babies."

The stranger asked Mara, "Is that Erdikun?"

Mara nodded.

"The same Erdi that beat prince?"

"Yes - why?"

"First the wild cat now this. Wait 'til I tell back home!"

Approaching Erdi he asked, "Can I shake a hand?" His face was flushed with excitement. "I was told you live somewhere in local, but didn't expect to atually meet you."

Erdi gave him a patient smile. It wasn't the first time this had happened and his father had informed him, even now, it was still talked about it up in the market. It was, quite frankly, a bit of a worry. The greater the acclaim, the greater the likelihood of retribution once Smarm put his mind to it.

He let himself be led to look at the wildcat and kittens. The same silent threat spread across the animal's face. Erdi could see trouble brewing. Penda would not take kindly to be actually nurturing such predators right there in the midst of them.

When time came to enter the house and decide on a fair trade for the mushrooms, Vanya remained by the playhouse fascinated by its occupants. Erdi had warned her to her stay well away outside, nursing mothers whether placid cow or a cuddly looking wildcat could be potential killers. Vanya widened a small hole where the playhouse roof met the wall, to peer inside.

Erdi, listening to the small dark stranger and his mother exchanging opening shots of a deal, suddenly had second thoughts. He shouldn't have left Vanya out there alone with a wild animal. It was too risky. What had he been thinking of? He hurried outside.

"Leave her in peace, Vanya. Too much attention will scare her off."

"She's got five babies, Erdi."

"That's good, Vanya, but come here. A mother with young can often be more deadly than the male." He watched her approaching, "Why are you looking so sad?"

"I think they're all blind."

"They're not really blind, Vanya. Their eyes will open soon I expect. The same as happens with puppies."

"Are you sure Erdi? Can we give her some food?"

"No Vanya. She'll find her own food. The best thing we can all do is stay well out of her way. Now come on, leave them alone."

When Penda was shown the new additions to their family his response was immediate and unwavering. He'd frighten the beast off at first light and drown the kittens. The children were to be told the mother had taken the lot of them off into the forest, back where they belonged. No amount of beseeching by the women would change his mind.

Mardi listened and said nothing. Later he was seen crouching by the playhouse door.

Erdi asked what he'd been doing, but he'd just shrugged and walked back inside the house. His young brother was as ever, a bit of a mystery.

Early next morning Penda returned from his early chores and Mara with hand on hip asked, "Well? Did you do it?"

"No. They've gone. She's carried them off. Probably all the attention scared her."

"Are you **sure**?"

Penda's glare warned it was best not to probe his veracity further and giving him the benefit of the doubt, she returned to her cooking.

It was a quite few days later, all the men folk were off working and Mara, drawn by the flitting shape she'd glimpsed from out of the corner of an eye, wandered outside. Quickly rounding Dowid's house, she caught sight of the wildcat, a mouse dangling from its mouth, as it sprang to the top of the palisade, to disappear far side. Walking beyond the fencing, there was no evidence of the creature, but then following her instincts, Mara lifted the small gate to the animal enclosure slightly, so it didn't drag when opened and she walked inside. Creeping up to the cow byre, to peer into the shadows, there was still no sign, but on turning to leave, the definite rustle of something moving drew her back and craning forward she peeped behind the baskets of stored charcoal. A small den had been created and inside, their faces as pretty as primroses, were the kittens toying with the live mouse the mother had brought them. Mara told no-one of what she had found.

On a warm spring evening Vanya and Talia came running into the house full of excitement. "Come and look! Come and look! Minchy's babies are running all over the place."

All hastened outside to watch the young wildcats. They were creeping up on one another, jumping almost vertically in surprise, skitting side tail in and around the playhouse, around the apple tree and even up and over the playhouse roof. The whole gathering, adults and children, just stared in amazement, then went into raptures at their antics. Even Penda pushed his hat back and roared with laughter.

Next day the wildcats were gone. They'd disappeared into the forest where they belonged.

One day out of the blue, Blade paid them a visit. He'd hoped to announce the news to the whole family, but had to make do with just Mara and Yanker, the only ones home when he called. He did have misgivings, thinking, 'anyone but Yanker,' but unwisely decided to press on. "Our dad says, I have to come and tell you." His eyes stared wide as he excitedly, almost frothing, told them he'd passed selection for training in readiness to join Prince Gardarm's band of soldiers.

"We're very pleased for you, Brone" said Mara not quite convincingly.

"Hey Blader!" Yanker called with a wicked grin spreading. "Has His Royal Highness recovered from the beating Erdi gave him?"

"Course he has. That was just down to luck. Erdi was just lucky that day."

"Yes we know he was Blader. But d'you know something?"

"No, what?"

"Ever since that day his luck's got even better. It's unbelievable! He just can't seem to miss!"

Mara suppressed a smile.

Blade, with a growing look of discomfort, made his way towards the door.

"What you've got to remember though, Blader."

The young man paused wishing he hadn't come. "That prince of yours shouldn't take it to heart. No, he shouldn't blame himself. After all, what you have to consider is," Yanker narrowed his eyes and wagged a forefinger, "that last shot of Erdi's would have beaten a better man than Gardarm."

Mara's clamp of hand to mouth, failed to stop an involuntary hoot of laughter. Blade, looking troubled, departed, his brain still churning over the meaning.

When he'd gone Mara chided. "That wit of yours will get you into serious trouble one day."

On a late spring day feeling almost warm enough to be summer, Penda watched Vanya and Talia playing horses. They had made low jumps from branches, setting them out in a circuit and pretending they were mounted, galloped around the course. His heart went out to his daughter. She still begged him for a horse, but everything they did, everything they toiled for, went into survival. Apart from a few minor exceptions, if they needed anything, they simply made it themselves. Their community couldn't justify obtaining and feeding a luxury as nonessential as a pony, just there for children to ride. There were of course wild ponies they occasionally glimpsed when out hunting, but the thought of the time and effort trapping and breaking one in, had put him off even contemplating the notion. They did, however, need a good hunting dog. Harka had been sadly missed. A dog of his quality would be hard to find, but Penda, having put the word out, was rewarded, by a fellow marketeer telling him of a litter of puppies that could be of interest.

They belonged to a man known simply as Trader. He owned land to the south west of the fortress, but didn't bother farming it, preferring to reward those in his employment for their efforts. Penda told Vanya and Talia to ready themselves, for they were off on a surprise trip - no mention of the puppies of course - and full of excitement the two girls climbed aboard the cart to straddle the goods that had been loaded in

143

anticipation of a trade. Erdi had been told of the impending trip and on impulse, ran to join them, taking Blackie's bridle in hand so his father could also climb aboard. On downhill sections all four sat on the cart, the girls laughing at the gathering speed as the horse was urged to trundle into a trot.

Trader was home and welcomed them in for refreshment. He knew why they had called. He was a tall raw-boned man with a hearty manner and generous countenance. A strange white streak across the top of his forehead, his wife explained, was caused by constant wearing of a cap whether, rain or shine, adding, he would even wear it to bed if she let him. The lady was introduced as Gwedyll and the mere sight of the her sent Erdi into quite a strange dither. With colour rising, he felt tongue tied and petrified into silence, lest he should suddenly blurt something stupid. Dark, slender, with the most beautiful brown eyes, she spoke with an accent that sent shivers through his whole being. Needing all his concentration to understand what she was saying and loving every moment, he leant forward to listen, hanging on her every word. Even when Penda and Trader swapping local gossip drew him into their conversation, he found his eyes straying to the willowy creature. She was chopping vegetables to add to the meal cooking in the massive bronze cauldron hanging above the fire. On feeling a firm grip clamp his right shoulder, his heart leapt, thinking he'd been caught in the act. He gave a sigh of relief on hearing Trader boom out, he wished to hear the story of how he'd bested Prince Gadarm at the slingshot.

Gwedyll called out, "Tywy!" and a small boy entered. He ran and reaching up to hug her waist, turned to give the two strange girls a look that left them in no doubt as to whose mother this was. Gwedyll led the three children out to see the animals. Erdi was about to launch into the story, but pausing, asked Trader if he would first mind answering a question.

"That cauldron?" said Erdi.

Trader burst out laughing and said that the damn thing could well be the end of him. It had been given as a dowry

144

payment. She was from the Skreela nation and her brothers were keen to have it back. Erdi gently probed further, hoping his interest wasn't straying into impertinence. "But the cauldron. It's of fine beaten bronze----Those faces and the way the handles loop through the mouths, I've never seen anything like it before."

"Oh I know. I shouldn't be owning it, but Gwedyll, she has the right. Gwedyll's the real thing. A chieftain's daughter. You look surprised, but she is. No doubt about it. But then the whole thing got in a tangle. There was a lot of snarling back up in the mountains. Families falling out and here's me a simple trader with a Skreela stock-pot hanging over m'fire. The daft thing is, when I look at her." His voice rose in volume and he slapped a thigh. "Can't believe my luck. Should have been me paying the dowry not the other way around!" His laughter was infectious.

He suddenly became serious, "Have had to watch my step lately though. Now her brothers have come of age, they've begun making threats. Getting quite nasty in fact. It could only happen to me. They'll have to have it back one day, but let 'em wait I say. Now tell me about how you bested that prince, that bag of lard." Squatting, he pushed his cap back and leant closer in anticipation.

Later, once Erdi had told his tale and had been clasped in appreciation like a long-lost son, Vanya and Talia came bursting in verbally falling over themselves in the excitement of trying to tell them about the puppies they'd seen.

"Can we have one? I want the little wriggly one. I held him. He's got needly teeth. And he licked my finger."

"Oh, I don't know," said Penda. "Do we really need another dog?" He teased her a little more and then all went out to see the puppies.

"Can we have one?" pleaded Vanya, hopping up and down with hands clasped together.

"That all depends," Penda replied and with a confident air took Trader over to show him what was on offer in the cart.

145

The cover was thrown aside. He could take his pick. Silence followed. Trader pushed his cap back and scratched his temple clearly struggling to find the least hurtful way of explaining why he would have to let them down. In the end he gave up and just said "Come with me." He took them to a large storage hut which from door to back wall was crammed to bursting. Dried and smoked meat of every variety hung within. There was smoked fish, salted fish, baskets of wheat, peas and barley and even pots of honey. He took them to another store, crammed full to capacity with wheat and barley, there being no room left in the grain pit.

He explained that the litter of puppies were from true hunting stock and listed the details regarding the bitch's ancestors and those of the dog that had sired them. As much as he had taken to Penda and his family, he was not willing to trade one of the puppies for yet more food.

Penda was a bit taken aback, never having done business with a man quite like this before. Trader put an arm around his shoulder, "Tell you what. A certain man I know has a bit of an itch to be owning a pair of hunting birds. Get young Erdi here to bring me a couple of young falcons and I think we can have ourselves a deal."

"What about training them?" said Erdi. "I wouldn't have a clue about that."

"You can leave that bit to me. There's a man I know can handle that side of things. You just bring me the birds. I need 'em sharpish mind. Need to tell my client his wish is all but granted, otherwise he'll be away getting 'em elsewhere."

On the way home, a disappointed Vanya had it explained that the puppy she had fallen for was too young to leave its mother. Maybe they could go back another day when it was a bit older.

Penda was quiet and out of sorts. He'd never had his goods turned down before.

Erdi trying to break the silence, "There's something about that cauldron story that doesn't quite add up."

"Not really any of our business," was snapped that gruffly it managed to kill at birth that particular attempt at conversation.

After another long moody tramp, made longer by deafening lack of talk, Erdi asked brightly, "Do you really believe all that stuff about the dog's heritage. It's a bit of a yarn surely?"

Penda growled, "He didn't get the name Trader for nothing." And the rest of the journey was endured in silence.

A few days later, with chores completed, Erdi took the opportunity to mount Blackie and head off in search of their mushroom gathering friend. Enquiries had informed him of the foresters' last location and he thought they'd not be that hard to find provided they'd not moved on. They hadn't. If any group of people could quickly locate and capture a pair of falcons it would be them.

Considering their nomadic lifestyle, he was not surprised to see the shelters they lived under were makeshift, but he hadn't expected find them quite so meagre. The hut walls were enough to hold up a scrap of roof and to stop a curious wolf nosing in, but gave no hint of home. Savage looking hunting dogs leapt about at their tethers making a frightful racket, barking and screaming and Erdi found it difficult to shout above the noise in his attempt to inform a squint-eyed woman what he'd come for. She screeched sounds that made no sense, but it seemed to be an offer of food. Eyeing flies swarming around the bloody strips of meat draped to dry in the sun and noticing the warts on her hands, he politely declined. Children ran everywhere, dirty, half naked and unshod and he wondered if he had indeed found the right camp. With relief he recognized the mushroom trader emerging. He smiled, shook his hand in welcome and invited Erdi to meet the rest of his clan squatting around a fire blazing down in a hollow away from the mud, flies and noise. There looked to be at least four families and every member was eager to shake the hand of the man who had vanquished the prince. All the faces grinned, whether they had lumps on, teeth missing or were attached to shoulders without hint of a neck. It was not hard to see why the mushroom man had been their chosen representative to go trading beyond their gloomy world.

Erdi's attention was drawn to three youths approaching, probably drawn by the earlier din of dog barking. Although seeming surprisingly free of blemish they still didn't approach a look that would generally be considered normal. They weren't similar enough to be considered triplets but having said that, they did share the same high cheek-boned, gaunt look and the same piercing wolf-eyed stare devoid of humanity that made Erdi glad he'd not met them earlier when riding alone. They had it explained in their completely incomprehensible dialect, exactly who he was and immediately their faces broke into smiles. He still found it amazing his fame had penetrated so deep into the forest. He was slapped heartily on the back, but still didn't trust them.

Erdi told his mushroom man what was required and that quick delivery of two young falcons would be met by a fair trade in smoked eel. When this was related to the three youths, they nodded--- nodded some more, replied briefly and the man turned to Erdi and said it wouldn't be a problem. Erdi wasn't convinced. It all sounded too simple. He repeated the request to make sure all had been understood.

There was more jabber and finger pointing back up into the forest.

"Don't worry. It's not a problem. They know of a nest high up in a lightning tree. They'll go and investigate."

Another string of words and serious nodding of heads was translated as, "They say they know of other nests. It won't be a problem."

Erdi found himself head-nodding along with them, smiling and replying, "Thank you. Thank you." In reality he couldn't wait to be clear of the place.

One of the youths drawling a laconic utterance to no-one in particular brought a loud burst of laughter, leaving Erdi looking on with an uneasy smile.

The mushroom man, assuring that the falcons would soon be delivered, accompanied him back up the bank to where Blackie was tethered. An angry shout and gabble of words sent two boys leaping from the animal's back, to disappear, bare flesh, dark through ragged clothing, as they scampered behind the houses. An equine wary eye mirrored Erdi's feelings exactly and both were glad to put the encampment behind them.

A few days later, Erdi was surprised by the sight of the mushroom man emerging from the forest to deliver two young falcons flapping their wings near ready for maiden flight. It was hard to imagine anything so perfect and beautiful being delivered from what he'd witnessed.

"Those three that managed to capture them," he asked, "are they brothers?"

The man's face had a look of suppressed mirth when replying, "Well sort of."

Erdi set out alone to do the deal for the chosen puppy. Penda for some reason had no wish to renew contact with the man known to all as Trader. Erdi wasn't troubled by this as he'd immediately felt an affinity with the man. Hospitality was again shown and he wasn't quite the same dithering wreck when talking to Gwedyll, even though sudden first sight of her when approaching the compound had still delivered a terrific jolt inside. It wasn't just her beauty that sent him into a state of confusion it was the way she moved and the glow that seemed to radiate, whether in motion or merely sitting.

As Erdi was leaving with the puppy tucked safely inside his shirt, Trader said, "Your father's a strong character, Erdi. What folks say and the little I've seen of him tells me that. Look! I don't want to meddle in family business, but if ever you need a place to sort yourself out, a person to turn to, you're always welcome here. I need a bright mind about the place. Someone keen. You're certainly a winner, you've shown that. You've got a fair bit of your father in you, no denying, but things, even when similar, don't always work well together you know." For emphasis, he rubbed fist knuckles together. "Just remember, keep it to yourself of course, you've always got a place here." The unexpected offer, quite took Erdi's breath away. He thanked Trader and rode home mulling the opportunity over.

Vanya of course was in raptures at the sight of the tiny puppy wriggling its whole body in an attempt to wag its tail, before rolling over to have its soft belly scratched. She immediately named him Brownty, the wriggler.

The Teller, looking at the sky, hunched his body in a shiver. The sun had gone behind a cloud and it felt quite chilly. Time we all went in, *he said and then added,* I need to ready myself for this evening, but I'll tell you one last bit before we go.

Grandma Vana still busied herself with tasks about the house and also had never lost her skill at pot making. She showed Vanya how to roll out the clay coils, curl them into a circle to form the cylinder that was then pressed and coaxed into the final shape required. With a pattern incised, the pot was ready for firing. Vanya was quick to learn the art, but also busied herself making a range of small hollow balls.

"What are those things meant to be, Vanya?" her grandmother asked.

"I'll make them into faces, grandma."

"Oh faces. I see. But you'll need to pierce them or they'll break in the fire."

"I know **that**, Grandma," she said in a matter-of-fact grown-up way, "I have to do that anyway so there'll be holes to thread a chord through."

Small balls, black from the fire were dabbed with paint, features added in charcoal, to be hung up inside the house as decorations. All the faces were different, each supposedly, a person she knew.

"If I hit my head one more time on that…."

"Don't break him, father, that's Gang-gang. I'll move him."

Mardi laughed at her occasional use of her baby name for their grandfather. He asked if he could have two of the balls, but unpainted. One big and one small. He disappeared with these into the playhouse.

Vanya's inventiveness never failed to surprise, but it wasn't so much the faces she was painting that caught Erdi's eye--- "Why have you got those, Vanya?" He picked up two tiny white, perfectly round, pebbles.

"They're my lucky stones, Erdi. I found them in the stream. One's Minchy and the other's Brownty."

Closer inspection revealed both stones to have little faces etched on them and the one face had whiskers.

Meanwhile a thin shaft of sunlight through the hole Vanya had made in the playhouse roof whilst wildcat watching, lit the smallest of the clay balls Mardi had hung up, which in turn threw a shadow on the other.

With that the Teller stood up and thanked them all for listening, but explained he really did now have to go and prepare for the evening's saga to be related up in the Great Hall. The whole gathering, parents, youths and children clapped and warmly thanked him.

Part 3

Chapter Fourteen

The Teller prepared himself for the trials of the evening. He requested to dine alone and ate sparingly, preferring to feel light and alert, with residual hunger giving an edge, rather than the opposite experienced when weighed down with food. He drank barley water rather than beer as he needed a clear head. Its sorrel flavouring brought a slight shudder and sharpening of the senses. He had to concentrate, be in the right frame of mind. Perhaps the two sessions he'd gifted the youths and families during the day had been too ambitious. He struggled to remember what he'd covered the night before. There couldn't be any omissions otherwise parts of that to be related would make no sense. He'd told them all about Elsa, but not the two youngsters running in fright from her. That was not the thing to tell a hall full of battle-hardened warriors. Also, other than their interest in Donda the voluptuous, he had not told them of the boy's escapades. They'd liked that, always relishing something of a bawdy nature. But it wouldn't have done to have regaled fighting men with anecdotes of children and fairy stories. He'd briefly mentioned Zak in legend shooting the giant's hair off. That had to be mentioned, but he certainly hadn't related the cousin's unwillingness to bear arms for their lord and master. How could you explain to devotees of heroics that it was equally heroic to question the path led by the majority. To go one's own way and not become swallowed up and carried along by the clarion call to arms. The Teller shuddered. That could have ended the night prematurely with a humiliating meeting with the water trough. The youths that afternoon, had initially looked puzzled at the prospect of listening to a tale where two main characters had shunned the chance of combat, but had then warmed to them as the slingshot saga went into full swing so to speak. That reminded him. 'Don't slip in cheap jokes. They puncture the mood. Make them laugh by all means, but avoid appearing smart, cocky.' He was merely the vehicle for the story. It was about the characters, not him.

As he sat and cleared his head, memories of the previous night began to drift back. Yes, he'd told them about Scratch, also Vanya's dream of the bear, the Fire Feast, the visits to Trader and the tale of how Erdi had come into possession of the sword. 'Had he told them that? Yes of course he had.' He went through it all again to make sure, counting the episodes on his fingers. When he felt certain of his approach to the evening's telling, he put aside the day's clothes, washed in refreshingly cool water, donned his performance apparel topped by the cloak, took a few deep breaths and walked at pace towards the Grand Hall.

It was packed. Whole families had been permitted to attend. He'd whetted their appetites during the day and they wanted to know 'what happens next?' The majority stood as he entered to give him a rousing welcome.

He thanked them, bowed to the chieftain, stern and unmoved in his seat of office, gave a welcoming smile to the royal family now in attendance and took his seat up on the dais.

Now, *said the Teller,* I'll take you forward, yet a further four years in time. Erdi and Yanker had grown into quite handsome young men and had somehow managed to stay free from Prince Gardarm's clutches. The playhouse was still a focal point, although not for Vanya and Talia, but for younger ones growing up. Erdi made it his job each year to keep it

156

weatherproof and to check his secret was still safely contained within.

Vanya had been tireless in her constant search for invention which had led her into the world of weaving and sewing. Talia and Luda had been willing accomplices. She paid no great heed to the fact she was growing into a beautiful young lady and hadn't, even when two years previously they had crowned her as Spring Queen. A certain Skreela boy had certainly taken notice, but still hadn't the courage to walk that long lonely walk from his side of the camp over to where Penda and his family had their pitch. Caution told him it could be an even longer walk back.

Mardi felt certain he'd stumbled across startling discoveries, but had been begged by all to tell no-one of them.

More babies, born to Inga and Morga, had not only swollen their community, but looked like surviving and Old Tollan and Vana, understandably less active now, reveled in tiny chores helping the daily round of bringing up the growing family.

Donda had her eye on Erdi, probably with material gains in mind, for the moment flattery came from elsewhere, both he and Yanker were completely ignored. Her brother and others recruited with him were now warriors trained to a junior level bearing sword and tattoo of rank to denote their accomplishment.

Trader still had incongruous ownership of the Shkreela cauldron, but was feeling the time to relinquish it to be close upon him.

The chieftain of their valley was still in power, in name anyway, being in the unenviable position of having to explain why yet more bronze offerings exacted by his Seer had not made any noticeable improvement to the deteriorating weather. Apart from all this life had gone on much as before.

So, we come to the Spring Fair. The baskets they had woven were hanging from the sides of the carts, joints of dried venison and cured wild boar flitches and hams were aboard

157

for trading, but much of the load was taken up by garments and other accoutrements the young ladies had spent the winter creating. They shared a mixture of apprehension and excitement at their venture.

A narrow wooden bridge had been constructed at Nant Crag border crossing making their journey to the Feasting Site almost sublime compared to the old days. Charge the tallyman, now gone grey, was across on the far side to record contents and quantities in the loads trundling past.

As they approached the Feasting Site one of the traders ran to meet them. He was gasping for breath and keen to negotiate a trade on their complete load of baskets. The haggling went on as the carts rumbled and with the perimeter fence of the Feasting Site looming ever closer, minds were forced to concentrate on closing the deal. They pulled into the site and a woman asked, "What's the very best you can do on one of those grain baskets? The very best for **me**." As if she was someone special.

"I'm really sorry," said Penda "they're no longer mine. They're all spoken for."

A man from a nearby pitch, also with baskets on offer sneered, "How do you always seem to have the witches' luck?"

"Easy," called back Yanker. "Better we make 'em, luckier we get!"

"Enough of that!" growled Penda. "D'you want to turn the devils against us?"

He meant the spirits always listening in for the chance to humble or ridicule.

Their usual pitch was vacant. Newcomers would have been warned off claiming it. It was Penda's by rite of tradition dating back to the first fair attended by his father Tollan. If there was any screeching and shouting on first day of setting up, knowing looks were enough between veterans, 'Pitch jumpers!'

A frame was rigged up to hang and display the cured meat and a board was laid on x-frame trestles to show off the textiles. Other items of clothing hung on display beneath the half-retracted awning on the cart. Bracelets woven from cow hair hung on chords. Fragrant perfume of violet was on offer in jars. Above all, creating an impression of entering a tent, were hide awnings stretching from cart uprights to supporting front poles. This gave shelter if it rained, shade from the sun, but also an exclusive feel to the cavernous interior. Vanya's little world. Each evening chords joining the front covers were undone for the hides to be used as ground sheets.

The first morning didn't go as well as Vanya had hoped. Women picked up and examined the more adventurous items of her creation, said they liked them, only to put them down again escaping with the excuse, "I'll think about it." The bracelets woven in various designs, went well enough, as did woolens and the perfume, but Vanya was beginning to feel a panic welling inside as regards the bodices and chorded skirts. Maybe she had been a little too adventurous. The traditional long brown look was stubbornly hanging on.

Penda seeing his daughter struggle gave Yanker a 'I warned you!' sort of look to remind him not to gloat in future.

Then a rising murmur amongst the throng and heads turning to look followed the approach of Gwedyll, Trader's wife. She had a young man with her, who stooped slightly as if trying to duck from the prominence the latest spurt in growth had given. He was handsome, but looked like one going through that awkward, easily embarrassed, occasional squeaky voice phase. Gwedyll's smile greeted all and she turned to Vanya to ask how the morning was going? When Vanya gave her the truthful reply, she looked genuinely surprised.

"But your things are wonderful." She held up one of the bodices to admire. "These people don't deserve you, Vanya."

"Thank you, but who else can I offer them to?"

Gwedyll suddenly put a hand to mouth. "Forgive me. I haven't introduced my nephew." Then on seeing Vanya eying him beneath lowered lids asked, "Or have you two met already?"

"You took your time!" snapped Vanya playfully, her toss of head adding to the youth's embarrassment.

Gwedyll gave a hoot of laughter. "Don't you realise who he is?"

"Yes I know," replied Vanya with a meaningful look. "He's the one who keeps smiling at me."

"He's Prince Bonheddig. Heddi we call him. He was keen to make your acquaintance, but too shy to make the first move. Weren't you Heddi?" On suddenly realizing her nephew hadn't understood a word, didn't speak the local language, her laughter preceding the explanation in what the locals called, Skreela, chimed like music. Heddi's bright look was clouded by a frown on hearing his shyness had been laid bare, but then on hearing of Vanya's opening comment and understanding its implied meaning, his spirits soared and he gave her a smile. On being introduced to the family, he was charming and gracious, then looking directly at Vanya made what could only have been interpreted as an earnest request whatever the language spoken.

"He would be honored if you would attend the competition this afternoon," translated Gwedyll. This of course was the event that had so captivated her four years previously and this year the prince would be taking part himself. Vanya replied that she would love to, but only if blessed with more good fortune trading her garments.

On being told this, the young man became thoughtful. Suddenly brightening, as an idea occurred to him, he explained to his aunt and then cajoled her playfully, to act upon it.

"Heddi suggests I model these for you."

Vanya clapping her hands with excitement, ushered Gwedyll behind a draped cloth in order to change.

160

She reappeared wearing a tight bodice, and below bare midriff hung a short hip-hugging chorded skirt, that each time she moved, parted to reveal a flash of slender thigh. Erdi looking on had heart palpitations and Yanker, nudging him, stared open mouthed, with not a sound emitting. Vanya, commanded Brownty, "Stay! Good dog." and accompanied Gwedyll and Prince Heddi around the enclosure pretending not to notice the attention they were attracting.

On returning to the family pitch, they found a man waiting. He had, on first glimpse of the modeling tour tracked the clothes to their source, but his attempt at doing a deal with Penda had got him nowhere.

"AH! Here she is," said Penda with relief.

The stranger asked Gwedyll what was expected in exchange for one of the outfits? He held up an item in each hand. Gwedyll told him it was not she he needed to talk to, but Vanya. He paused, his face a picture of incredulity, but then on eyeing the girl, tall for her age though barely into womanhood, considered the situation, although highly unusual, to have enough credibility for him to suggest they enter into a business discussion. Vanya took this in her stride and in fact an onlooker might have thought she'd been trading for years. You could see he admired her pluck, but smiling, he pointed out the need for him to also make a little something from the trade and if satisfied would be back for more next spring. Wasn't this better than dealing with all the picker uppers and put back downers? How much better could she do if he took the lot? He was told how many outfits that amounted to and as calculations commenced, Penda was quite taken aback by his daughter's seeming command of the situation. A firm shake of head, shamed the number of fingers held up as an opening offer into crumpling. An improved amount was met with a polite thank you, but yet another shake of head. Then came the man's theatrical imploring look, plus open armed plea that made Vanya giggle. When a further attempt at reason was rebuffed, he gave an exasperated downward sweep of arms and turned as if walking away from the deal. Vanya, patiently standing her ground, arms folded, waited. He reluctantly dragged himself back, and with a deep sigh, as if drained of all energy, gave an improved final, final offer, another half finger. Now hurried marks were made on the tally board to check they had both arrived at the same total. This was followed by smiles and a firm hand shake. He would be back later with bronze in payment and to collect his goods. When he'd gone Vanya sank backwards against the side of the cart, looked to the heavens and mouthed, "Thank you."

Then as if prompted and goaded out of sheer devilment by the whispering spirits, the clamour arrived. The ladies were told they had missed the chance. Some were quite indignant, "But I told you I was thinking about it!" and "How can they have all gone I was only here moments ago!?" Plus one women became quite irate, "You can't have traded them all. I've promised my daughter!"

Some ladies in the Teller's audience shuffled uneasily realizing with discomfort, they could have quite easily featured in such a scenario themselves.

A new tally board was put to use as orders were taken for the next fair.

When things had calmed down and they had neatly stacked the dealer's goods for collection, there was chance for a snack of bread, crispy fried back-bacon and thirst-quenching dandelion root drink.

Gwedyll, still in her new attire, returned just after middle day to collect Vanya. Talia and Luda, left in charge of the afternoon's trading, accepted the challenge and responsibility with relish. Faithful Brownty looked up and spotting an opportunity followed at Vanya's heel. He had spent the morning, best out of the way of things, under the cart in the shade. His long dark coat with flash of white beneath collar and tip of tail, gleamed and his eyes were alert to all around.

People looked at him as if they'd never seen a dog before, when of course they had; tied to a post for life, guarding their homes or occasionally unleashed for hunting, but not one that looked like part of the family.

Women muttered as they passed, some looking jealously at Gwedyll as if, given the slightest provocation, they'd have gladly snatched the very clothes off her body.

"You know she's only a Skreela don't you! Not one of us!" A woman snapped at her husband like a call to duty. Studying his wife, standing dumpy, brown, unswayable in her belief that tribal affiliation alone surpassed all else and being forced to compare her with this foreign female of her scorn, so free and slender in the clothes of Vanya's design, I'll leave you to imagine his thoughts. Please forgive him, when following the ladies' graceful progress, for that deep, 'Oh if only,' intake of breath, that when soft emitted from puffed out lips, that almost inaudible, "Phew," sound. Feel for him when his wife's flinty glance and repetition of, "Not one of us!" forced his sigh of resignation and a "Yes my love," reply through gritted teeth.

Skreela was in fact a derogatory term for a tribe that referred to itself as Y-Dewis. They became rather tender to say the least on hearing the word Skreela, which was slightly hypocritical in view of the fact their name for wild cousins living even higher in the western mountains was Y-Gwyllt. The untamed.

Halfway to the compound fence Vanya spotted a boy bowling along a willow hoop. She caught it. He looked up slightly startled. Vanya laughed and holding it waist high said, "Watch." She called to Brownty who glad to oblige, ran and jumped silkily clean through without touching the sides, returning for a repeat performance. Vanya said, "Thank you" and handed the hoop back to the boy who stood wide eyed and gaping as if watching the progress of two shimmering visions fresh landed from another world, passing locked in conversation out through the north gate and on to the open ground.

On spotting them, Heddi urged his pony into a gallop and pulling up in a sharp turn and halt, leapt from its back to land lightly beside them. He glowed with confidence, seeming almost unrecognizable, now comfortable in his element. Gone was the stumbling embarrassment of the previous meeting and standing before Vanya was the youth as would soon be the man. She looked at eyes bright with life, smiling face flushed from exertions and hair tousled by the wind and remembered that clearly as being the pivotal moment. The moment she had made her mind up. But first she'd have to 'learn language,' as she had put it years before.

Gwedyll translated that he was honored by their company and that he hoped he could conjure up a performance commensurate with having the event graced by their presence.

With this he returned to the fray and the two ladies joined by the dog sat and watched in the cool dappled shade of an old broad oak. They perched on its roots and Brownty panted and slurped almost smiling as he lay soft in the dust left by countless sheep that had taken similar refuge over countless years.

Meanwhile Erdi had taken the chance to wander the camp to see what was on offer and to renew old acquaintances. Everyone had heard of Vanya's success, it had been talk of the fair. That was until the start of the rumour. For the very first time it was said there could be slaves for sale and the whole place now buzzed with talk of it. How the rumour had started no one knew. Some confided they'd had it on good authority, that even as they spoke, slaves were being shipped down the North River, the Dwy. Talk of slaves over the years had always eventually come to nothing, but this time it felt different. 'Where were they from? What would they look like? Who could afford to possess them?'

A man Erdi vaguely knew from previous fairs was curious to know about the dog he'd seen earlier jumping through a hoop. Erdi told him he'd been trained for hunting, but was more or less Vanya's dog. She'd taught him to sit, lie down, not pester them for food at meal times and various other things including not to cock his leg on convenient house support posts.

"You mean you let him in the house?"

"Yes he's sort of become part of the family." Erdi left the man scratching his head.

There was as yet no sign of his friends, the brothers from the eastern tribe, known to his people collectively as the Salters. As he wandered further it became evident not much was new. Goods on display looked more or less the same to those in previous years. Then he was drawn towards a small pitch for no other reason than to find out why such an unusual number of people had gathered around it. Was there a conjurer, a storyteller or an exotic creature maybe? No too quiet for that. So what was the attraction? He managed to nudge and weave his way through the small crowd to see nothing more interesting than a board holding a large earthenware pot and horn drinking vessels. Behind was a fire for heating water and beneath the serving board was a large closely woven basket. The man at the centre of all this interest, although small, virtually bald and looking like an unlikely candidate for such attention, was obviously used to it. He reached into his large basket and theatrically put a pinch of dried leaves into each mug and then as if a wide-eyed magician, scooped a jug of hot water from the large pot and holding it up to maximum height, carefully poured into each mug in turn. Erdi was at least expecting small puffs of smoke or plants to spring to life. But no, the man then simply handed out the mugs of liquid as if offering everyone a blessing. Blowing to cool, then carefully sipping, each recipient seemed compelled to turn to a neighbour in order to nod, grin and join in the general smacking of lips. The man beamed as if he'd just transported them into another world. How could a few dried leaves and hot water cause such an outbreak of nodding, grinning and lip smacking? Was it some sort of drug? Whatever it was, it seemed they couldn't part with scraps of bronze fast enough to receive a package containing the stuff. The man was doing a roaring trade in dried leaves. Erdi tried it dubiously, but was then equally stunned. He'd never tasted anything like it in his life. The man was from the south and used sign language as he wasn't conversant with the local tongue. A twist of the fingers to mid cheek region and pursed smack of lips indicated incredible flavour and a rub of a hand around the stomach area explained it was also good for digestion. He called the stuff, mint. Erdi was keen to return to tell the family of his discovery.

That was until his gaze was caught by the sight of a young lady approaching a small stall over by the perimeter fence. She was struggling towards a cart lugging a huge bundle and even with leverage of her right thigh at each step, was scarcely able to keep it off the floor. He ran and arrived in time to help her deliver the bound package of leathers up on to the boards of the vehicle.

She leant on her arms against the cart for a moment, regaining breath, then turning to Erdi, gave a smile of relief and mouthed, "Thank you." He asked if she needed further help, but she replied, while busily re-arranging items on display, she appreciated his offer but could manage. Her every movement gave an air of independence.

Apparently, she and her father made shoes and leather jerkins. Erdi commented on her sandals. They were particularly attractive, pretty in fact, suiting her trim foot and ankle, with criss-crossed bindings adorning her lower leg. The hem of her skirt had bold patterns embroidered and on the curve of her hips hung a slender leather girdle. A small white calfskin jacket surmounted a pretty embroidered blouse and looking up beyond brown tresses Erdi's observations were brought to a sudden halt by a narrow glint of eye and firm hand on hip stance which asked, 'Well? What are you staring at?'

"Oh" he said surprised. "I was wondering. I hope you don't mind me asking. Your clothes look different. Where did you get them from?"

"I made them of course!" Her avowal was emphasised by eyes widening and Erdi noticed they sparkled blue. He didn't have the courage, but wished he'd been able to follow his compulsion to hold her gently and brush the softest of kisses on her brow. A gentle kiss on just where it glistened would have disarmed that beautiful glow of vehemence. Or have invited a slap! He gave thanks to the fact she wasn't aware of what he was thinking.

"What is it?' She asked. "Why are you standing there grinning?"

He was heartened to see a teasing smile spread as she spoke and he wished he'd had the courage to say he'd never felt this way before, but instead said, "Perhaps you would like to pay us a visit and meet my sister Vanya. I think you may have a great deal in common."

"How can you say that? You hardly know me."

"It feels as if I do."

She waved a hand over the contents of the cart, "I'm sorry I daren't leave this."

"You just did. I saw you."

"Only for a few moments. I had to help my father."

She explained that just the two of them managed the small stall and so she couldn't really abandon it. Her father had gone to settle up for the leather bale Erdi had helped her with and there was no telling how long that would take.

"You come from over by Five Pools don't you."

Looking slightly mystified and feigning indignation, "How do you know that?"

"You say your words slightly differently."

"You're trying to say I talk funny!"

"No, I like the way you talk."

"No you don't. You're making fun of me. I shan't say another word."

"Please," said Erdi daring to touch her arm, "Talk as much as you want. I'll not tire of it."

"Look my father will be here soon." She seemed genuinely fearful and he'd noticed the look of worry, each time she'd checked for his approach. "You'd better go."

"But we're not doing any harm."

"I'm sorry," she said, "it's not your fault. He angers very quickly. He worries about me. I suppose he's been a bit overprotective since my mother died. None of the boys dare approach me. He's scared them all off. He thinks most men are only after one thing."

"Well he's probably right there," said Erdi laughing, "but I assure you my intentions are honorable."

"I believe you." Then with lowering of eyelids she added throatily, "just."

Erdi laughed and slightly theatrically, clasped the region of his heart as if severely wounded by her implication.

"But please," She continued with an agitated look, "If he sees us talking it will put him into one of his moods. I'll have to suffer it for the rest of the day."

"Why? For all he knows I could be a customer." Said with a pair of ladies' sandals dangling from a forefinger.

She laughed and snatched them from him. "He's not stupid you know."

"Have you tasted that stuff they call mint?" Was asked brightly, trying to lengthen his stay.

"Yes I have, but please, you'll get me into trouble. Thank you for your help. Now go. Goodbye!" Erdi left, turned to wave and when she smiled and waved briskly in reply he carried on his way, not so much walking as floating. Shaking his head in disbelief and unable to suppress a smile, he was so much in another world, he hadn't noticed Trader approaching.

"You look pleased with yourself, young Erdi."

"Don't you think it's a most wonderful day?"

Trader gave him a slightly puzzled look, then asked if he'd discovered anything on his travels.

Erdi replied, "I was going to ask you the exact same thing."

Trader shook his head, but then conceded there were a couple of items he had had an interest in. He'd of course admired the clothes Vanya had been so successful with, but that wasn't his line. He owned to not having a clue how to rate the value of ladies' apparel. Erdi asked what he thought of the new mint sensation? Trader although admitting it was certainly different, said he hadn't let himself get carried away by it. Instead, he'd had a little chat with a friend of his, also from the south, who had told him, where he came from, the plant was not difficult to find. In fact, the man had been that annoyed at not having seen its potential, he'd let slip the gem, the plant was common to the point of going rampant if not held in check. Trader tapped the side of his head and smiled. "We have a bit of a deal sorted, But now let me show you one little item of merit I've rooted out."

He led him to a lone man sitting cross-legged with a blanket spread before him. Erdi looking down was puzzled, for on the blanket lay nothing more than flint blades, scrapers and a handaxe. "Ah good you've kept it for me," said Trader. He handed the man the tiny scrap of bronze agreed as payment and received the napped handaxe in exchange. When at a polite distance Erdi asked, "What's so special about that outmoded tool?"

"I'll show you in a minute." Once out of sight of the vendor Trader held it up between finger and thumb.

"I can see it's finely napped," said Erdi.

"Finely napped? That my boy is the finest piece of workmanship you're ever likely to see. How the man made it, well, refined it really, without smashing the edges I'll never know."

"Didn't you ask him?"

"What for? You don't think he made it do you?. I bet the thing's ancient. Its maker's probably been back with his ancestors since the time of the circle stones. Look at it! It's not just a tool, it's a work of art. That man couldn't have made it. If he had, he wouldn't have parted with it for next to nothing."

"Why was it still on show if you'd said you'd have it?"

"Ah. Just an old trading trick, Erdi. Sight of things sold makes others keener. Shows he's a seller. Stuff's in demand. Have to make their minds up."

He handed the axe to Erdi who held it up, revolving it slowly and having had its merits pointed out could now see what Trader saw.

He studied it and as if in a trance said in a far away voice, "It's beautiful, simply beautiful."

"Are you sure you're alright, Erdi?" asked Trader slightly nonplussed. There was something different about his young friend, he couldn't quite put his finger on.

Erdi's face snapped back to life. "Yes fine and I've never felt better," he said with a laugh.

He obviously had no inkling of what his father was busy planning.

Out beyond the palisade things were drawing to a dramatic conclusion. The whirling of horses had drawn quite a crowd and now only two riders remained in contention for the prize. What had started years back as just an impromptu way of having fun, had become by the intervention of tribal elders, more formalised with definite rules and even a small award given to the victor, the coveted bronze arrow-brooch. This senior involvement had almost certainly been driven by political undertones. A message to the gathered tribes. 'Look what mere Y-Dewis boys can do. Any of you brave warriors fancy challenging their fathers?'

Gwedyll and Vanya had stayed on into the lengthening shadows and so when young Heddi cantered over with the said brooch proudly on display he was surprised to hear, "Oh it's over. Did you win?"

He of course couldn't understand the words, but from the tone knew it to have been a question and when Gwedyll stumbled and reddened slightly during translation, instinct

170

told him the finer details of the afternoon's hard-fought affair had not been as riveting to them as he'd imagined.

He of course had made the same mistake most men make in assuming the little ladies are as fascinated by male pastimes as they are. Gwedyll and Vanya had had a great time, true, but for the most part it had been spent talking about things they liked, things they didn't, plus they laughed on realising they shared utter disbelief at certain conventional nonsense still being shown respect when long beyond the time of warranting it. They might have originated from two completely different tribes, but that afternoon realised they shared more in common than with many close relatives. In fact they had dared to divulge inner feelings they'd not think of revealing to those supposedly close to them. One could bet the afternoon had passed like the click of finger and thumb. Any distant watcher not knowing could have easily taken them for sisters.

Heddi hadn't up to this point understood how different were the workings of male and female minds. He wasn't alone in this. For in fact men in general, when toiling to exhaustion on certain muscle sapping tasks carried out under trying circumstances, probably think their efforts are viewed with a certain amount of admiration and sympathy by the fairer sex. They certainly don't imagine such comments as, "When's he going to stop making that dreadful racket?" or "I hope he's going to clean all that mess up when he's finished!"

There were gasps of disbelief from the Teller's audience and anxious looks towards the chieftain's family. Some women were thinking, 'Surely he can't get away with saying that in front of the chieftain!' When the craggy old warrior's wife smiled, laughter broke out.

Anyway Vanya had enough innate guile to recover the situation and asked brightly, "Can Heddi show me his wonderful brooch?"

That, plus a warm smile and a few artful words of query and admiration was all it took. To Heddi it was the best day of his life. The spirits of the Spring Fair had certainly been going full-sword to the hilt, casting their magic. In that bewitching glow of the moment, he asked Vanya if there was anything, any small gift he could bestow on her? All she had to do was ask. This was translated, as was her answer.

"A horse," she said.

There was a moment's silence and then all three burst out laughing.

Erdi keenly awaited Vanya's return. He told her about the mint and then trying to sound as casual as possible, ventured on to the subject of the young lady he'd chanced upon. The fact Vanya would probably have things in common with the girl was stressed as a screen to enable him to describe her without divulging his true feelings. The more he talked, however, the more her smile grew into a knowing look. With head on one side and eyebrows arched she asked, "Do I detect something here? Has my big brother fallen for this," she paused "what's her name?"

"I forgot to ask and anyway who said anything about falling?"

"We know these things," said his sister laughing. "You can't fool me, Erdi. Is she pretty?"

He attempted to keep his expression blank, but no matter how hard he tried to suppress it, his eyes betrayed an inner smile.

"Is she Erdi? Look at me Erdi. Is she pretty?"

"Stop it Vanya!" His pretence of annoyance, was met by her calm, inquisitive gaze, until pressure within forced his face to crack into a slow spreading beam of joy to reveal the truth.

She started to whistle the piper's tune played at every joining ceremony, but it became impossible to continue once she'd started laughing.

"What makes you think I'll like her, Erdi?"

"She seems to like the same things as you and doesn't seem the sort to talk about babies all day long." He'd managed to regain some composure.

"Mmm. Perhaps I'd better meet this ----. Fancy not asking her name!"

The next morning Erdi was busy re-hanging the awnings in front of the cart, but was interrupted by his father, "Leave that. Yanker and Dowid can do that. Can you get changed there are some people I'd like you to meet? Oh and you'd better scrape those whiskers. I've put a blade and water ready."

It sounded particularly ominous, but his father wouldn't answer any questions as they walked in silence to where a family camped near the East Gate, slowly rose in greeting.

They seemed very pleasant, ordinary, but pleasant and when a fairly tall girl, a bit on the hefty side, gave a gappy smile and firmly shook his hand, Erdi suddenly realised what this little meeting was all about. It felt like a bronze fist had just clutched his heart and a white panic in his brain, accompanied the desire to get up and run from the place as fast as his legs would carry him. As the full horror of the situation dawned and with the girl eying him warmly, he felt anger at his father for having put them in this situation. He couldn't help but feel a little sorry for her. She was wholesome enough, was probably a hard worker, but he felt not the slightest glimmer of attraction. He managed to quell his feelings for decency's sake, but couldn't wait to get away.

"Well you didn't have much to say," said Penda when marching back, looking pleased with himself. "A bit shy perhaps. Not surprising at the first meeting. You'll have more to say, the more you see of each other. Her father's a good man. Good family all round. Good breeding."

The colour had drained from Erdi's face. The term, 'Good breeding' hadn't implied admiration for the girl's background. It had been said more in the manner of relishing her strength and girth of child bearing hips. Erdi felt as if his whole world had fallen in. The spirits had obviously witnessed his happiness the previous afternoon and were willfully playing with his life for their sport. He felt helpless.

While this little drama had been unfolding Vanya had asked Talia to accompany her for the pre-arranged meeting with Heddi. It would not have done to have gone alone. Brownty padding along behind made it a threesome. Heddi had said he would be proud to show Vanya how the arrows were launched to fly so far by hand. She, the little madam, had played the roll of helpless female and hadn't owned to the fact she already knew. Talia, slightly embarrassed, winced when Vanya made pretence of fumbling with the throwing strap and she couldn't believe that the poor lad, even though besotted, couldn't see the game her friend was playing. It was obvious he was blinded, just loving the chance of being close to her; being able to hold her hand and show her the correct grip. "Then you stretch your arm behind and arch your back." He showed her thus overcoming the language barrier.

"Like this Heddi? Am I doing it right?"

"Oh stop it Vanya," Talia muttered to herself.

On understanding what she'd asked, "Yes perfect. See if you can reach that clump of weeds." He picked similar from amongst the grass, showed her and pointed to those growing about forty paces away. Talia groaned and Heddi's mouth fell open when the arrow winged twice the distance.

"Oh I like this game," thrilled Vanya. "Don't run Heddi." She held his arm. "Brownty will get it. Brownty? Fetch!" The dog sprang to life and was soon effortlessly racing in a rippling motion, eating up the distance to return with the arrow in his mouth. Vanya pointed and on hearing, "It's dead," he dropped it at Heddi's feet. Bright eyed, the dog half turned eager for another go. From that moment on young Prince Bonheddig began to feel love sick at the very thought of Vanya. How would he manage without her in his everyday life up in the lofty valleys of home? The spirits looking on rubbed their hands together with glee.

It was about mid-morning when a horn blown loud enough to be heard away in the hills, announced the commencement of the broad-staff competition. It was held out on the same open ground the Skreela youths had used the day before. Each competitor had a staff and the object was, not to beat the living daylights out of the opponent, but to score five points against him before he managed to do the same to you. Points were scored by rapping the opponent's knuckles, jabbing the staff on his foot or by simulating a blow to the head or jab to the midriff. Any crack on the knuckles severe enough to force release of the staff, signaled end of contest. Any potentially lethal blows were not followed through, but just made clear enough for the judge to shout, "Hit." Any of the older youths could take part including junior ranking warriors.

Erdi noticed the family he'd been introduced to were watching and the girl gave a wave. He returned her a weak smile.

Both Erdi and Yanker survived the early bouts, but as the competition stiffened Yanker was eliminated and he left sucking the blood off his knuckles. Erdi wasn't a huge man, but made up for that with speed and agility. He survived the various rounds and even beat the youth who'd vanquished his cousin. Then almost as if it had been pre-ordained, Blade stood facing him like an angry bull in the final. With the soldier's diet and training he'd become huge. He nodded at Erdi as if to say, 'Now you're for it.'

Erdi stood his ground and matched the young warrior point for point which everyone could see was making him wild and erratic. Then he finally lost control completely, yelling "Magic stones! Magic stones! I'll give you magic stones!!" The soldier boys had obviously had a word in his ear as regards the little jape years before and he came at Erdi thrashing his staff in determined attempts to bash his brains out. Any one of the blows had that lethal potential.

"Magic stones!! That old shovel trick!"

175

He was that committed to attack he left himself wide open, but Erdi's scoring jabs to midriff that would have normally had him declared the winner were ignored. Blade's blood was up. Rules and conventions didn't matter anymore, he wanted revenge and continued thrashing and swinging wildly. The judge, at the risk of getting himself brained, stepped in, trying to end the madness. deftly ducking, recoiling, but to no avail. His final tumble backwards, brought a loud, "OOOH!" from the crowd. A few made a move to intervene but then thought better of it.

Erdi could see the hatred, blinding any semblance of reason flashing from Blade's eyes and with it came the cold reality that this could be a matter of life and death. Blade had completely lost control. He emphasized each attempt to kill with words forced out from bottled up frustration and humiliation. Obviously recent life in the junior ranks hadn't been the heroic, romantic notion he'd dreamt of, with him instead becoming an opportunity for light relief and butt of their jokes.

Only words admittedly, but we all know how cruel young men can be in such circumstances and Erdi was now reaping all that had been sown.

"I'm a warrior!"

Erdi caught the blow with his staff.

"But do they call me Blade? No!!"

Erdi ducking, felt the draught from the swipe.

"Do they call me Brone? No!!"

Erdi somehow contorted his body to evade the thrust.

"Thanks to you my name is…"

Erdi arched his back as the broad-staff whirred, nearly taking his face off.

"Bone Head!!" He shrieked and the crowd gasped as the blow, cracking Erdi's stave, drove it down on to his temple. All held their breath as he swayed sickeningly. They waited, but he didn't go down. The judge having recruited two, brave enough to help, had managed to disarm Blade before he'd been able to follow up with the death blow. He was led away raving like a madman. Absolutely ranting. "Magic stones. AHHHH! They thought they were SO CLEVER!" His voice could have been heard across in the Skreela hills. "Their fault! Not mine. It was that Yanker! Yanker and the STONES!"

The onlookers turning to one another, looked completely puzzled and said things like, "No, me neither."

"Well what a thing to do," piped Yanker as if totally mystified by his inclusion in the tirade.

As Erdi, visibly shaken, swayed, cracked stave in hand, a young girl lifting embroidered hem of skirt, ran lightly to the centre of the contest ring, to put an arm around him and gently mop the blood from his brow.

"Looks like Erdi's picked himself a pretty young doe," said Dowid.

"I think you'll find," said Mara, eyes narrowing. "I think you'll find the young doe has just picked him."

There was a general hum of voices from people, obviously wondering who the young lady was, but her father stood back from the scene with a face like thunder and as if attempting to bring a sense of balance, Penda standing directly opposite, glowered with a face to match. The family of the hefty girl, having proudly let slip their lovely daughter could soon be betrothed to Erdikun, took the final scene of the drama as a personal insult and the poor girl herself felt embarrassed and foolish. Those spirits hadn't had so much fun in years.

Prince Gardarm, turned away in a fury. Not only had one of his men made a spectacle of himself, but had lost to the very same peasant who'd humiliated him years before. The scars still hadn't healed, so to speak, but time was on his side. He would even things up. He would have his revenge. His younger brother, Prince Aram however, was of a totally different disposition and took the opportunity to wander over, approaching Yanker as if they might have been friends, equals even. This brought a sense of unease, not helped by the sight of people, as puzzled as he was, now watching. He calmed inner tensions, however, managed to radiate a smile and listened, obviously curious to know the reason for this unexpected familiarity.

The prince praised him and Erdi for their skills. Skills that if used in combat, could bring them accolades and reward. Furthermore, men of their caliber could consider themselves destined for high rank. They had the brains to devise solutions when in difficult situations. "Not like some," he confided. Would Yanker and his cousin consider volunteering for the elite squad of warriors loyal to him, Prince Aram? It would be taken as a personal favour. To gain such a triumph where his brother had failed, would bring him untold satisfaction. He could even arrange for Yanker to be later enrolled into the Queen's own guard. He said this with a wink.

Yanker thanked him for his suggestion and said he would give it considerable consideration. After all one can't be expected to give more consideration than that and with his usual jaunty manner fully restored, plus thinking, 'why miss an opportunity?' he edged closer and muttered the following, as if passing on a secret of huge import, "Has Your Highness heard of that amazing piece of flint, Trader managed to get his hands on for next to nothing?"

The prince looked mystified, suspecting Yanker could well be trying to make a fool of him. 'Flint? What could something so antiquated have to do with anything?'

"I can understand you looking like that, Your Highness," said Yanker. "I felt exactly the same. The thing's a relic. Yet in another way, having seen it, I think it is in fact, more of a jewel. It's a handaxe napped to perfection. Best you'll ever see. Might be something our lord and master might appreciate. Would I be right in thinking he did well on the tin exchange?" (He had negotiated slightly better than the usual ten to one exchange rate of copper for tin)" A little congratulatory gift like this could be well received." It was common knowledge the chieftain had had a sword cast, so massive, it was too heavy for use. He was also proud owner of a lance tipped with gold. Useless other than for ceremonial use. There was also his revered bronze shield. Totally impractical. So why not add the best handaxe ever to become available, to his collection? "I suggest Your Highness might be pleasantly surprised when looking at it. I might be wrong. You might just think it beneath your father's dignity, but it can't hurt to look, Your Highness." Yanker studied the prince, judging the effect his words. Emboldened, he continued, "Rather you didn't tell Trader I suggested this. He told me he wasn't fussy about trading, what he calls, his gem. But please, have a look Your Highness. I'm sure he'd be honoured. He's proud of it. He'd be proud to show you."

On returning to camp Dowid asked his son, "What was all that about?" He wouldn't have been the only one wanting to know the answer to that question as not much got missed at gatherings like this. It certainly hadn't been missed by an eaves dropper who had remained hidden behind an awning and had heard every word.

"What me and my new best friend Ary? We're," he screwed up his face as if struggling to pull his two hooked forefingers apart, "like that!" he said with a laugh.

"You watch it my boy," warned his father. "Dangerous consorting with princes."

"It's Donda that needs to watch it. Off with the soldier boys again."

"She's probably safe as long as there's a crowd. They'll all make sure no particular one gains an advantage." He squatted where his bowl had been placed ready. "It's when there's only one of them you might see growing evidence. Evidence one of 'ems parted of her whiskers."

A large wooden spoon, as if out of nowhere, delivered a resounding Thwack!

"OWWW!! What was that for?" Dowid asked, looking up at Mara and rubbing his skull.

"Less of that sort of talk," said she, arms folded and culinary weapon still erect in a fist.

"But I'm only telling the truth!"

"I'm not putting up with that sort of talk. Not **here**. Remember this is the **Feasting Site!**"

Dowid spread his palms and frowned a gesture of, "What?"

The other men laughed silently into their soup. Penda, who still wasn't in the best of moods having witnessed a certain young lady, as if a spirit-sent agent of destruction, smash his match-making plans, even he couldn't help his rugged face cracking into a smile.

Vanya looked across at Erdi and obviously referring to the mystery girl who had rushed to his aid, mouthed, "she looks nice." It was some consolation as he sat quietly, head bandaged and throbbing. None of the family had made a fuss regarding his injury and he hadn't expected it. If you played rough games you had to expect rough consequences. That was their way.

Meanwhile as the day turned into one of those pre-summer scorchers the excited atmosphere around the Feasting Site began to feel almost inflamed, simmering as if ready to boil over at any moment. The slaves were due. The interest it caused seemed almost unhealthy. Some, without any notion of dignity, ran to the north gate to gain first sight of them. Eventually when the throng spilled out on to open ground, there was that much bad-tempered jostling and pushing, warrior power was required to restore a semblance of order. They were not armed, but no less effective. No-one really knew what to expect. All eyes were on the track that led north through the trees. Young boys pelting towards them as if pursued by devils, faces overheated and voices hysterical, yelled, "They're coming!"

"I've seen them!"

"One's locked in a cage!"

Gradually, almost painfully, a small group emerged, led by a squat bald man. He walked slowly, hindered by the obvious disadvantage of a massive stomach. With what was generally on offer to eat, a stomach that huge was in itself a thing of wonder.

"Don't try and tell me that's what a slave looks like!"

"No. More like he's just eaten one of them."

"I wouldn't trade our old dog for a fat lump like that." Such banter and laughter was their way of dealing with the unfamiliar situation.

Then as the file drew closer, scuffling of weary feet, plod of horse and squeak of cart axle were the only sounds heard other than a baby crying. The crowd parted in silence, their eyes fixed on the three men roped together, a young girl following and finally the cart driven by a bare-chested brute of a man. On the cart was a cage and in it was a filthy, wild-eyed occupant hanging on to the wooden bars as the vehicle rocked and jolted over the ruts. Carts and stalls had been moved in readiness, creating an open selling area and now at last all could see what a slave looked like. They made for a pitiful offering in the centre of the Feasting Site. Most disconcerting, however, was the fact that, but for the whims of the spirits, it could have been any one of the onlookers standing in a similar situation paraded in front of strangers to be regarded as nothing more than a commodity. This would be the final business of the fair. Well almost.

The three roped men were hollow eyed, ragged and filthy. One went to sit down but winced and rose again when the lash hit him. The young girl was also unbelievably dirty made all the more obvious by white tear streaks on her face. Her feet were bleeding and she half-heartedly brushed flies away from a cut on her brow. Up in the cage glaring down at them was a creature with long straggling hair, whose sudden snarl, caused a tiny girl to scream and hide behind her mother's skirts.

The three chieftains, guards, plus clerks there to translate, entered the circle and terms were explained. There was to be an auction. This was open to all except of course only the wealthy few had the wherewithal to compete. Trader could

181

have put in a few bids, but other than having satisfied his initial curiosity, he distanced himself from the whole thing.

An empty cart was rolled forward to act as a selling platform. The bald slave trader, resembling a gasping, over-sized toad, was helped up. He stood and now everyone could get the full benefit of his gut. Its weight took it well below belt line and along the top curve, greasy food stains darkened a shirt bulging as taut as a suet pudding cloth.

"Fair play, that's some sort of belly," said Yanker to no-one in particular. Then thinking, some of the old ones are the best added, "Bet he hasn't seen **his** for a while," He basked a little in the mirth this engendered until suddenly shocked to rigidity by the burning look from the slaver. The man laconically pointed him out to the brute in his employment.

Somebody said, "Now you've done it, Yanker. He heard you."

"Didn't think he knew our language!"

With sweat glistening off every muscle the colossus leapt off the cart and Yanker fled for his life. There were hoots of surprise plus sounds of general merriment as he scrambled through the crowd. It parted for him, but the pursuer found his way blocked by those apologizing for their clumsiness. The bald man, his face gleaming with sweat, sat impassively as he waited patiently for his man to return. Empty handed thankfully.

Some children had gathered in the shadow of the cage and were taunting and pulling faces at the snarling occupant. The slave trader flicked a hand, sending his man into action and they scattered. "Have a care doing that," he called after them. "If they catch you pulling those faces, they'll change the way the wind blows. Those ugly faces will stick for life!" He was referring to the willful power of the spirits of course.

He then raised his arms for attention and said, "I have the pleasure of offering you today these lovely creatures brought here for sale." Suddenly looking down he added, "Don't touch the goods please. You can do whatever you like once you own her." A few hoots were heard from the women and cheers from the men. "But until that time please keep your hands off! All of them are healthy specimens. In fact, there's nothing wrong that a good wash and feed won't put right. Now I want you to bid briskly and when I clap my hands consider the deal done."

One by one, the three previously roped, were led up on to the improvised selling platform by the slave handler. Flicks of his leather persuader, forced them to stand straight. They were obviously terrified of the man. The Skreela chieftain had turned his back on the auction having apparently said, "If I want slaves, I'll come and catch my own," and so the bidding was between remaining two chieftains. Following each clap of the slaver's hands, he pointed to their new owner. All three would be heading south.

Many of the onlookers were unnerved by the realization, at the current rate of exchange, their own lives in a similar circumstance, wouldn't stack up to very much at all. There were sounds of female consternation when the young girl was pushed up for sale.

"Don't trouble yourselves," called out the slaver. "Don't make the mistake of thinking they have the same feelings as you or I. They have no more feeling than a cow or sheep. She'd still keep you warm at night though. And there could even be a bonus, hidden in that belly of hers." There came the odd cheer from the like-minded and he beamed in response. Erdi felt a loathing for the man.

Ownership of the girl was hotly contested, but eventually she also passed into the possession of their lord. Many wondered why he had need for slaves considering many of them were virtually slaves themselves.

Then came the turn of the caged man. The handler asked for two volunteers to help drag him out. He was immensely strong and flung them against the bars, causing the whole cart to rock. Finally entangled in a net and arms pinned behind, he was dragged from his prison to stand up alongside the slaver.

183

The net was removed and and his shirt ripped open for the benefit of prospective buyers. Two guards flanked him, each holding a noose that girded his neck ready to throttle at first sign of trouble. Muscles shone as his chest heaved. His wild hair, when caught by the breeze, showed a red tinge and fierce hatred burned from dark eyes.

"I know he looks like a bit of a handful," the slaver called out, "but a little training and you'd have yourself a one-man army. Or geld the brute. That'll calm him. He even comes with his own house." The cage was indicated and it was obvious a few found his remarks suited their sense of humour. The Salter chieftain shook his head and declined to bid, forcing the slaver to bid up the value of his own possession. Needless to say, he didn't push his luck and ownership was relinquished for quite a reasonable sum.

It took a number of men to slide the cage down from the cart and the prisoner was dragged back inside. He offered his arms to the bars for the bindings to be undone. The muscle-bound handler obliging, suddenly leapt back as if avoiding a snake strike and ruefully rubbed his throat. He would obviously be glad to see the back of the man.

Penda's family consumed the last meal of the Spring Fair in a subdued mood. What they had witnessed had been unsettling. Mid-way through, without warning, Vanya got up and disappeared carrying the remains of a meat joint. Erdi stood and followed. Brownty had beaten him to it and was on Vanya's heals. The cage was still centre site, and pausing, she approached the bars. Before Erdi could run and stop her, the meat was offered. It was taken gently. The man's eyes stared a warm thank you, before he tore at the food with canine ferocity. Vanya turning, ran to the nearest wagon to ask for water. Men already standing, had been poised, anticipating a need to be called to the rescue. Erdi, watching as the wild man drained the beaker and tore into the meat once more, called, "Vanya."

His sister turned and speaking through huge tears said, "Wolfy was starving, Erdi."

The man stopped eating and eying her intently, extended an arm through the bars. She reached towards him and their fingers gently touched.

The next morning all was fuss and bustle as those remaining, broke camp. Some with less to pack had departed the night before. Mardi told his brother he had at last located one of their friends from the high citadel, but something awful had happened. Erdi followed his brother to where the youth stood waiting, upwind of the cage. Erdi asked, where had he been? He replied he hadn't even wanted to come to the fair. His people had forced him. Not being able to face the throng and their questions he'd spent most of his time outside the camp.

Now as you know they only had a certain amount of language in common, but to keep things simple, here is the gist of what was said.

"Where's your brother?" asked Erdi.

"That's the problem. He's dead."

"I'm really sorry. What did he die from?"

"I'm sad to say he killed himself."

"That's terrible," said Erdi. "Whatever made him do that?"

The caged man was watching them intently.

"No-one really knows. He was there one minute. Next thing we knew he was lying dead at the bottom of the cliff."

"Didn't he give any indication?"

"Not really. Of course, I'd asked him, why had he been so sad, but all he said was…." he paused wondering whether to continue. "He said he was tired of wiping his backside every morning."

"Oh I'm sorry I shouldn't have laughed."

"Don't worry," was said through tears. "You're not alone in doing that."

The man in the cage looked puzzled, watching as Erdi put a consoling arm around his friend.

"If his death weren't bad enough the Seer then pronounced that my poor brother had been possessed. The evil ones had got into his very being. His body was carried to the black hole, where they're known to dwell and it was cast weighted down to sink into the cold bottomless waters."

Mardi joined in his brother's effort to comfort with words of sympathy, but it was a job to know what to say for the best. In the end their efforts were curtailed by all the bustle around them.

Walking back, to continue helping with the dismantling and packing Mardi asked, "You wouldn't let them throw me into the cold black waters would you, Erdi?"

"Of course not, Mardi. What a strange thing to say."

The activity in the Feasting Site, with so many trying to avoid becoming trapped behind the largest, slowest carts, had become frenzied. It was not surprising therefore, that when one of the Seer's acolytes approached Trader, he was not given the warmest of greetings.

"I assume you were the buyer. I've been sent to enquire about the axe you acquired."

Trader looking up annoyed asked, "Are you some sort of poet?"

The man looked mystified.

"Buyer, enquire, acquired," said Trader. "Oh never mind. Anyway, who sent you?"

"I've come to ask about the stone axe on behalf of Prince Gardarm."

Obviously, this man had been the eves dropper and had rushed to ingratiate himself with the prince, wanting the glory of procuring the rare axe before Aram had the chance. But first he had to satisfy himself it was as good as described.

"Have you indeed. Well you can go back and tell the prince, if he wants a deal, come and look at it himself."

"How dare you! I can't say that."

"Well fine. I'm not in the mood for parting with it. You don't think I'm going to sully the value of this gem of a stone by offering it up for the opinion of a minion do you?" Trader stopped suddenly, "By the stars you've got me at it now! On your way. I'm busy. Go on; off with you! I'm willing to offer it, but to Prince Gardarm alone."

Shortly after, the prince, visibly annoyed, stomped into view closely followed by his failed negotiator.

"Come on man. Let's get on with it. I don't have time to waste."

"With all due respects, neither do I," said Trader. "And I hope it's not impertinent to point out, this deal was not my idea in the first place."

"How dare you speak to His Highness like that," said the minion, attempting repair work on his recently dented status.

Trader enunciated calmly and clearly, "The proposed deal was not my idea," he gave a slight bow, "Your Highness."

He showed the stone and in fairness Prince Gardarm could appreciate its uniqueness, but was still in no mood for nonsense. "Alright. So how much? Four bolts?" (equivalent to half a rond, half an axe-head)

"Oh I'm sorry, Your Highness. Bronze won't acquire this."

"The cheek of the man, my Lord!"

"Quiet! Don't try and **slime** me, you idiot!" Then turning to Trader, "So what will then?"

"Gold. Just one small ring of gold." (a standard trading unit often used by the wealthy)

"Come on," said the prince to his aid. "The man's clearly mad!"

They had turned to leave when the utterance, "Well. If you don't know how to rate it, best it stays with me," stopped them in their tracks. This not surprisingly had got under the prince's skin. "Watch your tongue! I'll have you whipped! Of course I know how to rate it! That's why I'll not part with gold for it!"

"Fine Your Highness. However, one ring of gold is much like another, but this," holding it up, "is unique. Yes we've all seen handaxes before, but not the like of this, Your Highness"

It's facets caught the light as he turned it temptingly between finger and thumb.

"Damn you! I'll think about it."

"Sorry Your Highness, I treasure this stone and it's not for thinking about." He tucked it back in a pocket. "I acquired it on its merits alone with no thought for gain. However, if you want it this instant," Trader clapped his hands, "it's yours. Otherwise Your Highness, I'll not part with it. Not to anyone,"

All about them, the bustle for departure with stalls having been dismantled and carts moved, had reached a point that left their little deal being negotiated pretty much out in the open. This of course didn't trouble Trader, but Prince Gardarm was now clearly uncomfortable, uneasy at the amount of attention they were attracting. He realized he'd made a huge mistake demeaning himself in this way. The man should have been compelled to bring the stone to him. This was Trader's territory and the prince was beginning to feel foolish, exposed. He wanted the axe and needed a quick way out. Then as if things weren't bad enough already, he couldn't believe it, his brother Aram was approaching. "Damn you man! I'll have the thing!" And being shoved aside with a growl of, "Out of my way idiot!" his aid did well to remain upright.

"I'll send him back with the gold," was snarled over a departing shoulder.

As people left the fair one last snippet of gossip buzzed around. Trader had turned flint-stone to gold. The fair had been a memorable success, but two young men returned home quite love-sick at heart.

The Teller pulled from his cloak the same strange instrument he had used once before. He raised it to his mouth and a guttural sound of laughter clattered around the walls. He called out, Was similar laughter heard blown on the wind, heard blowing through the trees and over the water as these mere mortals left the Feasting Site?

Chapter Fifteen

Once back home, Penda, who had been keeping his anger under wraps, summoned Erdi for a good talking to. The time had come for him to realise his responsibilities. It was appreciated that soon he would be a man and if he decided to strike out on his own, as his grandfather Tollan had done, taking up with a woman of his own choosing, there was little they could do about it. He might not have the families' blessing and would almost certainly be landless, but if his mind was made up, he'd just have to make the best of his choices. While he was still under the family roof however, he had a duty to them all and any desire for freedom of choice, held serious consequences. No one could force him into a life not of his choosing, but Penda had found him a good woman from a good background, strong, apparently a good worker, who would bear him strong children. Affection and respect would surely follow. If Erdi was to stay as part of their extended family then it was his duty to sacrifice his own personal wishes for the greater cause. Furthermore, her father had pledged an ox and twenty axe-heads for their union. (*Bronze axe-heads had become a proto-currency*)

On seeing Erdi roll his eyes, not a wise move under the circumstances, his anger was enflamed to such a degree his words resounded for all to hear, each being emphasized like a regulated drum beat. "Don't you make light of THIS!" was how it started. Then it was pointed out Garrow their ox was getting on in years and that his replacement would not only be invaluable, but very soon, essential. Also, the bronze would provide his sister with the sizeable basis for a dowry. "Would you deny your sister a good man when the time comes? Would you be that **selfish**?"

Even Dowid and Yanker, exchanging pitying looks on Erdi's behalf, had winced and instinctively raised a hand to hat as the last word, **selfish**, had blasted their way. Even the nearby fish-pool willow had seemed to quiver.

Erdi hadn't expected the last twist of leverage. "Father," he began carefully. "The young lady who showed such concern after the recent broad-staff encounter; I hardly know her." He wasn't at this point going to admit that he would very much like to get to know her. In fact he thought of little else. "The one you introduced me to, I have to admit, I didn't like to say it at the time, but I feel not the slightest hint of interest for."

"Don't you talk to me in that manner. Who d'you think you are? You sound like some sort of, grown beyond his sticks, court advisor! Recent broad-staff encounter! Not the slightest hint of interest! I don't know where you get it from! You've got a bit above yourself, my lad. What you're really saying is, your mind's set on a course that denies Vanya her chance of a dowry. And don't think that Skreela boy will come riding to the rescue. You know as well as I do his folk won't condone a union between one of the royal line and a girl off nothing but our scrap of land."

"Father. I know I have a duty to my family and I certainly love my sister and wish her all future happiness, but I don't see why this can only be achieved by me living a life of misery."

"I see! Well let me tell you something. I did a bit of digging. Now you're listening aren't you!" Penda's voice was again on the rise, warning others within earshot to grab hold of the nearest solid object and brace themselves. "That lady of your desires is a nobody, descended from nobodies. Her father probably couldn't provide one cured ox HIDE for the match, let alone the actual living ANIMAL!" His hand slapped the ground in emphasis and he stood and left having said all that needed to be said.

Through the ensuing silence, Erdi continued to squat, alone with an aching heart. He felt sick and trapped by the dilemma. He hadn't been able to concentrate on anything but seeing the girl again. He couldn't even call out her name in a cry of anguish to the spirits. He still didn't know it. The thought of her plagued his waking mind and cost him untold loss of sleep. Deep in thought he remained as if frozen, motionless and thoroughly miserable, knowing his only chance to pursue his dream, would be to leave home. Having done that, how could he support a family? He had nothing. She had nothing. He could hardly invite her to share a life of misery. To make things worse a notion kept taunting, causing him to groan "I can't believe it. My whole future for an ox."

Mara, whether wanting to or not, had heard all her husband had said and walked quietly out to where her son remained, head in hands. He knew, without looking up, who had just softly touched his head. Erdi pulled himself upright and looking down with a beseeching look asked, "Do you agree with him?"

"It's a hard life Erdi from the day we're born until the day we die. Your father is simply looking at the long term rather than romantic notions of the present. A sure way of gaining an advantage in this life, whether prince or pauper, is by taking a few easy steps forward courtesy of who you spend the rest of your days with. A mighty chieftain often gains more from who he ends up in bed with, than ever he could have gained from warfare. Once our family had nothing, but in just three generations we have become the strong unit you see now. We need you to build on that Erdi."

"Oh, not you as well. I was hoping you'd see my side of things."

"You obviously feel deeply for this girl, but you're young, feelings can change. I doubt you'll see her until Summer Fair and by then all could be forgotten."

191

"Not the way I'm feeling at the moment. I couldn't settle down with that, that **thing**. That thing that supposedly brings such advantage to us all. I swear I'd be physically sick!"

"Oh Erdi. She's not a thing. She's a fine young woman. With having children and working together, you'll find love will grow. I've seen it happen many a time."

"Oh I know I shouldn't call her that, but compared to what's in my heart that's how she appears, a joyless thing with no appeal whatsoever."

"Give it time Erdi. You will grow to admire her."

"So you're asking me to sacrifice my happiness for the sake of the family?"

"It's not so much a sacrifice, as a duty. We've produced a fine son…"

"So you mean I'm a commodity. Like the slaves were!"

"No you shouldn't say that, Erdi. That's unkind."

"No worse than forcing me into something I'd hate. Forcing me to ignore this invisible arrow that has struck me out of nowhere like a gift from the spirits and accept instead the hand of a woman I'd never have chosen. And for what? For the vague possibility I'll feel admiration for her. You've swapped my chance of happiness for that thing and an **ox**!"

Later grandma Vana, managing to find Erdi alone, took both his hands in hers and looking up into his eyes whispered, "Follow your heart, Erdi."

Erdi looked at her amazed.

"Follow your heart." She put a finger to her lips, then smiling, hunched her shoulders and squeezed his hands, giving Erdi a brief glimpse of how she might have looked as a young girl.

Now I don't know whether it was the spirits intervening, who can say, but some time later an opportunity came Erdi's way. He had been strictly forbidden to go up over the east ridge in search of the girl and Penda had done all he could to keep his son's mind off the young lady by occupying his time with burdensome tasks. Erdi was now taking on the full workload of a man and wondered if this was to be his lot in life now, being tied to the smallholding and ending up as stuck in his ways as his father.

It was his uncle Dowid who offered the glimmer of hope. Being basically the one in charge of catching eels, it was only to be expected, he'd found out a few things about them. He hadn't however come close to solving the biggest mystery. He had seen immature eels wriggling through the dewy grass early on spring mornings. They headed for the two pools the family had rights over. But where had they come from? Nobody seemed to know the answer. He had known years of plenty and then years of want. As far as he could work out, they didn't seem to breed like other fish. In their holding pool he'd had every chance to witness their behaviour, but apart from eating ravenously, sometimes even each other and getting fat they didn't seem to do much else. He had never ever seen their offspring in the pool, meaning they didn't mate there and their eggs couldn't have arrived with the rain, or stuck to avian feet for if they had, there would have been evidence. He would have seen eel tiddlers. Perhaps they bred in faraway rivers, perhaps in the sea or maybe they grew from the mud like worms, but whatever the answer it didn't solve the immediate problem, it seems they'd run out of them. Traps laid in the Black and Offering Pools had been pulled up empty for a number of days now and turning to Penda for ideas, they decided the problem would be best laid at the chieftain's door. As he and his court were the main beneficiaries of their catch, it would be to their obvious benefit if they could provide a solution. The path to finding this solution could be eased, done subtly of course, if the notion happened to be slipped in, that they be given the fishing rights on the Habren river and other likely sources in the area. It would be just an emergency measure of course, but sometimes emergency measures can become permanent. Dowid chose his moment. When hearing that Prince Gadarm had undertaken a grand tour to display his might and effulgence, he was in like a hawk supplicating the chieftain's main advisor. A hint at the solution to the eel problem was dangled and Dowid awaited a reply. In due course the plea was put to the chieftain and after less than a day's wait, the concession was granted. They could fish the Habren river and amazingly, also the Five Pools. Just like that. If anyone took exception to it, they had the chieftain to answer to. Strange how some problems are like pulling teeth and yet at other times the answer can pop out just like a squeezed apple pip.

Anyway, Dowid, Erdi and Yanker were now free to take Blackie and a cart loaded with all the necessary on an expedition down to the great Habren river. Penda had been happy to release his son on these fishing duties not realizing that the Five Pools had also been included in the concession. Naughty uncle Dowid had kept that little detail to himself.

They left in high spirits, for it always brought a sense of liberation, each time the chance came to break free from their small contained world. They were armed, but didn't expect trouble and they had food, but expected to catch enough fish to feed them.

"Stay clear of Hanner Bara!" shouted Penda as they left.

"What's Hanner Bara?" asked Erdi.

"You'll see," said Dowid laughing.

It was slow going on account of the lumbering cart, but they were in no hurry. All that was required on the first day was to throw the baited traps into the river to lie for the night, so compared to their normal routine this was almost like a small break. They followed the main trail south as far as the prominent outcrop, home of the Ridge People. It would have been enjoyable to have stayed a night exchanging views and news, but they pressed on taking a smaller track that cut away to the southwest. By mid-afternoon they had reached the confluence between the Nwy and the main flow, the Habren. Both rivers had cut deep channels forming a formidable barrier between where they stood and the land to the south and west. A straw rope-bridge spanned the tributary and Erdi and

Yanker made the crossing, partly because they could, but also to talk to a shepherd on the far bank. The walkway itself was no more than a foot's breadth and the man said, when using it to shoulder his lambs across, he needed one hand to hold the animal in place around his neck and the other to tightly grip one of the hand-lines. They were told, rope stored for the purpose was used to renew the bridge each spring as most years it got washed away by the floods. He could normally swim the adult sheep across, but not when the river was up. "She's a killer," he said. "Flows as fast as a galloping horse. Whirlpools and waves looking to suck you under. Huge trees comes a-swirling down in the torrent. Some years when she's full and raging, she swells up 'oer the banks and turns pastures into lakes. Water as far as the eye can see. She's a killer," he warned with relish.

"Whose is that hut?" asked Erdi pointing across to the opposite bank.

"Oh that. It's just for the lambing. But look!" he clutched Erdi's sleeve anxious to pull his attention back to the river. He bent and picked up a stone. "See that bank yonder." He lobbed the stone across the Nwy. "She's just the little sister, but when she's up and a'ragin' sweeping the bridge downstream, there's no place to cross 'cept way up where the bears still roam." He pointed to the western hills. "T'would take a full two full days hard going to get all the way round to where that stone just landed."

They re-crossed, had a snack and followed the Habren east, scrambling down the banks to toss the traps in as they went. They had all been narrow-entry eel traps, but the final one dropped where they set up camp, had an opening large enough for most fish to feel invited.

The contents were what they started the next day with. The river had been kind. She had given up a bountiful catch. Each trap they hauled up had occupants that were kept alive in the huge hide bag on the cart. It was topped with a fine twine mesh to prevent any of the catch escaping on the slops of water when the cart rocked. By middle day, they were back to their campsite and more driftwood was hauled up the riverbank, added to the smouldering embers and the fire blown into life. Dowid had remembered to bring a generous twist of salt and the trout impaled on sticks to bake, were delicious.

During the course of the afternoon, traps were re-laid as they followed the Habren's generous loops further east. They worked on in a state of total oblivion, as if the task was nothing but recreation. Why hadn't they thought of doing this before? It almost seemed too good to be true. Behind them, quivering huge above the western hills, the sun's colour was beginning to deepen, its light gradually spreading into a rosy glow, long shadowing their movements on the sheep cropped grass of the riverbank. Catching the tang of woodsmoke drifting on the breeze, they paused. Up ahead amongst the shadows of a stand of trees was a small settlement. On approaching they caught the wafting aroma of food cooking intermingled with the sweet scent of the enkindled oak cooking it. The cluster of houses stood on a ridge above the Habren, their location determined by the fact that that particular section of river was regularly fordable. When not, a ferry was on hand to carry wayfarers and animals between the two landing stages. It was a clever system that rose and fell with the water and the ferrying raft was hand hauled across by a rope spanning the river.

"But not when she's a-ragin,'" said Yanker mimicking the shepherd. "She's a killer!"

They pitched camp near the straggle of houses, took care of Blackie's needs and heralded by dogs barking, wandered into the tiny settlement. They could sense unseen eyes watching their progress and hearing the heavy thumping of hysterical dogs against a pen gate, gave thanks to the fact it had been adequately secured. Dowid knocked on the sounding board of the largest dwelling and they ducked through to the interior. Eyes adjusted to the light and it quickly became evident this

196

was not a home. Not primarily anyway. It had boards to sit on with rails as back rests, all fronted by crude wooden tables. Two men they took to be fellow travelers nodded a greeting. Sight of a pale strip of cloth betrayed the movements of a third man busying himself by the central hearth. He moved into the slab of light thrown by the entryway, cloth draped over one shoulder as he briskly served food and with no more than a, "I'll be with you shortly," to the newcomers, carried on fulfilling the men's needs by taking them drinks. He finally turned to Dowid and asked how he could be of help? He had a matter-of-fact tone and looked the type to value quality and efficiency over wasteful pleasantries. It turned out he made his living by feeding wayfarers and with the help of a local lad, ferrying them over the river. Dowid enquired what was on offer and asked if it could be paid for with fish. The man stared at him with a look of tried patience, "Fish?" he made a slow finger jabbing motion towards the clusters of fish traps hanging from the rafters. Erdi had never seen his uncle colour-up before, but he did when the realization suddenly hit. The man lived above what was probably the most bountiful source of fish in the whole surrounding territory. Dowid apologized for his foolishness and explained they had not a scrap of bronze between them. The answer was wood. It was needed for cooking. They had axes and when it suited, could work for their supper. Obviously they could have fed themselves from their own catch, but having a meal given in return for payment was a completely new experience, one not to be passed up and Erdi couldn't wait to tell Mardi and Vanya about it. Then to add to the wonder a friendly, slightly chubby woman drifted in and even though there were other spaces available, urged the three to budge up a bit so she could sit beside them. Then in quite a matter-of-fact manner, she enquired, were they in need of someone to be nice to them? Erdi and Yanker looked at each other puzzled, but Dowid realized he'd at last come face to face with the notorious Hanner Bara and she was not what he'd imagined at all, looking more like a friendly aunt than a woman of pleasure. He politely declined her offer, to which she answered haughtily, "Huh! You've obviously not been on the trail long enough!" before rising with dignity to proposition the other two travelers.

When she later departed, with one on each arm, as if off to a celebration, Dowid explained she had got her name from the Skreela in whose language, Hanner Bara meant half bread. She would apparently do it quite willingly and not even trouble the client for a whole loaf in reward for her services, for she was quite happy to oblige for just half the amount.

It had been a fascinating trip all round and remarkably successful as regards their catch. Beginner's luck as it happens and it was just as well they had kept their reason for being there to themselves, but I'll explain about that later.

Now they had proved fishing the Habren was viable, Dowid suggested they give another location a try. Erdi and Yanker were told to keep the details to themselves, for he'd no wish to anger his brother-in-law, but soon they'd be heading back up to where granddad Tollan had laid his traps so many years before. News of a few untimely deaths had reached his ears. This left a possible opening, plus their recent blessing from the chieftain gave them a certain amount bargaining power. The next little adventure would be over the east ridge and into Five Pools country. Erdi's heart skipped a beat.

On the morning of departure, they left as if heading south to the Habren once more, but after a short distance swung east and mounted, what Erdi referred to as Elsa's ridge, taking the only path a horse and cart could manage, the one he and Yanker had fled down years before. Even this was tough going as in places the way through required widening and at numerous points all three were needed, backs heaving into the task, to shove the cart up and over steep, rough patches. Frequent rests were taken.

On one of these Erdi thought it wise to point out to his uncle that things had changed a fair deal since Tollan's first arrival in the area. More people had settled throughout the tribal lands, families had burgeoned and things weren't so free and easy as they had been back then. Erdi hadn't brought this up previously, for he'd not wanted his misgivings to cause the trip to be cancelled, but he did now feel the need to voice his doubts, thinking it highly unlikely that those living around Five Pools would simply allow them to roll up and help themselves to fish.

"We've been granted the right. Let them try and stop us!" said Dowid.

Erdi bowed to his uncle's seniority, but still had serious misgivings. He wasn't looking forward to an almost certain confrontation and began trying to concoct a solution in readiness.

They arrived and on a suitably lonely shore the cousins paddled out in the pair of circular crwgs they regularly used for pool work and dropped their eel traps into the lake. Meanwhile Dowid, humming to himself, cut staves and osiers to fashion them into hurdles of a particularly tight weave. Stout poles were driven into the lake bed, to bind the hurdles to and the resulting half circle formed their holding pool.

Later a fire was lit, they satisfied their hunger and had a surprisingly good night's sleep. The next morning the traps were retrieved with spectacular results.

"There I told you not to worry," said Dowid beaming, but then wondered why Erdi and Yanker weren't looking at him, but at something over his shoulder. Turning, he was alarmed to see a group of men marching towards them with an urgency that didn't bode well at all, plus there was such an air of anger bristling, you'd swear it was visible.

It started with, "What exactly d'you think you're doing?" and descended from there into a particularly ugly scene. Nobody in fact owned the lakes or their contents, but Erdi couldn't help but sympathize with their point of view. As he'd suspected it had been imprudent and disrespectful to just help themselves like they had. Not Dowid though. His blood was up and he was happy to slog it out verbally, as loud as his lungs could manage. He didn't care if they were outnumbered. He'd take the lot of them on. After all, "The chieftain had given his blessing."

Their answer to that was blunt, to say the least and the three were left in no doubt, that a blessing granted by an ageing leader living beyond the high ridge, didn't amount to very much where they happened to be standing. Erdi could imagine this going on for some time, with ultimate prospects not looking at all good, especially in view of the right of might being firmly in their opponents' favour.

As he'd planned, he quietly climbed up on the cart, raised his axe and struck the woodwork with the back of it. Blackie reared up from his tether under the trees and all the men stopped and stared up at him.

"Enough!" said Erdi sternly.

Dowid gaped in surprise, "But Erdi -----"

"That includes you Uncle." The mouth closed again

"We can stand here arguing all day and still get nowhere. If you will allow me, I have a plan to put to you that could benefit us all."

He got down from the cart and one of the men said, "He called you Erdi. Are you the Erdi who beat Gardarm?"

Yanker knowing his cousin was hardly likely to bathe in any hint of glory said, "The very same," adding a bow and sweep of an introductory arm as if presenting an exclusive offer of something rare and famous. It was like a magic charm. The mood changed completely.

Erdi explained the details of the trading concession, granted to grandfather Tollan many years before, which still gave them the right to supply the chieftain and his court with eel and any other fish taken from certain allocated locations. Unlike here, any royal concession granted on territory within immediate control of the fort still had total respect. They did, however, automatically forfeit a tenth of each consignment as payment for this concession. Erdi avoided disclosing their supplies had all but run out, but said that if they worked together the abundant resources from these pools could be traded for bronze to be shared between them. On seeing Dowid about to object he said, "Before you say anything, uncle, please imagine how you would feel if these men arrived and started laying traps in what we call **our** stream. Nobody actually owns the stream, but there again, how would you feel?" He turned to the group of locals and explained, "This leaves control of how much is taken entirely up to you. You can do the catching and we'll haul and trade the catch. Believe me the hauling of it will be no easy matter."

The men laughed in acknowledgement and went off into a huddle to talk the matter over. On returning their spokesman asked, "How do we know we'll be getting our fair share? How do we know how much you trade the fish for?"

"I'm glad you asked that. The procurer at the fort keeps a tally board and so do we. Each amount scribed on our board receives the procurer's mark. You are free to examine those tally boards any time you like."

With the deal seeming a good one all round, the men couldn't have been friendlier and the three were invited back to take food and drink as a way of sealing matters. They were ushered into the headman's house and those who not so long ago had had violence in mind, now treated them like long lost brothers. Ample sustenance was offered and out of respect for the ritual, they were expected to make a decent show of consuming it. It was at this point that Erdi's heart skipped a beat, he'd seen the girl from the Spring Fair walking past, out in the sunlight, leaving him in a dilemma, for he couldn't break from the throng for fear of causing insult. It was hard to stay focused on the conversation mind you and when finally able to make his excuses, he ducked out from the house, only to find she'd gone. There was no sign of her. A woman spotting his troubled look, asked him what had he lost? Erdi described the girl and with a knowing smile she explained that the young lady in question didn't live in the village, but in a lone hut with her father, near the track leading to Newt Pool.

She explained the directions. She told him the same thing, but in another way. He struggled to leave, but had to listen to a repeat of the first version. His arm was tugged as she warned not to take a path, forking off to the left at the fallen oak. He could still hear her calling as he ran along the track towards Newt Pool, "Just go straight! Don't take that other path!"

The girl turned, alarmed at the sound of running feet, but on recognizing Erdi, gave a hands-to-openmouthed look of amazement. He hurriedly explained all that had happened and why he was there, then stopped, "I'm sorry, I don't know your name."

She told him, "Gwendolin." A touch on his arm sent a thrill shooting up it as she added "No need to tell me yours. Certain tales seem to precede you.---- Oh no it's my father!"

The man approaching with menace said, "Inside please Gwen. Myself and this young man need to have a little chat." He took Erdi's arm in a firm grip and briskly led him away from the house.

"I suppose you must be feeling quite pleased with yourself."

Erdi looked puzzled, "I'm not certain what you mean?"

"Leading my daughter on the way you have. Now you've had your bit of fun, flattered your self-importance, I want you to leave her alone."

Erdi of course tried to impress upon the man that he had genuine feelings for his daughter but was stopped by the question, "And your family?"

"It's up to me, not them."

"Don't be a fool. I've no way of raising the dowry they'll expect, so all you'll be doing is breaking her heart. I don't know your father. Penda isn't it? But I know those who do and they tell me there is not a chance he'll condone this. He has high expectations, does your father. Now do us both a favour and leave us alone." With that he walked away, leaving Erdi to trudge the path back to the village.

It is said that love finds a way and yes up to a point it did. The two young lovers managed to meet on a number of occasions courtesy of further fishing trips. Erdi would sound the signal, an owl hoot blown through cupped hands and make his way to wait beneath the trees near Newt Pool. Gwendolin's father had become used to her pool vigils, as it was where she often disappeared to, lost in memory of her mother. Newt Pool was where her ashes had been cast. The spirits had welcomed her. They also welcomed the flower blooms often tossed to colour the dark water like tiny, slowly entwining flotillas. Gwendolin, when standing thoughtful in the shade, believed her mother's presence sighed with the breeze off the mere as it riffled dark leaves to light and wafted strands of her hair, weightless as prayers whispered soft in the hallowed glade. She now shared this special place with Erdi.

The Teller paused and with eyes brimming with amusement, Now you are probably wondering how they fared on further excursions to the Habren. Well bluntly, the rather spectacular success experienced on their first outing was not repeated. Word had somehow spread that three interlopers from north of the river had simply turned up and had had the cheek to help themselves to a massive catch. On their return a reception committee awaited. The audacity of it was the thing that most incensed. Had they been caught in the act, they were told they would have lost the lot, their catch, horse, cart and fish traps. Dowid's mention of the concession they'd been granted brought general laughter. What gave the ageing chieftain, the right to grant complete strangers, permission to help themselves to what had been theirs since time immemorial? Obviously the old man's powers were waning. They conceded that people had a right to fish for their supper, but an undertaking done on the scale they'd embarked on, well it was beyond belief! This was where Erdi's diplomacy once again came to the fore. The same deal was struck as that agreed at Five Pools and in fact quite a bond grew between the two parties. The river people went as far as admitting, they'd actually had sneaking respect for the audacity of the fish raid and lubricated by a drop of cider, all ended up laughing about it.

So time moves on. The swallows arrived swooping up into their homes to nest, but it wasn't much of a summer they heralded. It was one of flies, muggy weather and dull leaden skies. If the sun broke through at all, it was usually in the early evening, as if to mock the people with the fact another dull day was nearly over.

The Summer Fair with the usual fabrics, clothes, utensils, fortune teller and tattooist on offer, came and went, but Gwendolin and Erdi were closely watched and so could only manage smiles at a distance. Vanya's prince had also had his wings clipped, not even allowed to venture east with the rest of his tribe, but his message of explanation reached Gwedyll who passed it on, translated of course, to Vanya. The only one still fancy free seemed to be Donda. As she played queen bee, she appeared happily oblivious to how it was being looked upon. Mara was not the only one to view her activities darkly. Previously her actions, those of a silly young girl, had been forgiven but now flaunting her womanhood the way she was, 'What was she thinking of? What were her parents thinking of?' Respect for her entire family vanished.

Time was fast approaching where a meeting of the elders could be put off no longer. Soon Dowid would have to reveal to Penda the exact nature of the business conducted during the previous few months. It would then be obvious that the bronze they had accumulated was only half that to be expected from the amount of fish they had delivered for trading. Dowid didn't relish the almighty row that was sure to follow as Penda realized his son had had countless opportunities to keep his forbidden relationship alive. As much as Dowid hated the thought, the truth had to be faced. The hot ember had to be grasped, as they say. The meeting could be put off no longer.

Penda's roar nearly blew the roof off. Even when he'd calmed down somewhat, his feeling of hurt at the deception of it all, kept the anger burning. No credit was given to Dowid's initiative or the diplomatic skill Erdi had shown in gaining them such bounty. This was a serious rift. Penda seemed impervious to the logic, that a half share was better than no share at all. It was the deception that really rankled. He was blind to the fact that obtaining this new source of fish had probably kept their concession alive. No, he was deeply hurt. His own people, his own son in fact had deceived him. He, the head of the family, had been kept in the dark about the whole enterprise. Like a wounded bear retiring to its cave, he became unapproachable. The atmosphere and tension in their hamlet became almost palpable.

One evening Erdi whispered to Vanya that things might improve if he disappeared for a while. Next morning the family awoke to find him gone.

Chapter Sixteen

Erdi arrived at Trader's about mid-morning to be asked, "So? What's happened?"

Erdi told him and listening patiently he finally asked just the one question, "Do they know where you are now?"

Erdi said that Vanya would have told them. He felt drained and in a state of dilemma. On the one hand his father had made his continued presence unbearable, virtually impossible, but on the other it felt like he'd committed the worst form of betrayal. He also felt vulnerable, now having struck out alone into unknown territory.

"I suppose you're feeling a bit strange, young Erdi. You'd better come inside. Gwedyll will find you something to eat. Cheer you up a bit! You look like a hot nosed hunting dog." The friendly punch he gave his shoulder, hardly made contact.

"Gwed!" he called. "I've found us a young wanderer. She'll put you right, Erdi. Don't take things so much to heart. It can be a healthy part of growing up, a young man clashing with his father. Almost to be expected with two strong characters under the same roof. Here she is."

Under Gwedyll's care, Erdi instantly brightened. He also felt quite at ease with her and they conversed with a freedom that lifted his spirits. Now his heart had been so completely captured elsewhere, the silliness he'd admonished himself for when previously in her company, had gone. Also, once in tune with the way she spoke, the accent that had once seemed so strong, was now hardly noticeable.

Trader thought it best to mount up and visit Penda. Have a good talk. It wasn't a job he relished, so was best done immediately and got out of the way. No good letting bad feelings fester. "There's something I'll show you when I get back, Erdi. It could be the start of a new venture."

When Trader returned that afternoon, he answered Erdi's questions with just one sentence, "We've cleared the air a bit." Then he led him on a quick tour. Not only were there full storerooms, those held up off the damp on their pole supports, as seen previously, but beyond the palisade two open barns had been erected and enclosures constructed for farm stock. In one, pigs grubbing and rooting had turned the whole area to mud and slime, in another sheep grazed the broad pastures, in small pen with its kennel a bitch patiently endured the playful antics of her litter and bold alone in its corral stood a formidable looking stallion. It snorted as they approached and started a white eyed, agitated tour of its enclosure as if expecting an escape route to open on the next circuit.

"What d'you think of him? Isn't he a wonder?"

It was one of the larger southern horses, a breed favoured by the warriors. They were huge compared to the local wild ponies and were built for speed rather than farm work, as was Blackie. This particular beast also looked unbroken and ferocious.

"What do you intend doing with him?"

With a slightly unsettling ring of confidence, Trader said airily, "Oh just train him a bit and move him on. You couldn't have come at a better time. We'll give it a crack in the morning."

"You're not asking me to get in there with **that** are you?"

"No. Don't fret Erdi. You just rope him off the rails as he goes past and I'll haul him in."

Erdi looked at his friend and trying not to sound too perturbed asked. "How much of this sort of thing have you done before, Trader?"

"Well none really, but it can't be that difficult."

207

Erdi tried to remember the last time he'd heard that phrase and a little alarm rang in his head.

A farm worker approached and at a respectful distance, stood waiting. Trader excused himself and joined the man in conversation.

On returning he said, "Oh that was just Delt. It's easier if I tell him what's wanted and he tells the others. I don't bother myself with all this sowing and growing stuff. It's best left to them. What's the point of having a dog, then go yapping and barking yourself? I could actually do with someone similar to handle the animal side of things. The dealing side, I mean. Delt's alright seeing to work here, upkeep, welfare and the like, but he's not the sort you'd send out trading for sheep and horses. I must admit it's all a bit new to me. Never got into livestock before, not on this scale anyway, but we can see how it goes. You know me, have a go at anything within reason. Nothing ventured nothing gained."

Erdi took another glance at the pacing horse and had serious misgivings.

Back in the house he remarked that the cauldron no longer hung over the fire. "Did the Skreela have it back?"

Trader flashed him an alarmed look and a hand-fanning motion indicated, 'not so loud!' "Don't say that word here. It upsets her."

With a wide grimace of embarrassment, Erdi sucked air through his teeth as if possible, to inhale the very word Skreela back in. "Sorry. I wasn't thinking."

Trader leaning closer, said quietly. "It's alright she didn't hear. Thought it wise to give the cauldron a bit of a rest. Too many affronted princes about. Not just her lot, but ours as well. In fact our lot are worse. That Gardarm! Well you know what he's like."

The day was crowned by a splendid meal and entertaining conversation that fortunately took Erdi's mind off the worry of what he had done. Also the beer helped. It temporarily dulled his emotions and eventually helped bring the gift of sleep. It wasn't just the fear of the unknown that had clamoured with such discord in his brain it was the terrible guilt knowing he had upset his whole family.

He awoke to a day set fair for an encounter with their hoofed friend. It was almost as if an equine instinct had told it there was likely to be a little something in the offing that morning. Something it might not be partial to. With coat gleaming with sweat, it repeatedly threatened one end of its enclosure, to half rear into a turn, before pounding the short distance to the threaten the other.

"Are you sure this is wise?" Erdi asked.

"It's only a horse," Trader replied.

"Only! How does a thing get that big just by eating grass?"

Trader slowly approaching the enclosure in a crouched posture, made noises he imagined wild, unbroken horses liked to hear. He had the rope firmly tied around his waist and slipping the noosed end to Erdi hissed, "Like I said," in a voice was little more than a whisper, "when he comes round you rope him and I'll climb over and haul him in. We'll both calm him. By this afternoon he'll be as gentle as a lamb. I promised Gwedyll she'd be riding him before supper."

"Gwedyll? Has she seen the brute?" Erdi hissed.

"Yes of course."

"And what did she say?"

"Nothing exactly. Just one of those looks. But what do **they** know about horses?"

'Nothing,' thought Erdi, 'other than her people seem born to ride them.'

The one in question had now started doing circuits eying them guardedly. Erdi, more by luck than judgment managed to collar it first go and surprisingly there was no visible reaction. Neither did it react too badly when Trader scrambled over the fence to command the centre of the enclosure. It was only when he'd pulled in the slack and the noose gripped that the beast suddenly understood. Then there was cause for alarm. It screamed, reared, thundered around the fencing, but unable to distance itself from the man spinning in the middle, took off, sailing with the grace of a bird, to thud down beyond the fence rails. The rope was ripped from Trader's grasp and watching the slack play out, there came the horror of the inevitable, for with a crack it yanked him hatless into involuntary pursuit. With a look of panic, legs scrambling to catch his midriff, his effort to emulate the horse made the first rung, but not one splinter higher. Sheer force smashed him through the railings and he was dragged bumping headlong as if bodily trying to plough a furrow. Erdi watching from atop the rails, was witness to the silhouette of the madly galloping horse diminishing and the line of Trader's progress being hinted at, by the snaking disturbance through the long meadow grass.

He followed the sound of groaning and found Trader bruised, bloodied and badly shaken, still prone amongst what he'd flattened.

"Are you alright, Trader?"

The Teller said he was not conversant with swear words from so far back in time and so asked his audience to fill in with their own to embellish Trader's groaned reply of, "What the ----'s it look like?"

He helped him to his feet. Nothing was broken and fortunately the rope had snapped otherwise he'd probably have pioneered a new crossing over the Habren where the animal was finally located. The horse was moved on in a deal and Erdi thought it diplomatic not to ask the details. His stay with Trader was obviously not going to be without interest.

His next task was to master the skill of sitting astride one of the nimble mountain ponies and all the business of caring for its needs. Plodding along on Blackie was not Trader's idea of horsemanship. Having Gwedyll accompany him whilst achieving this helped blow any doubts about leaving home clear out of his head and once gaining the required proficiency he was sent out as a messenger, deliverer and at times envoy, paving the way for future deals. He couldn't imagine returning to a life that often required standing around from dawn to dusk guarding grazing livestock. Every day now seemed different, with him never quite knowing what to expect.

One morning he returned from his rounds with two generous mounds of dead hare bouncing like a macabre collar either side of his pony's neck.

"Where in the land of darkness did you get that lot from, Erdi?"

"Gam was hauling them up to the market."

"Oh, I know. Oddie's brother."

"No not that Gam, Gam, from down by the slow stream."

"Oh, that Gam. I know who you mean. Gam the Gimp, lives with Big Helda."

"That's the one. I'm sorry, I should have asked you first, but there wasn't time. Hope I've done right."

"Why what have you pledged?"

"One peg of peas."

"Done alright? You've robbed the man."

"Oh and there are these. I said we'd throw the basket in the deal for them." He untied a brace of woodcock.

"Now that's something I've not had in a while. Hang them for a day or so, then we'll have 'em roasted with a bit of fat bacon. You've got what we call a lucky face, Erdi. Couldn't have bettered the deal myself. Think I'll send you out roaming again."

Gam with the crooked leg got, his large basket of dried peas, with a twist of salt added for luck.

On another occasion Erdi was woken before daylight and instructed to fetch the ponies. They set out north in the grey light and it was not until passing under the dark outline of the fort, that they heard the first awakening of the dawn chorus. The morning was cool and misty and both had fleeces tied tight. Dangling from a strap on Penda's horse was a caged pigeon. Within hailing distance of Nant Crag, the border stream, they waited in the trees.

211

Muffled voices could be heard urging their mounts forward and hooves clunked, displacing rocks in water and skidded, scrambling footholds up the bank. Five men appeared astride the smallest horses Erdi had ever seen, the riders looking comical, bouncing towards them with feet raised in order not to scrape the ground.

Erdi couldn't help but laugh and the lead man who spoke their tongue said, "I know they look on the small side, but I'll tell you what, you wouldn't like to try and stop one if it had an awkward mood on." They all rode to a clearing, judged a safe distance from the border and the deal was conducted quietly and without fuss. Bronze axe-heads were the payment. The caged pigeon was handed over and an empty cage taken in return. Their payload was shared out for ease of carrying, the axeheads being slotted into loops on their belts. Long undershirts hid all evidence and coats were drawn tightly round to complete the concealment and of course, keep out the cold. The sun was still no more than low angled beams, lighting misty glades. Erdi watching the men, turning to wave before slipping from view, waved in return and asked Trader where they would now be heading. He said, they would be taking the same trail back across the stream, before cutting across to the Feasting Site, where just beyond, a boat could be found to take them north up the Dwy.

Tax had been avoided on their way south, on account of duty only being liable on what was transported, rather than on mode of transport. They had managed to joke their way past Gwal, a defended toll point on an outcrop above the Dwy, the tally man there having found the mere sight of them hilarious. On the final toll, however, they hadn't wanted to push their luck and so had avoided the obvious crossing completely. Apparently, certain tally men there had the habit of asking potentially awkward questions such as, "Where exactly are you going and why are you going there?"

"It's not as if we could go unnoticed," their leader had said with a laugh.

To avoid all human contact, Trader took a circuitous route along western higher ground and they finally descended into the broad flatlands of home about the time swallows skim low for flies. They had not rushed, as their string of horses had already been through quite an ordeal.

"One thing puzzles me," said Erdi. "How did you know when they'd be arriving?"

"A little bird told me."

"Oh they let the pigeon loose when a day away."

Trader nodded.

"But how did you know where to meet them?"

"We usually meet there. If it's to be the toll crossing, twine tied to the bird's leg tells me. First time it's been horses mind you. What d'you think of them?"

"First, I thought they were a joke, but having handled them they're sturdier than they look. What will you do with them?"

"Hide them of course. They can't stay here. Can you imagine the reaction if they're spotted? We'd get no peace. Then all you need is the wrong caller. A smiling face hiding jealous eyes."

"Then the tallyman comes calling. What would it be, a heavy fine?"

"Confiscation more like. It's obvious they're not from around these parts. They couldn't have flown here. There's obviously no record of the entry dues having been paid, so for smuggling....yes I think they'd probably confiscate them. But fret not. I've just the man. He'll spirit them away until required and can be counted on to keep his mouth shut." He added with a wink, "You could say the same for his little friend. Well not mouth shut exactly, you can never say that about a woman, but you'll see what I mean."

They were away again before sunrise, leading the five half sized horses up into the western hills. Game abounded as is often the case when not hunting it. From the position of the sun, at last showing itself behind, Erdi judged them to have changed course slightly, to now be heading south west. Their

213

ascent followed the tumbling windings of a small stream and they picked their way beside it, taking a more direct route than one evident from faint traces of cart tracks. Up ahead the way was blocked by a forbidding looking palisade, denying further access to the narrow valley.

Trader dismounted and pulled on a chord hanging beside the gate, the distant ringing sound starting ferocious dog barking. They waited. "You might get to meet his little friend, Mad Aggie," said Trader. They waited and with still no sign of the occupier, Erdi thought, perhaps the man had gone out for the day. Then on reflection and trusting his instincts, he waited patiently, for the place didn't evoke that unmistakable gaunt, devoid of humanity feel. His instincts proved right. From behind a raised portion of the palisade, a single eye peered at them. The owner of the eye slowly emerged, his hair a wild tangle and other eye covered by a patch.

"Oh it's you Trader. Wait there I'll lock the hounds up. Whatever are those you've got? What ever d'you call those things?"

"Those **things** Patch, are horses!"

Finally the gate creaked open and to the continued merriment of the one eyed man, they led the ponies in. Tethered in the shade of a clump of hawthorn, they stood patiently, ears twitching and tails flicking to ward off the surprising number of flies within the compound. While Trader explained his business Erdi had a look round. All within gave off an air of neglect and chaos. The decision of where to site the midden seemed to have been dependent on the location needing to be within convenient flinging distance of the house door. As a pig sty is best sited near a midden, logic must have followed that pigs and all that went with them would be best kept adjacent the residence. Birds hopped amongst the steaming mess gorging on the flies. Its spread had caused the stream to alter course slightly as if disgusted at the prospect of contamination. A sapling grew through the roof of one of the storage huts. A small cart sporting an admirable growth of grass lay at a drunken angle, sadly wasting away and in places the thatch of the house roof was sagging, black and glistening. The only thing that seemed in good order was the palisade.

With the business of secreting the ponies sorted, all three perched on a convenient lip of banking. Trader declined the invite to enter the house and the offer of water was turned down in unison.

From over by the trees came a shriek. A young woman of no great height but ample build, stood pointing at the five small ponies. Evidence slowly grew, until finally there was no doubt, as to which of the five was the stallion.

"Oh come away from there Aggie," called Patch. Turning to Erdi he explained, "She's harmless enough. It's just something she gives off. Has the same effect on the dogs."

She came running towards them with every part, whether body or clothing, in motion. She stopped and grinned at Erdi as if she'd just spotted something delicious to eat. The combination of gabbled noises and frantic wild-eyed pointing was slightly unnerving. Patch explained she used words only he understood and was telling them about her excitement at seeing the ponies. Erdi almost felt sorry for her until, with a wicked grin, she hooked out a giant lump of snot and after a moment's hesitation, wiped it on his shirt.

Trader and Patch rocked with laughter and the latter said, "Look out! You've done it now. That means she likes you."

Months later when relating the tale to his cousin, Yanker had said, "Snot? She liked you? You wouldn't want her falling in love with you!"

But meanwhile Trader had caught Erdi's anxious glance and flick of head meaning, 'Let's get out of here,' and told Patch they'd best be leaving. Aggie caught the drift of this and wide eyed in panic, pulled up her blouse and desperately holding on to Erdi, started to frantically suck on a nipple.

"No Aggie, don't!" shouted Patch, but too late. Erdi was on the receiving end of a two handed, generous squirt of milk, full in the face. He looked stunned, she looked triumphant,

Trader moved out of range in case he was next to be anointed and Patch yelling, "Bad Aggie!" smacked the top of her head and then pointing, angrily barked "Inside!!"

She hesitated, saw he meant it and with drooping bottom lip turned and walked forlornly towards the house. She gave Erdi one last backward sad-eyed look.

"Is she pregnant?" asked Erdi wiping his face.

"Pregnant? No, just one of her tricks. She's always at them. Full of the stuff. Look upon it as a sort of love token."

"Poor Aggie," said Erdi as they left the compound.

"Never seen her quite like that before," said Trader shaking his head.

Of course, Gwedyll almost cried with laughter when later told about it. "Nose pickings? Breast milk? Love tokens?" Managing to draw enough breath, she gasped, as if all one word, "You certainly know how to charm them, Erdi," before having to prop herself against him, helpless with laughter.

He bore this with a resigned grin and said in a deadpan voice, "I actually felt a bit sorry for her. But there again you can't blame me for wanting fast out of there can you? There's only so much in the way of love tokens one man can take."

"Stop!" she pleaded holding her sides.

"Before we left Patch asked if we fancied trying one of Aggie's specials? A rather rare type of cheese?"

"No!" Gwedyll shrieked. "Stop it, Erdi! I'm nearly wetting myself!"

So without being anything other than himself he seemed to have enriched their lives. Even Gwedyll's son Tywy had given up viewing him as a competitor for his mother's attention and in fact admiration had grown as Erdi's innate ability became evident during regular honing of Tywy's slingshot skills.

A big attraction and reason for satisfaction in this new life came from the way each day could lead to the unknown. It offered new ways of looking at things and the chance of liberation from their small valley world. There were new subjects open to him, such as the heritage of Gwedyll's people and she rewarded his interest with tales of their history, their legends and even how to speak cymry, their language. He never uttered the word Skreela again as long as he lived and although of course he couldn't have told you things like various plant names in this new tongue, he was eventually able to make himself fairly easily understood.

Adding to his new sense of freedom was of course the fact it wasn't that difficult, if his rounds happened to take him over Elsa's ridge, to grab precious moments meeting Gwendolin by Newt Pool. They yearned to be together permanently, but meanwhile their brief encounters were treasured, keeping love alive.

One morning, even before first bird song, Trader's household was woken by a terrible racket of dogs barking. Trader with a cloak tightly containing his annoyance stomped in boots, laces trailing, out to the palisade to investigate.

On returning he said, "It's the Bleddi."

He didn't rush to open the gates, but when they eventually yawned in the dim morning shadows, Erdi looking on, thought similar freedom of entry would not have been granted where he came from.

Other than their woad ringed eyes taking in all around them, the three Bleddi warriors used no motion other than that needed to seem as one with their ponies. Each led a pack horse laden with pelts and strapped to these were bronze tipped spears, bows, arrow quiver, cloaks, bedding and cooking paraphernalia. They wore leggings, fleece lined leather jerkins and hanging behind, head-borne, crowning all with a menace that easily matched that of their battle-worn swords, were wolf-head capes. Their arms were patterned with tattooed tribal marks, plus those of witchery to exude power and fend off evil. Each one was a trained fighter, valuing valour over life.

Before even the slightest mention of business, they were given food and drink. Then talk was of their journey and the hospitality offered when passing through the tribal lands of Gwedyll's people. They told Trader, they'd had no difficulty avoiding detection, east of the fortress, when entering the territory and laughed as if the mere fact of being challenged would have been an insult to their dignity.

'Pity the tallyman who tries,' thought Erdi.

Amongst themselves they conversed in an indecipherable cymry dialect that not even the Y-Dewis themselves understood, but for general communication they spoke, though heavily accented, the universal cymry. Erdi could hardly understand what they were saying, but gradually, as his ear tuned in, he began to get a rough idea. He made the same mistake as most, thinking conversations in foreign tongues were almost certainly on subjects of vast importance, when in fact they are often no loftier than discussions on the weather or details of the last meal eaten.

Being of warrior class, talk naturally moved on to the comparable merits of their steeds and then on to anecdotes describing trials and tribulations involved in accommodating various equine moods and personalities. Erdi had been introduced to the men and so felt free to listen and was helped by the odd word of translation from Gwedyll. He heard Trader ask them how copper extraction was progressing in the great mines up on their north coast. He thought he'd misheard the answer, but Gwedyll whispered the miners had indeed tunneled those vast depths Erdi had thought to be dubious.

Trader asked how the ore was extracted from so deep underground and was told the men struggled out with laden baskets. When asked why they didn't use horses he was told in no uncertain terms, that such a notion was ridiculous owing to strictures of the tunnels themselves. Then Erdi felt sure Trader told the men, not the truth that he owned five tiny horses perfect for the job, but simply knew of their whereabouts. When he described their size, the men obviously thought he was joking.

He did eventually convince them, however, but then dismissed the notion on account of the inflated value the owner had put on the animals. The story was spun further, with the telling of another party interested. He assured them this hadn't bothered him, however, as he'd never been one to rush into a deal headlong. He hadn't got where he was by being pressured into making rash decisions, even if these ponies did happen to be incredibly rare. The Bleddi leader was now as keen as a tiny mouse smelling cheese in a trap and asked how much? Trader revealed the sum shaking his head at the sheer stupidity of it, but was reprimanded and told not to be so faint hearted, grasp the ember, get the deal done! He then pointed out he'd be needing a small amount of reward for his trouble and was impatiently urged to get on with it. That was the nub of it anyway.

When the conversation then centred on the rumblings coming from the Y-Dewis, Gwedyll's people, Erdi sensed her tighten up slightly and from that point on, she offered no further insight into the conversation. The tension mounted until there seemed sudden cause to go outside with Tywy, her son. Talk of the revered cauldron seemed to have been the cause. When told it was only to be expected that the tribal leaders would want its return, Trader looked angered and stubbornly averred his intention to retain possession. An insult had poisoned relations somewhere along the line. Was it that Trader couldn't forgive that particular insult? Was there mention of gross ingratitude? Then Erdi became completely puzzled. Was trader being reminded, he was merely guardian of not only the tribal emblem, but in fact of Gwedyll herself? This last revelation shocked Erdi like a face slap from an ox-blade shovel. Trader looking decidedly uncomfortable, attempted to change the subject. If true it would confirm Erdi's suspicions of things not quite adding up all that time ago on the first trip there with his father. It was something his senses had picked up rather than anything specifically said or done and whenever having these feelings, Erdi had learnt to heed them. Equally important, was to listen to that little ringing sound in the head, heralding a warning, such as when seeing the look on the face of the eel stealer's father, or the edginess felt when anywhere near Crown Prince Smarm.

When the Bleddi leader eventually smiled and apologized, saying the cauldron was of course, really none of his business, the mood brightened somewhat. On seeing Trader still eying him warily, he smiled again and added, he'd merely thought passing on information regarding his neighbours could be of some use to such a respected friend. Erdi could see from Trader's studied gaze, he had also spotted the warrior's smile hadn't quite masked the cunning glint in those woad ringed eyes beneath the wolf-head cape. When at last, all stood to wander outside, Erdi was relieved that Trader, with composure restored, looked fully back in control. In a brusque commanding manner, he gave instructions, telling the warriors where to offload their merchandise and where to stack weapons and possessions in the dry, out of the way. The deal was underway at last and it turned out, not to be an easy one. Pelts were put into various piles on the wooden boarding. It was a facility adjoining the palisade wall, built to ease inspection of goods, keep them up off the damp and out of the weather by virtue of a thatched awning. Once all was laid on display the haggling started. After a not very promising start, hides were put back on the ponies in disgust, only for further negotiation to have them taken off again to be added to a completely different bundle. Trader stood calm amid the well-orchestrated routine, that ran the full range from guile and persuasion through to animated vehemence and fury. Three on to one, but from where Erdi stood, his friend still looked to be slightly ahead. The mere effort of trying to keep track made the head spin. Erdi shuddered to think how he would cope if ever called upon to deal with such people. How they all knew what had been agreed and what hadn't seemed a mystery. Finally, the Bleddi leader, supposedly driven to the limits of frustration, angrily thumped the boarding as if on the verge of calling the whole deal off. A companion, the self-appointed intermediary and apparent saviour of the transaction, cajoled Trader saying that if his offer were to be upped just a little ---- a gap between forefinger and thumb indicated the amount ---- he was certain his partner would see sense and take it. He was now supposedly Trader's ally and berated his companion for making such inflated demands, shouting, "You're asking too much! Let the poor man earn a living!" Then to Trader, the beneficiary of his, oh so reasonable intervention he urged, "Just offer two bolts more for each stack, he'll take them." His wheedling was endorsed vociferously word for word by the third Bleddi warrior. Trader, having heard it all before, didn't budge. Finally they capitulated and the leader slapping Trader's hand to seal the deal said, "You're a hard man, Trader. Why are you always so hard on us?"

"I'm doing you a favour really," he reasoned. Erdi couldn't help but smile to himself.

"Favour? How d'you work that out?"

Erdi strained an ear to understand the answer.

"Well you could have taken your skins to ------" he mentioned two other known traders.

"Well I know we could, but they can only come up with the bronze once they've traded the pelts on."

"There you are," said Trader. "If I was as loose in my dealings as they are, I'd be in the same mess. By being hard but fair I'm certain to keep the deals moving and have payment ready each time you call. So as I said, I'm doing you a favour."

The man grumbled the reply of, "Never looked at it like that before," and eying Trader suspiciously added, "You'd better not be joking about those ponies."

An arm enfolded to accompany the words, "I've got more sense than that my friend, but remember, gold. Not pelts. Not bronze. Gold."

The man's hand had gone instinctively to his sword hilt which was only released when Trader, oblivious to the momentary freeze of the other two Bleddi warriors, had removed his embrace. Erdi at last dared breathe.

When they had gone and all the tension with them, he asked whether it troubled him to deal with such people?

"To start with it did, but it's something you get used to. Something you get hardened to. Let's be honest, there's nothing to stop them just riding in and taking everything, but fortunately they take the longer view."

"What about the deal itself? From the little I know, it seems you did well."

"Yes. It feels lucky, Erdi. When a deal feels lucky it usually comes good. Makes up for those that turn out a bit disappointing."

Erdi smiled and then remembering tales of tight constrictions and rock falls in the Ogof copper mine to the south of them said, "You don't really believe horses could be put to work in a copper mine?"

Trader simply put a finger to his lips, "Shh."

Erdi once again realized, he was a long way from being able to tackle such a transaction himself. "Why didn't you do a deal on those ponies right here and now?" This really did seem puzzling.

"It's no good expecting the seller to suddenly switch to being the bold buyer. It's like asking one person to instantly become two. It never works. Best to tease the interest a bit first. People always want what they can't have. Make it too easy and they can go cold on the whole idea. As it stands now, they already look upon them as their horses. All I'm doing is supplying them."

Erdi was lost for words.

That is not to say everything Trader did, turned into a spectacular success. To arrive at the destination of being a respected trader involved taking chances, being willing to experiment, using gains to fund the broadening of knowledge, the exploration of speculative trails that could result in some ventures turning out, as he freely admitted, 'a bit disappointing.' The trick was, not to make the same mistake twice.

His tangle with the stallion had been an obvious example and on returning to the compound one day, Erdi spotted the potential for another. Standing prominent and strangely immobile were three mature stags. Their lack of movement was on account of them being stuffed deer hides held upright by cleverly concealed wooden supports.

Trader was full of confidence regarding these acquisitions and couldn't wait to try out what he described as, his 'new wonder lures,' the leap of ingenuity that was likely to transform the way deer were hunted for ever more. One would be taken into the forest and positioned to entice a live stag. A mature male, seeing it as a challenger, would feel compelled to drive it off. When close, Trader and Erdi, lying in wait, would dispatch the unwary quarry with bronze tipped arrows. They had these to hand. Erdi had instructed Tywy on how to straighten the shafts, attach flights and finally bind metal tips to shaft-ends using pine resin. Between the two of them they'd built up quite a supply.

"What could be simpler?" asked Trader.

'Those same fatal words again,' thought Erdi.

The next day, as often happens, didn't go quite as well as expected, meaning the two didn't set out on their quest until the sun was dipping towards the western hills. A stuffed deer was loaded, strapped on the cart and Trader chose a spot beside a game trail, clearing branches and vegetation to place the lure to look as natural as possible.

"Seems to me it would be better put out in the open. Somewhere more obvious, perhaps next to where the does are known to feed," Erdi dared suggest.

"No this will be fine, you'll see." His ebullience left no room for doubt.

They returned early evening and just as Erdi had suspected, were perched like fools in a nearby tree until the uselessness of the enterprise became obvious even to Trader.

The next attempt was Erdi's suggestion. Trader had already tired of his new wonder lures and had had to be coaxed into, yet again, loading a stuffed stag, but this time it would be placed ready for an early morning luring in a nearby clearing. They returned as dawn was breaking, lying in wait upwind from the stuffed stag and Erdi peering across the open ground, spotted something moving in the wreaths of mist. A young stag approached. It had spotted the lure, but looked caught in that dilemma between curiosity and caution. Then, with ears flattened and neck hairs bristling, it made a stiff legged advance on the supposed intruder. The hunters watched, notched their arrows, the only sound now being their heartbeats. Almost within range the stag stopped, nose twitching. It turned suddenly and was off, white tailed, bounding across the open ground.

"Whatever made it do that?" asked Trader. "Spirits warning it?"

"No I think we did. Our scent is all over that stuffed stag. It warned off the real stag. Next time we need to cover our hands when positioning the thing."

"Next time? I've had enough of stuffed stags already! I've better things to do with my time."

Later Erdi, trying to keep a straight face called out, "Trader, what shall I do with these stuffed stags? They'll be ruined if left too long out in the open."

There came a wry laugh, "Huh! Stuff the things under cover somewhere, I'm sick of the sight of them."

Erdi smiled as he packed them away. How quickly the allure had worn off the new wonder lures. Task done he walked over and asked Trader, "But how will you get rid of them?"

"It's an old traders' saying but true, Erdi: 'everything goes in the end.'"

So there they stood stuffed and forgotten, apart from when trying to squeeze past the vicious antlers, in an attempt to access something beyond.

It was about this time it became evident why their chieftain and lord of the valley had so avidly thrown himself into the slaving business. It had started as a rumour, but then became accepted as the truth, he'd been persuaded to enter the venture by his son, Crown Prince Gardarm. The young slave girl had been put to work on menial tasks such as basting and turning meat, fetching and carrying and of course helping keep the Great Hall clean. The little bonus that had been hinted at by the slaver had died at birth.

There had been an attempt to enroll the wild man into the fighting force, but even though armed with no more than a stave had quickly put an end to that notion, almost braining his three restrainers and vaulting the perimeter fence. He was ridden down, brought back and put to work on heavy duties. Never unchained, let it be added.

The other three had been put to use on the land of an avid recipient and were worked all the daylight hours, clearing and draining wetland for future agriculture. Their welfare was the responsibility of their new owner as was recompense to the chieftain should they escape. There was a little catch in the deal. Half of all the first three years' produce from the new land, alive or dead was to be gifted up to the fort in gratitude for having use of the slaves. From then on, the annual tithe was set partly as an average of those first three years production and partly according to an estimate of what such an area of land could be expected to produce. It was a fifteen-year contract. If any year, the yield didn't meet expectations the contribution was to be topped up by produce from the owner's share off the new land or failing that, from the rest of his farm. Any further land added to the smallholding after the first three years was subject to the same terms.

The eel stealers were the lucky trialists for this new scheme and the father of the two boys had taken on a sickening air of grandeur as the families' fortunes looked set to burgeon.

"How can it fail?" he'd been heard to say to wiser heads than his.

General distaste for the man, however, didn't deter Trader from flattering his ego a little and suggesting livestock could produce good returns on the new land especially during the first years while still draining.

This was partly why Trader had involved himself in the sheep business. In the short time he'd been there, Erdi had come to realise his friend's natural talents didn't necessarily lie in that direction. Trying to be helpful, he dared advise caution. Like everything, there was probably more to the judging of sheep than met the eye.

"Nonsense, I know just the man!"

When the first flock was driven over from the south-east, just beyond where the Habren starts its flow due south, Erdi couldn't put his finger on exactly why the little warning rang in his head, but sensed something didn't seem quite right. It was Trader's main man Delt, who pointed out there could be a difficulty. His eying of the flock had brought on quite a worrying puzzled look. He wasn't one to be rushed into judgement, however.

"Would it be in order to ask what you think you have here, master?"

Trader never failed to be slightly irritated by the way he dragged out the **a** when saying 'master,' almost like a sheep bleat. With a look of impatience he said, "Sheep of course! What sort of fool question is that, Delt?"

"But forgive me master, what would you be wanting with the sheep?"

"To trade of course. What d'you think?" An uneasy look did begin to creep in at this point.

"Forgive me for being so bold, master, to trade on as what?"

"This is getting ridiculous, Delt! To trade on as breeding stock." He shot Erdi a look of exasperation expecting the feeling to be mutual.

"Ah!" said Delt.

"What d'you mean, AH?" He waited. "Well come on, out with it man!"

"Then there could be a problem, master." He moved amongst the flock and grabbing one of the largest animals by the scruff said, "This one here for example won't be doing any breeding on account of having its breeding tackle cut off. It's a wether, master."

"How can it be? A wether that size doesn't look like that. They have a lumpy look."

"Lumpy look, master?"

"Yes, the lumpy skull of a ram."

"Not if it's bashed with a rock, master. It's an old trick and one you shouldn't be blaming yourself for falling for. All this one's good for master is the knife. Oh look! Here's another. He's had the exact, same treatment, bashed to make him look like a breeding ewe." As he warmed to his task, the more Trader looked crestfallen. Five were found in all.

"But wouldn't bashing them like that kill them?"

"Evidently not, master. The blow isn't always fatal if done at an early age. How much did he make you part with for these, master?"

The question, especially put like that, had a sickening sound to it.

Delt winced at the answer and shaking his head sadly continued, "Like I said, master, an easy mistake to make."

With Trader having gone exceedingly quiet, Erdi thought it best to leave him to his thoughts and help Delt corral the flock.

Delt's voice had a way of carrying, "See Erdi, what look like the pick of the bunch are in fact the worst."

Trader couldn't have helped but overhear and Erdi watched him heading towards the house with the look of a man under a heavy burden. It wasn't so much the actual loss that would have irked, it was the fact a man he'd trusted had tricked him, made a fool of him. His son emerging to greet with a smile, worked like a magic charm, seeming to immediately lift the oppressive cloud and with a paternal arm around the boy's shoulder, they both disappeared inside.

It was quite a few days later, that Erdi was called over to where Delt had corralled the sheep for inspection. Trader was leaning on the rails examining the flock, fresh arrivals mixed with the old.

"Can you pick them out, Erdi?"

He searched for a while until satisfied he'd located all five members of Trader's little embarrassment and said, "Well yes I can, now I know what to look for."

"Good, then you can come and help next trip. Make sure the robber doesn't best me again. He's putting another flock together. A few here, a few there. He should have gathered enough by now. Plus, there's meant to be a tup in the deal."

"You're not going back for more?"

"Certainly. Just one more lot. I've an idea in mind. I want you to mount up and fetch two of those small mares ready for tomorrow."

Erdi pulled a face.

"What's that for? She won't bite you."

"I'm not so sure."

"No Erdi. I don't think it's biting she has in mind."

Erdi remembered his way up to Patch's place. He had taught himself to take note of certain landmarks, not only those lying ahead but those when viewed looking back down the trail, thus hopefully avoiding loss of way when retracing steps or reusing various routes. The chord at the gate was pulled for attention and almost colliding with the man on entering, told him he had come for two of the horses and there was no time to spare. Aggie, perched with legs up on the banking, in a way she felt offered the best possible view of her assets, screeched and waved. Erdi pretended not to hear.

"I think she's calling to you," said Patch unnecessarily.

"I've no doubt she is." Erdi busied himself with bridling the two selected mares.

"It's just a comfort thing you know. Sooths her mind."

"I'm sure there are those willing to help in that respect, but forgive me, my duty is to Trader. I've been told to have these ponies back, rested, fed and watered ready to travel at first light tomorrow. Explain that to Aggie for me. Hopefully she'll understand."

As the compound gate shut behind him there came a hidious wail. It was heartrending and the pain in the sound, haunted inside his head even when well out of earshot. Dusk had descended by the time he got back.

Trader asked, "Well?"

"Was not an easy task Trader. Can we go there together next time? Poor thing's kept little better than an animal." He hadn't wanted to question Trader's business, but couldn't hold his curiosity any longer, "Trader? All the way back down here I've had this question troubling me. Are you really thinking of trading these ponies for more sheep?"

Trader simply returned an arched look.

"Forgive me for asking, but what about the deal with the Bleddi?"

Trader just tapped his temple lightly, indicating he had a plan in mind and said, "We've a fair bit to do in the next few days, Erdi."

The next morning Delt received instructions; he and another hand were to set off with three days rations and one of the dogs. Trader and Erdi followed on behind and being mounted, caught up and overtook them just south of Elsa's ridge. The trail followed was well defined, being the main route south on the slightly higher ground that avoided extensive marshes to the west. They reached a cluster of houses at a place known as Medle. Trader was known to the people there, who expressed delight at the notion of putting the travelers up for the night once their tiny charges had been delivered south. It was difficult to leave, however, on account of the children's interest in the tiny ponies. When eventually managing to pull themselves away, they were accompanied by youngsters running trying to keep up until tiring to be left in a graduated line, youths down to toddlers back along the trail.

Once they reached Habren island, not in fact an island, but a huge loop in the river known as such, Erdi needed to pay full attention, for his job was to return and guide the two drovers to the final destination.

As usual, arrival was signaled by dog barking. The man advancing to greet them was all smiles until seeing the small ponies, at which point a worried look clouded his brow. Erdi wasn't told the man's birth name, but as he was introduced as Tupper, that is what he called him. The fellow's jocularity gave Erdi an uneasy feeling, for he looked a little too pleased with himself and his immediate familiarity didn't entice, as it obviously did with some folk, but repelled like a warning. They were offered the customary food and drink and after having been regaled with tales of Tupper's latest love tangles, the subject eventually got around to business.

"I hope those aren't for me, Trader," he said nodding towards the two small mares.

"What d'you mean not for you? Course they're for you. I've been saving them specially. I've had to fight people off. You won't have any trouble trading those on, Tupper my friend. Everybody's been after them."

The man groaned, "Nooo Trader. I do sheep. Not horses you know that. Sheep for bronze that's me."

"Well it's time you tried something new."

"Granted they're a rare sight, but I simply don't have an outlet for them."

Erdi left them to it and wandered over to where the flock was grazing. He counted five full hands plus a large tup making twenty-six in all. As before the man had included five wethers in the deal, hoping them not to be noticed. Obviously, his approach to women, honesty and trading could be politely described as imaginative. The subject of horses could still be heard as Trader and Tupper approached, with of course,

Trader needing to examine the sheep. Unseen by Tupper, Erdi signaled five.

Trader nodded he'd understood and said, "Fine looking flock, Tupper. You've done well. Was a bit reluctant to let the ponies go, but now I see the deal it looks to be a fair one."

Erdi left them and as arranged, rode to meet up with the two men following. They were waiting for him to the north of the huge loop of the river that bore the misnomer Habren Island and having learnt the route, he guided them to where the two traders were still locked together in negotiation.

"I don't think you two will be needed," Tupper called out to the two drovers.

"Course they will. Look now Tupper, you know me to be a man of my word."

"Yes of course Trader, no-one doubts that."

"I tell you what. Give me your hand. If you get stuck with these horses, I give you my word, I'll have them back. Give me your hand."

"No I'm sorry Trader."

At that point Trader's manner changed completely. Gently moving Tupper from blocking his line of vision and staring intently at the flock, he said slowly, "Hang on! Is there something a bit strange about one of those sheep? And that other one!" He went to get up, but was stopped by the question, "You said you'd give me your word. You'll definitely have those mares back if I can't shift them?"

"Yes but you mustn't say where you got them. Don't worry they're not stolen. Just doesn't do to have everyone knowing my business." All was said this in a faraway voice as if something about the sheep still troubled him.

They slapped hands on the deal and Delt went to work with the dog rounding up the small flock. As they headed back north, Trader gave Erdi a wink. "I don't want to bring bad luck on the deal, but I would gamble a sack of bronze on our friend Tupper being stuck with those horses. It's all clay round here. Too heavy for things that size to manage. Also they're not what you'd call cart pulling material. Not unless someone went to the trouble of building one small enough. What else is he going to do with them? Teach children to ride?" His ruddy face was a picture when he laughed.

Erdi's mind was full of questions but he'd learnt it best on certain occasions to keep them to himself. He would watch and wait as the plan unfolded.

Partway back they stopped as arranged. The children of Medle were disappointed, hoping they'd still have the small ponies in tow. As compensation, Trader volunteered Erdi, asking him to show them his skill with the slingshot while the food cooked. Erdi, giving a sarcastic grimace of thanks, dragged himself up and went outside, marginally revived by the youngster's enthusiasm. After the meal a flute accompanied a woman with a most haunting singing voice entertaining them with renditions of traditional melodies.

They arrived home about the middle of the following day to be told by Gwedyll one of their pigeons had just arrived back. This signaled an early morning start next day bound for the Nant Crag stream running along the northern border.

As they waited in the insidious misty rain Erdi resisted the temptation to ask what was to be expected on such a fine morning? It wasn't to be horses as from the sound, it was just a single rider approaching.

It was the same man they had dealt with previously. He had two large baskets strapped either side of his horse.

"You managed to get them then?"

"Two," replied the man and followed them to the same spot in the woods used before. The baskets were lowered to the grass and the lid of one was partly raised. A puppy's eager face appeared in the opening, whimpering to be let out. Trader peered in the other basket and the deal was briskly transacted. The bronze was safely slotted away as before and the man left without ceremony to re-cross the stream.

They took the ridge route back and only when they'd arrived at Trader's compound did Erdi get a proper look at the precious cargo. They were rough haired, grubby white in colour and had massive paws. Gwedyll gave a little squeak of delight as they scrambled from the baskets. One eying its surroundings nervously, squatted near the hearth, darkening a patch of the hard mud floor.

"This is where you come in, Erdi. Your next little job is to train them. And first lesson is to stop them doing that in the house."

Erdi was provided with a specific list of things Trader wanted the dogs proficient at and of course top of that list was hunting.

That evening they heard, the dull clank of bells and bleating from along the track. They all went out to watch the sheep being driven home. Delt was still mystified as to why his master had again, and this time knowingly, taken charge of a flock that had five wethers included. He had done as instructed, however, and not mentioned a word about it.

Eight wethers were traded on for their fleece and meat and two were kept to be slaughtered that coming winter. The rest of the combined flock were put to graze heath and woods with the idea of having their lambs as bonus the following spring.

As the days went by, now riding as if born to it, Erdi went about his business and wherever he went locally the dogs went with him. He found them intelligent and easy to train. When fully grown no wolf would dare approach livestock they happened to be guarding. Already at not yet a year old they were larger than any hound living locally or for that matter, any still alive in people's memories. If required to show ferocity they duly obliged, otherwise they were gentle, playful creatures.

Chapter Seventeen

The approach of the Autumn Fair, sometimes referred to as the Harvest Fair, started to figure large in peoples' talk and daily lives. Erdi was counting off the days as he was beginning to miss his family badly. This hadn't been helped by Yanker calling. Erdi had been out on his rounds at the time, but a message had been left, Mardi desperately wanted his brother home and Vanya had been missing him that much she had been heard crying at night.

Going to the fair with Trader's family instead of his own felt peculiar and almost traitorous. They were setting up camp in the usual spot, when Vanya appeared. She approached in an urgent manner, but on spotting Erdi, stopped and stared as if trying to hold herself together. Suddenly her face crumpled and she flew the last few paces hardly touching the ground to bury her head in her brother's chest, her shoulders heaving as she clung to him crying. His sister was loath to let him go and looking at him, eyes glistening, hugged him again as if to prove it was not just a dream. When calmer she begged him to come home. She implored Gwedyll and Trader to try and patch the rift so he could return. They pointed out he was free to leave at any time and meanwhile of course, would do their best to try and smooth things over.

Later Mardi ghosted into the glow of the fire to be hugged by his brother and he quietly explained they needed him back. They all missed him, but also there had been some worrying developments. Reportedly, a wild band of raiders had been seen riding in the area and even worse, no official move had been made to challenge them. The chieftain had of late been leaving such matters to his eldest son and the crown prince, when told tales of theft and rape, had simply dismissed them as hysteria. He had remained smug and inactive even following reports that two young girls had gone missing. 'Go and breed some more,' had allegedly been his answer, but you can never be certain, for rumours can never be trusted entirely and what people want to believe travels like the wind.

The next morning a collective mood of agitation went through the whole Feasting Site, as if a truth, decipherable to all, had come windborne rustling through the trees. The Bleddi and Y-Gwyllt were riding in together. They were rare visitors and the wildest of those collectively known as the Skreela. Their approach would be by way of the ford, where the track led out to a vacant camping spot beyond the palisade. The wooden bridge had been swept away and not rebuilt, but with recent weather having been kind, the waters were low and fordable.

Sounds of splashing echoed as hooves slipped on riverbed stones, carts creaked, a horse snorted, but dark faces peering from beneath the awnings remained mute. The ferocious look of their proud mounted men-folk, with tattoos, woad, feathers and wolf pelts stunned the watching throng to silence.

Until a lone voice said to no-one in particular, "Must be snow on the hills." Erdi didn't need sight of the man to know who had spoken.

All around him were still chuckling at the remark, as he eased his way through to where Yanker greeted him with, "Oh, so you did decide to come then?"

"Only to snuff your rush!" Erdi replied. (rush referred to a rushlight made from reed pith dipped in tallow to give a dim light when lit. To snuff it had the broader meaning, to put your fire out; quench **your** glory.)

They left the crowd still silently staring, enthralled, as if expecting something wonderous to transpire, flying warriors maybe and they walked to where they could talk more freely.

"You seem different," said Yanker eying him up and down. "Don't know quite what it is, but you do. You seem different."

They swapped stories and were soon laughing and joking like old times.

Then, realising time was short with them having to be back helping with setting up duties, their mood became more serious.

"I've missed you cousin."

"And I you, Yanker."

"You have to come home, Erdi. I'm not joking. You're badly missed."

"I would, but as you know it's not that simple."

"Let's try and work something out. I know your father's stubborn, but even he's worried by the rumours."

"Has anyone seen these men?"

"Everyone says they know someone who has, but no-one I know has actually set eyes on them."

"I've obviously heard worrying things myself, but I've been too buried in what I've been doing to pay much attention. Thought it might just be women's talk. Half my time's been taken with the dogs."

"What dogs?"

"I'll tell you another time. I've lots to tell you in fact. I miss you cousin."

The fair was one of those times when everything seemed to beset and beleaguer. After a trying day when he'd said, "Some days it's best to just stay in bed," Trader went on to explain how he'd noticed over the years, problems seemed to arrive in waves. He had become aware of definite cycles during his trading life. They were troublesome and seemed to come around no matter how much one tried to avoid them. Knowing how to cope at such times, actually acted as a good lesson for dealing with life in general. They'd had quite a long talk about it deep into the night, following a particularly difficult first day at the fair, details of which I'll tell you later.

Trader explained that if you're attempting to do a certain thing, in his case trading for a living, first and foremost, there were no short cuts, it was essential all should be done diligently and to the utmost of one's ability. There were no substitutes for planning and rigour, plus the essential large dash of self-belief, needed when the best laid plans are wrecked by circumstances, seemingly beyond control. There were two definite cycles of good and bad fortune and anyone in the trading game had to learn how to deal with them. He didn't know why things happened the way they did, but offered the opinion, perhaps the spirits were to blame.

The first cycle tends to be lengthy, he said, lasting about eight years, at the end of which, everything as regards trading and perceived values seems to crash. This is the time for maintaining a steady hand and keeping a low profile until things improve. He added, "It's a time of survival when nothing seems to go right." If patient, however, things just seem to slowly improve of their own accord, but even then, it can take up to a year for doubts to be banished, to regain that feeling, at last you're basking in the sun. The most important thing was not to take the bad times personally. It was essential to keep believing. Keep doing the right thing. He added, in consequence, a strange thing often happens. Something positive, as if out of nowhere, often pops out when least expecting it, resulting in the goal achieved, although of great benefit, not being what you'd actually been aiming at. But if you hadn't made a positive effort in the first place you probably wouldn't have gained any result at all. It was those spirits again, as if they could see you pressing with all your might attempting to force one huge door open, so to speak and for a little joke, probably sending them into raptures, opening another at knee height you didn't even know was there.

The second cycle Trader described, was like the one they were in now. You think all is going to plan then from nowhere it hits you. And he said, bad things tend to come in threes. Why? He didn't know. All three things seem to hit at once, but if you pick your way carefully, they soon pass, like the ferocity of a dry bush burning. The trick was again, to never stop believing. Another piece of advice given, was regarding those times when you can seem to do no wrong. With finger raised in warning, "That's the most dangerous time." He thought scheming spirits and those meddling little goblins were at the back of it. They would lay a trail of plenty to lure you into feelings of infallibility, making it the time to be most on guard. The time when you could make your biggest mistake. "You're offered something you wouldn't normally consider and you're on such a run of luck you think, 'how can I fail?' Then those fateful words escape your lips, 'Ah, go on then'"-

---- he clapped his hands --- "and the trap closes leaving you looking at the worst move you've made in months. In fact, as we know certain mistakes can last a lifetime." He paused before adding, "When I think about it, the best time to do a deal is when you're short of the wherewithal to do it with. That's when you're at your keenest."

I'm just giving you a brief summary of what they talked about. Like I said, their discussion went on deep into the night. Into that witching hour when you feel confident enough to confide inner thoughts you would never dream of revealing in the cold light of day.

Erdi was also warned, never to make the mistake of thinking things go on for ever. "Nothing goes on forever. What everyone wants today can look tired and forgotten in no time at all." He felt the spirits were to blame, for as if overnight, for no apparent reason, the value of the most prized and coveted commodity, could suddenly collapse. Looking Erdi in the eye, he said, "It could even happen to bronze."

So what had actually taken place that day was the following. Shortly after Erdi had returned from meeting Yanker, Tupper came calling. He was a rare sight at the fairs and so for this reason alone his being there had to have a pretty strong reason. Trader had expected there to be a day of reckoning, had even planned for it, but the sound of Tupper in his face, first business of the day, like a fox-head hat come to life had not been in his plans at all. He stayed calm, however, asked him to keep his voice down and told him he'd be there to trade the horses back second morning after finish of the fair.

Tupper snarled and yapped some more. He certainly wasn't all geniality and smiles now and flecks of spit had to be wiped off as the man advanced seemingly oblivious to the fact that Trader had acquiesced.

"He's agreed," Erdi said.

Tupper stared back with that clouded look people have when anger has scrambled the brain.

"Trader's agreed. He'll be there first thing after the fair."

"Well, that's all very well!" He sort-of ran out of pathway here and began to backtrack. "You mean he'll have the horses back?" A tiny light of reason now flickered in his eyes.

"Yes, that's what he's just said."

"Oh! Well I suppose that's all right then. But you can understand my position can't you. You can understand me getting a bit overwrought."

"A bit overwrought?" said Trader watching the departing figure. "I should say he was. Surprised he knows the meaning of the word!"

No sooner had he gone than, as if they'd been waiting around the corner, the three Bleddi warriors appeared. They refused offers of hospitality, rather wanting to get straight to the point. They had managed to set up a transaction involving the five ponies and were just checking the deal was still to go ahead. They were in no mood for forgiveness if they were being made fools of. Trader said with an air of munificence, "Have no fear. Everything's in hand. Be there third morning after the fair and bring pelts as well as gold, I might have a little bonus for you."

This was more like it. They at last accepted the gift of beer and wheat-cake.

239

With them finally gone, there was still no respite, for as if the spirits had concocted it, Erdi caught the unexpected sight of Luda fast approaching and an inner sense told him he was not going to like the reason for her visit.

Completely out of breath, she gasped it was good to see him again, but he had to come quickly. "It's Donda, she's pregnant."

Erdi frowned, mystified, but made his excuses to Trader and accompanied Luda, wondering why Donda's pregnancy was any of his business.

A reception committee awaited. There were his parents of course looking very concerned, Ma and Pa Blade looking self-righteous, Blade himself, looking puffed up and vengeful and Donda, not looking particularly pregnant. Perhaps a bit fuller, bearing the signs a woman might notice, but hints too subtle to alert the attention of the average male.

"You've done it this time," sneered Blade. "Our dad says....."

"Your father's right here, Blade, let him speak for himself." There was an edge to his voice. It was their first meeting since the broad-staff encounter and had they not been in the confines of the Feasting Site, Erdi felt certain Blade would have instigated an immediate rematch.

Pa Blade spat with anger that there was no doubt his daughter was with child. Donda had confessed. Erdi was the father and now they expected him to take up his responsibilities.

Penda's first words to his son after all that time of not seeing him were, "So what have you got to say for yourself?"

Erdi didn't reply as such but asked Ma Blade, "When exactly was I supposed to have had such intimate knowledge of your daughter?"

"How are we expected to know? How can we know when you came creeping around?" Ma Blade blustered, certainly not the friendly 'auntie' now, but all bosom and haughty sanctimony, above tightly folded arms.

Here Mara intervened. "You're not trying to tell me as a woman, you don't have a rough idea. I credit you with a little more sense than that."

Had a man said this to her, an explosion of indignation would have thrown him off track, but the same trick wasn't going to work on a woman.

Ma Blade made a rough calculation, told them and everyone else rewound the course of recent events in their minds.

"So Donda, would you agree it happened somewhere about the time of the Summer Fair?" Mara asked.

It looked like the spirit had been knocked out of the girl, but she obliged calculating on her fingers and whispered, "It must have been just after."

Erdi reasoned, "If I'd been the father, Donda, you wouldn't need the finger counting pretence. You'd remember the time exactly. Well I hope you would. Why are you blaming me like this?"

Penda still hadn't forgiven his son, but wasn't about to see an injustice done. "Well either you two ladies have forgotten how to count or someone else must bear responsibility for the child."

"How d'you work that out!" sneered Blade.

"My son was nowhere near your property at the time you're suggesting. Firstly, every day, he was under my close watch, until the time he was up at Five Pools with Dowid and Yanker and from then on he's been working at Trader's."

"He could have still come poking around our place," said Pa Blade.

"Business never took me near your house," Erdi replied "and for your information I don't go poking around. Not your place, not any place."

"You must have done that time years back, over at Scratch's!" Jeered Blade before his father could reply.

Erdi looking directly into the bloodshot glare of hatred said, "Do you think it wise to bring that up?" He then

241

suggested to all, "Why not fetch Trader as witness? He knows exactly where I went and reasons for going."

Vanya was sent, seeking Trader's help, who arriving with a grand professional air, told them that Erdi's time had been too full for him to have possibly courted and taken advantage of their daughter. He knew some of Erdi's trips over Elsa's ridge had been a little protracted, but as he couldn't see what relevance that had, didn't mention it. He of course, had also known why Erdi had tarried, but had dismissed it with the thought, he too had been young once. Trader then went to great lengths explaining, he had in fact specifically avoided sending Erdi in their direction on account of the recent difference of opinion between him and his father.

"I'm sorry Donda," said Erdi. "I'm sorry for the situation you're in, but you'll have to tell your parents the truth. You know full well I'm not the father."

After they'd dragged themselves away, huddled around Donda, crying inconsolably, Mara said, "Well we don't need the help of some wonder-wizard to know how this little accident happened. You only have to cast your mind back to the Summer Fair. I couldn't see the point of stating the obvious though, poor girl's distressed enough as it is. If they'd have persisted mind you ----- I tell you--- I was on the verge of it anyway. I'd have let them have it. The whole barbed quiver full!"

"She's only got herself to blame," said Penda.

"And her parents," Mara reasoned. "They should have stopped her antics. A bit of flirting, yes. But she was flaunting herself."

"I told you one of 'em would part her whiskers," said Dowid backing away as if expecting another whack from Mara and even she laughed, this time saying, "You can see where Yanker gets it from."

So that's how Erdi began to reconcile with his father.

When he eventually returned to help Trader, he found him in a withdrawn mood. Gwedyll took him to one side and told him that they'd had a long and not very pleasant visit from her people. They had demanded immediate return of their emblematic, bronze cauldron. She leant close and whispered, "Their reminder that there was nothing to stop them simply taking it along with Tywy and myself, drained the colour from his face, Erdi. I've never seen him look so shocked. Went as white as milk poor lamb!"

Erdi couldn't quite picture Trader as a lamb, but avoided comment, asking instead, "Why doesn't he just hand it back. Why is he being so stubborn?"

"He's too proud, a bit like your father. Thinks I have an equal right to it by birth. Talking of birth. When are you to be a proud father? I was told why you had to dash off."

Erdi explained what had happened, much to Gwedyll's amusement and then asked, "Why do you think she blamed me? Also in the past, in the games we used to play; you know the sort of games -------"

"Games, Erdi? Whatever do you mean?" Gwedyll's teasing look reminded him of how he'd felt on first seeing her.

Blushing slightly, he managed to continue, "It always seemed to be me she picked and I never knew why. Yanker used to make all the jokes, but she seemed drawn to me. It didn't make sense."

"Well you tell me. Come on now Erdi, why do you think young miss buxom chose you?"

"Buxom? Didn't know you'd ever met her."

Gwedyll simply returned him a patient look and said, "Well?"

He thought for a while. "Was it my slingshot victory? Was she was looking for a share in all the fuss people made?" He looked up to see Gwedyll staring back at him, an eyebrow raised.

"That battle with the broadstaff?"

Shake of head.

"Hunting?"

"Closer."

243

"I'm not the worst looking man in the valley."

Gwedyll's look of fast losing her patience, prompted Erdi to struggle for yet another answer. "Family? Our family has survived fairly well. Better than many."

"Closer, but what word have you missed?"

Seeing Erdi's completely blank expression, she gave him the answer, "Security---- Yes, you have skills in combat and hunting, you come from a strong, respected family, you have a calm way about you, but what matters above all in the mind of a girl like Donda, is security. Put everything together you've mentioned and it amounts to that and more. We live in dangerous times, Erdi. With this strange bad weather, food is becoming scarce. Alright, so the silly girl had her head turned. She knows she's made a huge mistake and couldn't be feeling more vulnerable. So out of sheer desperation she's made an attempt to ensnare you. The perfect protector and provider. Plus, you're not a bad looking young man."

He thanked her for the compliment and then a thought suddenly occurred. "And what about you? When you and Trader first met, dare I ask? Security?"

"It was a bit more complicated than that in my case and don't you say a word, but basically, yes. Plus of course----" She leant a little closer, "We **are** quite fond of one another. Life's never dull with him as you might have noticed. Never without incident. Just wish he wasn't so stubborn at times."

"Oh, the cauldron problem. It seems he needs a way out of that without loss of dignity?"

"Yes. You're right, Erdi, but how? The more I reason with him the more he digs his heels in."

Left alone with his thoughts, Erdi gave the matter serious consideration. To this was added yet another problem as the day wore on.

It started with bellowing and shouting from across the other side of the site.

"Sounds like two of them are going at it," Trader said cheerfully, having recovered somewhat from the in-law's recent visit and little thinking the storm could be blowing their way.

The sound of the angered voices growing louder stirred up that ominous feeling within Erdi, that no matter how unlikely it seemed, where they now stood was to be the eventual destination of those so heatedly arguing. His feelings were right. Two men approached, both red in the face and the way they still growled at one another, neither had given a finger's width of ground. They led an energetic huddle that looked almost willing to break into a run to avoid missing the outcome. Trader recognized the one complainant and asked what the problem was? It transpired that two young bull oxen Trader had handled could have been stolen. The second man said, he knew they were his by their markings. They had gone missing months back, but there was no mistaking these to be the very ones. Trader told him it was not really his problem as he'd handled them in good faith. The next question of course was, 'who had brought them to him?'

When he divulged, he'd traded them off two brothers, the one's Erdi referred to as the eel stealers, everything dropped into place. The man's property adjoined theirs and they'd been the first people he'd gone to when looking for them.

Thus, the vociferous and mobile disagreement moved on to where the eel stealers were camped, attracting an even bigger audience with a number starting to take sides.

With much vehemence and anger, the brothers declared their innocence, saying the animals must have wandered onto their ground and they'd simply assumed them to be theirs. With oxen being prized to the extent each was given a name, this seemed highly unlikely, but how could the rightful owner prove it and how could he force the brothers to pay for what was in fact theft, other than by offering violence. Also, their story now differed completely from the denial of all knowledge when he'd first enquired about the animals months back, but it was just his word against theirs. Even though the ultimate solution of a bare-knuckle encounter or something of that nature seemed fairly imminent, all had enough sense to hold back, as coming to blows within the confines of the Feasting Site risked immediate eviction. Not to worry, however, those relishing a set-to could yet be rewarded if all remained diligent. The burgeoning flames of the conflict were stoked by artful goading and encouragement until it escalated into such an inferno, a trial by battle was organized to be fought beyond the perimeter fence first thing the following morning. A limit of four protagonists each was agreed and staves were to be the only weapons permitted.

Erdi felt there had to be another solution. He needed a quiet place to think. Sitting in the shade of the lone oak out on open ground, ideas began to formulate. He returned, fired by what he'd dreamt up and enthusiastically explained his plan to Trader. It hinged on the fact that for some strange reason, Prince Aram had of late been seeking Yanker's friendship and he felt certain that if his cousin laid the problem before the prince in the right way, he'd be glad to see justice done. It seemed, Aram was opposed to using his brother's strong-arm tactics, preferring to be viewed as a measured voice of reason and being second in line to tribal leadership, was a symbol of power both sides would respect. Aram's judgement regarding plausibility of each plaintiff's standpoint would be listened to and it was essential all was done without Gardarm's involvement.

Trader was suspicious at first, not thinking it likely a lofty prince would take the trouble to intervene in a petty squabble, but gradually with more persuasion, he warmed to the idea. He said to Erdi as he was leaving, "Tell your cousin, if he manages to twist the princes' arm, to come and tell me immediately. And I mean immediately."

Yanker had been more than glad to help. It appealed to his innate sense of mischief and of course sense of fair play. Later that day he ran back to inform Trader, Prince Aram had agreed. He would ask his father's permission to sit in judgement of the case. Trader went straight to the man, who was still voicing grievances to anyone still willing to listen. "Wasn't he right to offer violence? Wouldn't they do the same if someone stole their livestock?"

Trader calming him somewhat, explained, not what had already been set in motion, but told him the tale as if he was on his way to seek Prince Aram's intervention. Then he asked, for going to this amount of trouble and being the only person having sufficient influence over the prince, would it be unreasonable to expect favourable terms regarding the acquisition of one of the oxen once they'd been returned to him? He gave his idea of what he thought to be favourable terms.

"But that means you'd only be giving me half value for it!"

"Plus you'd be getting your other bull back."

"It's hardly fair though, Trader."

"Make your mind up! Do you want me to fix it or not? Perhaps you'd rather risk battle and injury in the morning."

"No you're right. Try and persuade the prince to bring some justice if you can. I must admit I'd never manage to get anywhere near the man myself and as you rightly say one and a half is better than the nothing I've got at the moment."

Erdi and Trader awaited developments. Finally, the summons went out for the contesting parties plus witnesses to present themselves to the prince, for the pleas to be heard.

Erdi gave Trader moral support, but Yanker was thanked and advised to stay away. Prince Aram gave both arguments a fair hearing and after probing with a few searching questions, gave the matter serious consideration, before finally delivering his verdict. Firstly, he declared Trader and the present owner of the bulls to be completely blameless. Then he told the aggrieved party he needed to retain better control over his livestock, but turning to the eel stealers, told them this in no way exonerated what they had done. As they protested innocence, he slapped down his rod of authority, saying he didn't believe a word of it. The bulls were to be returned to their rightful owner and the eel stealers were ordered to pay their present owner their equivalent value in bronze. That knocked the stuffing out of them. They said, with not having such an amount readily available, they couldn't possibly, especially when bearing in mind the value of the beasts had doubled since their handling of them. The solution therefore, this stunned them, was: either the pair would do a half year's work for the plaintiff as a form of repayment or would lose possession of a slave for a whole year to accomplish the same. Furthermore, the injured party had the right to take his pick of the slaves. The man soon to be two bulls short said he wanted the brothers nowhere near his property and so would make his choice of a slave as soon as the fair was over.

Later that afternoon Trader was seen in deep discussion with the man who was shortly to be in the happy position of being two bulls to the good and on the sound of a hand slap onlookers knew some sort of deal had been sealed, but eying Trader's brisk departure, were left to watch and wonder. The solution of course had not been a crowd pleaser. They'd been keenly looking forward to the massive set-to planned for the morning and already, wagers had been made.

That evening Erdi wandering into the Y-Dewis camp, found them all downing beer while waiting for the pig to roast. They obviously wanted answers as to why he'd suddenly taken the notion to intrude, but managing to quell interest with an air of vagueness, he scanned in the hope of spotting his ideal intermediary, Prince Heddi. But as often happens with carefully laid plans, there was no sign of him. So, with no other option available he took a deep breath and approached the chieftain and his cohort of senior warriors directly. Removing his cap and with hands clasped in front, he gave a low bow. He was eyed suspiciously, very suspiciously, to the point he expected to be ejected from their sight, but when humbly thanking them for allowing him to stand before them, spoken in their own language, he could sense surprise and a little respect growing. Having said that, there seemed no sign of their tolerance extending to the offering of refreshment. Under the chieftain's stern gaze, he explained his plan, then waited as the precipitous silence yawned. He asked whether he should leave while the matter was discussed, but was motioned to stay. The ensuing talk was rapid and contained words beyond his comprehension, but from their body language he could see his idea had gained favour. A senior advisor smiled and thanked Erdi for his trouble, saying the plan was worth consideration. If it failed, they could always resort to the easy option, force.

They actually had a fair amount of admiration for his impertinence, especially with him looking to be no more a youth off a smallholding.

There was one other significant memory from this particular Autumn Fair and happened to involve the wild men from over the water, slave Wolfy's people. Their language was incomprehensible and they knew nothing of protocol expected at the Feasting Site, nothing of the power structure established over countless years and did it trouble them? Not one bit. They arrived the second morning of the fair with their strange talk, strange ways, like merry kings of the world.

All the major business had been done. Salt had been traded and of course the copper and tin. Animals driven and hauled there had been dealt for on the first day and rush for tools, clothes and domestic goods, always frenetic at the start was now down to the odd deal with the slow deciders and hardest bargainers. It was an actual tactic of some to leave their dealing until sensing which of those present wouldn't relish returning home with leftover stock. These were known as dag-enders. The hardest bargainers. They weren't much respected, but the odd one ended up with more accumulated wealth than those proud to be known as "proper" traders and certainly more than many that spent a lifetime sweating a brow for it.

So, it was on a slow second morning that the merry kings of the world arrived. Their leggings and cloaks were of a striking plaid weave and unlike the local men they sported beards, grown wild enough to match their persona. They greeted all as if they'd known them for years and their huge dogs loping beside them were a wonder to behold. Any who had witnessed Erdi riding out recently would have recognized the breed, but the six they had, were fully grown and large enough for children to ride. Their progress towards those gathered at the North Gate was slowed to the pace of the ancient ox they led. It could only have been obtained locally, there was no chance it had endured any sort of trek, for as Yanker had commented, the thing looked to be on its last legs. Quite prophetic in fact, for they butchered it and were watched as they skinned and dismembered the carcass, hacking it into small cuts and joints. Stout wooden posts supported the water-filled hide, hanging like a huge cauldron and the meat was dropped within, followed by barley and salt. Hot stones dragged from the fire, were brushed clean and added to bring the stew to the boil. Using long staves, glowing embers were coaxed from the fire and prodded into place beneath the improvised cauldron to keep the contents simmering. Ox cooked in its own hide must have been one of their specialities, for those that had pronounced the old beast likely tough enough to make the jaw ache, had had to eat their words when a taste of the meal was proffered. It was succulent, tender and delicious.

If that weren't enough to make them a focal point, the haggling over possession of their dogs reaching desperation, certainly did. Red faced envoys with looks of panic, became quite unseemly at the prospect of failing to procure a hound for their lord and master until the solution of the pack being split three ways was decided on. Two dogs going to each of the leaders. The Bleddi and Y-Gwyllt chieftains, on being reminded of their subordinate role to their main Y-Dewis overlord, got nothing.

Trader was obviously aware that Tupper had witnessed the panic trade on the dogs, as had those same three Bleddi warriors he had regular dealings with. Telling Erdi they had much to do, they broke camp early, leaving that afternoon before the official end fair. There had been enough time for Erdi to tell his family it would not be long before his return to the fold. He just needed to attend to one last item of business. The sadness and tears as he left them again, I'll leave to your imagination.

The next morning, as always immediately following a fair, much time was spent on such tasks as stashing goods away, answering Delt's questions and giving detailed instructions regarding various tasks required of him and the men. The main task being, the immediate collection of the three small ponies, with strict instructions to take the circuitous route back, so not to draw any unwanted attention. Before departure, Delt helped Erdi load the cart with the three stuffed stags.

"I hope this is the last time I have to look at these things," he said. "The number of times I've been jabbed ------" his voice trailed off. "What's he going to do with them, Erdi? Thought he might have been saving them for his pyre."

"I really don't know, Delt. Sometimes I can follow the logic but at other times I don't know what he's up to."

In the grey of a late afternoon Trader and Erdi accompanied by the two hunting dogs set out for the southern end of Elsa's ridge, where the track met the main trail south. Progress was slow and it was almost dark by the time the aroma of hearth cooked food drifted towards them. They were again entertained by the good residents of Medle and to show his appreciation, Trader gifted them dried mint he'd procured from his southern contact at the fair.

Just as the children of Medle hadn't wanted to see the small ponies leave they were as equally sad at the sight of the departing hounds the following morning. Trader had managed to brush aside, the many questions asked, with barely contained merriment I have to add, regarding the stuffed stags, but undeterred, the locals persisted with their probing and jesting, right up to the point of departure.

"You're not really putting those in a deal are you, Trader?"

"No he's just hauling them round for a wager."

Trader ignoring the banter, busied himself with checking the harness and tightening the straps on the load.

"He's not. He's taking them as far as he can, aren't you Trader? Get 'em lost so they can't follow you home."

"I doubt that. Like as not they'll be passing here again later. Hope for your sake, Trader, I'm wrong. Tell you what though, if I am, I'd like the custom of whoever ends up with **those** today."

"Well, whoever ends up with them," said another, "they won't take much feeding."

Trader, taking it all in good part, smiled and thanked them again for their hospitality. The villagers waved them off and stood watching, as the strange cargo staring back at them, rocked and jolted away down the track.

The day was still young when they reached Tupper's place. His dog barked then skulked out of sight on seeing the pair of hounds. Tupper on the other hand could hardly contain his excitement on eying them. He'd witnessed the interest the breed had caused at the fair and now feared what was now heading his way, might be too good to be true.

"Told you I'd keep my word, Tupper. Hope you've been looking after my ponies." He was taken to inspect them.

"I'm sorry Trader, there's nothing wrong with them, it's just they don't suit for round here."

"Don't worry, Tupper the dogs will put things right."

"What! Just two of puppies for a fine pair of fully grown ponies? How much more can you put, to square the deal up?"

"So now they're fine ponies all of a sudden. I suppose you noticed the stir caused by those hounds at the fair? These are the exact same breed. You won't have dogs like these on your hands for long. And please, not puppies. A pair of trained hunting dogs….. Believe me they'll be gone like.." He clicked his fingers.

Tupper with a fearful look, nodded in the direction of the stuffed stags. "What do you hope to do with those?"

"What d'you mean, **those**? They're the latest thing in hunting. You don't have to go crashing about the woods any more, the deer will be lured to you. Lured right up to your door."

Trader saw greed in Tupper's eyes for the dogs, but a wavering look towards the stuffed stags. "If you don't want the dogs, don't worry, I'll have no problem shifting them."

"They're trained you say?"

"Course they are. Trained hunting dogs fit for a chieftain."

"What about the dogs and a couple of ronds thrown in to make up the difference?"

"I don't think you understand, Tupper. I'm here to get you out of trouble on the horse deal. I'm a busy man, I should be seeing to other pressing needs, but I said I'd be here and here I am offering you the tastiest deal you've had in years." He glared at him, "Now you've the cheek to ask for bronze! I'd better make myself clear, it's the dogs and deer or nothing!" He nudged Erdi, "Come on, get the dogs! The man wouldn't recognise a decent deal if it slapped him in the face." He made as if to turn the cart round.

"Wait Trader. You win."

"What, you'll do the deal?"

Tupper sighed and said those fatal words, "Ahh, go on then,"

Erdi, mightily relieved, un-roped the stuffed stags and Tupper helped him unload. "Put them over by the trees," he said, before cursing, as an antler caught him drawing blood. Erdi groaned and thought to himself, 'That's the stew in the fire! He won't want them now.'

"Yes, you have to be careful," called out Trader in an unbelievably bluff manner considering the circumstances, "they can be a bit willful."

Erdi, watching the slow trickle of blood down Tupper's right cheek and the worried look creeping across his brow, muttered to himself, "Shut up, Trader!" Shuffling backwards, helping the man move his recent acquisitions, he gave a silent prayer, a plea against a sudden change of heart. "Magnificent pair of dogs," he said trying to divert Tupper's attention from the wounding. "I'll be sorry to see them go."

A cold piercing look of disdain was the response. The glare a hardened trader might give an enthusiastic junior on realising the public face of geniality was no longer required. Erdi said no more.

The cart seemed incredibly light as they left, almost like riding on air. Their two small ponies seemed glad to be leaving the place and trotted along merrily behind. The day had brightened by the time they rumbled back empty through Medle and mouths fell open as if stuffed stags had been miraculously transformed into two tiny ponies, which in a way they had. It was one of those days to savour, one to never forget. Adding to the magic as they headed towards the sunset, now spread like a beckoning homecoming beacon across the western hills, was the movement of something alongside the cart. Erdi looked down and his heart lifted at the sight of his two hounds loping along beside them. They panted, tongues out, obviously tired but visibly happy.

"You trained them well," congratulated Trader.

Early the following morning, as Trader conducted his business with the three Bleddi warriors, the trail east was given the occasional concerned glance. Only when the pony transaction had been concluded did he show them the dogs. The sheer sight of them was enough to secure a deal. There was hardly need for words and no thought of haggling. Their day's trading was turning out to be like the deal of a lifetime and hardly believing their luck, couldn't get the pelts off their packhorses quick enough.

Which was just as well for no sooner had they been hurried on their way than a lone rider, whip arm in action, was seen fast approaching from the east.

"No prizes for guessing who this is," said Trader.

Tupper swung down off his horse and said in a desperate voice, "My dogs have gone."

"Don't tell me you've lost them!" admonished Trader.

"I didn't lose them. One moment they were there, next thing they were up over the palisade and bolting north like they'd got scent of a hare. Never known dogs scramble over a wall as high as that before. Thought they might have come back here or maybe got lost in the woods between here and Medle. One of villagers spotted them on their way through. Are they here?"

"No they are not," answered Trader quite truthfully.

Tupper looked crestfallen. "Thought I'd start by coming here to ask." He gave a sigh of exasperation. "Now I'll have to work my way back and search for them."

"That's a mighty patch of ground we're talking about Tupper. Finding them amongst that lot would be as hard ---" he paused as if struggling for a comparison. "It would be as hard as getting new born lambs from a wether."

"What d'you mean by that?" Tupper snapped.

"It's just a saying around these parts."

"I've never heard it before."

Trader gave a few words of consolation and followed it with, "At least you've still got the stag lures."

"Those things!" he wailed rubbing the abrasion one had left on his cheek. "I had to chase the local urchins off. Bold as bronze! Using them as target practice!"

"Well you know what they say," said Trader escorting him back to his horse.

Obviously expecting a small crumb of comfort, "No what's that?"

Said with solemnity, as if a piece of revered ancient wisdom, "Some deals can turn out a bit disappointing."

Tupper stared open mouthed, not knowing whether to laugh or cry. Erdi ducked behind a convenient cart and leant back against it shaking with suppressed laughter. There were tears in his eyes and he clutched his sides in agony, absolutely aching from the pressure of not being able to laugh out loud.

On seeing Tupper's departure and Trader returning to the house, Delt who had been busying himself in the nearest hay barn, leant his wooden fork against the stack and wandered over to where Erdi was standing. The man seemed to open up when Trader wasn't around.

"Looks like sheep-cheat got sent home with a hole in the arse of his leggings," he said nodding eastwards, with a merry twinkle in his eye. He of course now wanted to know every detail of how his master had managed to climb out of the stuffed stag deal. Erdi was glad to relate the tale and told him how he thought the whole plan had been thwarted by the stab of an antler.

"What? Spiking the deal so to speak?" They both laughed.

As I said, the man tended to open up when Trader wasn't about.

With the loss of his dogs making Erdi feel like part of his body had been severed, was to a certain extent ameliorated by the knowledge he'd soon be going home. Yet he still somehow expected to see them, tails thumping the floor as they sat awaiting his approach. He still expected to feel a wet nuzzle on the back of a leg, to hear their excited squeak and panting when an outing was imminent.

One afternoon he spotted Delt returning down the northern trail leading a young ox. Erdi was amazed to see, it was one of the bulls recently hotly contested for at the Autumn Fair. Trader gave no explanation, but thanking his man, instructed him to lead it round to one of the stalls. Erdi didn't know if it was just his imagination, but Trader had seemed a bit cooler towards him these past few days.

That made the approach of Prince Heddi one bright morning all the more nerve racking. He was accompanied by a young warrior and the three spare ponies they led. The plan that had seemed so promising when concocted beneath the oak tree at the Feasting Site, now, as he watched it coming to fruition, had a most alarming look of interference and meddling. He could imagine Trader in a stern-faced fury demanding, "Erdi! Was this your idea?"

Trader pushed his cap back and scratched his forehead trying to work out the reason for the visit. Heddi dismounted, touched Trader's extended hand in a very formal manner and said, "My father sends his utmost respects." Erdi was given just a hint of a smile to accompany a nod of acknowledgement and even his aunt Gwedyll and cousin Tywy, emerging from the house, received no more than the same. The young prince continued. "He realises that relinquishing the cauldron is an act of great sacrifice and magnanimity and he admires your spirit of co-operation and even handedness in restoring this emblem, where it will hang exalted in the Great Hall of my people, the Y-Dewis. The extent of his gratitude he hopes will be implicit in the gift he sends to your son, Prince Tywy." He led one of the spare ponies forward, "I present one of the finest horses of the royal herd."

Trader staring at the prince and then at his son said, "Now just a moment!!"

Gwedyll beside him, clung to an arm and implored, "Please. Please let's put an end to this."

"My father intends to make this a bond for life," added Prince Heddi.

Gradually with feminine smoothing, soothing words and smiles, and the reasoning that her decision in the matter ought to have an equal weight to his, Trader's troubled brow was calmed and his resistance began to melt. The cauldron was disinterred from its hiding place to be wrapped and strapped to a spare pony. It has to be said, with its cast bronze masks and sheer size, it did seem incongruous for it to be in its present location.

Trader asked, "What's the third horse for?"

Heddi led the animal forward, turned to Erdi and said, "This is my personal gift to your sister, Vanya."

Gwedyll, seeing Trader, obviously weighing up the sinking esteem of his son's gift, when now witnessing a gift of exact same value being awarded to a slip of a girl not even present, reasoned, "All we've done is return a cauldron, Vanya has given her heart."

If the gift of a horse hadn't been enough to shock, a few days later on the morning of Erdi's departure the young ox was led round and after a short speech of thanks from Trader, was presented to him. He was stunned. Everyone was there, Trader's family plus the hired hands, all assembled to bid him farewell.

"Tell your father, that's our thank you for all you've done here."

Erdi felt embarrassed by their generosity, but they all looked so pleased, brimming with it in fact, he found it impossible to refuse. He went to embrace Trader, but was told with a smile, "Be off with you." The man's coolness of late had obviously just been an act. "If you ever have need to stay again, there's no need to ask." He didn't divulge, this was the deal he'd worked out with Penda, way back on that second day of Erdi leaving home.

Gwedyll kissing the side of his face, squeezed an arm and whispered, "Thank you again." She hadn't needed to tell him she was referring to the recently resolved cauldron impasse.

Delt, leading the bull, accompanied him and Erdi turning to see all waving a farewell from the middle of the track, had a vision to be treasured for the rest of his life.

Chapter Eighteen

You can imagine his mixed emotions as he slowly made his way home. You can imagine the strange feeling at being under the family roof once again, the emotion shown by all, the prickly first few days in his father's company. He looked and felt like a changed person, but slowly he eased his way back into his former existence.

Vanya wasn't long in giving the appearance she'd been riding ponies all her life and Mardi, coaxed by his brother, also mastered the art. He had something extremely important to impart, but waited for a time when he would have Erdi's full attention.

For Dommed the return home with the bull didn't compensate for the extra burden that had been placed on him and the rest of them by Erdi's absence. He didn't show his resentment, he hadn't needed to, Erdi sensed it. He recalled another of Trader's pithy summaries on life, "You can't please everyone."

One late sunny afternoon Mardi, managing to find his brother momentarily free of tasks, told him there was something in the playhouse he wished to show him. On the way there he said, "I think I know why the sun goes cold."

The wattle door was pulled shut behind them and hanging in the gloom, Erdi saw two clay balls. A thin shaft of sunlight pierced the darkness by way of the small hole Vanya had made years before when peering in at the wildcat. It lit the larger ball and a sliver of the smaller orb behind. Mardi's face was radiant. He pointed, "Imagine this is our world. If we were on the dark side here." His finger marked the spot. "See it's black just as it would be during our night and," then indicating the light area on the smaller ball, "this is how much we'd see of the moon at a certain point during its cycle."

There was that word cycle again, the one Trader had used. Patterns of life controlled by mysterious forces.

"The cycles of the moon are repeated, as are those of our world. Erdi, I think we live on a giant rotating ball that goes round the sun and the moon goes round us. So we don't have to make sacrifices to the spirits and pray for them to renew the sun. It all just happens whether we make sacrifices or not. We have always asked, where does the sun go at night, when what we should have been asking is, where do we go? I think I know. The sun doesn't go down into the cold distant waters at night. In fact it doesn't go anywhere, it stays where it is. It's us that moves, I couldn't wait to tell you, Erdi!"

Erdi feeling stunned, simply staring blankly back at his brother.

"On this giant ball of ours, when it slowly turns away from the sun, it takes our part the world into night."

"World?"

"Yes, Erdi. We call all around us our world. So if we all live on this big ball, it must also be, our world. It slowly turns giving us day when we face the sun and night when we've rotated away from it."

"Rotated? Goodness Mardi, you've grown up while I've been away!" He crouched in the gloom, his mind spinning with visions of worlds and moons, then asked, "So why do we have winter then?"

Mardi picked up another clay ball. He tilted it slightly so the hole through centre was slightly off vertical. "The only reason I can come up with is this. What we call our earth is slightly tilted. If we were up here somewhere and this other ball is now the sun," he slowly moved it round the larger suspended ball representing the sun, "this would be our summer." As he continued the circuit he said, "now you can see the tilt has us positioned away from the sun putting our part of the world into winter."

The Teller explained to his audience, All this took much longer to theorize than I've just indicated. I am just relating the essence of the matter. Erdi had been able to follow his brother's logic, but that didn't mean he necessarily agreed with the findings. Which of course you may not either.

"I'm sorry, Mardi, it's hard to believe. It's too much to take in."

"Oh there's loads more to tell you about yet."

He told him of eclipses, explaining how the moon sometimes positioned itself, directly between them and the sun and how their world in turn, occasionally came between the sun and moon to such an extent, its light went out. He then stunned him with the fact that if you set off west or east you would in theory, end up back where you started from.

"What keeps us on this ball of yours, Mardi? Why don't we all just fall off it?"

Mardi laughed. "I don't know. I've spent a long time thinking about that. All I know is, there's some huge force in operation and I don't yet know what it is."

"You're a strange one my brother. It's all quite amazing and neatly explains everything, but I still can't believe it's true."

"I can prove it, Erdi. In the middle of spring the moon will darken. From my calculations it will be followed, roughly one moon later, by a darkening of the sun."

"How do you know that?"

"Never mind how I know. If that happens will you believe me then?"

Erdi looked completely mystified, "How do you know all this stuff, Mardi?"

"I've told you before. I get these strange feelings. Things come to me as if from somewhere back in time, as if I'd somehow forgotten them. They just sort of emerge like a memory coming back."

"Mardi you must keep this secret. It's dangerous." He was deeply worried especially when considering his habit of blurting things out. Not to the same extent as he'd done when a youngster, but one could never really relax. He could still say the oddest of things. Erdi had learnt to interpret the signs, for if Mardi, with a slight cock of head, began studying one person in particular, then an utterance could well be imminent. If quick enough about it, there was a possibility of forestalling, but at other times there was no chance. Out would pop the words and the damage was done.

Vanya had only been given a broad picture as to the paths Mardi's celestial investigations had been taking. She had been more interested in his other gifts and explained to Erdi, their extent as far as she knew. She showed him the tallying system he'd invented. It was based on the five digits of the hand. Up to four short vertical lines represented the obvious and crossed through as if by a thumb meant five. She used charcoal on a riven piece of wood, to illustrate. Two lots of five were denoted by a small square. Four lots of five was the square with one corner triangulated, six lots by two triangulated corners, eight fives by triangulating the third corner and ten fives by a fourth triangle, completing a diamond pattern in the middle of the square. Triangulating the diamond shape formed an even smaller square and gave further multiples of 60,70,80 and 90 and a tiny circle in the middle of everything denoted one hundred.

"It really works Erdi. I can keep a record of what we do. I've shown some of the people I deal with. They use it now and it makes everything so much easier."

Erdi drew the shapes in the dust with a stick. "What if the amounts aren't exactly these convenient two lots of five. What if it's a triangle in the square plus one full hand and a finger?"

She showed him on the piece of wood. "You just draw the diamond in the square plus the little gate shape I showed and then add one more vertical line and so on."

"So the diamond in the square plus two would look like this," he scratched the shapes, "and the amount short of one more full triangle would be," He drew the gate pattern then scraped four more verticals.

"That's it Erdi. The thing is, after a bit you don't have to work the figure out, you sort of get used to the shapes."

So we move forward to the time, when once again, the Fire Feast was close upon them, but first as always came the Day of Offering. Talk, as everyone gathered by the pool, was about how the value of bronze had soared. It had gone beyond any had previously thought imaginable, driven mainly by the scarcity of tin. There had been tales of boats sailing from far off shores bearing merchants prepared to barter goods of untold value in order to sail home with the magic ingots. The frenzy to procure the metal made it almost impossible for local chieftains to compete. Those controlling its source had become a byword for wealth, 'As rich as a Tin-King.'

It was a gusting, bitter wind that morning when the chieftain's wagon rumbled to a stop by the lakeside. The fabric of the royal standard cracked like a whip and it took two men at arms to hold it to as near vertical as they could manage. Dried leaves blown from hollows scudded past and cloaks required holding tight lest when billowing full, they caused the wearer to stagger off balance. Into this wild day emerged the frail chieftain to be furnished with his regalia. A sudden flurry, causing him to totter backwards, brought a gasp from all, but the courtiers leaping to his aid, managed to hold him erect while they adorned him in his finery. The crowning glory, the bronze helmet, was held aloft, poised ready. As if seizing its last possible chance, a willful gust swirled a snaking pattern across the lake and deftly whisked his complete head of hair off leaving him vainly fingering for it, on his bald pate.

"Zak shot his hair off," piped a lone voice.

The collective gasp of surprise and looks of disbelief, preceded the whole crowd dissolving into laughter, their helplessness, worsened by the shock of all realizing their once mighty chieftain was now naught but a little bald man and the fact that they shouldn't have found it so funny.

Two men at arms were ordered into the throng. This stifled the laughter, as did the sight of Mardi being manhandled out from amongst them and on Prince Gardarm's instructions, marched back to the fort, his feet hardly touching the ground. Erdi and family were ordered to remain. Only at the end of the ceremony could they follow and learn his fate. The majority wished him well, expecting the comical young fellow to be given a severe reprimand and an order to give humble apologies, but nothing more. They hadn't had a good laugh like that in many a day, but within Erdi, there crept a feeling of extreme unease.

The family was ordered to wait outside the Great Hall. There was a degree of shelter in the lee of the building, but the cold wind whipping at exposed flesh, bit like sharp tweezers on earlobes and soon they were visibly shaking. Finally the big door groaned open and they were admitted. Men at arms stood stiff to attention around the room. A fire crackled in the central hearth and their eyes were drawn to the far side as a rattle and creak let in a grey shaft of light. Looking grim and formidable in their full regalia, Prince Gardarm, the Seer, and court advisors swept in to take their places on the far side of a long trestle table.

Mardi was led in and then abandoned by his guards to bow and stand alone before them. "You know why you're here?" demanded the prince.

Mardi said, "I am truly sorry Your Highness. The words just came out before I could stop them."

"For insulting the chieftain, my father, I could have you whipped. Whipped so hard and for so long you could die from the pain of it. I could throw you in with the dogs. They would make short work of you. I could have you stripped and flung in the prison. I doubt you'd see the night through."

The family was petrified and Erdi realized his instinct had been right. No sane person would have threatened a punishment this severe for what in fact had been, no more than a simple jest. Yes, he couldn't have picked a worse person to insult and couldn't have chosen a worse time to do it, but not even the chieftain himself would have thought it warranted any more than a sharp lesson in manners and respect.

Add Gardarm into the scheme of things, however, a man still smarting from his humiliation down on the Arrow Field and you had a recipe for a judgement that defied all reason. Erdi felt the grip of doom slowly clenching their future and felt helpless in the face of what he sensed was an impending disaster.

"Not only did you insult my father, your words were a vile blasphemy uttered at a consecrated shrine on the most hallowed day of the year. Think yourself lucky a lady's soft heart and dulcet tones have influenced my father."

Was there hope? Erdi's instinct told him, it was nothing more than a brief reprieve. Merely a twist in the cruel game the spirits were playing with them. He waited for Gardarm's pronouncement. "You are to be enslaved here in the fortress and given a daily round of demeaning duties until the eve of the Spring Fair. Following that, your case will be reviewed. Now what have you to say for yourself, slave?"

All waited nervously. The sentence had been severe, but not as bad as Erdi had feared. He stared at his brother willing him not to blurt out anything contentious.

"I know things," he said.

Fists clenched tight, Erdi groaned.

"We all know things slave. What exactly do you know?"

Vanya rushed forward and giving her brother a shake said. "I'm sorry Your Highness he says the strangest things at times."

"Let him continue. What things?"

Vanya bowed, daring to approach further. "May I help, Your Highness? He needs but a glimpse of something to be able to remember and draw every detail." She was petrified, breathless and her eyes darted around for inspiration.

"Would you let him show you? He'll need charcoal and board to draw on. Can I ask him to approach, Your Highness?"

The prince wanted none of this nonsense, but with the request coming from a young lady, he eventually nodded and the requested implements, were furnished. "Would it be possible for my brother to have full view of the tusk necklace worn by our most respected holy man, Your Highness?" She hoped and prayed the diversion would work. Her heart was pumping and her hands shook.

The Seer pulled back his cloak and taking off the necklace laid it on the boarding in front of him.

Mardi glanced at it and Vanya asked for it to be immediately hidden again.

Mardi picked up the tally board and sketched what he'd seen. The necklace was placed above the drawing for comparison. It matched exactly, not only the correct number of tusks, but their exact lengths, curves and locations.

"Well that **is** a clever trick," said the prince with undisguised sarcasm, "a clever trick indeed. However, it has no bearing on the case. Does he think an ability to draw, licenses him to insult my father?"

Here the Seer added his observation. "Your Highness, if you would please allow me, I don't think that was what he had in mind when he said he knew things. I am right aren't I Mardikun. Tell me, what other things do you know? Come on Mardi, you know my calling compels me to help the people, I the Seer, won't hurt you."

"No Mardi!" shouted Erdi.

"Ah! The sling man himself. I wondered when you'd make a noose for yourself. Step forward!" demanded Prince Gardarm in triumph.

Erdi did so and squeezed his brother's arm hoping it conveyed, 'Shut up! Say nothing more.'

"What else do you know Mardikun?" The Seer's mellifluous tone masked the lethal trap. "Tell us Mardi."

"The moon will darken."

A surge of fear lancing through Erdi's body, told him his senses had been right. They were perched on a precipice, requiring just one more indiscretion to send them crashing to their doom. What was happening had surely been preordained and the inevitability sent a blizzard of panic around his brain. He felt as if floating outside reality, watching a nightmare unfolding, but helpless to stop it.

"Yes we know sometimes the moon darkens, Mardi. But when? Surely you can't be saying you have such knowledge."

Picking up the tally board again, Mardi rapidly sketched a pattern.

"And what is that meant to indicate?" sneered the prince.

"It means nothing Your Highness. It's just scribble," said Vanya in a petrified whisper.

Gardarm slammed his fist on the boarding making the tally board jump and roared, "Tell me, or you will all hang this very day."

"It means fifteen full hands of nights from now. (75) That is when a full moon will darken." Distraught at having to reveal this, Vanya hung on to Erdi for support, her face buried in his chest. Her words, although barely audible, had caused astonishment.

The prince summoned the Seer to join him and their muttered, agitated discussion could be heard, coming from the depths of the hall. Time crawled as all awaited the outcome.

On finally returning Gardarm, drawing himself fully erect, boomed down at Mardi, "For you to have wisdom of this nature is exceptional and possession of it can have but two possibilities. Firstly, you are a Seer yourself," laughing, he looked either side for support and sickeningly, they all duly obliged. He continued, "But the more likely reason is, you are in league with the purveyors of evil. If your prediction is wrong, you will be set free earlier than stated, on the night of the supposed moon darkening, but your family's land holdings and fishing rights will pass to your neighbours - those loyal subjects who have put my slaves to work. From that point on, you and your family will be given three days to leave our tribal lands. If not beyond our borders by the time allotted, all will be at liberty to hunt you down like beasts of the forest."

He waited for this catastrophe to sink in, before relishing, "If, however, you happen to be right in your prediction," he paused enjoying the suspense, "you will receive the full punishment due to those who consort with evil. ----You will be hung by the neck until your legs have ceased their death dance, until your fingers have ceased their vain effort to claw at the rope strangling you, until all evil has flown from your body. Your cleansed carcass will then be cut down and cast into the drear, cold black waters, to be received by the evil that lurks there. I must of course add," looking directly at Erdi, "for contempt of court, attempting to prevent revelation of your association with forces of darkness, your brother Erdikun will join you in slavery until the night previously specified." He smiled in that sickening way of his and with head aloft as if communing with the spirits, it wasn't hard to imagine him saying a hearty, "Thank you. I've waited a long time for this."

Chapter Nineteen

So just like that the sky had fallen in on their lives. Needless to say, none of the family attended the Fire Feast that year and yet their plight was in actual fact, talk of the fair. Early in the time of the new sun, a very worried Gwendolin risked her father's ire, risked attack from whatever lurked in the woods and risked being turned away by Erdi's family, in order to visit and obtain clarification of events. She was warmly welcomed and Mara, with now at last being face to face with the girl, couldn't imagine her as anything other than a daughter-in-law. All thoughts of fixed marriages and dowries had been blown away by recent circumstances. It seemed Erdi had found himself a young lady with a golden heart and at that moment in time, such a simple blessing counted for everything. Yanker was asked to escort her home. He tried to comfort, promising he'd do all in his power to have his cousins released. Soothing words, but in reality, what could he do?

Erdi was severely worried for his brother in the short term, never mind the terror of the death sentence he was under. Their daily work of latrine cleaning, hauling water and the toil of mucking out pigsties and stables was arduous and soul destroying and Mardi hadn't his brother's strength and stamina to cope. Also, being constantly cold, soaked and stinking and forced to struggle on through each day whether wind, rain or snow, they were likely candidates for a fever. Erdi was certain Gardarm relished the thought of them simply being worked to death. He struggled in the attempt to lift his own spirits, let alone his brother's. Mardi looked that distraught at knowing his indiscretion had brought either a death sentence or family ruin, Erdi was petrified he might lose all will to live completely. Each day he attempted to impress upon him: it was not his fault; malign forces had been at work; he was not to blame himself; he must keep believing.

For reasons he couldn't explain an inner voice told him, that against all common sense, against everything stacked against them, they would both come through this somehow. There had to be an answer. He had to keep Mardi's spirit and will to continue, alive until this was found. His determination was bolstered by remembering Trader's advice: never stop believing; keep doing the right things until such time the spirits decide to favour once more; then eventually things will come right of their own accord. When on water duties, with every visit to the stream to refill the skins on the cart, he prayed for the benign forces therein to save them.

Of course, when time allowed, Blade couldn't resist the temptation to gloat and taunt, "Our dad says you've had this coming for a long time. Look at the state of you both! Your family's not so great now is it!" Dangling a length of looped twine in front of Mardi, never failed to send him into rapturous laughter. He seemed oblivious to the time-honored belief, that hidden forces were keenly watching for such smug elation, for whether it be from great or small, good or bad, they were ready to dash low the self-satisfied with impartiality and relish.

Back at home the eel stealers and their father came calling on a mission to examine what was soon to be theirs. They felt compelled to ensure, considering the circumstances, standards hadn't been let slip. It was after all, soon to be their property and so an inspection of it ought to be theirs by right. Surely the present owners would understand, the weight of responsibility they were under and not have reason to take offence. The three, especially the sons, looked extremely full of themselves until Penda asked, "Tell me something? How exactly do you expect to get off my property?" He had blocked their way stave in hand and Dowid had sidled up to stand beside him similarly armed. When they launched into attack, the three had no choice other than to run from the flailing onslaught yelping as whirring slingshot added even greater vitality to their departure. They were driven deep into the woods, bloodied and forced to go the long way home and didn't come calling again.

Back up at the fortress it was brought to Prince Gardarm's attention that Erdi, for some reason, had a certain calming influence on the slave they still referred to as the 'wild man' and so suddenly their daily routine was changed. The brothers were led into a fenced off area of the fort's enclosure to spend each day smashing rocks. These weren't just any rocks, but those with green flecks, mined from southern scarp slope of a ridge overlooking the Nwy river. This was then loaded into a furnace to extract the copper. Most of the that used for smelting into bronze arrived in refined form, having been sailed down the Dwy, but when another pay-dirt seam was struck, ore from the local Ogof mine provided a valuable supply. It was whilst doing this work, that a bond struck from having been thrown into the same circumstances, developed into a friendship between Erdi and the man Vanya had referred to as Wolfy. He had picked up a rough understanding of their language, but Erdi took the trouble to teach him more. He was rewarded with tales from the man's homeland across the water, how he'd been trained as a warrior, the cattle-raids he had been on, the love of his life he'd been separated from and how he'd been betrayed and sold into slavery. He toiled every day chained to his work surface, a rock. It took two to move the rock and two to stand over him spears held ready while the rock movers relocated him. The only time unfettered was in his wooden cell at night, The brothers had first been forced to sleep, tied up like dogs in the straw and muck of the cow byre, but when they'd eventually been put into a cell of their own, close enough to communicate with the wild man, they were able to share with him their anger, frustration and dreams of hope for the future.

One day smashing rocks as usual, Wolf, as they both called him, asked Erdi to recall something that had happened at the fair the day after he'd arrived to be sold. He said he hadn't been able to understand how such laughter and tears could have gone together in the same conversation.

Erdi remembering the time in question, told him of the sad suicide and also what the surviving brother had said that day. He told Wolf that when he'd asked the reason for taking such tragic action his friend had told him the words his brother had uttered the day before he'd thrown himself of the cliff. The poor, sad youth had simply said, 'he was tired of having to wipe his backside every morning,'

Wolf gave a look of disbelief, then a laugh from deep within turned into such shoulder shaking, chain rattling convulsions Erdi thought he might die from lack of breath. He concluded that this reaction hadn't been sparked by the hilarity of what he'd said, but was more a matter of it having somehow released an obstruction - tension locked inside the man since the day of his enslavement.

Being as close to bronze smelting as they now were, it was only natural that Mardi should take a keen interest. Initially the guardians of the knowledge were reticent to have him anywhere near them, but as he was either to be not much longer for this world or more likely, forced from the territory a pauper, they couldn't see any harm in it. From the very start he looked to the job born. They were amazed at how quickly he picked up the basic skills and then how quickly he exhibited mastery of the finer arts. They called him their little magician.

He learnt to carve intricate shapes from wax and encase them with clay. Baking the clay mould melted the wax leaving a void that liquid bronze could be poured into. One effort turned out particularly well and he was shown the pin fixing technique to complete it. The brooch of a mythical river beast in swirling rapids was polished until it gleamed.

One day Prince Gardarm gave them an unexpected visit proudly swaggering into view with his step-mother, the beautiful Lady Rhosyn on his arm. Her hair was prettily pinned up and walking light of step, she looked not that much older than her escort. On catching sight of Mardi working by the smelting oven, he turned purple with rage. Lady Rhosyn's reaction to the outburst was velvet-soft, simply disengaging her arm from his.

The two foundry workers, on being asked to explain why a slave was working with them, looked literally terrified. Then taking a deep breath Gardarm turned the full might of his wrath on Mardi.

The young man simply blinked, fished inside his shirt and as ingenuous as ever held out the piece of jewellery and said, "A pretty brooch for a pretty lady."

Lady Rhosyn thought it exquisite, the young man charming and by the time Gardarm had the men hauled up before his father she had interceded on their behalf. A mild rebuke was given and they were ordered back to work. Mardi's apprenticeship continued and the old chieftain gave quiet consideration to the impossible situation his son had put the young man and his family in.

When not smashing rocks Erdi was put back on water supply and latrine duties, during the course of which he was able to witness comings and goings at the fort. Taking note of merchants, locals, armed men and whoever else happened to be passing, helped alleviate the bitter anger and frustration locked up inside. One afternoon four mounted warriors entered leading two pack horses and from their casual air Erdi surmised this not to be their first visit. Their mode of dress suggested they were from foreign parts and yet one could obviously speak their language, for Erdi saw him and Prince Gardarm in deep discussion some time later.

Owing to the fact he and his brother had taken on their demeaning duties with hardly a word of complaint, they were often offered words of sympathy and encouragement by a few who not only gave them a sneaking regard, but if the opportunity allowed, dared to converse with them. From such a contact was gleaned the information, the four men were almost certainly Tinners from the distant kingdom in the southwest. Heavy leather satchels had been seen, hauled from their pack animals, but what sort of transaction had then taken place, remained entirely open to conjecture. The most likely commodity that warranted journeying all that way to trade it was of course, tin. But tin in exchange for what?

It was shortly after this little incident, talk of the planned raid reached Erdi's ears. It was not the time of year for cattle raiding and yet with spring not even remotely in sight, the bustle of activity in the fort made it obvious, the plan persisted. All was being made ready for a strike at a supposedly soft target to the south.

'Fourteen brave men and Blade,' was how Yanker later described the would-be marauders, adding, 'led by a maniac.'

The jaunty little force, led by Prince Gardarm, set off with an unsettling degree of bravado and were gone a mere six days, to return in the dead of night, not like heroes, but fugitives. The following morning observers were shocked at how cowed the men seemed, having no trace of their previous vainglory and in fact no trace of spoils of war. One of their number had been captured in battle and presumed dead and those returning looked spent and hollow eyed. All except Blade, who if rumour was true, hollow looking or not, had only the one eye left. He was judged lucky to still be alive. As much as Erdi detested him for recent goading of his brother he wouldn't have wished this upon him. But there again, without requesting it, it had happened and so Erdi offered a quiet prayer of thanks to the spirits responsible.

Two days later Delt appeared at the fort. Erdi had never seen him astride a horse before and from the look of it, his mount had been pressed to gallop the whole way. With message delivered and surprising adroitness, he wheeled his mount around and set off at pace towards the gate. Erdi, waving, managed to slow him, but Delt's usual air of calm had vanished. He shouted, "No Erdi. The Bleddi are coming. We've got to move everything. Tell your people!" He left at full gallop and the gates were swung shut behind him. The two guards having slid the beam across, turned on Erdi driving him away. He knew the pair, each from a large family, who having viewed them as the least gifted as regards tilling the land and thus surplus to requirements, had somehow managed to have them enrolled into Gardarm's service. Now circumstances allowed these dolts to treat him, natural heir to his father's domain, as if he were nothing more than a stray dog.

He and Mardi were now put on fulltime water duties. Under guard they spent the day filling the skins for carts to transport the precious cargo up to the fort. With relief, Erdi noticed the fortress beacon had been lit and was being answered by beacons on all surrounding hills. His family would see this, put their stock into hiding and take refuge in the fort.

Across the valley, cattle, sheep and horses were being driven north to be hidden in emergency corrals in the forest. There was not enough water or in fact room for them in the fort.

That night he and Mardi forced their weary legs back up the hill, source of the clamour they'd heard, from the day's incessant activity. Inside the fort, the scene was frenetic, with the whole circuit of the palisade swarming with those reinforcing it, slingshot was being placed to lie in piles atop the fighting step, food was cooking ready to sustain the besieged and stakes were being prepared, ready to drive in and slow any direct assault on the fortress gates. The largest of these faced east and a smaller entry gave access to the west. It was a scene of sweat, smoke, hammering and barely controlled panic.

The following morning, worried looking families straggled in with whatever food they could carry. Erdi's family was amongst them, but Dommed had been left behind to mind their livestock, secreted in the forest. Prince Aram was busy locating the refugees, losing patience as some got his instructions wrong or just stood there dithering in the way of everybody.

Erdi and Mardi were again on water duty. Their guard seemed to gain little comfort from being told he would be given ample warning of any imminent attack and took it out on the brothers for being the reason his life was at risk. Malicious flicks of the whip set them in motion as he followed aboard the cart. At least they were untethered, being hardly likely to attempt an escape with their family now ensconced and available as hostages and the enemy almost upon them. Erdi politely asked the man if he knew why their wild western neighbours had suddenly taken the notion to attack, but on receiving a stinging whipcrack in reply, decided from that point on he'd remain silent.

That evening all seemed calmer. The last of the stakes having been hammered in on the path, forced the brothers to scramble round and haul themselves up the steep incline for readmission through the West Gate. This ascent was too severe and craggy for the cart which returned going the long way round, entering by way of the East Gate.

The outriders, later thundering back through the portal, with terror on their faces, shouting the Skreela were almost upon them, hardly had a calming influence on those seeking their protection. Some in fact, looked white with shock. The final stakes, preventing further access, were hammered home, the gates were swung shut and bar slid across. Then they all waited. A baby cried and others around the camp took up the chorus.

Erdi was now at an extremely frustrating disadvantage, for with no prisoners allowed up on the palisade, he was unable to witness the enemy's approach. He could hear the advance, however, initially sounding more like a mass drive of stock to market, with sheep bleating and cattle lowing, obviously the gains so far on the way to battle. He was told their number looked to be well over a hundred fighting men and if including camp followers, double that. Perhaps nothing would happen that night.

He was wrong. A loud howling was followed by a deep throaty response and thunder of weapons on shields. With each repetition, Erdi could gauge the extent of their advance. Although a blood curdling sound, Wolf sat looking completely unmoved, saying, "Fire arrows next."

Almost as if he'd ordered it, they arrived in showers over the palisade. Their flames guttering in flight looked harmless until landing on thatch, where an initial ominous crackle was followed by a roaring blaze sending thick, blinding smoke everywhere. The brothers were instructed to join those already on ladders raking the little infernos to the ground where the women could beat and stamp the life out of them.

Then came the heads. The whole attack had probably just been a show of strength, a sample of what was to follow, a tasty morsel for the inmates to sleep on and of course to get the Bleddi close enough to sling the heads over the wall. One of them was Patch's.

That seemed to be it for the day apart from the sound of their visitors making merry and feasting. There were still howled threats and the firing of the odd stray arrow, but no-one now expected an attack until dawn.

A cold uncomfortable night was followed by a cold grey miserable morning. Huddled folk with worried faces tried to coax warmth back into their limbs. Erdi was told to patrol the camp with basket and blade-shovel to scoop up what had been exuded during the night. The stinking loads, full to the brim, were put by the East Gate ready for their contents to be dropped from atop the palisade on to the unwanted visitors. Mardi had been given the job of covering smeared remnants of offending patches with straw.

Erdi managed to snatch a few moments to ask Yanker, if time allowed, could he keep them informed? The brothers then returned as ordered, to where Wolf was chained and all three sat and awaited their fate.

More fire arrows made their pretty arc and soon the camp was in smoking chaos once more. The main clamour of battle, resounded from over by the East Gate. There were screams, cries, clash of metal and urgent orders bellowed. The Seer and his followers, from up on their platform, screeched madly for divine help and howled down curses on the foe.

Suddenly Yanker, running, bent low to avoid the smoke billowing from the houses, said with eyes streaming, "You'd better come and help. They're almost in on us, smelling like dungheaps and mad as wasps about it. I've been sent to find Aram."

"We've been ordered to stay here," Erdi replied.

"Forget orders Erdi. You're needed!"

"Ask him how many in attack?" Wolf didn't ask Yanker directly knowing that he'd probably not understand his strange accent.

"He says at least six hands." (*30*)

"Then it's just a feint. Tell him to look to the West Gate." Erdi passed on the message for Yanker to relay to Aram.

Then Wolf said, with at last a hint of urgency, "Now Erdi, head there yourself and grab all the help you can. Hurry my friend I don't wish to sit here as a target for spearing practice."

He and Mardi ran to where their family had last been sighted. Looking severely shaken, Dowid and Luda were there, having returned to re-arm and slake thirsts before rejoining the fray. When told of the more urgent danger likely at the West Gate, all armed with spear and sling, ran across the camp leaping over debris and ducking low under burning

278

posts thrown askew by the intensity of the infernos. Erdi shouting to a warrior, urgently making his way up to the fighting step, warned, 'keep low, an attack could be imminent.' The man turned, peered down, saw who it was and was in the middle of shouting, Erdi had no right to be there, when his face froze in shock. He'd felt the draught from the salvo aimed at his head. Following a quick look through a viewing slit, he waved frantically, summoning them all up for action. Ammunition had been strategically placed and although, initially only five in number, with well-aimed slingshot, they managed to keep heads low. Thankfully, the bristling row of stakes had done their work, preventing a massed storming. They were joined by others running along the fighting step and fire was concentrated on the Bleddi warriors desperately wrenching at the stakes to force an opening. When two were worked free, warriors poured through the gap and under the cover of shields, two assault squads, carrying siege ladders made it to the palisade.

By the time Aram arrived, heading the relief force, he was greeted by the splendid sight of Erdi and Luda thrashing and spearing to drive the attackers down rung by rung. The second ladder had been flung aside and the assailants sent tumbling down the hill. The difficulty of the terrain plus extra numbers swarming up on to the fighting step, forced the raiders into a retreat and Prince Aram was amused by the sight of one bloodied warrior, staring up at Luda with a look of utter disbelief. The stone she had been swinging to wing in his direction, had been removed from its sling and lobbed to land at his feet.

By mid-morning all attacks had been beaten off, giving the defenders time to quench thirsts, attend to the wounded and drag away the dead.

Prince Aram in all fairness gave credit where due and seemed almost embarrassed at the plight the brothers and their family were in. It prompted Erdi to suggest, it might shed a little light on matters, if Yanker, for some strange reason favoured by Aram, approached the prince, in the hope of teasing out the motive for the surprise attack. The Bleddi were a ferocious tribe to be sure, but it made no sense them risking loss of life attacking a well defended fortress for no apparent reason. Also attacking at such an unfavorable time of year hinted that motive must have been extremely important.

Yanker reported back, it was obvious the prince knew the answer, but unfortunately for them, hadn't felt obliged to divulge it, especially not to naught but a low born farm boy. He still had a certain sway over Aram, however and had at last begun to sense an inkling why. It was nothing tangible, but he noticed a strange change come over the prince on the few occasions they'd briefly been alone together. So at the very next opportunity, emboldening himself, he gained the prince's attention and with a winning smile passed on the knowledge that Erdi was probably the only one amongst them able to speak the Skreela language. If circumstances required, he could be sent down under a branch of peace, to open up a line of communication with their attackers. The prince did not dismiss the idea.

There came a change of tactic at this point. The Bleddi force was again split, though not for attack but for siege. Any route to water was blocked. On the third day the besieged were taunted by the sight of their attackers offering up water skins in mock salute before pouring the contents over themselves. Cooking fires raged and they contented themselves feasting and waiting.

On the seventh morning Erdi was summoned. Things had become that desperate the two princes wrangled openly, not caring who heard. Prince Gardarm argued, their meager remaining water resources should be reserved for exclusive use of nobility, warriors and men of fighting age. He was vehement in his insistence that women, children, the aged and all others not necessary for defence should be ejected to throw themselves on the mercy of the Skreela. There was of course the option of the defenders pouring down the hill in attack thus lifting the siege, but recent dealings with the enemy had persuaded Gardarm this was probably not a wise move. So the truth was now out. The lie had been spread that the recent cattle raid had been to the south. But the fool had attacked the Bleddi to the west and now all were reaping the benefit. Aram for his part argued, he wasn't prepared to see loyal subjects, people of his own tribe, having sought their protection, being ejected to die of thirst and starvation beneath their walls. He felt certain the Skreela would prevent clear passage, for the horror of watching their own people slowly dying, would increase the pressure on the defenders to capitulate. He championed the idea of sending a man amongst them to try negotiate a deal.

Gardarm went into a foot stamping, pot smashing fury when the old chieftain came down on the side of common sense and Erdi, armed with nothing more than a rowan branch was ordered to approach the enemy. While waiting to be thus armed, he stood communing with the spirits, praying his would not be the next head to be lobbed over the fortress wall.

Branches of the revered rowan and oak had been used to bedeck the interior of the Great Hall at the time of the Harvest Feast and then in mid-winter had come the time for holly and mistletoe. Having served their purpose, these adornments had been taken down and tossed over the palisade wall and now lay in the ditch beyond. A man was sent on a mission of retrieval.

The rowan branches, a symbol of peace, were presented and Erdi, eying them dubiously, asked Prince Aram, "Excuse my impertinence, Your Highness. You and I know these to be rowan branches, but how is the enemy supposed to know?" He held up the bare twigs.

"I suggest you employ your powers of persuasion."

Erdi, shaking inside, started out on the walk that could well have been his last. As he approached, with quivering branches held aloft and free hand spread open to show absence of weaponry, he heard "One, two, three," shouted in unison followed by a roar and female screeching.

It happened again and when close he witnessed a surreal sight. Mad Aggie was being tossed aloft by way of sheeting made from sewn deerskin. She loved it, maniacally kicking her legs in the air and it appeared the men shared her delight.

A warrior who recognized Erdi from the dealings done at Trader's asked his chieftain's permission to approach, and with this granted he drew his sword and met Erdi on the track to ask him his business. This was explained and from then on, the man acted as go-between. Erdi was not allowed direct communication with the chieftain who, before any other business, insisted on knowing why such a stripling had had the temerity to approach their camp brandishing a bunch of twigs? Was it meant as an insult? Erdi tried to explain it had not been his idea, but one forced upon him. They were rowan branches, considered by his people to be a sign of peace. The twigs were tentatively reoffered, until the look on the chieftain's face felled the notion like an axe chop.

So, with furrowed brow and considerable concern, Erdi awaited the outcome. The atmosphere was tense--- cold sweat trickled down his back and as he watched his fate being debated, the chieftain's woad ringed eyes never left him. It was not certain at this point whether it would be Erdi, full in body, returning to the fort or just his head.

Just then, a huge dog that had been sprawled out in front of his master sensed something it recognized. A large shaggy head popped up, then drawing itself to full height and with tail wagging furiously, the hound whimpered and strained at its leash to reach Erdi.

"How does the creature know this man?" the chieftain demanded.

After conferring the warrior replied, "The man trained him my Lord."

The old warrior's face cracked into a smile and he watched with enthusiasm as his dog was led forward for a reunion.

There was huge merriment at the sight of the animal, front paws on Erdi's chest, almost knocking him backwards in the effort to lick his face. It was as if the faithful hound had conferred on him honorary membership of the tribe. Not only was he beckoned to approach the chieftain and his officers, he now at last heard the truth.

What unfolded was a strange tale. The recent unprovoked raid into Bleddi territory had not been for cattle. Four young women had been stolen and the Bleddi were not leaving until they had them back. The man they'd captured in battle would be exchanged as part of the deal and there was the small matter of twenty extra cattle, they demanded, for having been put to this much trouble.

Seemed reasonable enough on the face of it. Gaddarm threw such fury at Erdi, one would have thought it had been his idea. Once calming slightly, he ordered him return with the message, 'they'd think about it.'

Erdi replied, "Permission to speak Your Highness?"

It was reluctantly given.

"The Bleddi chieftain, I'm afraid, expected you to say exactly that and has given until morning for the decision to be made." A back handed slap was the reward for his endeavors.

The wrangling that night, Erdi was not a party to, but by the morning he was instructed to go down once again, twig-less this time, to request safe passage to enable drovers to collect the requested twenty head of cattle. About middle day four frightened, but very pleasant looking young ladies blinked in the first daylight they had seen since arrival at the fort. Thankfully, it seemed they'd not been harmed or molested. The besieged families stared at them as if they had just grown straight from the ground.

Erdi accompanied them down to their people. There was much rejoicing and their bound captive, as agreed, was bundled forward. Bruising on his face gave evidence he'd not had an easy time of it, but at least he was still alive. Erdi was turning to accompany him back up to the fort when a familiar screech caused him to stop. Mad Aggie, skirt hitched up, bodice swinging, ran to waft half clenched fingers under his nose. His instant recoil and bout of coughing, brought a cheer from the Bleddi warriors. Much encouraged, Aggie grabbed and squeezed him as if she'd won Erdi as a prize at the Summer Fair and finally standing on tiptoe, she landed a huge sloppy kiss on his lips. The more the men roared the more she beamed. His erstwhile go-between yelled in his ear, "Isn't she marvellous?"

Erdi nodded and shouted above the noise, "Yes. I must admit, she fair took my breath away." Relieved he'd not been given the milk treatment and happy now Aggie obviously had no shortage of comfort, he made his way back up to the fort feeling as if he'd dreamt the whole episode. The warrior, now free from his bonds walked on ahead, not wanting to be seen in association with a latrine-cleaning farm boy. He now carried a huge burden. Not only shame at having needed such help, but shame that one so low born had succeeded where his fellow warriors had failed. He would make the serious avowal, "Death would have been preferable."

The Bleddi departed taking their dead, their wounded and their booty with them. The faint melody of their marching song could still be heard as they disappeared back into hill country.

The scene within the fort, was one of stark contrast. Burnt remnants were being loaded up for dumping beyond the palisade, and families ghosting around, gathered belongings for leaving. They were a people in a state of deep shock and departure was slowed to a crawl by the injured. The dead, still uncorrupted thanks to the cool weather, were carried out on litters. The spirits had been kind to Erdi's family, all had survived. Approaching to bid a sad farewell, the brothers found them over by the East Gate and Erdi was a little surprised at hearing Luda humming the Bleddi marching song. He went to embrace his parents, but had been spotted by Prince Gardarm, whose rasped order had him and Mardi manhandled away and beaten by the very man Erdi he'd rescued. His jeering shouts and the sickening crack of wood on bone could still be heard resounding when sight of them was lost.

Penda, Dowid and Yanker had watched with murder in their hearts, the women had watched through tears. Erdi and Mardi were put back on water supply duties.

In the days that followed, Prince Aram took it upon himself to lead a small troop of soldiers on a tour of the valley. He thanked all for their bravery and commiserated with family losses. When hearing him give special commendation to Dowid and Luda for their part in defending the West Gate, Dowid took the chance to remind him that Erdi along with his younger brother had been equally courageous.

The prince looking him in the eye said, "I am well aware of that." He went to say more but paused, realising his rank forbade such familiarity, unless of course--- His thoughts turned to a certain young man.

Meanwhile, don't forget, the time of the full moon was relentlessly approaching.

Fortunately the brothers were left little time to dwell on the fact. Once the problem of water shortage in the fort had been addressed, they were put to work helping the squads still clearing up. The warrior Erdi had helped free, occasionally found time to show gratitude by gifting him the filthiest of tasks as if pleasure derived from his victim's misery helped erase his sense of shame. Other warriors showed solidarity by making it their business to trip or push the victim into the mire he was trying to clean up, thus helping the offended warrior's painful ascent back into the brotherhood.

Then picking their way through this scene of misery and mess, emitting an air of nonchalance and levity, came the four Tinners. They led their mounts up to the Great Hall. All disappeared within and weren't seen to re-emerge until early evening, by which time, looks of insouciance had been replaced by dark scowls. Grimly mounting their ponies, they departed at an uncalled-for pace.

Not long after, Erdi caught sight of a figure in the shadows and from the way it moved he thought it must be Blade. If it was truly him, it was almost as if something had shrunk him to half his former size. Erdi calling out, saw the face turning towards him in the moonlight was wearing an eye patch.

Chapter Twenty

As the days progressed and the moon waxed further, Erdi asked his brother if anything could be done to alter their impending fate.

Mardi replied, "There's nothing I can do. It happens of its own accord."

The tension became unbearable and Erdi noticed, even Prince Aram had a decidedly grim look. He had been summoned into his presence, where he was given thanks for the bravery shown at the West Gate, a commendation regarding his diplomatic dealings with the enemy and was told, Lady Rhosyn had asked, in fact entreated, 'could anything be done to alter the darkening of the moon?' Erdi gave the same answer his brother had given.

Aram then informed him of Yanker's visit. His cousin had come specifically to plead with him to intervene in some way. Try to somehow persuade the chieftain to give a stay of execution. Aram had promised to do all in his power, but this was limited, with his brother having the loyalty of the majority of the fighting force. Erdi had heard the rumours. Gardarm had bought loyalty with bronze and promises, to the point that even the chieftain himself now feared him. Mardi's fate therefore looked sealed. If Gardarm, backed by his troops, demanded a hanging there wasn't much to stop him getting his wish.

"You might be able to help indirectly, Your Highness."

Aram eyed the young man.

"Where will we be assembled whilst witnessing the darkening?"

"Right here in the fort I presume. Why?"

"I have an idea. Could you persuade your father to have it witnessed down on the Arrow Field?"

"Yes I don't see why not. I can try. Can't see what difference it will make, mind you."

"And could the people be informed of the fact?"

"Yes I can arrange that. My brother hasn't bought support of all the troops. There are enough loyal to me to carry this out, but what difference will it make?"

"We could make an appeal for the people to intervene. It might prove a vain effort, but it's the only thing I can think of. We have to try something, Your Highness." As he was leaving the prince said, "You can thank your cousin for this meeting. He's a charming young man."

Erdi thanked the prince and in his cell that night prayed to the spirits for help like he'd never prayed before. Could they gift them a cloudy night?

On the 75th night, the time of the supposed darkening, the brothers were taken down to the Arrow Field. Gardarm had been vehemently opposed to this, but with much persuasion and beguiling feminine input from Lady Rhosyn, the old chieftain had granted Aram his wish. The prince had used the logic, the people needed to be witness to a fair outcome. If judgement and sentence were carried out within the fort, they could be brewing up trouble for themselves, especially considering pent-up hostility following the recent Skreela disaster.

Fair outcome? Poor Mardi was visibly shaking. Gardarm had thought it a dramatic touch, which humoured him greatly, to hang a noose around his neck.

"Don't let them throw me in the cold dark waters, Erdi," he pleaded. Erdi promised, not letting his brother see his tears.

Down on the Arrow Field a huge throng awaited.

"Nothing like a good hanging to draw a crowd," muttered Trader. Penda's family were there of course. Vanya, Talia and Luda had tears streaming, but Mara stood fists clenched, white with fury.

Blade's father was there as expected, but his mood of jocularity suddenly clamped shut, the moment someone said they'd knife him if he so much as uttered another word.

The eel stealers had their little circle of support, all watching the sky keenly, waiting for the moon to bring the hoped for, unbelievable uplift to their fortunes.

All waited pallid in the moonlight. The spirits looking on must have thought what strange entanglements these humans weave themselves into. Would they help or just let things take their course? They could be perverse, vindictive or just plain arbitrary as the mood took them.

It was a chilly night to be out there, standing in the damp grass and it was quite amazing really that just one sentence uttered by a young peasant boy, "I know things." had them all assembled looking up at the full moon.

A loud groan accompanied the first hint of encroachment, followed by silence as a dark shadow began to edge across the moon. As the light dimmed a single wolf howl was chorused by all the packs of forests and hills. People fell to their knees, a woman fainted and all eyes turned to Mardi in wonder. 'How could he have predicted this?'

With a malignant glint, the Seer made an upward jerking motion in region of his neck, to which Gardarm nodded, 'Mardi would hang.'

The holy man called for everyone's attention, the eerie light and enormity of what was happening lending power to his words---- "For communing with the evil ones, Mardikun will be taken to the hanging tree for the prescribed sentence to be carried out."

The collective groan of horror was topped by piercing screams. Troops sent amongst the people, raining blows and threatening murder, reduced the hysteria to low wailing and inconsolable sobbing.

"It is done for your own good!" shouted Gardarm. "Ridding you of evil! How else could the boy have known the mysteries of the moon? Evil will spread through him to you! Devils in human form are the the bridges evil uses to enter our world!"

He turned inviting more from the Seer. "It is a sad thing we have to do this night, but do it we must. By dabbling in the secret knowledge, the boy has brought this upon himself. He obviously had no idea of the potency of the dark forces he was playing with. I should know, I have spent a lifetime battling evil. Saving the people from its malevolent power. His family should have known better. Should have put a stop to it. Surely they knew the dangers." Looking around, he smiled, "It makes no more sense than allowing a child to play with fire."

"Give the lad a slap then," shouted Trader. "He doesn't deserve to hang!"

At this point, Prince Aram intervened, telling all of the brothers' quick thinking and bravery, their anticipation of the attack on the vulnerable West Gate of the fortress. He called out, "Without regard for their own safety, they threw themselves into the breach to hold off the Bleddi attack, fighting against overwhelming odds until support arrived. Their actions saved the fort and all within. Even having been treated as slaves, the lowest of the low, they still risked their lives for us. Hasn't this youth, Mardikun been punished enough? Yes, he insulted my father, your chieftain? But hasn't he done enough to redeem himself. His ability to predict the workings of the moon should be looked upon as a gift, not a threat to our people. Such knowledge should offer us an advantage over our warlike neighbours. I feel you the people ought to be the judge of this. Is he a force for good or evil?" Turning to the old chieftain he said, "Now I appeal to you, my father and lord over all here, throw open the question. Ask the

290

people, should the brothers go free. Free to return to their families without further duress or threat of eviction?"

"He's been sentenced to hang and hang he will!" snarled Gardarm.

Surprisingly, at this point a female voice could be heard clearly chiming, "Now just one **moment!**" All eyes were on Lady Rhosyn who with calm authority, holding simmering anger in check, strode through the gloom, across to her stepson. There were gasps as a severe prod in the chest sent him into a backward step, "What gives you the right to carry out this sentence? It was only the fact your father was indisposed on the Day of Offering that you were actually allowed to hold court that day. Surely such a rare gift as this young man possesses should be cherished, not snuffed out."

The cowed look and shock, on the prince's face, as if memories of similar scoldings from his late mother had been stirred up, brought jeers and lusty cheers. These faltered and silence descended at the sight of a small fire flickering to life, mid height on the fort's embankment. The strengthening blaze lit a female befrocked in white, who bent, offering her hands to the fire, causing the flames to gutter and rise in intensity. Then with arms raised aloft she called out, "Mardikun is a force for good not evil. He is innocent of any wrongdoing. You the people must save him. You the people must decide."

As one, all were awestruck, silenced, many sinking down on one knee, gently thumping a fist against heart, before what they imagined to be a vision. Voices were then heard whispering, "It's Elsa." The woman revered as an Earth Mother had come to save Mardi.

Prince Aram bent down, requesting his wavering father's judgement. "Will you let the people decide?"

All attention was now on a frail old man squatting on his stool and breathing seemed to stop as they waited. He who had once been so mighty, now seemed to rule in name only. Was there still enough strength remaining to overrule his eldest son, or would he crumple and bow to Gardarm's wishes? All prayed there remained enough of his old spirit burning. Lady Rhosyn crouching attentively beside him, softly tucking his scarf tight against the cold night air, whispered in his ear. There came a collective sigh of relief as the old man waved his ascent.

Prince Gardarm, seeing things slipping from his control, took recourse to the only weapon remaining, fear. He shouted to the warriors, fist pumping the air, "Hang him! Hang him!" The support in unison from his troops, their guttural cries, foot stamping and shield hammering from out of the blackness, was spine chilling.

In reply came the haunting cry from the lady in white. "He must be saved." She pointed. "Look the moon has given her answer."

A loud gasp accompanied the sight. A bright crescent of light peeping from around the dark shadowing circle, began to broaden white, flowing with fronds to reveal emerging, the moon goddess, unfettered by darkness, full face restored to glory, victorious. Their chant of "Save him! Save him!" reached such deafening levels of hysteria it became obvious what they, the people had decided - and it wasn't support for the man who had so recently brought catastrophe into their lives.

Prince Gardarm stormed from the Arrow Field, the second time a loser. Suddenly turning, he pointed at Erdi shouting, his voice almost cracking into a shriek, "Don't think you've won yet!"

There was a sickening feel of inevitability in the words. Would he ever be free of this madman's hatred? What else had he planned? It reminded him of childhood battles, tantrums and spite, not the behaviour expected from a grown man. A man in power. A prince. Erdi sensed some mighty unknown force of change was pending. Whatever it was, its imminence seemed to be hovering over them and the man who should have been leading, the warrior Prince Gardarm, was losing control. His actions would likely be ever more unpredictable and they would have to remain watchful at all times.

Erdi had wanted to say farewell to his friend Wolf, but he'd not risk that now. Mara hugged her sons, then recoiling slightly, scolded saying they both needed a good dip in the stream once home. Prince Aram and Lady Rhosyn gave them the unexpected honour of a few words of congratulation and many in the crowd clamoured to do the same. All melted apart as Elsa, enveloped in a dark, ground-sweeping cloak, giving the impression she was gliding rather than walking, drifted through the throng towards them. Mara had been the one, who out of desperation, had sent for her and against all expectations, their Earth Mother had not only arrived, but had delivered Mardi, safe from the noose.

It was dawn by the time the reunited family reached home and still firing on whatever surges through the body in times of stress, they stayed up for a while to discuss their miraculous delivery from the nightmare. Then finally fatigue and delayed shock won the day and all fell into a sleep as if drugged. Not before the animals had been seen to of course.

Once all had had time to recover, once things had begun to return to normal, once they'd lost the fear of it all having been naught but a dream, they dared to go about their business without dread of the squad of troops arriving to drag the brothers back into captivity.

Erdi thanked his cousin Yanker for his intervention. He had set the things in motion that had saved Mardi's life.

"I'm afraid it came at a price," he replied.

"What sort of price?"

"I gave my word to Aram I'd join his guard."

"You're joking. You'll be giving up your freedom. You're not even the type to be taking orders."

"Obviously. That's why soon I intend to be giving them. Anyway, what sort of freedom have we here? We think we have, but our duties dictate our daily round."

"But you'll be in the clutches of that maniac of a brother."

"No Aram has assured me, I'll be directly answerable to him and him alone."

"I don't understand. Why has he chosen you in particular?"

"I'm not that bad surely? No, joking aside, I have my suspicions, Erdi. I think he might run with the tups."

"I don't follow you?"

"All right, to put it another way, I don't think he's one for the ladies."

"Yanker, you wouldn't!"

"Don't worry. There's no hint of anything physical, I just think he likes having me around. I make him laugh. And to tell you the truth Erdi, putting aside his personal preferences, which of course are not those of my persuasion, I actually like the man."

"When are you expected to report for duty?"

"Next new moon. The extra I get will help offset the fact the family will be one man short from now on."

They were interrupted by the sight of Luda running and leaping on to Vanya's pony and while going at full gallop, swirling her sling to send a fragment of pottery flying off the top of a post with a direct hit.

"That's amazing!" said Erdi. "What's happening around here?"

"Oh there've been some big changes while you've been taking it easy up at the fort."

"Taking it easy! Look at me I'm all skin and bone. Oh --- there are two things you can do for me when you report for duty. First impress on the prince, it was Wolf's advice that saved the fort. As you know it was him that warned of the impending attack on the West Gate and secondly, I'd like you to search the cell we were locked in. Mardi made me a cloak-pin brooch. I think it's still in there. In all the confusion I left it behind."

Yanker gave a wicked grin and said, "No problem, cousin. I'll ask Blade to keep an eye out for it?"

"Don't ever change will you, Yanker."

One sunny morning Erdi, relaxing while looking out on a scene of tranquility, still hardly daring to believe their nightmare was over, heard his mother call. She was at the hearth as ever, tending to numerous tasks, stirring, stoking, mixing, reaching up to feel if the clothes had dried. She looked up and said to him, "You'd better ride over to Gwendolin's. Poor girl must be beside herself with worry. Do it today and don't worry about your father. He won't mind."

There certainly had been big changes. Erdi borrowed Vanya's pony and rode over Elsa's ridge to Five Pools. I won't go into detail, for it was a private matter, other than to tell you, Erdi was now even welcomed by Gwendolin's father.

On leaving, he uttered those fatal words, "Soon we can be together forever," said right there, beneath the trees with the spirits listening. The ecstasy of love must have muddled his mind, for he'd thrown caution to the wind.

Then days later they had visitors. Dusk was falling when they first heard horses approaching. Penda immediately locked the compound gate. Out from the trees cantered the four Tinners. This was the closest Erdi had been to them. Their unkempt, unwashed state and the way they moved with their ponies, gave the impression they spent night and day on them. The leader's greasy plaits, clasped by tin rings, bounced and danced like a head full of serpents, in rhythm with the horse. All four were armed with enough to render them a small army. Spear, bow and shield were strapped to their mounts, axe to their backs, sword and dagger to their sides.

One translated his leader's wishes saying, they expected hospitality.

"Tell him, he'll not get it here," rasped Penda.

"No need for that," was said with a sickening smile. "We were told you were friendly people."

"You were told wrong. Be on your way!"

The leader dug into his satchel and holding up a horn beaker, called out cheerily for it to be filled.

It was translated, "My leader says, look we've even brought our own drinking vessels. You'll surely not deny us a little beer."

A shot from Erdi's sling sent the mug flying from the man's grasp. His smiling face instantly flashed into one of writhed anger and shouting vile curses, he wound himself into such a screaming fit, it became deeply disturbing, almost as if Erdi's stone had unleashed an unstoppable force, likely to transform the man into a giant reptile right before their eyes.

"Amongst other things, my leader says you'll regret doing that," was said with such calm it could have been laughable, but for the fact the departing warriors left an extremely shaken community in their wake.

Two days later, Luda rushing back from the ford, face distorted by panic blurted, "Something really bad has happened. Vanya's missing!"

With that the Teller bowed and stepped down from the dais.

Part 4

Chapter Twenty-One

The Teller went straight to his bed and had no intention of allowing himself to be talked into providing more impromptu entertainment during the following day. Even though he'd grown accustomed to the prolonged sessions required for the telling, it still left him feeling drained. What he offered the people was part of himself and time was needed to replenish strength and build himself up for the next performance. Even for a man of his experience he'd never managed to conquer the initial nerves felt before stepping up onto the dais. Once into the story, however, an energy surge came from somewhere enabling him to give out his best, almost as if another persona had taken over. Even though on occasions, when prior to starting he had vowed to hold back, keep something in reserve, that strange invasive spirit still seemed to take over as if using his body as a vehicle to achieve its own ends, leaving him once again, utterly drained.

So he didn't appreciate the loud knock on his sounding board disturbing his slumbers early the following morning with the sun hardly yet glinting atop Elsa's ridge. He was summoned for a meeting with a senior court advisor, a ruddy faced man, brimming with an air of self-importance. It was explained, the chieftain had been quite unsettled by the section of the saga that had highlighted the main disadvantage of living in a redoubt strategically sited on a prominent hill, scarcity of water.

The Teller requested his apologies be forwarded to the chieftain, but asked the official to explain, he had only been trying to faithfully relate what had actually happened. He assured him no mention of water availability or lack of it would be made from thereon.

The Teller spent the rest of the day relatively undisturbed and so felt refreshed and ready for the evening. He looked at the array of eager faces gazing up at him. Each one seemed to be asking, 'What's happened to Vanya?'

So, Vanya has gone missing. You can imagine, the worry, the panic. All rushed down to the ford where she had gone to fetch water. Their desperate cries rang out from every direction, until Brownty was discovered. The poor faithful hound lay on his side, with two arrows through him. So that was why he'd not warned of danger. All returned to where Penda and Erdi were examining hoof prints in the mud. They looked fresh and on further examination, it was established there were four riders in all, heading south.

Feelings of devastation grew as the enormity of the situation sank in. Obviously, instincts told them to give chase, until Penda reasoned, they'd have no chance catching them on foot and one man on Vanya's pony would be no match for four mounted warriors. Maybe one could follow the trail, but what then? Instead, sick with worry the family hurried to the fort to request the benign, elderly chieftain, send his warriors in rapid pursuit. As the people kept him, his family, his Seer, his soldiery and all the rest of his retinue it was only fair in this time of crisis to ask for something in return. It was time for the much-vaunted, brave band of warriors to show their worth.

What Penda encountered, however, was a scenario that incited such frustration and rage, he would have had no problem biting a bronze skewer in half.

Having caught a chill on the night of the moon's darkening, the chieftain had taken to his bed and hadn't left it since. So rather than having a reasonable old man to deal with, Penda faced the prospect of seeking an audience with Crown Prince Gardarm reigning supreme in his absence. There had been no point searching out his brother Aram for apparently, he'd been sent, so rumour had it, safely out of the way on a tour, his small force accompanied by two warriors loyal to Gardarm. The ascension of the crown prince was beginning to feel like the constriction of a tightening bronze band, for the purpose of Aram's tour was to inform the people they now required permission from Prince Gardarm if wanting to leave the territory. An emergency measure enacted to clamp down on bronze smuggling. Gardarm wisely reasoned, such a controversial edict was better coming from his brother's lips rather than his own.

Prince Aram, now power was in the hands of his brother, was told his help and influence were always welcome provided his opinions complied with those of the official view. To show gratitude for this compliance, Gardarm had allocated the two warriors mentioned, pick of his own guard no less, to ride along with Aram's men to help guarantee his brother's safety, night and day and it had only seemed fair that Lady Rhosyn and her son should be offered similar consideration. Their every move was watched and reported back to Gardarm. Never again would they be allowed to intervene as they had done down on the Arrow Field.

Having managed to glean all this, Penda was given the mind-numbing news, direct access to the crown prince was denied. Erdi knew his father well enough to realise, he was now well beyond the point of caring about his own welfare and had his mind entirely focused on his daughter. His family was facing an injustice beyond belief and that famous temper was on the verge of boiling over like a pot of sour fruit. When his shouting and pounding on the door of the Great Hall erupted, Erdi used the diversion to slip away unnoticed. The fort interior was of course well known to him and most occupants had been drawn towards the din his father was

301

making. Who would dare roar like a bull and hammer and kick the main door of the Great Hall? He walked, trying to appear as casual as possible, to one area he had cause to know particularly well. With finger to lips in a sign to Wolf, he secreted himself in what had once been his prison. He was taking heed of one of his instincts. Reason told him, following the recent humiliation down on the Arrow Field, there would be absolutely no chance of Gardarm's help. Also, their slender chance would have been rendered completely useless if he, the one person guaranteed to evoke feelings of cruelty and revenge, had sought succour from the very man seething with it. The prince's look of satisfaction, as if the spirits themselves had gifted him the rare chance to gloat, would have glowed to such a sickening degree, had Erdi bowed before him, even his most ardent sycophant would have probably vomited. Only Mardi knew his plan. A wild notion really, but he was desperate to try anything, otherwise Vanya would be lost forever.

Back at the Great Hall Penda continued to hammer and roar until eventually, angered by the racket, Gardarm sent out two men to haul the miscreant in to stand before him. The family was allowed to follow.

"So! You wish to hear my new edict regarding boundary restrictions," said the prince, seemingly unaware of the danger his smarmy smile put him in.

"Boundary restrictions! Travel bans!" Guards grabbing Penda, were just in time to prevent him launching himself to throttle the prince right there where he sat. The whole of the man was shaking, including his voice. "You will have heard by now our daughter has been taken."

The prince, idly examining the beauty of a gold torque looked up and nodded.

"And yet you talk to me about travel bans! What about getting off your royal backside and ordering a travel ban on those who've stolen Vanya. Don't you understand," he yelled, "they've stolen my **daughter!**"

"You do **not** talk to me like **that**!" At his signal, a guard clubbed Penda to the floor. Mara close to hysterics screamed, "Why do we pay you homage, give up tithes each year when you fail to protect your people?"

"My warriors are for the security of the realm, not for chasing after a peasant girl you have failed to keep an eye on. Take them out of my sight."

Erdi had anticipated this outcome, but not the final twist.

The prince, fascinated by the effort needed by Penda to struggle to his feet said, "As a special concession, I'll permit your two sons to leave the territory if pursuit of your daughter requires it."

"What chance would they have? They're hardly more than boys," said Penda.

"Well it's time they grew to be men. Get thee gone before I change my mind." Gardarm obviously cherished a deep longing, that the brothers be rash enough to pursue beyond their borders. Two youths in hostile territory? All sorts of accidents could befall them and then relishing the thought of them meeting the four trained killers, he sighed thinking, 'More's the pity that probably won't ever happen.' In all likelihood they would simply become swallowed up or get hacked down never to be heard of again. At least that gifted sweet revenge without him having to take blame for their demise. With a smile of satisfaction, he returned to the beauty of his torque, obviously unaware of the extent of Erdi's dealings with those described as occupying hostile territory and only when too late, did he drop his knife mid-meal on remembering the young man could converse in the Skreela language.

Penda's family understandably looked a sorry huddle as they were taken under guard towards the East Gate and Mara gave Mardi a stinging slap for choosing that moment, of all moments, to cup his hands and blow the noise of an owl hoot. Erdi heard the signal. The note of failure.

He remained hidden, wishing he'd thought to bring some food for he was starving, but he had to remain patient. It was no use him making his move too soon. He was awaiting evening's change of guard up on the palisade. He had nothing with him but sling, knife, length of twine and the bare bones of a plan in his head. The longer he sat there with darkness descending, the more stupidly inadequate it all seemed.

A guard arrived. Erdi shrank back hardly daring to breathe, making the hammering of his heart seem all the louder. He took shallow breaths, willing the man not to turn. He would hardly fail to miss seeing him huddled at the back of the cell. Wolf cursed the soldier and cursed the slop he'd been given.

'Good man, Wolf.' Erdi gave silent thanks.

The guard kicked the door of the cage opposite, rattled his sword across the bars, cursed the occupant and departed.

Most folk living then as now develop an awareness that gives a rough idea of time passing, but those on guard, needing duration of the duty to be more exactly timed, had their sessions governed by the burning of a candle. When the candle was all but extinguished the man completing his watch would tug on a cord to rouse the relief guard, taking his ease in the room below. On being alerted, or in many cases actually awoken, this man would carry up his candle to be lit and placed in the lantern-pot to mark the commencement of his watch. If they timed it right the 'watch light' as they called it, never went out and the post was never unmanned. Erdi had taken note of this crude, but effective system whilst a prisoner in the fort.

As he sensed the time of the handover approaching, he crept from his cell and lifted the lever on the bar of Wolf's cage. When he'd aligned this with the opening slot of the barrier, fixed to prevent access to the mechanism from within, he swung a small bronze toggle upwards to allow free passage for the handle. This locking bar was slowly pushed across into its far holding brackets and the cage door eased open. He whispered his plan to Wolf and they crept towards the nearest

304

sentry post on the palisade. The guard up on the fighting step was looking out, as duty demanded and they had no problem entering the tiny guard room, a dugout chamber in the base of the fort's embankment. The man asleep within was gagged and tied up before having chance to shout an alarm, offer resistance or in fact have the slightest clue as to who had trussed him up.

They now waited. All seemed to be going to plan. Erdi had armed himself with the guard's sword and shield and crouching in readiness with the man's cape draped across his shoulders, held the new watch candle in his hand. The cord was pulled from above signaling change of guard and he rose in readiness to ascend the steps up on to the palisade. His pulse was racing. As if the tension weren't bad enough, the sound of a conversation above jerked him erect like an internal shriek. He stood mid-stride, face frozen in a grimace of disbelief at their bad luck and his mind raced trying to think of the next move. In the shock, he noticed he'd snapped his watch candle in half. Turning, he held it up lamely.

Wolf smothered a laugh, pulled a wide-eyed face of mock horror and pointed as if saying, 'Now you're for it!' A swiped a finger across his throat implied apt punishment for such a heinous crime. Erdi couldn't believe it. Wolf was quietly laughing as if the whole thing was just a game. Emboldened he thought, 'With this man I'm going to rescue Vanya.'

"So, anything to report soldier?" It was the voice of the warrior Erdi had rescued from the Bleddi.

"No sir. It's been a quiet night."

"I didn't catch you dozing did I, soldier?"

"No sir. Certainly not, sir."

Erdi thought it was just their luck that the warrior still seeking self-worth had taken it upon himself to undertake extra duties. One of which was inspection of the guard.

"So where is he then? Your watch light is almost out."

"I've pulled the rope, sir, but he's not come up."

"Well go down and fetch him you idiot. And leave the sword. Unbuckle it man. I can't stand up here unarmed!"

They heard his footsteps descending. The dark shape ducked into the guardroom to be met by a hand clamping his mouth and a length of signaling cord securing his arms. He was gagged and placed to lie neatly alongside his companion. The two could wriggle in voice-muffled anger together,

At last, Erdi began his ascent of the steps. In the shadows he could see Wolf creeping up the embankment to outflank the officer above.

"So there you are man. What took you so long? Hurry along! A snail could climb faster!"

Erdi kept his head down, hoping his slow deliberate climb would draw the officer's attention, to allow sufficient time for Wolf to position himself.

Sensing something was not quite right, the warrior's face took on a puzzled look. What was it about the guard approaching that troubled him? Putting hand to sword hilt, he uttered the one fatal word, "Erdikun?"

Wolf was on him and broke his neck. He eased the warrior's body down on to the fighting step and relieved him of his sword and dagger. Erdi's instinct was to immediately leap over the fencing to safety, but instead, forced himself to return to the guardroom. It was vital they had the second shield. Only then did they slip over the palisade. Both shuffled, as silently as they could manage, in a squat and slide down the steepest section of the embankment and then crept down the lower slope well aware they were in full view from above. Erdi braced himself, expecting a challenge to ring out at any moment. With relief they were finally swallowed up by the cover of trees.

Both pausing for breath, Erdi said, "You killed him." He had heard that unmistakable crack. He was horrified. "Why did you do that? Makes as much sense as poking a stick into a hornet's nest."

Wolf looked at him and shrugged, "He looked like he was tired of wiping his backside every morning."

Erdi began to wonder whether he'd misjudged the man completely, until he followed it with, "Erdi, the man recognized you. They would have known it was you who'd released me. If they weren't able to hunt us down, they'd have punished your family. I had no choice. As it is, they now won't know how I escaped."

The man was right. As tough as it seemed, he'd had no choice. They had until the end of the next watch in the fortress, to reach Erdi's home and then lose themselves in the forest.

Penda was still up nursing his throbbing skull. He was obviously relieved to see his son home safely, but then his jaw dropped and he stared in amazement at the sight of the hirsute figure ducking in through the doorway behind him. With his eyes still on the man, he shook his wife and Mardi awake. Stories were quickly swapped. Erdi was told he and Mardi had been given leave to travel and he in turn told how he'd managed to unleash the so called 'wild man' to help in their quest. Wolf could now do what he had been trained for. They had in their service a professional fighting man who, could also if necessary, be an efficient cold-blooded killer. He would help track down Vanya and hopefully bring her home.

While this was being discussed Mara busied herself putting together food and clothes for travel and rousing the fire to heat stones for dropping into their largest water pot. Wolf could not be seen to be ranging the countryside like one's worst incubus come to life. They cut his hair, clipped, then shaved his beard and he gave himself a much-needed wash before donning the clothes put ready for him. Erdi rooted around in the thatch of the playhouse and re-entered with the sword he'd hidden so long ago. He presented this to Wolf who feeling its balance and obviously struck by its quality, asked with a puzzled look, "Where you get this?"

Penda of course was asking himself the same question.

Erdi replied, "Where it came from is not important at the moment. I'll explain later."

The Teller then paused and said, Before I continue, I'd like to point out that of course Wolf had only a basic understanding of their language, but if I labour the point, he'll appear to talk like carved wood come to life. He was in fact the opposite. He was deep thinking, tactically astute and at times had a wry sense of humour. So I won't attempt to convey exactly how he spoke, but merely give the odd hint that Erdi's mother tongue was not his own.

The sword was without scabbard and so Mara sewed a leather loop for attaching the weapon to Wolf's belt. He picked up a shield and standing proud, full height, looked like a handsome warrior prince. His chin needed a touch of sun, mind you, for after all those years shielded by hair it now had that white bare-bum look.

Erdi and his parents checked the assortment of items needed for the journey. They now had a sword and dagger each, two leather shields and added to this was the following: bow, arrows, three slings, one spear, one axe, hook and line for fishing, fire making kit, one fire stone, a pouch of dry tinder, clay cooking pot, three water skins, wooden spoon, wooden bowl, flour, barley, dried peas, salt, dried meat, needle and thread, medicinal leaves, four complete 'bolts' plus numerous 'bits' of bronze, long lengths of twine, Mardi's boar tusk necklace and finally three amulets for luck.

A plan was discussed. Erdi pointed out that when Wolf's escape became known the search would be immediate and vigorous. On being told why so immediate and vigorous, Mara, with the vision of her sons' battering, courtesy of an axe handle still vivid in her mind, leant forward and clasping one of Wolf's ample hands in two of hers, let her eyes say thank you. Erdi reasoned, this search was likely to be concentrated to the north up towards the Dwy river. They would expect Wolf to head there in search of a boat sailing north towards home. This would hopefully leave the way clear for their quest to the south and the obvious place to head for was the Habren Ford. From there they could hopefully ascertain which of three trails to follow, south, south west or due west. The need to consider north or east was thought unlikely in view of Vanya being most likely in the hands of the four Tinners.

To avoid the fort their path would skirt to the east of the slow stream. They would be shielded from any direct approach from the west by the marshes lying between them and the main trail south from the fort. There were ways across, but these were not easy and after heavy rain, in fact impossible unless by boat, for the whole area became a lake. Perfect eel country as Penda had once stated vehemently into the face of a neighbour, as you might well remember.

Their course would take them near Elsa's ridge and Mara suggested they seek her out to ask for much needed spiritual help and also to rest up briefly as they would need all the strength they could muster for the task ahead. One thing was certain, they couldn't remain where they were now.

There were sad goodbyes, prayers, luck wishes and the three set out on their journey south. Erdi had had no chance to say farewell to Yanker and the others as the dogs, on recognizing it was him approaching, hadn't barked to alert them and he was loath to disturb their slumber. Luda had begged to join them, but Erdi on hugging and thanking her, explained she would now be needed more than ever with him and Mardi gone. "Please get word to Gwendolin for me," was Erdi's last request before leaving home for possibly the final time.

Dawn was just a hint beyond the trees by the time they reached the rough locality of Elsa's house. She had told Erdi years before that smoke would give hint of its whereabouts. The slight aroma of smouldering wood was augmented by the night air gently wafting from the south. With no other sign to go by they followed the scent and to their relief chanced on a definite path. This led to what appeared to be the source of the smoke, but look as they might, there was still no sign of a dwelling. In the strengthening light they could see grey swirls, that seemed to wreath from the ground itself, seeping from the steep banking up ahead of them. They quietly searched and on finally finding the opening Erdi called softly hoping the lady would be in residence and not out in search of night enhanced ingredients for one of her mysterious potions. The wattle door slowly opened and Elsa, hair neatly pinned, peered out. The brothers were recognised and with a look of pleasure at such a surprise visit, she beckoned them in.

The fire was stirred into life and a brew placed near to boil. Rushlights were lit, giving a dim eerie glow to their faces. The place was packed to the roof timbers with storage pots and baskets, sun bleached animal skulls and innumerable sprigs of dried plants and leaves. The house was located in a natural three sided hollow, but wattle walled within as was normal. Elsa explained that water exuding from the banking beyond the walls was taken around the house and away down a stone channel. A roof of thatch and turf spanned the hollow.

She listened intently to what had happened and to what they intended to do. She said she would of course seek spiritual help, but first they needed food. Cured pork and bread, then poppy seed cake was washed down with a hot nettle-leaf brew. Her attention then turned to Mardi.

She rummaged amongst belongings stored to the rear of the house and eventually pulled out a slender circular deerskin box held together by sinew lacing. With the box on her lap, Elsa unwound the binding loop and lifted the lid to reveal tightly packed, graduated rings of bronze, centred by a metal cone. She pulled this upwards and as if by magic a conical hat was drawn from its casing. The lowest and largest ring was splayed out to form a flat, circular rim. Small rivets were twisted to lock the rings into place and she put the hat on Mardi's head. He wore it well.

"Do you know what the patterns signify, Mardi?"

"Yes the round and crescent shapes are sun and moon."

"It was my father's. It's a Seer's hat." She then bestowed upon him her father's blackthorn wand. Mardi removed the hat and turning it slowly, the studied look on his face hinted that hidden meanings in the embossed spiraling decoration were in some way calling to him.

"It's yours now, Mardi. I think you're going to need it."

Mardi was of course stunned, but his bashful protestations were brushed aside. There was no time for that sort of thing. The rare hat and blackthorn wand were now his and that was that!

She asked them to stay just a while longer and rest, but the day was already brightening and so reluctantly they dragged themselves up and left the warm nest. She promised prayers to the spirits to aid their mission, for which they gave thanks. Mardi clasped her in a massive hug as would a brother a sister, her presence seeming to draw out a new confidence from within him. On finally leaving, they heard deep rumblings in the western hills.

"You need to take care," called Elsa, "there's a storm brewing."

They headed south along the forest trail, luckily meeting no-one. Any wayfarers had to be avoided, hidden from, for the warrior in their company had to be kept a secret until beyond home territory.

They reached the settlement lying to the west of Medle, perched on its convenient mound surrounded by water. The houses, smoke seeping from their roofs, yellow glint of hearth from an open door, looked snug and secure, packed tight above their shimmering reflection. Mardi and Wolf had remained hidden in the trees, leaving Erdi to call out to a boatman far side, requesting to be ferried across.

Storm clouds rearing up like rumbling monsters, flashing thin jagged tongues of flame, would soon be directly overhead. He would have to make haste.

He returned with the encouraging news that the Tinners had passed nearby and what was puzzling, had seemed quite brazen about having four captive women in tow, almost as if granted licence to enslave them. A pair of them had ridden close to hail a request for a boat and admittance. The headman, obviously having heard the rumours, took one look at them and this was denied. The course he had seen the small party take, put them on track for a meeting with near neighbours, occupying a hill fort on the ridge to the south west. A warning beacon had been lit and they had received a reply. The raiders would not be welcomed there either. The headman sympathizing with Erdi's plight, had urged him to make haste. If the storm suddenly broke, the placid slow stream, actually the river Preye, would swell to full spate and in no time at all, become impassable.

Rain had begun to fall by the time they reached the ford. It was crossed without difficulty and Erdi noticed, all but hidden in the trees, a hut he'd not seen before. Mardi and Wolf, once again took a circuitous route to conceal the latter's presence from enquiring eyes and Erdi approached alone. A dog stopped its vigorous scratching of a bald, blood-flecked rash and started to bark. A woman stared at him from the hut doorway, her round face blotched with angry spots. Two girls appeared looking as wholesome as thin twists of dried pigskin and Erdi asked whether four horsemen had recently passed that way?

She answered that they had and one had bragged about possession of slave girls. She added, sounding almost disappointed, the riders had not seemed in the least bit interested in taking her two daughters. As she walked closer Erdi noticed her hair seeming to move of its own accord. Suddenly realizing the reason, he thanked her and backed off as quickly as circumstances demanded, but not so rapid as to cause offence. He gasped with relief when rejoining Wolf and Mardi.

"Talk about disgusting! The woman was alive with vermin!" He shuddered and scratched as if the mere sight of her had made him itch.

They continued west almost at a stumbling run, constantly checking the storm's progress. Rain had now become persistant and sky ahead, the colour of a deep purple bruise, looked solid and threatening enough to herald the end of the world. It was pointless going on. They needed temporary shelter and backtracked to where they'd passed the trunk of a large tree, flattened in a previous violent rage from the west. Its roots that had once slowly writhed below ground now pointed skywards dark, shining in the rain. Branches were hastily axed from nearby hazel, trimmed and jabbed in the soil to lean against the prone trunk. Over these were tied leafed branches, multi layered to maximise shelter and over all were leant two weighty branches of dead wood to prevent the whole structure being blown away. They edged their way down into the hollow left by the vacated roots. There was barely enough space for the three huddled in the gloom.

A deafening crack of thunder overhead, as the storm hit, almost seemed personal. The rain blew across the ground in sheets and their little shelter trembled and juddered as if straining to be whisked up to join the detritus flying past. Trees hung on grimly, their branches out like ragged flags, losing fresh spring leaves ripped and whipped to join the swirling mayhem. From the bank above a stream blubbered from out of nowhere, its torrent the colour of dirty milk. When their make-shift home started to drip, it forced them to huddle ever deeper beneath their sheltering forest giant. Erdi wondered, 'Where's Vanya during all this?' Then came the hailstones as big as pebbles in an intense bombardment, rattling and bouncing off trunk and canopy.

Sometimes the worst of people seem to have luck of the devils. As the storm broke the Tinners and their captives were safe and dry in a herder's hut and their horses tied up in the vacant byre. The same two Tinners refused shelter at the island village had requested admittance up at the ridge-top palisade. Along with failure to gain entry went their last chance of snatching more captives, before heading south. But as I said the devils seemed to be looking after them, for undaunted, they had stumbled upon the empty hut at the base of the ridge. Neither Erdi nor Vanya realized it, but at that point, weather permitting, they had almost been within hailing distance of one another.

The worst of the storm moved on, but the rain persisted keeping the gallant three huddled in their flimsy shelter. Mardi asked his big brother to tell him a story.

"Aren't you a bit too old for Zak stories, Mardi?"

"No they remind me of the safe times before all the bad stuff happened."

He wanted to hear about Zak and the terrifying forest being, the Boggerman. It was a traditional tale going way back to the time when such people had abounded. It was said that amongst other things, they exchanged their ugly offspring for pretty human babies and dined on the flesh of captured maidens. Probably all tribes had a similar legend, the gist of each being, a sacrificial maiden is offered annually to buy peace from the beast during the ensuing year. In the local version, Zak had dug a pit in the path that led to the sacrificial post and had disguised himself as the maiden on offer. Then the Boggerman, apparently having not the slightest scrap of sense, approached his prize from exactly the same direction as he'd always done, fell as simple as you like into the camouflaged pit, allowing hero Zak, who was not really tied up at all, to triumphantly leap forward and give him a good spearing. In gratitude the local chieftain bestowed upon Zak the fine sword mentioned previously in the Zak and Big Hendi story.

"And before you ask, Mardi, Zak's spear was hidden behind the post. That's why the monster man hadn't seen it."

"Was the sword as good as ours, Erdi?"

He gave Mardi's shoulder a squeeze.

"What was that for?"

"You sounded like our little Mardi again. Zak's sword was good, but not quite as good as ours."

314

"Tell me what you really think, Erdi. I know people still say, 'Look out, or the Boggerman will get you!' But were there really things like that living around here?"

"Yes, so they say. They were immensely strong and didn't mind the cold. Our ancestors weren't all fruit and honey mind you. It's said they hunted these strange creatures as food and stole the least ugly of their girls. They realized, once these matured, their immense strength could be harnessed when passed on to resulting offspring.

"You mean the children were captured for breeding, like animals?"

"I'm afraid so, Mardi. What's the matter? Why are you looking like that?"

"Poor Vanya. Do you really think we can rescue her?"

"We have to keep believing, Mardi."

The man with the exceptional sword, that even outmatched that possessed by the legendary Zak, was hunched up and dozing.

The sound of a blackbird chortling away as if the day had been the finest in its life, heralded that the worst of the storm had passed. They emerged from their shelter, stretched and looked around. Every tree had an encircling mantle of fresh green leaves and at the bottom of the bank lay a strange long white mound. They approached it barely able to keep their footing. None of them had seen anything like it before. Erdi scooped up a freezing cold handful to examine. It was like snow, but made up of tiny individual globules, hail stones. The rain had washed them down into a drift. He grinned and tossed the melting ice into Wolf's face.

The man smiled, gripped Erdi's wrist, squeezed it and was still smiling when down on one knee Erdi begged to be let go.

"Sorry Wolf," he said rubbing away the pain and making a mental note not to take similar liberties in the future. Then something came to mind that had been puzzling him. "Wolf -- when we were in the fort, just before our escape -----?"

Wolf nodded to indicate he was listening.

"I have to be honest I was petrified. How were you able to treat the whole thing so lightly? Almost like a game."

"Oh **him**," meaning the warrior he'd sent to meet his ancestors. "Erdi, that man was nothing. Just like baby compared to where I come from."

The thought recurred, 'with this man we'll rescue Vanya.'

Their progress up to the hillcrest on the slime and mud of the trail was painfully slow and in certain places, was so treacherous it had to be abandoned altogether. Drenched foliage was grasped to help drag themselves up. One bonus was the discovery of a dead hare, obviously caught out in the open and brained by the massive hailstones. This was offered in exchange for hospitality, once finally gaining entrance to the small fort on the hill.

Here they learnt how close they had come to intercepting the raiding party, but were so cold, wet and exhausted they couldn't contemplate continuing further. All three had gone two days with hardly any sleep and had eaten nothing since leaving Elsa's house that morning. They would set out at first light and hopefully be there to confront the Tinners still waiting to ford the Habren. The village headman had vindicated their decision advising rest, seeing little to be gained by immediate pursuit. He told them that after such a deluge, the river would be in near flood and too dangerous to cross for at least two days. So why press on in their exhausted state? He added that if such wild weather had come from the southwest rather than due west, the whole Habren valley below them would have been inundated on the morrow. Then nobody could have gone anywhere. Certainly not due south anyway.

They of course now had to explain to the headman who Wolf was. They'd had to abandon the notion of trying to keep his presence a secret. The man could hardly have been expected to shiver the night away hidden in the woods. Erdi said he was a warrior on his way south, who on hearing their plight had offered his services. The headman's eyes narrowed

316

into a disbelieving look, but he decided not to enquire further. There was something about the stranger that reminded him of someone, but as hard as he tried, he couldn't remember who. Their neighbour's signal from down in the valley had warned him of a single armed voyager approaching, but here before him were now three. He studied them. He'd heard tell of Erdi's family and one thing was certain, from what little he knew of them, they certainly would not have had authorization for the swords they carried. They were frighteningly young and obviously desperate to rescue their sister. He smiled at their courage and wondered what exactly the young bucks weren't telling him.

The Teller paused and said, The folk back then of course didn't have the sophistication of you people today, but there again, like the headman just described, most had a fair instinct as regards body language and what sounded plausible. You couldn't get away with much.

The following morning, with a watchful eye on the weather, they set out for Habren Ford. Another storm was gathering, but this time blowing in from the dreaded southwest. It was as if the spirits were joining forces to block their progress.

They reached the ford as huge face stinging raindrops started to pelt down again. The river was already a swirling brown torrent and branches swept along in its grip, quivered as if horrified at having been caught in a terrifying race beyond their control. At least the Habren hadn't burst its banks. Not yet, anyway.

They were told the Tinners had arrived the previous evening and on viewing the state of the river had not lingered, choosing instead to head west. This decision had been made easier by the owner of the hostelry refusing to serve them. Rumours had reached him regarding four raiders, but rumours were rife amongst river travelers and these scraps of gossip hadn't been his concern until standing right there before him, fully armed, were the very four men everyone had been talking about. He was a brave, independent sort, not afraid to speak his mind and told them, he considered theirs to be a despicable trade. With a hand on the latch of the dog enclosure, he threatened to unleash its vocal occupants if the Tinners didn't move on immediately. His courage and candour prompted the sneered reply that proved so invaluable. 'If he thought sight of a mere four captives was despicable it was a pity he'd not be there to witness the full number they expected to return south with.' They had further business with their friends dwelling in the uplands of the Gwy river. "Now those are what you call, true slavers!" the man had said.

Unlike his previous visit to the ford Erdi had bronze to exchange for food and they decided to sit out the storm lashing and crashing about them. It made no sense to try and make up lost ground in such weather.

Then from out of the shadows emerged Hanner Bara sensing a business opportunity. She smiled, drew up a stool and sat facing them. They waited, but knowing time was on her side she merely eyed them and then, as if preparing herself for business, reached inside her jerkin to pull the wayward left breast back into line, shook tresses free and then said calmly, "It looks to me like you fine gentlemen could be in need of a woman's touch."

Erdi had an immediate mental flash of Gwendolin and worried sick by the thought of Vanya out in the storm, thanked the woman for her offer, but declined.

Mardi looked at her in horror and not wanting his first ever sexual encounter to be with such a woman, fiercely shook his head.

Wolf, however, remember he'd been caged and tethered for over a year, asked the lady what was expected for such a service and with the help of Erdi's translation of his words into a version she'd understand, a price was negotiated. The bronze they carried was for emergencies only, but considering Wolf was prepared to lay down his life for them, parting with such a small scrap seemed only fair under the circumstances.

Hanner led Wolf to a small adjoining room, allowed her in such days of inclement weather and they were gone some time.

On re-emerging the big man wore a slightly bashful grin and Hanner, fussed about him straightening his clothes.

"Thank you Erdi," said Wolf as they skirted hut drainage channels and ducked away from dripping thatch, commencing their way west at last.

"What I can't understand," said Erdi, "is how you actually managed to do it. It's not like the woman's one you'd dream about. She obviously keeps herself tidy and has plenty for a man to grab hold of, but she's just so plain and ordinary."

"You'll find," said Wolf, "as you get older, Erdi, your standards can slip a bit."

They followed a trail that cut off most of the river's more exaggerated loops, but it was still quite late in the day by the time they reached the confluence of the Habren and Nwy. The rope bridge was still up spanning the tributary.

There were hoof prints nearby, but obviously no horse could have crossed by such means. They followed the trail along the bank and came to the shepherd's hut. Hoof prints and mounds of horse manure in a small corral adjoining the building told them the Tinners must have sheltered awhile. Again they'd had the devil's own luck, but at least Vanya would have been in the dry. Wolf, examining the prints along the river, said they were not fresh and had probably preceded the storm, meaning the small hut had been occupied the previous night putting them a full day behind their quarry. Fresh prints led west along the Nwy. In a small eroded fissure of a fence upright Erdi spotted something small and white. He picked out a tiny stone. There was a round face scratched on it. He was showing it to Wolf and telling him, Vanya must have left it there, when both suddenly froze at the sound of horses approaching. They hurried back to the bridge, now barely above the raging waters, meaning the surge they had been warned of, must be fast arriving from the mountains. The

319

rope bridge, nearing its time of renewal, was looking disconcertingly black and frayed in places, but it had to be trusted, they had no choice. The shepherd had told Erdi that by just taking those few steps, would save two hard days travel.

He was on the bridge when the order to halt rang out. Another order, had the troop, undulating in unison, closing fast and almost upon them. If the bridge snapped now, he would be sucked into the raging torrent and gone. It rocked wildly in the wind and the whipped-up spray, soaked his feet and leggings. He reached safety and one at a time, ignoring the howls of anger from their pursuers, Mardi and Wolf followed. The latter then crouched and busied himself as if his belongings had needed rearranging. Even shorn and shaved it would not have been wise to have shown his face.

The soldiers dismounted on the far bank and not having the same incentive to cross, took one look at the swaying rope structure and pulled back.

Their officer called out. "I ordered you to halt!"

Erdi put a hand to his ear and with a strained look shouted, "Sorry, what?"

"I ordered you to halt and now I'm ordering you to return!"

At last, it seemed the spirits were with them. Erdi watched the majestic advance of a huge tree, roots foremost, swirling around the bend, bearing down on the bridge until, as if frustrated by its tangle with inundated bank-side shrubs, it started to judder and tremble in the torrent. Accumulation of pressure caused wild thrashing as if being wrestled by a monster from below and once freed, it leapt unleashed, like a huge black leviathan to go on a crazy ride down towards the Habren taking flying remnants of the bridge with it. The stunned look on the officer's face remained, an unforgettable picture in Erdi's memory.

He smiled and gave the warrior an exaggerated shrug, Yanker would have been proud of.

"I know who you are," came the shout. It was the same officer who had been judge of the slingshot contest years before.

"Then you'll know we have permission to travel."

"Prince Gardarm has rescinded it and who is that other man with you?"

"A fellow traveler offering the help you should be giving."

"We have our orders. You know that. That man has no permission to travel and now neither do you!"

"He's not of our tribe. He doesn't need it. And our return? With the best will in the world, that has been made a little difficult. Do you expect us to drown in the attempt?"

The man, with a resigned look, slowly shook his head.

With that Erdi gave a wave and they proceeded west keeping swords well hidden beneath their capes. The officer had proved himself to be a fair man at the slingshot competition and so would, as like as not give a true, unbiased account of what had happened. It was just hoped that serious questions would not be put to his family regarding the mystery man in their company.

The officer stood watching the three receding figures. He shook his head sadly, giving them little chance of reaching higher ground before the full surge swept them away. Whilst puzzling over who the third man was, the thought suddenly struck him, "Were those army issue shields strapped to their backs?"

Erdi scanned the meadows ahead. They were flat almost inviting to be swamped and the waters were now dangerously high. Above the line of the river bank, brown rolls and curls could be seen flying past and in the pastures behind them, water had already crept as if in sinister pursuit. Hollows were beginning to well-up as if fed by hidden springs and a tiny brook had swollen to become waist deep. They waded across and started into a loping run as water brimming from it spread across the land as if some oozing water god was stalking to suck them under. A freshening wind now blew into their faces. They stopped to check they weren't heading into a trap. All around the grass whispered a deathly song and ominously filling the impressions around their feet, small pools of brown water seeped up. With a sense of panic setting in, they ran all the faster and the splash of each step through the creeping flood warned, 'Only high ground can save you now. Run for your lives!' With the force of the wind buffeting his shield and dragging him back, Erdi actually contemplated flinging it, for it would be no earthly good to a drowned man.

The dull grey sky had given way to even murkier twilight by the time they eventually made higher ground. They were gasping for air with Wolf suffering the worst, hardly fighting fit after his year's confinement. Their sweat-shined faces broke into smiles as they looked at one another, soaked through, mud splattered from the waist down, but at least safe. Behind them, the land they had hastened across between the Habren and Nwy, was fast becoming one huge brown lake.

Now they needed food and shelter and cutting and trimming stout branches as they went, spotted in the fading light, the chance of a potential haven. A steep east facing bank. Two poles were pushed into ground at roughly a bodies' length from the banking, their longest pole spanned these and the remaining four, ran from the top of front uprights and connecting bar, back into the earth topping the bank behind. Their twine held the box-like structure rigid and branches were cut to cover top and sides. The front was left open.

Next, needing to provide immediate warmth, Erdi busied himself with the fire kit. This comprised of a board with a central groove, a flat stick of the same timber and some dry tinder. While the others went in search of wood, he cut a blunt point on one end of the stick and rubbed this up and down the groove in the fire board until embers began to smoke. He pressed on, rubbing harder until these sent up a small billowing cloud. The tiny glowing embers were carefully tipped on to a handful of tinder and teasing this loose to allow air flow, but not so loose that smoking shards lost contact with dry fibers, he gently puffed to blow the whole bundle into flame. Wolf had hacked off wet bark from dead branches to reveal dry wood, for peeling into shavings. These were carefully added to the flames and once past that most critical phase, larger pieces of prepared wood were added. Once the fire was roaring, they no longer had need to hack off sodden bark, as the flames with much smoke and crackling, soon did the job for them. The firestone was put in the embers to heat and Mardi filled their cooking pot with water from a nearby rivulet. Obviously there were stones to be had all around, but put the wrong muddy rock in the fire and you all know what happens.

The Teller made a near silent 'Pow' sound as his palms were spread upwards and outwards. Some in the audience chuckled.

Once the water was boiling, barley, dried meat and a pinch of salt were added. This was given an occasional stir and when ladled into their wooden bowl, was passed around. Erdi had wondered why Wolf had removed one of his boots, but was too tired to ask and they slept beneath the shelter curled up like bats in their capes.

The next morning the answer was clear, Wolf's right big toe had become rubbed and looked sore as a boil. The boots he'd been given were too tight a fit and with all the wet weather his softened skin had been rubbed raw. A piece of cloth was tied around the wound and the sodden boot forced back on. Then not wasting any daylight they followed the ridge south and by middle day caught sight of the Habren once more. They were now south of Gatekeeper's Ridge, looming up on the far side of the river and between its length and the ridge they were on, was a vast lake. A turbid torrent racing round in a tight curve showed the normal course of the river. Trees like sentinels in their own reflections told them the lake was not a permanent feature.

They pressed on weak from want of food, making do with dried meat in an effort to placate that hollow feeling in their bellies and stave off the onset of wobbly-legged stumbles. Occasionally through gaps between trees they caught sight of the river coursing below. It was high, but at least this far south, was still contained within its banking.

By evening they reached a small community safely sited on a raised spread of land above the waters. Dogs barked and people emerged to watch their approach. Erdi called out a welcome in the language he'd learnt from Gwedyll and with relief heard a man reply in the same tongue, enquiring who they were. Information was exchanged at distance, then satisfied they were not a threat, the man invited them into the community. They offered to work for their food, but the folk wouldn't hear of it. Two ladies with a giggle, said the men's leggings could do with a wash. Hung near the fire they'd be dry by morning. One noticed Wolf's bandaged foot. She fetched hot water from the fire and removing the filthy piece of rag, winced at the sight of the wound. As she washed his feet, she called out an instruction and a young girl brought her some sort of mash that was kept bound to the wound by a clean bandage. Erdi, remembering that first meeting with Elsa years before, suspected it contained beech leaves. The offer of their own medicinal leaves had been perused, but brushed aside.

Then the three, with the blankets they'd been loaned wrapped tight for warmth and retention of dignity, gratefully accepted the food offered. There was a small price to pay, however. Even though almost nodding off where they sat, they were still required to sing for their supper so to speak. To help they were plied with beer and around them, folk avid for news from beyond their own small world gathered close to listen. They wanted to know where they were from, where they were going, how Erdi had learnt their language and were stunned to hear he'd met and knew quite well, their young Prince Bonheddig. They sympathized with their plight, but said, there'd been no sign of the Tinners. After some discussion they felt convinced such a convoy couldn't have passed through their territory without being apprehended by their own Y-Dewis warriors. Erdi wasn't so sure. Those men seemed to carry the devil's own luck with them. When he described the route, the floods would have forced upon the slavers, the headman scratched a map on the hut floor. It showed the river Nwy, plus a second the Tinners would need to cross before being able to head southeast in order to take the ford over the Habren leading to the easiest trail up into Gwy territory. He scratched a line showing the route they would probably take and on the Habren he scraped an X. "This is where your paths should cross." He pointed with his stick, "Between here and here they need to somehow ford the Habren to gain access to that route I just mentioned. If you're planning to confront them it has to be done somewhere on that short stretch of river. Go any further and you might not be coming back. You could end up in the same predicament as your sister or," he made a swiping motion across his throat, "worse." He drained a mug of beer. Then by rocking a hand held horizontally, he indicated that maybe, given a bit of luck, they had a fair chance of intercepting the slavers. He took another deep draught of ale, belched and said they needed to be there before middle of next day. Then hopes were dashed on him remembering the slavers were mounted. More beer and slap of temple for overlooking the fact their captives would slow them down, brought him back to the hand rocking frame of mind. Not looking entirely happy with that prediction, he took yet more generous slugs of the magic liquid, wiped his mouth with the back of a hand, raised his beaker and pronounced loudly, "I have every confidence in your shucshesh!"

The three went to bed not knowing what to believe and slept like babies. They left with clean leggings warming their lower regions and a meal warming their insides. Wolf now walked with a jerking limp, but was at least free from burden as the brothers had redistributed his share of the load and had this plus the shields strapped to their backs.

The trail along the lower slopes of their westward ridge was well traveled and they made good progress considering Wolf now had to swing himself along aided by the crutch Erdi had fashioned. By mid-morning they came to the fork in the trail the headman had mentioned. One path continued straight on towards the western heights and the other south towards a long range of hills. They took the latter as advised and were soon rewarded by the glint off the Habren river.

Their hearts sank at the sight of hoof prints at the ford, for it meant they had arrived too late for any notion of ambush. The waters had settled considerably, but it was obvious no-one would have dared cross at this point. Backtracking, they saw the trail split again, north-west through a gap in the hills or south-west to where they knew not. Mardi found hoof prints along the latter trail and so trusting to luck they followed it. Their way over a small stream and up through low hill country was not that demanding, but Wolf was now in obvious pain. They gave him encouragement and helped him over the roughest patches, but the man would soon be in need of more than a few beech leaves or he could be losing a foot.

The sight of a cluster of houses beside a stream in a pretty wooded valley, lifted their spirits, exaggerating the sudden sinking feeling at seeing six armed horsemen approaching. These reined in, watched and waited, causing Wolf to mutter, "They not looking for trouble. They defending."

Erdi called out, to say they came in peace.

"Your friends passed through earlier," shouted the headman.

"No friends of ours. They're slavers."

"We could see that well enough."

"They have my sister."

There was a short discussion and the headman motioned them to approach. "What's the matter with his leg?" He jabbed his spear down in Wolf's direction.

"It's not his leg. It's his foot. He needs help."

The man looked unmoved but with fingers to lips he let out three shrill whistles. Women and children began to emerge from the trees and soon melted along with them silently as they threaded into the hamlet's enclosure. Sight of the slavers and their captives had obviously had an unsettling effect. The mood was decidedly muted.

Erdi asked the headman how many slave girls had there been and had one been quite tall and slender with dark hair?

"Would be hard to say. There were four women for definite and a wretched state they all looked in."

"You didn't try to help them?"

"Why? They were none of our business. We winged the men a few barbs as a warning to stay their distance and with that they obliged." He then muttered words in a dialect lost on Erdi and a young woman sprang to her duty and returned helping an elderly lady who carried a basket weave box.

While she was gently seated on a stool to tend to Wolf's foot, Erdi told the headman their story. He had no way of knowing the impression he was making as the man's countenance remained the same throughout, changing no more than the stern facade of the palisade wall.

Erdi paused to watch, as the medicine woman picked out tiny white wriggling objects from a small cylindrical box, to place them carefully on Wolf's wound and seal them in with a tightly wrapped bandage. She picked up Wolf's shoe, examined it, had a short discussion with one of the young men and made a beckoning, no-nonsense demand with her fingers for Wolf to offer up his foot for removal of the other shoe. The young man disappeared carrying the footwear.

Erdi continued to relate their tale of woe. A while later, both he and the headman turned to witness the return of the shoes. Darts of leather had been let in and the old lady leant down to help raise her patient's good foot for a trial fitting. Wolf beamed and she smiled. He gave thanks in his language, she replied in the local dialect and the two looked to have a complete understanding.

She turned her attention to Erdi and from her tone and manner was obviously offering him instructions and sound advice. The headman translated, "The man must keep the foot dry and stay off it for as long as possible. After four days remove the maggots and put on a clean dressing. Four days should be long enough for them to clean the wound."

Erdi thanked her, but explained to his host, resting the foot was not an option in the situation they were in.

Receiving instructions from the headman, a young warrior mounted and rode off towards the forest, the same patch the villagers had first been seen emerging from and on returning, led three horses. Erdi was told, these could be ridden as far as the Habren, at which point the three accompanying warriors would lead the ponies back.

Erdi's attempt at thanks were waved away. The medicine woman gave Wolf more indecipherable instructions as he mounted and smiling, he leant down to gave her shoulder a squeeze. Erdi remembered the time he'd first set eyes on Wolf, ragged, wild and snarling and smiled to himself at the transformation.

They forded a small stream and cantered to the top of what had seemed to be, before receiving the villager's help, an insuperable mountain. Beyond the crest the trail dipped and curved down through the trees into the Habren valley. On approaching the river, it became immediately obvious, here at last it could now be forded. A man was loading animal hides into a worthy looking log boat tied up at the bank. Erdi asked if he'd seen four horsemen passing through. He said, he had and added that if they hurried, daresay, there was a fair chance of catching them.

Erdi thanked the man. "Good news at last," he called. "We've been tracking them through floods and storms for days."

"I daresay," the boatman replied carrying on with his loading.

They urged their mounts across the ford, Wolf with infected foot raised above the flow to keep it dry. Once on the south bank it was time for parting of the ways and return of the horses. The lead man confided he'd have liked to have helped further, but didn't dare continue. Border tensions had eased in recent years, but they still risked losing their horses, with the prospect of an ignominious walk home, should they encroach onto the ridge that separated the Gwy and Habren valleys.

On seeing Wolf stagger with pain when alighting from his pony, the man winced and said to Erdi, "Tell that man to remount."

Against orders the three warriors cantered with them along the south side of the river and up the trail winding towards the ridge crest. Here he wished them luck, repeated they'd dare not risk going further and thus said, he and his companions left at pace abandoning them to their fate.

Wolf shuffled along using the crutch once more and they emerged from woodland onto open hillside. On scanning up towards the skyline, the only thing they saw moving was a buzzard swirling on the up-draught, but cresting the ridge and looking down into the valley far side, Erdi caught sight of movement. "There they are!"

Working their way up from a small stream, was a line of humanity moving no faster than a crawl, almost lost to view in the gorse and bracken. Luckily, they had spotted them before the trees ahead swallowed them up. Spurred on, at now being so close, they set off again with vigour down towards the valley bottom and even with Wolf's incapacity looked likely to catch them. As he helped his warrior friend across the stream, Erdi scanned the ridge-top cleared for grazing and his heart leapt at the sight of the column emerging onto open ground. There were now, however, only three mounted men, leading Wolf to conclude, one must have been sent ahead to warn of the column's imminent approach.

They hadn't realized, the small stream they had just crossed, was the Gwy river in its infancy.

As with most hills, you think you're approaching the summit only to find you've merely crested a lower ridge. The animal track they had been following disappeared into a deep oak and bracken choked gulley given extra life by the welling up of a small stream. Wolf now needed support from both, as they edged into it and pulled themselves up far side. His grimace at each step showed clear evidence of pain, but somehow he'd managed to restrain audible sounds of it.

They continued up through the stunted oaks, to finally stagger out into the open once more. The crest of the ridge was within reach and for the first time in days Erdi caught clear sight of his sister. His instinct was to call out, but common sense prevailed. She looked a forlorn figure forcing a hand on thigh with each step up the last of the ascent.

Vanya was now so close Erdi felt the spirits must at last be favouring them. Surely, even they couldn't be this cruel. Allowing their mission to come within an arrow shot of success, only to then deny them.

He received his answer. Along the crest riders appeared, spear tips glinting in the sun. On spotting them, they sent up a whooping cry of triumph. Erdi groaned in disbelief and rage. They the hunters, were about to be the hunted. "Vanya!" he called in desperation.

Vanya stopped, turned and stared in amazement at sight of her brothers on the slope below. Initial joy, turned to terror as she realized she might have inadvertently lured them to their deaths. She waved in recognition, but then pointing back towards the trees, pleaded with them to turn back. She called, begging them to run and save themselves. Erdi wondered if his fate was to endure an afterlife tortured by the vision of his sister being pulled back into line and dragged away into slavery.

The phalanx of warriors swept down off the hill towards them. Erdi's gallant attempt had come to nothing. They were surely soon be put to death or taken captive.

The Teller at this point asked if he could pause to take refreshment? This decision was met with a groan and looks of sheer incredulity. A few left the hall to relieve themselves, but didn't stay out long. He chatted genially with those nearest in the audience. They replied politely, but not at length for they were keen for him to return to the story. At last, he re-mounted the dais. So where was I? *The Teller continued in an almost self-mocking, animated, melodramatic fashion.* Oh yes, can you imagine our three heroes? Spot-rooted in terror as a host of savage, wild-screeching horsemen thundered and rumbled down off the skyline. Can you feel that gathering hoof-beat throb? Almost share the fear with the whole ground shaking. Almost smell the acrid, glistening horse sweat. Any thought of flight to nearest trees; would leave Wolf abandoned in their dash for safety.

"All stand together, we'll go down fighting!" Wolf cried to the sky and swords were drawn. The screeching hoard now close upon them, woad stripes on faces, savage glint of eye; low-bent as one, eager for spear thrust, eager to see bodies ripped and torn.

Imagine the three's gut-watering fear; bodies' shake to the beat on the trembling ground. No option left than to pray and brandish; bronze swords in hope, "Let's die with honour; yell to the Gods for a warrior's death. "AAAAAAAAHH!!""

The horse formation pulled up, skidding into a dust and rubble strewn, wheeling panic, to turn and gallop for all it was worth back up the hill. Erdi, Mardi and Wolf, the latter one-footed, were about to leap up and down and hug each other, when the real reason for the retreat thundered past. A troop of Y-dewis warriors accompanied by the six villagers encountered earlier pursued their quarry until driven out of sight over the ridge top. Satisfied with the job done they returned at a gentle canter. The officer in charge, moving just one finger, beckoned Erdi.

"We meet again," he said. "Get yourselves off this ridge. What's the matter with him?"

Erdi did his best to tell of Wolf's injury, his eloquence in the Y-Dewis language hampered somewhat by the trauma they'd just been through. He'd obviously conveyed the gist of the matter, however, as the officer barked an order for a warrior to dismount. The pony offered was received gratefully and they all made their way back down to the Habren, with Wolf, an odd sight, riding with throbbing foot, raised as high as balance would allow.

Erdi had of course pleaded with the officer to pursue their attackers and rescue his sister, but the seasoned campaigner had replied his men had fallen prey to their neighbour's traps on too many occasions before. The Gwy warriors, it seems, only fought if possessing overwhelming odds or from ambush. It would have been suicide to enter their territory with just his few men and six untrained villagers. Back at the river the soldiers dismounted, still in a cheery mood following their minor victory and the taciturn village headman, with face looking glad to at last be free from its somber strictures, told Erdi it had been one of the funniest things he'd seen in a long while.

"What was so funny about that?"

"The three of you thought you'd scared the Gwy off."

"Whatever gave you that idea?"

The man shook his head, he'd not been fooled and his craggy face became transformed into something quite unrecognizable, as a smile slowly spread across it.

The commanding officer set himself up on a raised portion of bank, where an arrowhead spit of land divided the Habren from its tributary. Thus ensconced and his men erecting a sharpened-stake barrier to protect their rear, he summoned Erdi. He had been present when the young man had boldly approached his chieftain at the Feasting Site and now wanted to know how and why they'd happened to have crossed paths again. Having listened, he said they'd been tracking the slavers for days, but each time he was convinced he had them trapped, they'd disappeared like phantoms. On two occasions he'd positioned his men to lie in wait in valleys, logic said they would have to use, only to find his quarry had slipped away over the hills. As you can imagine the man was not enamoured at having been outwitted, especially with it having happened in his own territory and didn't look like a man relishing having to explain the lack of success to his Y-Dewis chieftain.

On Erdi telling him the likely destination of the Tinners, another officer was summoned. With not wearing standard military jerkin and leggings, but clothes of woven plaid, topped by a dark green cape, rather than the usual utility brown, the man had a slightly outlandish look. His lank hair had four feathers attached by rings of bronze, that toned exactly with his weather-beaten face. He listened intently to his commanding officer.

With a flick of his head, he drew Erdi's attention and with his dagger sketched out a map. "This is the Gwy river. This here is the entry it makes on the broad funnel leading out to the sea. You've reason to believe those slavers have further business with the Gwy tribe?"

Erdi nodded.

"I would guess then, that that will lose them a day at least. Add to that the days needed, to travel between that ridgetop yonder and this point here on the estuary, you have a total of eight. They'll be slowed by their captives, but between here and here" he said pointing, "their progress will become easier by virtue of the Gwy river being navigable. They'll be able to float their captives downstream. But even though," he pointed with his dagger again, "between here and here, the river is certainly not navigable, don't think that gives you the chance to go after your sister. Try and you probably won't come back. It's rumored they eat their captives. I don't believe it myself, but dead is dead, whether you're eaten or not. On the other hand, look I'll show you. If you take this route," he scratched out a huge curve north, arching it east to finally etch it south, "you could be at this point on the river estuary in time to intercept. Provided you have a boat."

Listening and looking quite fascinated, his commanding officer sent one of his men to summon the boatman and on arrival asked him his destination. He was shown the map and he pointed to where the Habren began its journey south.

"That is where I'm bound."

"Good, then make room for three passengers."

"But that's not possible. I can't make room where there is none."

"Nonsense man! You have crwgs hereabouts I take it?"

The man nodded and mumbled, "I daresay."

"Then two of them can paddle ahead and clear the flood debris to ease your passage and the wounded man can ride on the load. Now wipe off that whipped dog look and make haste. They need to leave immediately!"

"With all due respects, sir, if I'm allowed to ask a question?" He wanted knowledge of the state of the river to the north of them and following Erdi's description of conditions encountered said, "Excuse me, sir, but from my experience of these waters it would be safer to depart at dawn tomorrow. Then I daresay the rage in the river will have subsided."

The officer was clearly annoyed by the man, but reluctantly bowed to his superior knowledge of the river and after a languid hand gesture to usher him from sight, he turned to Erdi and said, "Yes?"

"I am truly indebted to you and don't want to appear ungrateful, but this route means us going back the very same way we've just traveled. Believe me, that journey was not an easy one."

"This time you have the river with you, plus you don't actually have a choice. Go that way," he pointed south, "and

334

you're finished. In fact, walking anywhere's out of the question. Yon brawny limper wouldn't last a day. Your only way is on the river with him a passenger. By the time you reach the trading post, yonder gloom-trader is heading for, he'll hopefully be fit enough to travel on foot if needs be."

Erdi thanked the officer and despondently returned to Mardi and Wolf and as you might expect, their spirits were not lifted by the news. Wolf apologized for being such a burden. Erdi told him he wasn't and that they would pull through this nightmare together somehow. He did add mind you, that he found it incredible that such a small part of the mighty man's body, one big toe, could render him so incapacitated.

Wolf with one of his wry looks replied, "I've heard tell of whole kingdoms being lost over something not much bigger."

They were all in low spirits, but to take minds off having been so close to Vanya, only to see her being dragged beyond reach, they set about mundane tasks. They helped the boatman render the load watertight by strapping down cowhide; prepared a place on board for Wolf to recline; walked to a storage area to return with the two, skin lined crwgs, carried aloft like massive hats; gathered dry wood and tinder for use on the journey; cleaned themselves up, washing and shaving and Erdi even sewed up a split in his leggings. Mara had insisted he take the needle and thread and for this he was now grateful. The brawny limper, Erdi had had to smile to himself at the description, honed their weapons, drawing much attention from the warriors in camp. Well at least his sword did.

All but one of the village volunteer force returned home. It was the headman, who remained to act as guide to the commanding officer, taking him and three of his men on a mission all warriors relish given the chance, hunting. Shrill squeels echoing off the hills gave reason to believe they had been successful and a young bloodied sow, hanging draped across the officer's pony as he returned to camp, provided the proof.

The five men who had departed earlier returned that evening with bread and beer to complement the roasted carcase and they feasted, retelling the saga of the day, well into the night, all men together, not a woman in sight.

Chapter Twenty-Two

The next morning with the last wreaths of smoke from the campfire lazily adding a tang to the low hanging mist, the warriors broke camp to return west, the villagers departed with them and the cargo boat was pushed into the flow for the journey north. Farewells had not been emotional. The previous night's beer had dissolved barriers sufficiently for banter and camaraderie to flourish, but in the cold light of that following day, the usual warrior, civilian divide was re-established.

The boatman and his young assistant made great issue of Wolf being in their way and a huge burden extra to requirements and although sharing a look of gloom, seemed strangely lifted by it, as if having knowledge of some mysterious secret, dark and dire, conferred on them a sense of superiority. They weren't two you'd relish sharing a drink with or reveal your inner feelings to. Erdi named them Daresay and Doom and smiled at the thought of the sport Yanker would have had with them. He missed his cousin.

He and Mardi paddled ahead in the crwgs clearing debris and at one point were confronted by a huge tree blocking the main river flow. They had their own axe, plus use of the one included amongst essential boat equipment. The water that funneled down through the only clear passage beneath the trunk was flowing at such pressure, it roared and began dragging their fragile craft close to the point of destruction. Spotting the danger in time, they back-paddled frantically, managing to gain calmer waters and left the crwgs, two glistening black domes, upturned on the bank. Returning to the fray with axes and paddles, they straddled the tree to hack off the main impediments to its progress and only when the trunk finally slewed to float itself, did it suddenly occur to them, they were in danger of being swept downstream. Paddling madly to avert disaster, they managed to steer and beach their tamed monster on to a pebble shoal, thus preventing it reappearing to block them a second time.

They were soaking wet, but cheered by success. Deftly guiding their crwgs mid-river, Erdi sent his little craft into a spin of triumph and called out in a jocular manner to those in the awaiting boat, "That would have held you up somewhat."

Wolf who had been highly entertained by their struggle, laughed and nodded in agreement, but the head boatman looking up with face devoid of expression, simply said, "I daresay."

Their headway along the Habren could at best be described as steady and that evening, they had only progressed, if you can call returning in the wrong direction progress, as far as the village they'd passed through on their way south. Not the maggot village, the beech leaf village. Again, they were welcomed and helped to their mooring by folk eager to hustle them inside to glean how their venture had fared.

They were fed and given shelter and Erdi regaled them with the tale of how close they had come to success near the Habren - Gwy ridge, but then had to sadly reveal the reason for them returning the way they had come, empty handed. He knew enough of the language to communicate the basics and the headman, who for some reason was able to understand the slightly strange sentence structure, his none too perfect pronunciation and habit of using a handful of words to compensate for having forgotten the exact word needed or perhaps never having learnt it in the first place, was able to communicate the story to the rest of the assembly. The man was enthusiastic and inventive in the re-telling, helped of course by beer and had those, packed tight in the hut and others eagerly listening in through the doorway, almost wetting themselves at one point, but decidedly glum at the conclusion. Daresay and Doom sat in the shadows unmoved by any of it. Wolf having kept an eye on them, warned Erdi to be up early next morning. He didn't trust the pair and wouldn't have put it past them to have left him and the brothers stranded.

Erdi was up at first light and saw with relief the boat was still tied up to the small wooden jetty. It was quite a sleek craft considering it had been fashioned from a tree trunk. The prow had been trimmed to a pugnacious point in an attempt to aid efficiency through water and its sides had been trimmed sheer, managing to lose most of the clumsy log look. At the aft end a transom, a half circular plank, was slotted tightly into grooves cut in the trunk thus preventing water entering. Compressed moss in the joint ensured it was entirely watertight.

Daresay looked slightly shocked at the sight of Erdi there before him.

"Don't you trust us? Did you think we'd be away without you?"

Erdi resisted saying, "I daresay," and instead explained airily he had felt the need to check all their things were all still safely strapped down and accounted for.

A narrow-eyed look in return said all.

The villagers turning out to watch their departure, embarrassed them with generous gifts of food and even Daresay and Doom were included in the slightly festive departure. When presented with a fresh baked loaf, Daresay did attempt a smile in gratitude, but his expression looked more like one of relief mixed with uncertainty experienced when expelling a particularly smelly passage of wind. The day continued much as before, except the river's flow slowed slightly and there was greater evidence of flooding. Trees stood gloomily perusing their own reflections, as if the detritus entangling their branches had offended their dignity. On more open areas, sparkling expanses reflected the sky and

339

seabirds wheeled and gathered in flocks feasting on the unexpected bounty.

Wolf pointed out, that their presence inland often heralded bad weather on the coast and warned there could be yet more storms blowing in from the west. Erdi conferred with the boatman who, although not usually communicative, welcomed a good wallow in the gloomy and confirmed the information to be correct, adding with relish, if a storm came from the northwest flooding the Nwy valley, they'd be forced to change their plans. Meanwhile they were approaching a section below the abrupt, easterly range of hills, at the point where the river was often fordable. He hauled in the log they had been towing, it was used to roll the craft over the shoals. The river was still fairly high, racing over the stony bottom, but the man insisted on its deployment, obviously concerned about unnecessary abrasion to the craft's hull. He might have been a gloomy man, but there was no doubting his knowledge of the river or transportation of goods thereon. Obviously proud of this, he informed Erdi of upcoming slow-moving reaches where he and Mardi could climb aboard and ride the load. On other sections, he suggested a short walk across a narrow neck of land could be preferable to sitting aboard, while they worked boat around huge loops in the river. He had a horn to summon them if the way became blocked. He imparted his knowledge on account of being proud of possessing it, but the fact his passing it on, also helped ease the passage for others aboard, caused him to sigh with a look of sad resignation. By the evening they had yet again, made no more than steady progress, but at least Wolf's wound had been given chance to heal as he reclined, as if in state, atop the cargo.

They arrived at quite a sizeable village on the west bank and pulled in to rest up for the night. The place had not been evident on their journey south as they'd avoided the valley path, reasoning the higher trail along the western ridge to be the wiser option.

Their decision was soon vindicated. Villagers emerged as always, curious to see what the river had delivered up, but the headman, not looking too enamoured at the sight of Daresay and Doom approaching, merely nodded and offered a perfunctory greeting. As Daresay made to reply, he was left open mouthed by an ominous grumble of thunder coming from the north-west.

The headman rolling his eyes and addressing the three newcomers, his back pointedly turned on the two boatmen, said recent weather had been quite abnormal and added it was deeply worrying. He took Erdi to show him the newly gouged channel and explained, it was the first time in his life he had known the village to be completely cut off. The children had enjoyed being on a temporary island, but the parents had obviously been in fear of not only their village being swept away, but them along with it. To cap it all, he said his grandmother had been complaining all day. He confided, "She's had another of her twinges and we all know what that means. That right knee of hers has never been wrong yet!" He gave a sigh, raised his eyebrows and jabbed a finger at the storm grumbling in the western hills.

Erdi wandered down towards the water's edge. Just below the mound where the houses stood, all grass and vegetation had been swept flat in a northerly direction. These good cheerful people had been no more than a knees' depth from being swept away.

Again, they were all fed, the price as always being news from the outside. Daresay and Doom brooded in silence, their tightly wrapped capes hardly containing feelings of acrimony, which left Erdi, being the only other amongst them capable of conversing in the cymry tongue, to repay hospitality with his words. He didn't seek prominence, but the villager's eager questions drawing him into telling yet again their, quest, their saga, elevated him to special guest status. Some actually looked a little in awe of him. This rankled with the two boatmen, who although hiding true feelings with smiles, couldn't prevent Erdi's instincts sensing that even if he could have offered them the moon, they would still have relished nothing better than witnessing the spirits managing to ensnare him as comprehensively as a noosed hare. Wolf eyed them guardedly.

With Erdi's tale concluded all were drawn outside into the failing light to witness the spread of lowering, rumpled cloud across the far western sky being lit as if by flashes of daylight, followed by low rumblings you'd expect to hear if the Gods took the notion to roll lumpy boulders across the wooden floor of their attic. The headman opined philosophically, "Grannies' knee got it right again. It'll be up by the morning!"

Erdi gave an involuntary laugh at the image.

"I meant the Nwy river not her knee," explained the headman slightly hurt. To Erdi's relief, a friendly hand on the man's shoulder and an apology brought him back round to a smile. 'What a stupid mistake! Not good to offend this stalwart man who'd been so hospitable.'

The thunder rumbled on and he turned to Mardi and Wolf, deeply worried as to what this latest turn in the weather might do to their plans. North of them, the Nwy ran into the Habren and this new deluge would probably mean delay until the waters subsided. At this rate the chance of seeing his sister again, let alone rescuing her, seemed hopelessly remote. Seeing Daresay and the headman conversing, he was on the verge of interrupting, desperate to hear their view regarding travel on the morrow, but then thought it best to hold his tongue. His recent indiscretion and awareness of being very much a junior regarding matters pertaining to river flow and flood gave him reason to consider it wise to maintain a low profile and wait.

His patience was rewarded on hearing the headman proffer the idea, "So you'll be needing use of the cart again."

"I daresay," came the answer and terms were negotiated for two days use of the ox cart which, courtesy of the recent flooding having rendered the local ground totally unsuitable for any form of immediate agricultural activity, was luckily available. In fact the headman had said, once the cart was returned, its first job would not be farmwork but the relocation of goods and stores to higher ground. In the meantime, an adequate expanse would be cleared for new homes to be constructed.

The following morning an ox, forced to swim at one point, was drawn across the Habren, with the ring through its nose attached by twine to the stern of the boat. The cargo was transferred to the cart waiting safe on higher ground above the river. The crwgs strapped atop the load in case of further need, added extra water proofing in the event of rain. They all walked, apart from Wolf who again rode above all, infuriating Daresay, by reclining, hands behind head against one of the crwgs, as if having found the perfect pillow and enraged him still further by raising his feet up on to the other. He did deign to descend when the vehicle needed heaving and shoving over the most difficult patches.

They passed beneath steep forested Gatekeeper Ridge and struggled up the gradual incline to top a gentle scarp that offered a tantalizing view of northern land spread out before them. It was breezy up there, yet not a clear day. The home of what they called the Ridge People was visible as was Elsa's ridge, lying not too distant from their own hamlet. Shafts of light through cloud brought dull grey patches sparkling to life as they reflected off floodwater still lying in the flatlands. Daresay was as ever reluctant to impart anything remotely interesting, but couldn't help but divulge his knowledge of the Habren. Well, he was proud of it and almost looked in danger of seeming genial as he explained, the river described a huge curve running west to east and had so many huge loops along its course, it in actual fact made their current mode of transport quicker than paddling. It was just that he baulked at having to hand out bronze to reach his destination. Even though the Habren had been placid that morning, he pointed to the rough location where the Nwy joined it and said, continuation along it would have been too dangerous until the storm surge down the tributary had passed through. This is what Erdi had suspected. He cheered himself with the knowledge that at least the route they were on avoided the mounted patrols they would have almost certainly encountered, had they been afloat on that particular section of the Habren. Patrols hauling them ashore, travel no longer permitted and worse, a commanding officer demanding to know who exactly Wolf was?

Mardi looking down on their home valley bemoaned the fact they had slogged through so much, to be no further than a day away from their starting point. Erdi had tried to block out similar depressing thoughts by telling himself, very soon they would be journeying in the right direction and with luck, be at the Habren estuary before the Tinners.

Their journey became easier from here on and by evening, after fording a small stream swollen by flooding backwater, they emerged from trees far side, to be welcomed by the sight of a large settlement perched high on the far bank of the Habren, Amwythig, their immediate destination. Drawing closer, they were taunted by the aroma of food cooking, but their business was not with the inhabitants in their fortified redoubt, but with those whose lives were wedded to the river. They followed its course looping round to the north and approached a pleasant, wooded area where a small stream added its clear cheerful water to the sullen, turbid main flow. With the far bank, at this point, being no higher than the one they traversed and the river having broadened, Erdi suspected they could be approaching a ford. Sight of deep tracks down to the water's edge and out the other side confirmed it. Daresay, pondering the state of the water, predicted the possibility of a safe crossing at first light. There were huts on the far bank and further downstream log boats straining at their tethers, rhythmically rising and falling with the floating jetty, gave clear indication of the torrent's flow.

They tended to the ox, finished the last of the food gifted them that morning and settled down to sleep, three on the cargo of pelts, Daresay and Doom beneath the cart. They had been crawling along at the speed of an ox all the daylight hours and so it didn't take much rocking to send them into oblivion.

They woke to guttural shouts, shrill whistles and splashing. A cart midstream had an alarming look, as if likely to become buoyant and yaw round to take ox and driver with it, but the man obviously knowing the waters, stood, cursed and whipped the beast into such a fear of the lash, it dragged its burden, rumbling, rocking, to where it disgorged water on the far bank.

The sight spurred them into action. They checked the load, hitched ox and cart and headed down to the water. Erdi and Mardi paddled across in the crwgs, the flow of the river taking them close to the moored boats. By the time they had carried their craft upstream to the ford, the cart was safely across, glistening with water. The ox had an untroubled demeanor, Doom avoided eye contact, but Daresay seemed strangely pleased with himself. Erdi didn't like the feel of it. He didn't know why, but instincts put him on full alert.

He had noticed during his life that when certain people had visited and shared their home, the initial cheery phase following arrival and greeting could soon evaporate and certain habits or mannerisms of the guest could soon start to grate. If the stay became prolonged, the feeling of annoyance as regards these little niggles could build until the irritating habits seemed to be the only thing you noticed about the person. This would lead to shortness of temper and a strong desire to see the back of the visitor. However, when the desired day at last arrived, Erdi had noticed a strange sense of guilt would begin to overwhelm, to the point of feeling compelled to be extraordinarily nice prior to the person's departure. So, when Daresay went out of his way to introduce him to the boat crews ready to make their way south, he felt perhaps the man had been driven by similar feelings.

The boatmen, energetically eating and chatting in a hut similar to the one where Hanner Bara plied her trade, fell silent when Daresay and Doom entered and a lone voice said, "Hide all the ropes."

The noise level began to pick up again on their departure. Erdi ordered food, all three were made welcome as if late arrivals at a family party and there was a general shuffling along the plank to allow them space to sit.

One asked, "Have you been traveling long with those two?"

"Long enough," said Erdi.

This brought laughter plus a further comment from down the dining board, "You did well if you managed more than a day with 'em."

"Yes one day with those two's enough to make you want to hang yourself!" commented another.

"We called them Daresay and Doom," said Erdi. The abrupt outburst of laughter revealed sight of half chewed food and would have been heard way up in the town.

Most of the boatmen were only plying fairly local trade, but the two largest craft were traveling to the point where the Gwy joined the Habren in the widening estuary the Y-Dewis warrior had described. Erdi seemed to strike up an immediate understanding with the one boatman and his mate and was understandably relieved when they were offered places aboard. There were a few last details to attend to and then they'd be casting off. Erdi told them it would be a relief to be traveling in the right direction at last and they'd be ready as soon as they'd retrieved their belongings. It felt as if their luck could be changing.

They left the hut, walked to the ford and stood impatiently waiting for the return of Daresay and Doom. Erdi was annoyed with himself for not having insisted their things be dropped off before the business of trading pelts. Daresay had assured him the deal would not be prolonged, as it was a fairly routine transaction done annually. There would be no protracted bartering. The memory of Trader dealing with the Bleddi warriors came to mind. How could a deal involving hides and pelts not be protracted? This could lose them their chance of immediate travel south and he was just about to suggest they go looking for the cart when it re-appeared, empty but for their belongings and two bulging sacks. The sacks contained salt and had been tied high on the cart's stanchions to keep contents dry during the re-crossing of the river. Erdi was that relieved to see their possessions back, he never thought to question the lack of other trade goods on the cart.

All was there neatly piled ready for them, but for one item. Wolf's sword was missing. "Where's the sword?" demanded Erdi.

"You have those two swords" Daresay said pointing "and here's your spear, what more d'you need?"

"Would you like me to explain that to my friend?" Erdi said calmly nodding in Wolf's direction.

"You can explain all you like. That sword is now ours. Call it payment for the transport we've given you."

When Erdi translated, Wolf picked the man off the floor and snarled an aside to Erdi, "Tell the snake to go for his knife so I can kill him!"

Erdi obliged and asked again, "where is the sword?" But with the wretch starting to change colour, he suggested to Wolf, if Daresay were to be lowered, it might increase their chances of obtaining a reply.

The man coughed, rubbed his neck, blinked several times and managed a croaked confession that he'd hidden it earlier, tied to the underside of the cart. Mardi ducking below the boarding in search, reported back, there was no sign of it. When Wolf pushed Daresay beneath and growled, "Find it!" no translation was required.

"It's gone," said Daresay woefully, offering up the end of a loose piece of twine, "the river's taken it."

Wolf wrenched him from under the cart, forced him against it with one hand and put a knife to his throat with the other.

The terrified man wailed, "You can search me, search the cart, I don't have it. And killing me won't bring it back."

Erdi stayed Wolf's hand, he had noticed their boatman approaching. The genial fellow was jauntily making his way to inform them he was about to cast off, but what he witnessed stopped him dead and the way he stood staring at them open mouthed, indicated he was almost certainly having second thoughts about having them aboard. With his eyes never leaving Wolf's blade, he asked slowly, "What ever is going on?" He obviously found the scene deeply disturbing, not helped by the sight of Wolf choosing that moment to give Daresay a stinging back-hander that floored the man, causing him to whine, "I'm sorry it's a terrible loss for all of us."

"That sword was worth more than all your stinking skins put together," shouted Erdi down into the man's face. He couldn't help it. A certain something inherited from his father had simply snapped and burst from him. Still shaking, he turned to the boatman and realising how bad it had all looked said, "I'm sorry, if you'll allow me to, I'll explain later."

The man, with eyes like an alarmed owl and still rooted to the spot he'd arrived at, looked first at Erdi, then down to the prone boatman, to hear Daresay wail, "Oh don't, it's terrible. It was stupid of me. You probably think I traded it away up in the town, but ask who you like, I swear on all the spirits, the Habren has taken it. Maybe they'll see it as an offering. It might bode well for your journey."

Mardi was down by the ford staring at the water. The sword would have sunk immediately, but the force of flow would have carried it into the depths.

Erdi again apologised to the boatman for the scene and told him there had been good reason. "I know it looks bad, but believe me, I think even you will share our anger when I explain." This allayed the man's fears sufficiently for him to tell them time was now of the essence. They needed to gather their things immediately and stow them aboard. There was room in the barge they would be towing.

When busying themselves with this Erdi was asked, "So tell me, what was all that about?"

Still seething inside with anger, he did his best to calmly recount the details. but the tremor in his voice from the sheer effort of holding back his emotions, left the boatman in no doubt as to the seriousness of what had transpired. He gave a brief rundown of how they had come by the sword, how his sister had been stolen, how close they'd come to rescuing her and how this snake of a man had now lost their sword, had lost their talisman in fact.

A frown of puzzlement clouded the man's face regarding the final detail, but he didn't enquire further, as certain things needed explaining before the off. He gave him and Wolf instructions regarding where to sit, details of paddling and steering and that his orders were to be heeded at all times. He warned them of possible trouble ahead when navigating the gorge and admitted that to be the main reason they'd been offered transport. Puzzled by the sight of Mardi still standing on the bank. staring at the river, his voice trailed off and then he added, "Can you explain all my instructions to your brother?"

"Mardi," Erdi called, "time to get aboard,"

Mardi joined them at the boat and said "He's lying, Erdi. The river told me. He's lying. Why would he tie the sword to the underside of the wagon before undertaking such a hazardous crossing?"

The boatman with his previous misgivings confirmed asked, "Do you mean to say an experienced boatman tied a valuable sword to the underside of his cart before making the crossing of the Habren this morning? --------I'm sorry, I might not like the man, but I'd give him more credit than that. Not even he would do something that stupid. Your brother's right, the man's lying. An experienced river man would know better than to do that."

"So he's either traded it or still has it hidden somewhere on the cart," said Erdi.

"Look. I hate to see a snake like him prosper," said the boatman. "Run and catch them. I'll wait. But hurry!"

"Too late," said Mardi, "they're already back over the ford and gone."

The boatman explained it was not in fact too late. He would put them ashore on the far bank and continue on his way. The river took a huge loop north before eventually flowing south. They could force out the truth, or maybe even recover the sword and then take the trail across the neck of land to rejoin the boat. He would be around the loop by about mid-morning. Wolf was keen to join them, but Erdi advised him to stay aboard rather than risk his injury flaring up again. "We need you later Wolfy my friend. Fighting fit. Mardi and myself can manage those two."

Now they really meant business and caught up with the Daresay and Doom just as they were approaching the brook they'd forded the evening before. The cart was rolling along at quite a pace considering an ox was pulling it and the two men seemed to be chatting quite freely in a way that was quite unrecognizable. Erdi was determined not to be put off by shrugs and slimy smiles. He'd have the truth from them.

Daresay, suddenly turning was obviously surprised at seeing the brothers again. His face switched on a smile of greeting, but his eyes showed fear of having been found out.

"You'll miss your boat," he said hopefully.

"Never mind the boat! Where is it?" demanded Erdi. "Or have you hidden it up ahead ready for collection?"

"I told you the river has taken it."

"I'll ask you again, where have you hidden it? Or has your trader friend got possession of it?"

Doom looked worried, but Daresay burst out angrily, "I told you the river's taken it! Are you calling me a liar?"

"You heard my every word and I never once said liar, but as you brought the word up then it's best you own it!"

"Search us, search the cart, but you won't find it. Look up the beast's backside if you want," he said pointing at the ox. A sickening smile like a split in an over ripe plum spread across Doom's face.

Mardi drew his sword and Erdi, hands shaking with anger looked over and then under the near empty cart. He raised the crwgs, felt the sacks of salt now stowed beneath and the more he vainly searched, the more the looks of Daresay and Doom glowed into unbridled smugness. Then he suddenly remembered something -- Grik the Fish!

The bottom of the cart had three boards and two cleats front and back to prevent moisture being absorbed by the end grain. Erdi knocked on the wood and when the middle board gave a hollow drumming sound, Daresay's eyes flashed a look of alarm. Even with use of the sword, there seemed no obvious way of prising the plank to gain access, but he wasn't giving up ---- not now silence and worried looks told him he was closing in on the secret. The front cleat was pegged solidly in place but the one at the rear was slotted to allow it to be raised. Erdi rattled it loose and lifted. Revealed was a secret compartment. He reached inside and a wave of relief passed through him as he carefully withdrew the sword, ringing as if being unsheathed. Brandishing it, he took satisfaction at Daresay's flinch at the word, "**Liar!**"

Something else had to be lurking in the secret cavity. What had made the sword ring? Erdi reaching inside, withdrew a string of axe heads.

"These will make up for the trouble you've put us through. No on second thoughts," he cut off just three, "you can have the rest back as payment for transporting us."

"Pay us with our own axes?"

"Consider yourselves lucky!"

"You're putting us out of business," Daresay wailed. "We need those to fulfil the order."

351

"So," said Erdi, "you mean to say you're not even trading on your own wits. You're using another man's bronze. No wonder the deal was done so quickly. And of course, you wouldn't have offered your man the sword, because being beholden to him you wouldn't have been given its true value." Warming to the task, yet another realization struck him. "And you couldn't have dealt with anyone else because the news would have got back to him. A sword such as this would have been talk of the neighbourhood. You'd have risked losing the contact who supports your gutless way of making a living. I've no sympathy. What an utter pair----. I'm lost for words. An utter pair of sneaks!"

As they left there came a growling voice, "Don't ever come down our part of the Habren again. You won't get out alive!"

"I daresay," Erdi called back.

As they returned taking the path running east, Erdi noticed his brother was shaking with laughter. "What's so funny, Mardi?"

His eyes were absolutely brimming with mirth. He bent, drew a deep breath, straightened and wincing in agony from the pain in his sides, managed to point and blurt, "It's **you**!"

"What d'you mean, **me**?"

He gasped, "Pair of sneaks!" Then as if in sheer torture he clutched his sides again, tears streaming down his face. Partly with relief of regaining the sword and partly at how inadequate the words had sounded under the circumstances, they were both convulsed with laughter. They almost stumbled over aching with it. They laughed all the way to the clear water brook that babbled into the Habren.

They crossed and followed the trail that was fortunately raised, as in places flood water still stood in the pastures. On the bank of the Habren they scanned upstream and there, mid-river, was a beautiful sight. Their boat was being paddled towards them. Erdi waved the sword and a cheer rang out. They had their talisman back.

Chapter Twenty-Three

Whilst waiting for the boat's approach they quickly cut branches and osiers from riverbank willows and stripped the leaves. As they clambered aboard with the bundle, the boatman nodded approval and they swirled out into the full flow of the Habren. Erdi turned and presented the sword to Wolf, hilt first and the man took it before grabbing him gratefully in a bear hug. Erdi, sitting himself upright again, turned to give his friend a broad grin and then set about constructing the fish trap, cheerfully recounting the tale as he worked.

They followed the loops and winds of the river. Flood water still lay quiet, gloomy in places. Deer splashed in flight, white tailed through the trees; herons stood reflected, waiting to stab; overhead a phalanx; complaining grey geese. Rings from their paddles span fast off behind, each touch of the water speeding them south. The river was clearing not swirling with mud; dead fronds, sticks and debris flushed from the earth.

The boat was a beauty and seemed to skim along. It was wider, longer and more elegant than their previous craft. The lines of the prow were sheer grace and the sides had been trimmed to achieve the fine balance between lightness and strength.

There was time now for reflection. Erdi felt his heart lifting in hope and he prayed Vanya had not been harmed. He still couldn't quite believe their luck in finding immediate transport south and watching his brother paddling, where he

353

sat beyond the mid-boat cargo, he marveled at how on their travels he'd seemed to have matured beyond all belief. He was fast growing into a man. Wolf's wound had surely healed for he had lost the throbbing pain in his foot and it had started to itch which was always a good sign. Were the spirits beginning to favour them at last?

They pulled in for the night onto a shingle beach bordering a flat meadow where cattle grazed. The bull of the herd and a number of cows had been hobbled to prevent over adventurous wandering and a cowherd stood watching from the shade of a nearby wood. A clear-water brook running into the Habren provided water for cooking and washing and the five set about constructing a shelter for the night. Once done, Erdi wandered the meadow, flicking over dry cow pats looking for worms. These were used to bait his fishing line. The catch was their supper and the scraps provided bait for the fish trap. In his wanderings he had also found a pine cone. Bits of head and tail were forced into this for luring in night feeders and once weighted with stone the trap was plopped into the water. They had bread plus eel baked in clay for breakfast.

Time had come at last to remove the bandage from Wolf's foot. The cowherd had wandered over to take a look at them and leant on his broad-staff saying nothing. It was amazing how clean the wound appeared, still red, but having lost that angry swollen look. It now had to be kept dry and open to the air as much as possible. The maggots having successfully done one job were dropped inside a dock-leaf pouch in readiness for another, fishing.

As if suddenly gifted the power of speech, the cowherd gabbling excitedly, pointed downstream. The boatman, Garner by name, said that even though he'd learnt enough of the various riparian languages to aid his passing up and down the Habren, he'd not the faintest idea what the man had said. They humoured him, packed their things and the mate, name of Cymar, shoved them off before scrambling aboard.

The man on shore shouting out to them, pointed his stick.

"Yes, thank you," Garner called back. "I'll pick you up on the way back!" He laughed and said to the others, "I think the fool wanted to come with us."

"No, it seemed like some sort of warning" replied Erdi.

They didn't have far to go to find out. Things had been going too well. It was only to be expected the spirits would intervene. The river banks were now almost sheer, rising that steeply they blocked out the sunlight and all glanced up with a feeling of foreboding as they were drawn into the funnel of dark flowing waters. They were heading through the gorge. The boat rounded a bend with the grace of a swan and awaiting them was an ugly scene of menace. Up ahead, at the end of a long murky reach of water, a threatening assortment of men had begun to assemble on a broad patch of shingle. The river diverted by this, flowed fast down a narrow eastern channel. Paddles were raised as they assessed the situation, with every moment of hesitation, taking them inexorably closer. Details began to emerge, the most significant being, all the men were armed. The boat swayed picking up speed in the current. Gaunt faces and ragged clothes gave hint that the rabble awaiting had not been drawn together by tribal bonds, but desperation. The east bank rose sheer and avoiding the threatening mob required passing as tight as possible beneath its shadow. A shower of slingshot fizzing into the water ahead, put an end to that notion and urgently back-paddling, they turned the boat to steer for slower waters under the west bank.

Garner listened to the shouted demands of the gang leader echoing off the water. He explained to his crew they were being asked for payment for shooting the waters of the gorge; bronze, part of the cargo, whatever happened to be agreed upon. Without payment they wouldn't make it through alive, for not only were they a sitting target from slingshot above, but were equally exposed to slings and arrows from off the shingle. Garner said they needed to talk, to negotiate the best deal possible. Erdi asked whether there was any chance of a way around the trap, because to him they didn't appear to be the negotiating sort. They'd be more likely to take everything. Maybe even their lives.

Wolf stared at the rabble and frowned. It would seem he also had other ideas.

"Erdi," he said quietly.

Erdi leant back, the better to hear him. "Erdi, those are not trained fighting men. I need your help. They won't expect what I do. I need you to disarm the main mouth-man."

"There are too many of them, Wolf."

"They're not trained fighting men. Trust me Erdi."

They edged towards the shingle beach letting the current do the work. The sun, as if wondering what was going on, had just started to dazzle through the tree tops high on the east bank, lighting up the pale grey shingle and various shades of brown worn by the motley crew assembled upon it. Amongst the roots in a golden sunlit hollow beneath the bank, a trout's tail was visible, slowly fanning back and forth. The only sound was of wood scrunching over pebbles. Passing on the fact, they'd been instructed to leave all weapons aboard, Garner stepped ashore, to be joined by Erdi and Wolf and all three walked cautiously towards the armed gang. For the first time in days Wolf had both boots on. Mardi and Cymar hauled in the barge to prevent it yawing into the main flow and waited, ready to push their boat off.

Garner and the leader went into a fairly heated discussion that Erdi couldn't understand a word of, but basically the remonstration that no-one had the right to impose a tariff on those traveling through the gorge, had been met with the reply, "Try and stop us!"

Wolf did just that. He drew a knife from his boot and like a wildcat, launched himself at the leader. The man was dragged back, his feet rattling the shingle. There was a blade at his throat and Erdi's silent but firm insistence persuaded him to part company with his axe and dagger. The gang members,

356

stunned by the rapidity of the action, remained rooted to the spot.

Garner, not slow to see where events were heading, shouted what Erdi guessed to be, "Allow us free passage or your leader is a dead man!' Turning to their captive, he must have asked something along the lines of, 'do you still want to live?' for at the man's screeched order, weapons were heard rattling onto the shingle. Similar instructions were then called out to those high on the east bank.

The river pirate was held prone on the cargo, Mardi securing his legs and Wolf's blade reflecting a buttercup glow beneath his chin. Erdi, with a shield on each arm, protected his warrior friend against opportunist shots from shingle or banking. With the two boatmen paddling them into the rapids they were soon way beyond range and skimming across deep slower water. They emerged from the shadows to pass through more open country and having served his purpose their captive was pushed over the side. Lucky for him he could swim. He dragged himself ashore a drab addition to the west bank where sunlight dazzled like countless stars off the flow, merrily twisting and rippling its course across a shoal of pebbles.

Once clear of danger, Garner steered the craft into a small inlet and instructed all to disembark. Shaking his head in disbelief he grabbed hold of Wolf in a huge fraternal hug. He was almost crying with relief and admitted that in all honesty, back up at the ford he'd been close to denying them places aboard. The tiny gap between finger and thumb indicated just how close. "Now I consider myself to be the luckiest boatman on the river."

Wolf looking slightly embarrassed said, "But they were not trained fighting men."

"Come here you brawny limper," said Erdi flinging an arm around him.

They continued south and Garner taught them a boating song. Wolf gave a rendering of a haunting ballad from home and they were all still singing as they pulled in for a chance to stretch their cramped limbs and snatch a bite of food about middle day. Dwellings could be seen dominating a lofty sandstone outcrop immediately east and a round hill, like an upturned bowl, lay slightly to the south on the west bank. Curious strangers approached asking questions. By the time Garner had answered them, they left being waved off like celebrities.

The river ran fairly straight and deep from here and at times it felt like they were the only people still alive in the world. They could have traveled further, but Garner steered for a small island saying they would be safer spending the night moored up there, in view of what had happened that morning. They constructed a crude shelter, enough to keep out light rain and Erdi found the local fish weren't at all put off by his bait having been in such close proximity to Wolf's foot. The fish trap was later dropped in the depths as usual. That night, as Erdi gazed at the moon's long shimmering light on the river, he wondered where his sister was?

Vanya was staring at the moon's reflection in a completely different river. The day after she had last seen her brothers, she and the other captives had been allowed to rest and by evening were joined by a further five terrified young women all in a wretched state. They were forced to walk from dawn until dusk for three days following the course of the river valley. On the fourth day, to their relief, two boats were provided and they were paddled downstream. Vanya attempted to comfort one of the new captives, a girl roughly her own age and in doing so picked up some of the language she spoke, cymry. By the close of the fifth day since entering the Gwy valley, they were moored up near quite a large settlement on the north bank of its broad waters. As Vanya looked at the moon's reflection an instinct told her, her brothers had survived. She knew it was against all logical thinking, yet she firmly believed it. This still left the question of where were they now and also who was the warrior she'd seen accompanying them? There was something nagging in her brain; she'd seen him somewhere, but couldn't place where and each time an inkling seemed within grasp the notion faded like morning mist.

The Habren river now ran a fairly straight course south. In places Garner and his crew had to log roll the boat and its barge over shoals, but with four of them working as a team they weren't greatly delayed. Wolf remained aboard not risking re-infection of his wound, a likely outcome had his foot taken a soaking from the river, followed by the softened skin being rubbed against leather footwear. He had earned his passage back at the gorge, Garner told him.

They met two boats labouring upstream and with each crew, news was exchanged regarding possible hazards ahead, good places to pull in and predictions regarding weather. Of course, those traveling north were warned of the danger awaiting and when Garner's own little saga was related, the river men left in silence staring back at Wolf with undisguised awe.

Then it rained. The cargo was battened down, but they all received a good drenching. They let the flow of the river take them, just giving the odd flick of the paddle to steer and with their cloaks wrapped tight and hats hard down they sat hunched and miserable. Rain dimpled the water all around and pattered loudly on the leather hides protecting the cargo. As if not bad enough already, sheeting gusts then blew in, that most insipient skin drenching variety, obscuring any view and at times they felt as if trapped in a strange otherworld. Cymar up in the prow shouted instructions to Garner steering in the stern. Stranded tree trunks, gaunt branches and shoals seemed to ghost up out of nowhere, but knowledge of the river allowed progress, if only at a crawl. Garner seemed to have a mental picture of the Habren, knowing where the main flows ran and which side to take when skirting an island. He instructed his crew to stow their paddles and concentrate on bailing duties.

The day had cleared up slightly by the time they reached their night's mooring. There was a large settlement on the west bank and having tied-up they gathered the most valuable of their possessions and slopped in their soaked boots, like half drowned dogs towards the village enclosure.

The two boatmen were of course known to the villagers, who welcomed them, always avid for news from along the river, but the three strangers were a different matter entirely. They could have exotic tales to tell and the folk almost fell to arguing over who was to have the honour of taking them in. The headman put an end to all that and they were led to the main hut where women relieved them of their sopping clothes and hung them to dry, steaming near the fire. They sat swaddled in dry cloaks sipping the day's pottage ladled from the fire pot.

Once warm and with appetites sated, Garner was invited to stand and tell the tale. He knew enough of their tongue to relate what had happened at the gorge and after a few rounds of beer he was asked to relate the best bit again. Erdi was invited to stand and he briefly told their saga, translated, as best could be managed, by Garner. Certain details weren't quite understood and so copious quantities of beer were poured as if dulling the brain could be the answer. One thing was certain, Wolf's sword made double the impact it would have done, had it been passed around for a sober circle to admire. Then the singing started, with Wolf receiving a rousing cheer for his soulful rendering of the song learnt at his mother's knee and by the time necessity to sleep caught up with them, it seemed as if they'd all known one another for years.

Wolf and the brothers had the best nights' sleep they'd had in many a moon and when waking, although feeling a little bleary from the beer, looked forward to the day's travel with a feeling of optimism. The sun, just up and glinting from the east, helped of course as did the fresh look of the grasses and fronds riffled by the breeze. Everything appeared resplendent and grateful for the recent rain. If trees could smile, they would have done.

They were gifted food by the ladies and even some of the menfolk emerged, yawning, stretching and grimacing with a hand to aching brow. They'd thought it only polite to see them off. As they set off downstream, Garner told Wolf there'd been a request to hear his song again and a plaintive melody from another land rang out across the water. It held a sense of longing and as the boat was rhythmically paddled into the distance, women watching had tears in their eyes.

Now the mist and rain had been blown from the broad valley, Erdi could see a prominent range of hills to the south west and an even longer scarp running south, visible on the eastern horizon. Land to the west was still inundated in places and Garner, calling out and pointing, said the Tamesa stream was often the culprit for the flooding. When the Habren was too full to take further water, the pressure backed up until the shallow basin the tributary ran through filled up like a lake.

They stopped middle day where a large flow joined the Habren from the east. There were scant remains of two houses on the spit of land between main river and its tributary. Garner explained they'd been shepherd's huts swept away by recent floods. He'd seen bloated cattle and sheep littering the bank near here, this being one of the most dangerous spots on the Habren. Strange how peaceful it all seemed as they rested in the sun. The range of hills to the east looked far more prominent now and westwards, land rose in a gentle dense forested sweep up to the horizon.

They had one further stop before reaching the confluence of the Gwy and Habren rivers. Darkness had overtaken them, but Garner's knowledge of the waters had allowed progress to one of his regular moorings. They tied up at the very spot the brothers had heard of when regaled with traveler's tales. For some strange reason each spring and autumn, following a full moon, the river flowed backwards in a series of high waves, faster than the speed of a running man. No-one knew why.

Most years on the spring surge, tiny eels could be seen glistening as they were swept upstream. Mardi gave the matter serious consideration.

They battened everything down, but again took their most valued items with them not wishing to risk losing Wolf's sword again. They climbed the short ladder up on to the wharf. Higher up the bank an open fire was crackling, people were dancing and singing, their silhouettes moving and swaying in its light. There was some sort of celebration going on and no-one seemed to mind them joining the throng.

Food and drink was on offer for all and so thinking it might be rude not to accept, they gladly tore into cuts of meat using the bread sliced from the baking stone as platters. After the previous night's drinking, Erdi made do with an elderflower brew to quench his thirst.

Beyond the main fire a slingshot competition was in progress. The white target peg was illuminated by lamps. At Mardi's request Garner asked and discovered that the unusually strong light came from the burning of whale oil. Mardi then informed Garner, in more of an aside really, that his brother wasn't a bad shot with the sling. A few beers later and the boatman was up on his feet and into the throng volunteering Erdi as their man most likely to win the flitch of bacon on offer as the prize. It was only a bit of fun after all.

The young villagers didn't see it that way and when Erdi and their local champion, nicknamed Pegger, were the only competitors left standing, so to speak, things became quite vocal.

"Come on Peggerrr!"

"Show 'im Peggerrr!"

Encouragement was growled with emphasis on the last letter of the name the man had obviously picked up thanks to his ability to hit the target peg with slingshot. As Erdi began to get the upper hand the encouragement sounded more like pleas from miffed children.

"Come on Peggerrr, what's ailing yerr?"

"You can beat him Peggerrr. He's nowt but a slip of a lad!"

When Erdi was finally awarded the flitch of bacon there were some extremely disgruntled mutterings.

"Who is he? Did you invite him?"

"No fear! They say he 'aint even from around these parrts!"

"He never seemed to miss! That canner be right!"

Erdi obviously couldn't understand exactly what was being said, but knew enough to sense the mood turning ugly. Wolf as alert as his namesake crouched ready with an eye on things. In his experience the Peggers of this world didn't usually take kindly to being beaten by a stranger on home soil. Erdi presented the handsome slab of bacon to Garner and told him he just needed a quick visit to the bushes. Wolf with measured step and keeping to the shadows, followed. A movement ahead caught his eye. A man had crept into place and was crouching in wait brandishing a sizeable lump of firewood. Wolf, more silent than a whisper, quickly crept up behind and tapped him on the shoulder with his sword. The man turned to find the weapon at his throat and an extremely large individual slowly shaking his head and beckoning him out into the light. The lump of wood was dropped and the would-be assailant was prodded back towards the fire. A thwack on his backside sent him running. It was Pegger.

When Erdi returned Wolf said, "Tell Garner we need go. Need go now!"

As they ghosted towards the wharf, they could hear a rising clamour of voices. The sort of clamour you'd expect to hear from drunken hunters goading each other before the chase. Torches were being lit. A search had begun. It felt like they'd turned up uninvited to a wedding and having had more fun than the locals, had run off with the bride.

Their boat was now up on the tide making it easy to step down on to the load and regain their seats. They slipped their moorings and paddled soft into the night. Again they were thankful for Garner's knowledge of the river and steering around seeming endless loops, they finally entered a broad basin. Their two craft were log-rolled high up, to lie safe on the bank and they spent the night sleeping on the cargo. Erdi remained blissfully ignorant of how close he had come to having his brains bashed in. Mardi had his mind on the moon. Vanya, somewhere near, wondered where her brothers were? Then suddenly without even searching for it, a notion popped into her head. Wolfy! He had been the man she'd seen that day with her brothers on the side of the hill. His wild hair and beard had gone, but she remembered the eyes -- it had definitely been him. This filled her with hope. She needed to leave a message, a sign of some sort.

Erdi was first up, it was hardly daylight, but he was anxious to be on the move again. He looked down at the river basin they had glided into the previous evening, looked again in disbelief and stood wondering where the water had gone. The river still curved its way under the far bank, but immediately below where there had once been broad waters, lay a large sandbank and up where he stood, they were high, dry and stranded. He'd of course heard tell of coastal tides, but had never expected anything this dramatic.

Garner wasn't pleased to be woken and questioned, but the amazement on Erdi's face started him laughing that much, the others were roused from slumber. There was no use rushing, he told them, as they were dependent on the tide. They soon had a fire going, bread baking and bacon cooking. They all agreed it was the best bacon they'd tasted in their lives.

Wolf toasted Erdi with a swig of water from the skin they passed around. His words when put in the right order meant, "Sweet are the gains of the victor." Apparently, it was a saying his people used.

Bonded like a band of brothers, they talked over the events of their recent journey. Garner said that when next traveling north, he'd have to put things right with the elders of the community that had so kindly donated them their breakfast, for he couldn't afford to fall out with those likely to put trade his way. He hadn't recognized many of the disgruntled youths. He assumed the festivities had drawn in the young bloods from the whole valley.

The returning water gently rolling in over the sandbar told them the tide had turned, but they waited until Garner gave the instruction to launch the boat. He told them they might sense the right time, for everything would seem to stop momentarily, as if held in suspension, before the waters started their surge back to sea again. It was the easiest paddling they'd experienced on the whole journey and the river widened to such an astonishing extent, a bird soaring high would have viewed them as nothing bigger than two beetles in tandem, slowly making their way across the glistening vastness.

By early evening they were back-paddling, waiting in the main flow opposite the point where the Gwy entered the Habren. All around were sandbanks with rivulets winding between them. The next surge of tide swept them up the Gwy river and they moored near a small settlement on the west bank. There were other boats tied up, some the like of which, Erdi had never seen before. They were of a plank construction.

They entered the small settlement and Garner suggested Erdi join him while he spoke with the headman. It was frustrating, for he was totally reliant on the boatman to ask if there had been any sign of the Tinners and his sister? First, however, he was required to wait while the opening conventions to a business deal were tiresomely gone through, then finally, the headman was asked if the Tinners and their captives had yet made an appearance. The man nodded and pointed downstream. Erdi looking on, could tell from the man's expression, not to expect good news and so when Garner did at last explain they had crossed on the morning tide, the whole lot of them, horses included, ferried over on a raft, the catastrophe didn't have quite the impact it might have done. It was still mind-numbing mind you.

Then a question was put that stunned them both. The headman asked if the young man with Garner happened to be called Erdi? Apparently one of young girls had managed to break free from her captors for long enough to explain, in sign language of course, she wanted the villagers to look out for her brother. Obviously desperate, she pointed to herself, saying her name was Vanya and had managed to add, her brother's name was Erdi, before being dragged away by one of the foul-smelling brutes.

"Oh and she asked me to give you this." Garner translated as the man rooted inside his jerkin. With a look of success and a smile he held out his palm. In it was a small pure white pebble, upon which was scratched a tiny round face with whiskers.

With that the Teller gave a bow and swept from the hall.

Part 5

Chapter Twenty-Four

The Great Hall was packed and the Teller, a little late, was cheered as he entered. Perhaps this would be the night for completion of the tale.

In a way this portion of the story was easier in the telling, but in another, not so, for he'd had to pick carefully through the details of Erdi's voyage in his mind as nearly all the events were now dictated by the sun and moon. This far inland his audience would hardly have knowledge of coastal time and tides, but it was in his nature to pay particular attention to such detail. Without it, plausibility could fall apart. He really felt at this point he needed a good rest, but the characters in the story wouldn't allow it. They called to him. Each performance he gave, telling the tale, left him drained and spent. Each portion was delivered like a complete entity, a creation that could stand alone to be judged, then next day he had to pull himself out of a state of exhaustion and put together the next chapter. After all, he could hardly abandon the characters as he'd left them the previous evening, either side of the vast waters, longing to be re-united and yet hovering in a state of limbo until his body and mind were allowed to be used as a conduit yet again, enabling their story to continue its journey down through time.

He felt certain his mood would lift once he was underway, once that dormant spirit surged and took over his body yet again, but nevertheless he continued the tale that night in quite a muted fashion.

Erdi felt broken. It seemed as if they were struggling in a hopeless battle against fate. He returned to where his brother and Wolf were waiting and told them the depressing news. While they had been traveling downriver that morning Vanya had been ferried across it. With greater luck they could have waylaid the Tinners mid river, but now it was too late in the day to follow as the tide was against them and with the next high being at middle night no boatman could be expected to risk crossing those dangerous waters in the dark. The next opportunity would not be until middle day on the morrow and so all they could do was to arrange a passage for then and glean locally anything that could aid their mission of somehow snatching Vanya back from the Tinner's clutches. The fact the tides dictated their movements put them a complete day behind, but at least they now knew Vanya was alive and well. Mardi and Wolf were shown the tiny white pebble she had left as a sign. Mardi gave a pained smile, kissed it and briefly held it to his heart,

Erdi had of course asked Garner to press the village headman for more details regarding their sister. The man had given the reply, that of course Vanya had looked tired, but who wouldn't, having trekked as a captive for all those days. Her face had shown a fair degree of urgency when relaying the message, but it was only to be expected given the circumstances. Other than that, it hadn't looked like she had been harmed in any way,

'Harmed?' Erdi wanted more details, but the man had replied, 'How could he give them? Their meeting had been so brief.'

All three walked down to where the boats were moored, knowing attempts at finding a reliable answer regarding crossing the vast estuary would be hampered by the fact, all discussions would have to be done in sign language. Then suddenly Erdi's hopes were raised. He heard a voice not only conversing in his own tongue, but the accent used could have come from one of his near neighbours back home.

He introduced himself and the man with a beaming smile spreading, told him his name was Padlor and the youth he'd been talking to was Darew his son. The man was the owner of one of the remarkable plank boats, was a veteran on the river, was a regular up and down the coastline and what's more, knew most of the people in the little trading community on the Gwy river. Erdi was determined to stick to the man like goose grass. He gave a silent thank you to the spirits for putting such good fortune their way.

There was a house up on the crag overlooking a curve in the river that offered food for travelers. Garner had mentioned it to Erdi and had suggested that they all meet up there. It wasn't a business as such, but as the lady of the house was famed for her cooking, it had been thought logical, she should occasionally profit by it. So, if pre-warned, a scrap of bronze, a woven basket, a hank of wool, a half drum of shelled peas; any of these could be traded for a meal at a time requested. Even occasionally, before turn of tide in a dark hour of morning. That's if she liked the look of you. The Tinners had been told her services were not available.

Garner and Cymar were already there waiting, when the rest of his crew along with Erdi's new acquaintances, Padlor and son entered to take their places at the eating board. Two fellow travelers following close behind squeezed into the last available spaces to render the small room full to capacity.

Occasionally clients dropped off their own meat or fish to be cooked, but other than that you ate what the lady gave you. Her man tended the various plots of land they owned and although not a gossip, kept an ear open for any interesting snippets passed from one traveler to another whilst on their way through. He knew enough to keep a still tongue as regards things overheard beneath his own roof mind you.

Now he was amused to witness, what on the face of it was just another gathering of travelers thrown together by their own peculiar circumstances, turning into something more like an excited reunion.

Erdi briefly related their particular saga and made clear the need to cross the Habren on the next day's high tide, Garner regaled the company with details of the incident at the gorge and Padlor explained how he'd escaped a life of herding and ploughing by first taking to the river and then to coastal trading. He'd originated from a village up on the very ridge where Erdi, Wolf and Mardi had taken shelter the night following the great storm and he told them about the people living there, remembered from his youth.

The old queen had still been alive and Gardarm had been naught but a squalling babe in arms. He'd been close friends with a youth who'd lived to the north of the ridge. They shared the same independent spirit and a strong disinclination to stand all day guarding cattle and sheep. Padlor had taken to trading on the Habren, his friend had prospered, by deals done locally.

"You're talking about Trader," said Erdi in amazement.

"You mean you know the man?"

"Know him? More than that. I've actually worked with him."

That was it. They rattled on about all the people they knew in north Habren territory. You know the sort of conversation, like a thrilling ride for those who share so much in common, but something to be patiently endured by listeners who don't. Padlor had known Erdi's father, Penda, still only a young man when the rover first left home and he'd known Elsa's mother when Elsa was still a young girl. His mother's sister, Aunt Gade had married one of Garner's uncles making them in some distant way, related and they'd have continued wrestling with just how close or distant that happened to be, had the host not interrupted.

"Excuse me," he said to Garner, "I heard that young man referring to Tinners earlier." The little party fell silent at his mention of the word.

The man continued, "Just thought I'd tell you, I happened to be down at the dock when they were loading their horses. The ferryman overheard them talking and they imparted certain information you might find useful." Their host explained, he'd chanced on the details of Erdi's circumstances courtesy of the village headman and then said, "I share my wife's revulsion for the slavers and their trade and I'm only too glad to provide any information that might help."

Garner translated this for their benefit and the room fell silent to allow him to concentrate on what followed. Even the strangers, the two that had followed them into the dining place, took a close interest. From the dialect they spoke, Erdi guessed they originated from the southern regions. *The Teller stopped and smiled.* This business of translation. You people have been marvellous. Quite often I encounter someone who is more interested in finding fault in detail than actually listening to the story. If you notice such a person about to pipe up, please silence him and allow me licence to relate what went on in that cliff top hut without having to explain how they all understood one another. The tale will flow all the better for it. I humbly thank you. *The Teller gave the hint of a bow.*

The Tinners had divulged exactly where they were now bound and bemoaned the fact that although their horses had so far been indispensable, possession of such from here on forced them to take the laborious trek overland rather than the easier option of traveling by water. They had been cheered by the fact they'd be joining friends across the estuary who had also been trading for, more likely abducting, yet more women to be sold in the south. Back down in Tinner heartland. Once this had been told the mood in the small hut changed completely. For Erdi, it was time for harsh reality and worry. The previously conceived plan of tracking the slavers and somehow snatching Vanya back, no longer seemed realistic in view of the sheer number of raiders they'd now probably be facing. All of a sudden, their mission seemed hopeless and the shock of this numbed him to his very soul. Had they missed their chance? With this latest news hitting like a hammer blow, it was hard to concentrate. The spirits as ever, seemed to be favouring evil. When would fortune begin to smile on the good? On their own noble mission? All his reasoning seemed scrambled and as the voices clamoured around him, he slid his hands below the dining board not wanting hardy boatmen to notice they had started to tremble slightly.

The conversation gradually ebbed, but this was not for the better as it began to follow a scary more explicit path. Anecdotes were exchanged in awestruck tones and this brought the two strangers to the fore, topping each tale with one more chilling, clearly relishing the gory detail. They had a fund of horror stories and were keen to impart, until eventually they completely dominated the conversation in the small room. It was hardly what the brothers needed at this point. They already knew the fear engendered by the slavers. They had not only met them, but had had their sister stolen by them. They didn't need to hear tales of the Tinner's savagery and to be told even trained warriors dare not tackle them. But the two southerners, having everyone's attention, reveled in it. They said communities had trembled before them and one headman having led his people into hiding, doing all he could to avoid contact with the wild men, returned to find ------ "Guess what they found on their return to the village?"

There was silence as all awaited the answer.

"The whole place torched and the old couple too sick to be moved, impaled in the most ghastly fashion."

If this hadn't been bad enough, the pair emboldened by the reception of such revelations, took courage and began to drag up the sort of juicy detail certain to invite opprobrium if disclosed with women and children present. They actually relished the horror of it. I won't sink to the same depths they wallowed in, but be aware of the fact, the brothers had to endure hearing particulars of what befell certain young females unlucky enough to have fallen into their clutches.

Also, apparently, the wild men had at times even dined on, savoured in fact, certain severed parts of their male captives.

Cooked of course. *The Teller gave a wry smile.* So we're not talking about complete savages here.

The little touch of irony was not completely lost on his audience.

Erdi had his head in his hands, thinking, 'Stop! For the love of goodness please stop!'

I'll just add one last morsel to leave you in no doubt as to the horror felt by the brothers.

"Grandmothers!" The one stranger had said.

"No, I don't believe it." Came a gasped reply.

"Yes I'm telling you. Grandmothers! It's as true as I'm sitting here."

To try and put it as delicately as possible, *said the Teller*, in view of there being ladies present; they apparently even forced their attentions on these poor old crones, right there in front of their kinfolk. It was almost like a sport, wallowing in the joy of witnessing their victims' humiliation.

Erdi thumped a fist down on the dining board. Padlor suddenly realising the effect all this was having on his new friends, stood and grimacing, fanned a hand to indicate, 'Stop! Haven't you any sense or feelings?'

The strangers, looking highly amused by the admonishment, were just on the verge of recounting what they thought to be the hilarious climax to a tale regarding elderly ladies and barbarous warriors, when the sight of Wolf slowly rising hand on sword hilt stopped them. In wide eyed alarm both mouths snapped shut and they sank as would a pair of seals on eying a harpooner heading their way.

Silence followed. All now realised the distress the vicarious divulgences had caused. When conversation did restart it was in worthy, anxious tones. Too far the other way in fact, helping to hammer home Erdi's feelings of futility and despair. He needed a quiet place to rid his head of all its jangle of confusion, but didn't dare let Padlor out of his sight. He instinctively knew the man was reason for hope. Staying with him seemed their only chance of finding the narrow path out of this catastrophe. There had to be a solution, for even in these blackest moments, even when any notion of continuing seemed completely futile, a small voice still called from within. The same voice that had given hope when enslaved in the fortress. It told him not to give up. 'Somehow, somewhere there had to be an answer.' Also he remembered Trader's words, "Keep doing the right thing."

The Teller paused here and took a drink of water. He smiled at his audience. He could feel his strength and enthusiasm returning.

With the conversation going on to more mundane river business, Padlor took the opportunity to offer Erdi some comforting words and also advised him to disregard the exaggerated rubbish they had just heard. Erdi's spirits began to lift as he listened to details of the southern territories the Tinners would be traveling through and to the fact there was an alternative. Was this the ray of hope he had been praying for? He was told to abandon his plan of tracking his sister overland for it would be long, arduous and against the small army that had now assembled, suicidal. Padlor could see how the morning's revelations had hit his new friend like a body blow and putting a comforting hand on his arm he smiled, saying, "It's not all bad news, Erdi. Like I said there's an alternative."

Erdi looked up hardly daring to believe there could at last be hope. He knocked twice on the dining board in case the spirits were listening, then waited, silently praying. Mardi, sitting next to them, drew closer.

"Those Tinners will be forced to take the long way round. They won't know the hidden trails through fen country. I live there. Trust me. They won't dare risk it. They'll have heard tales of lives lost by those foolish enough to try. Going round the fens will cost them two days, maybe three."

Erdi was heartened by Padlor's earnest gaze, but didn't dare yet fall into the trap of thinking that at last something good could be coming their way. Fate had been too cruel to them.

"Erdi, your best option is to go by sea."

"But where can we find a boat going all that distance?"

Padlor pointed enthusiastically at himself.

"You mean you travel to the end regions? To the very edge?"

"Yes at least once a year, but it's not really the edge as you put it."

Mardi, nodded in agreement saying, "There isn't an edge Erdi. Remember, we live on a giant ball."

Padlor gave him a puzzled look and said, "Well. If you like. But the fact is, none of us refer to it as the edge. There are all sorts of lands out there."

"So why do we call them the boundless seas?" asked Erdi.

"You've been listening to sailor's tales," said Padlor laughing. "Those old salt riders don't want to pass on where they get their cargos from. Anyway, are you coming aboard or not?"

"Without hesitation. This is what I've been praying to the spirits for." He could have hugged the man.

Padlor smiled and said, "You don't know how lucky you are. This is my last trip, Erdi. I've done years on the salt waters and there could be no more fitting end than this."

"I can hardly believe it," said Erdi quietly, almost like a thank you to the spirits.

"I have to make certain calls along the way, but we'll still be there before the Tinners. I'd bet my cargo on that."

Erdi's head was still ringing with what the two strangers had regaled them with. "You heard those tales earlier. My sister Vanya is into womanhood. She's beautiful. Like a beautiful innocent flower. Those animals -------"

Padlor interrupted. "Comfort yourself, Erdi with this small fact. Your sister is a valuable commodity. It's in their best interests to keep her that way, looking as attractive and as intact as possible," He didn't entirely believe what he had said, but it was what the brothers needed to hear. Then the food arrived.

The Teller felt the strength of the tale starting to course through his body and now at last relished imparting the details of where it led.

So! Early next morning the little community was abuzz with news from up the Habren. It's amazing how fast word traveled on the river. Especially such a tragic tale blowing in with the dark hour tide. A boat had been ambushed in the Habren Gorge, the crew massacred and cargo stolen.

Garner was the worst effected on hearing this as the three crew members had been amongst his closest friends. He held back actual tears, but moist eyes and slight crack in his voice betrayed the pain as he explained to Erdi, the men had been amongst those he'd met in the dining hut, the morning they'd first cast off. They were the crew of the second boat to be traveling south that day. Erdi realised he, Wolf and Mardi could have also had a mention in the tragedy had they not been seated next to Garner at the dining board that morning and had had the luck of places offered on his boat. Also the lost crew hadn't had the likes of Wolf with them. Basically, they hadn't stood a chance. They'd been shown no mercy.

This news put Garner's return upriver in doubt. He now faced the choice of waiting where he was or mooring up just south of the gorge until receiving further news. Erdi felt like they were abandoning him as they took possession of all their things, but he had to harden his feelings. It was Vanya that mattered. That was his mission. He was going to rescue her at all costs.

He watched the two men push off from the dock. Garner had decided on the braver option and was leaving at low water to catch the incoming tide up the Habren estuary. They were given fond farewells and jocular calls were exchanged across the water, regarding maggots on wounds, river pirates vanquished, best bacon ever tasted.

Garner, with hands funnelled to help his voice carry, shouted, "Come on Peggerrr! You gonner let 'im bag all the bacon, Peggerrr?"

"I daresay!" Erdi called back.

He gave one final wave as the two boatmen floated out of his life. Even though recent events had thrown himself and certain people together with unusual intensity it was still hard to comprehend the strength of bond that had developed in such a short span of time. He had only known the pair for a matter of days, yet felt a wrench inside watching them go as if suddenly parted from lifelong friends. He shuddered to think how he would feel when knowing he was looking at Wolf for the final time, but part they must, Erdi could hardly lead him back to a life of slavery.

Their belongings were stowed aboard Padlor's craft and he then insisted they all eat something as they would be glad of it by the end of day. Their way was long and daylight hours on the water would be curtailed by their dependence on the timing of high tide. First Erdi asked if he would accompany him and help question the ferryman. There might be other useful details he'd be able to impart.

The ferry was moored further along the dock. Padlor knew the man, Erdi saw rising from where he'd been squatting talking to his crew and after an introduction, he joined them, walking slowly back along the river. It turned out he'd originated from Tinner country, had fetched up on the Gwy by chance on a trip north and liking the place had decided to stay.

Two of the men working for him were his sons. He proved to be a mine of information.

He told of vast wealth in his homeland. Exotic goods from over the waters brought in by foreign traders desperate for tin. Padlor told him, he had also witnessed this.

Yes, but did he know about the strange animals, bright woven fabrics, the magic amber, carpets, oils, henna dye, spices and wine? "It's madness down there," the little man said, "Pure madness!"

"So why did you leave? You've left all that wealth for a life going back and forth on the tide."

"Can't last," he said. "Nothing like that can last. What's more all that wealth is in the hands of the few. You don't think the likes of me and my folks saw any of it do you? Tun Mytern even had a bear brought down to dance for his daughter. A trained bear brought all that way just to dance for his darling princess on her birthday! And yet others living nearby are close on starving to death. I tell you it can't last. The man even had a copper roof put on a hut so guests can hear the thunder of his wealth when it rains."

"Yes, I've seen evidence of the poverty you mention," said Padlor. "and also, Copper Hall. Of course, I've never been inside."

"Copper Hall! Nothing more than a glorified hut! It can't last. Glad I got out."

This was all translated for Erdi who asked Padlor to inquire why raiders had traveled so far north to drag women back into slavery.

"Listen to the next bit," he said. "Sums up the madness down there." He told them that the wealth of the area had lured young men from distant kingdoms, turning up in a wild frenzy, panning the streams for tin. Most had given up everything in the mad dash for quick riches, abandoning all once the rumours had spread. The lucky few had struck it rich and could indulge themselves, gamble, bedeck their bodies with bronze, drink themselves silly and fight, but what they were all really lacking, what they craved for, yes you've guessed it, women. They'd part with all the tin in the river to get their hands on one.

"Now listen, it gets even more interesting." He drew them close and in a conspiratorial tone told them, various gangs of traders, in actual fact slavers, had been sent out with tin to barter for these elusive items of young men's desires. Foreign traders in their desperation for the magic metal had forced up its value to such an extent, certain tribal chieftains here on home soil had found they couldn't compete. They could, however if they were willing to trade in human cargo.

Erdi on hearing this, asked Padlor to tell the man his sister had not been traded for, but stolen. The ferryman, suddenly stopping mid-stride, turned and said, "Now let me tell you the best bit." The three trips it had taken him to ferry the Tinners, their mounts, pack horses and captives across the estuary had given him chance to glean all the information just imparted, but now he said there was one last juicy kernel. The Tinners, those that had ended up in north Habren country, had parted with the tin they'd been given as arranged, but only on the understanding that a certain chieftain by the name of Gardroom or some such name, provided them with four young beauties to return home with. Something had gone wrong, however and Goldarm hadn't come up with goods as he'd vowed he would. Of course, the Tinners became a bit upset about this and told him in no uncertain terms, that without the goods promised, he'd better not be expecting further supplies of tin in the future. So big chief Gridbum does no more than tell them to go and help themselves. Grab whoever they could from amongst his own people. "It's madness I tell you. Pure madness."

So now Erdi had the truth of the matter.

They finally slipped their moorings after middle day and paddled downstream towards waters, the like of which the brothers had never even imagined, let alone voyaged on. And

Wolf? He smiled to himself. He'd seen it all before and looked forward to their reaction.

Once into the Habren estuary their progress on the ebbing tide was rapid and the western shore became a hazy pale green line on the horizon. Wolf tapped Erdi on the shoulder when they first swept up, cresting the waves, to slip smooth into gullies, leaving stomachs behind. He threw his head back laughing heartily at Erdi's lower lip-biting, wide eyed look of mock trepidation.

They continued paddling into the early evening, the sunset throwing a rose glow on two islands ahead in mid channel, the western isle hardly showing above the water line. Steering as if guided by this, Padlor altered course for the shore. They arrived riding on a wave that rolled and then gently rippled them up on to a sandy beach. Things for the night were unloaded, the boat was securely anchored and they pitched camp up beyond high water mark. They dined on the mackerel Padlor had yanked and hauled aboard, hooked on the very same feather lures Erdi had viewed so incredulously earlier that day. They were blissfully rocked to sleep by the sand-sieved sighs of backwash as wave after wave flopped lazily to shore on the incoming tide.

They were in no rush to leave next morning as Padlor's first call was only a little further west. Erdi walked with Darew down across the hard ridged sand with its countless tiny reflections of the pale morning sky. It was cool and fresh underfoot and there was a stiff offshore breeze. They tugged on the painter pulling the boat in and held it steady while belongings were loaded and the others clambered aboard. They all paddled vigorously to warm themselves and to reach deeper water.

About mid-morning Padlor began steering back towards land. Erdi couldn't discern what particular landmark had prompted this, for as far as he could see there weren't any and it wasn't until close inshore that he spotted the mouth of a small river issuing from between high sand banks. Here they waited. Finally, Padlor called from the stern, "Right she should be up enough by now," and they all paddled the boat in over the sand bar and along quiet waters, through a seeming endless world of tall rushes.

Channels of dark water led off to the unknown and Padlor steered them with the same certainty as Erdi would have felt if negotiating known paths at home. The waters opened into a large pool reflecting cloud and sky and on the far side was a small settlement with houses perched on stilted platforms above the water. The homes were inter-connected by walkways and small reed boats sitting light as ducks, slowly yawed in the breeze on their tethers below. Cheery cries rang out and Padlor paused mid-pool for exchange of a little banter, but this was not to be their destination. They continued further into the forest of reeds.

Fish leapt for flies, ducks took to the air in a clatter of wings, coots patrolling open water piped abruptly and moorhens, heads eagerly jerking forward, busied themselves on the fringes of the water channels. Then came other sounds, children's laughter, an axe chopping, a loud splash, a baby crying, a woman's high-pitched call and above all, the perfume of smoke drifting on the breeze to tickle the back of their nostrils. They emerged from the reeds and directly ahead was an island village, reed-roofed houses, washing flapping, smoke drifting across the water, wooden walkways disappearing off into the tangle, a jetty lined with small boats, adults poised in mid action and children running down to greet their boat gliding in. Padlor was home.

They were deep into what locals referred to as 'The Lefels' and Erdi could now see why the Tinners couldn't have contemplated taking the direct line southwest to their destination. They were all made welcome and it became obvious to Erdi why Padlor had chosen this little haven rather than return to a life in thrall to a ruling elite. He had told him they of course needed bronze, like any other community, but no-one here dictated their lives by their need to possess it and no-one took an annual tithe of everything they produced.

Erdi left Padlor covered in grandchildren, neighbour's children and even his tail wagging dog, attempting to join in. He wandered over to where Mardi and Wolf, laughing like youngsters were pointing at fish weaving amongst the fronds and together, they toured the island and explored along walkways. A man perched fishing on the boarding leant forward to let them pass. They discovered other patches of dry ground where crops grew and on a tiny scrap of land near the main island stood a lookout tower. They climbed up to the shaded platform and gazed out on a sea of grass riffling in the wind. A heron laboured airborne and flapped slowly across its domain. Flocks of tiny birds, in flickering grey clouds, took to the air and as if of one mind descended to become lost again amongst the reeds. There were small patches of blue water dotted here and there and to the south smoke drifted from another settlement. Looking directly west they searched for a while and then finally spotted the smudge of smoke that in all likelihood betrayed the location of the stilted village they had paddled past earlier. There was a range of hills to the north, high ground on the south western horizon and directly east, rising like Mardi's Seer cap from the fens, a conical hill.

That night there was a grand gathering, diverse fish and fowl to dine on, music, singing, dancing and of course beer. Erdi noticed they were being stared at and quietly talked about. "They make me feel like a piece of breeding stock," he said to his brother.

Mardi replied, "To be quite honest, Erdi, I wouldn't mind living here." Alas, fate had another path in store.

Next morning Erdi helped Padlor rearrange the cargo, in slight disarray from the previous night's unloading of certain goods he'd procured for the village. Fresh items, individually wrapped, were tucked in below the main load out of sight. Once satisfied everything was stowed, tied down and tidy, he told Erdi there was someone he'd like him and Mardi to meet.

He led them along a walkway where on one side reeds had been hacked back to allow access for a boat, a provision also provided along the branching path they followed. It reminded Erdi of childhood games tunneling through the long grass. On an island deep in the reeds was a hut and two men working vigorously beside a vertical clay tube that spat sparks and billowed smoke. They alternated on the bellows to pump a constant stream of air into the bottom of the tube. Scoops of material were poured into the little inferno and the pumping was re-commenced. Mardi was transfixed.

Both men looked up and smiled, but were too busy for further niceties. Mardi investigated and recognized immediately charcoal and crushed limestone waiting in piles to be added to the alchemy, but he couldn't identify the contents of the third pile. He gave Padlor an enquiring look and received the reply, "Mardi, you're looking at the future."

He led them into the hut and both he and Erdi smiled at the sight of Mardi gazing around mesmerized. Familiar tools hung from pegs and racks, but they had been wrought and cast from a dull, dark metal which was definitely not bronze. A square block of the mysterious material stood on an oak stump and nearby leant a hammer with a head of the same metal. Mardi lifted it, felt the weight, ran his hands over the business end to feel the texture and then when tapping it down on the block, his eyes widened in wonder at the thin ringing sound. He repeated the tapping, laughed and looked as excited as if he'd just learnt how to whistle.

"It's iron," said Padlor.

"Where does it come from?" asked Mardi.

"From out of the ground. We find it when cutting turf for the fire." He led them back outside. The men had ceased their pumping and Padlor introduced them. The swarthy older man was called Bastinas, but Padlor said he was known to all as Basty and the youth was called Ardew. As you can imagine, Mardi was all questions and even though he and his new best friend Basty didn't have a single word in common they seemed to have an understanding that transcended conversation. Mardi handled the new wonder ore and listened and watched as Bastinas explained the smelting process. The man picked up an axe, its head wrought from iron and invited Mardi to thumb its keen cutting edge, then with a deft diagonal chop, let the weight of the blade slice a slender pole of hazel clean through.

Erdi and Padlor left them to it and the latter explained that Bastinas had fetched up on native shores four years previously. He'd first tried imparting his knowledge to villagers down in Tinner country and not surprisingly when the so-called Tin King heard reports of this strange new metal, a squad of soldiers was dispatched to bring him in. Fortunately news of the impending arrest had reached the villagers who managed to smuggle him down to the little port on Crooked River and guess who happened to be casting off that very day? It was a big risk to take, but Padlor had left on the tide with the fugitive aboard and made it out to the blue yonder without anyone being any the wiser.

"Where's he from? He looks like no other man I've seen before."

"A far-off land way out in the east. He's full of fabulous tales, but it's hard to tell whether they're truth, exaggeration or even complete figments of his imagination. He certainly doesn't think much of the food we forage for around these parts. He describes it in that way of his, almost spitting in disgust, saying most of it's bitter and he then goes into one of his dreamy descriptions of what's available back in his homeland. 'Basty's off again,' the women say. Or when they've really had enough they shout, 'If it's that good, why don't you go back there?' They all love him really, though."

"With this new wonder material, do you need to add anything to it, like tin?"

"No that's the beauty of it. A bit of lime helps, but there's plenty of that about, but other than that you can just help yourself. Pick it up and smelt it. It's right there in the ground."

"What about up on the north Habren? Are we likely to find any?"

"Yes it's obviously not quite as easy as I just made it sound, but there'll be some lying about somewhere. Where you see colours on marsh water, like the colours of the sky bow, search around there and you'll find it."

"I know those colours you mean. I've seen them. So no more need for copper. No more need for tin."

"And no more need for those controlling the trade of them."

"I can hardly believe it," said Erdi. "It's been lying there, under our feet all along."

"Erdi, there are going to be some big changes. This metal belongs to everyone. The days of the Tin King and people like him are almost over. This is why I'm on the last trip down there. I'll keep the boat. Isn't she a beauty? From now on I'll be hauling clay for the kilns, bog iron, lime and charcoal."

"Those sacks we heaved off last night?"

"Charcoal," said Padlor.

"And the things we put on board this morning?"

He replied with one finger to his lips. Erdi enquired no further.

They walked back along the causeway to the village. Wolf was sitting on the jetty fishing. He pretended not to notice the small children creeping up on him. When close upon him he turned and growled and they fled shrieking, dithering in terror almost pushing one another into the water in their panic to escape.

Wolf called out to Erdi, "The little devils are scaring my fish." He looked truly happy. The little devils in question were peering from the side of a hut plucking up courage for the next foray.

At the midday meal in Padlor's hut, Erdi noticed one of the serving girls, smiling at Mardi. His brother gave a low-lidded, bashful smile in return.

Later with the sun just starting its dip towards the west, the girl was on the jetty waving them off, prompting Erdi to say, "Looks like you've made a new friend."

Mardi's face took on a glow to rival that of the coming sunset.

They reached the sea at turn of tide and continued their journey with the line of the coast taking them west. They paddled through the remains of day and the sun was low by the time they pulled into a small cove beneath a southern headland. Mackerel was again the evening meal, cooked impaled on small stakes jabbed into the sand around the driftwood fire that sent sparks into the night. Nearby a small stream etched shallow, ever-changing gullies on its way to the sea and taking a short walk up the beach, they were able to refill their water skins. The following morning with no time for a snack, they loaded the boat, conveniently floating in exactly the same depth of water on the new tide as it had been when anchored on the old. The whole day was spent paddling with nothing to sustain them other than dried meat and water. The distance covered was roughly the same as on the first day, but this time there was not the power of the estuary tide to help. They were exhausted by the time they pulled into a cove of lake-calm waters sheltered beneath an imposing headland. It was late afternoon and they rippled in across the reflected picture of steep cliffs with the tide brimming.

They were setting up for the night and searching for driftwood, when as if out of nowhere, a man appeared. Padlor knew him, and started unwrapping items he'd dug out earlier from under the cargo. The stranger examined them, each being a tool fashioned from iron. After a short discussion bronze was exchanged and the man left as quietly as he'd arrived. Close to the ascent of the cliff path, he stopped on hearing Padlor call, waved an arm in acknowledgement and continued on his way.

"I was just telling him not to mention where he got them from. Dangerous cargo."

"You still take bronze as payment?" queried Erdi.

"I'll exchange it for gold in the south. Soon bronze won't be worth any more than the face value of the tool it happens to be. An outdated tool at that. And 'ronds', 'bolts' and 'bits' of bronze? Not worth a bowl of cold pottage."

"Why was everything so carefully wrapped."

"Partly to hide it, but mainly to keep the water off. That's the one drawback. It goes a dull red-brown colour when exposed to the damp. It can be rubbed clean with sand, but you don't want to have to explain that before you even start the deal."

"Pity you and Trader couldn't meet up again, you have a lot in common."

Erdi, deep in thought for a while, said, "There's something I don't understand."

"You're going to ask, 'How did he know we'd be here?'"

Erdi nodded, slightly surprised at his perception. He felt himself warming to this man, amazed at how his natural unassuming manner had given no hint of the depth of his wisdom and ability to calmly deal with the vagaries of the sea.

"I'd told him on my way north that if the weather stayed fair, to start looking out for me at high tide on the eighth moon before full."

"Fair weather? We had storms on the Habren."

"Not down here. Had our share of rain, but no storms." He pulled his cloak about him and gave a shudder. "It's colder up there. Another reason for settling south. Having said that, wind could be freshening tomorrow. Don't ask me how I know. Sometimes I wonder myself." With that he laughed and carried his creel, beyond where the boat lay stranded at a drunken angle on the black line of seaweed and crouched at the waterline cleaning his day's catch. Gulls flopped down from high ledges into a swooping lazy glide, then wheeled, screeching and mewing with excitement, sensing a snack in the offing.

Next morning, they awoke at first light and Erdi noticed Darew was no longer with them. Padlor saw the mystified look and grinning, nodded out towards the boat. Darew was on board, occasionally dipping a paddle. He had slept on the cargo to keep pace with the ebb of the fresh tide that had crept in and lifted the boat in the night.

"She's a bit heavy to be starting your day rolling her down the beach," said Padlor.

They followed the coast westward and rounding a headland to at last point the prow due south, they hit the heaviest swell so far on the journey. When cresting the waves, a small island was visible out to the west. As they swept down off each roller to rise up on the next, down into the trough, back up on the crest, wave after wave, flow unrelenting, down and then up, Mardi started to go a funny colour. He would have quite happily followed his vomit away on the water had Erdi not grabbed him. Padlor steering in the stern laughed to himself. Mardi sweating profusely, retched up again with limited success and would have given anything to have been lifted off that boat. He sat slumped forward with paddle across his knees, moaning to himself. Luckily the day's travel was not that exacting and the waters calmed as they headed inshore late morning. They rode the tide into a river estuary and up a tributary flowing from the south. By the time they nudged against a small docking area, Mardi was like a new man, fully recovered. With a glow in his face and colour restored, he was actually starting to feel hungry.

"Feeling better now Mardi?" asked Padlor helping him up on to the jetty.

"I do. But that was dreadful. Never felt so sick in all my life."

"Well you gave the gulls a good feed. They were fighting over it."

"They weren't, were they?" said Erdi. "That's disgusting." He'd missed the spectacle having been too far forward in the boat.

"Wheeling and diving," said Padlor enthusiastically with hand movements to match. "Squabbling over it."

Mardi thought for a while. "It's not that disgusting really, Erdi. We relish eating certain things, love the way it's cooked, but basically it all just turns to sick in the end. We're all walking round with bellies full of sick. In fact when you think about it, our bodies must be running on the stuff."

"I'm really glad you told me that, Mardi. How do you dream these things up?"

"It's the same when you're kissing someone."

"STOP! Mardi that's enough."

"Well it's true," Mardi grumbled to himself. "Only telling you what's true."

Padlor led them to a small shack where smoke billowing, sounds of sizzling from fish grilling and aroma wafting as they entered, gave them an instant appetite.

The rest of the day, as Padlor went about his business, his crew splashed and swam in the waters, relaxed in the sun and then made all ready for the coming night. Wolf's white chin had long ago blended in with the rest of his complexion and rising from the river, he had resembled a powerful water god. Erdi kept the observation to himself. It wasn't the sort of thing you divulged to a trained fighting man.

The sun wasn't up when Padlor roused them from slumber and they stowed their things aboard in the cool of a grey dawn light.

"Come on jump to it!" he called. "Wake yourselves or we'll miss the tide. We've a ways to travel today."

They left with the tide pulling them downstream into the main river and out to sea. Padlor steered westwards across a broad bay and then rounding a prominent point late morning, they headed due south. It was a long day on dry rations, but they did finally head inshore to a pretty little river estuary just prior to high water.

Padlor overheard Erdi say to Wolf, "Not mackerel again," and retorted, "Perhaps you'd prefer nothing."

Erdi instantly apologized.

"And it could be nothing tomorrow." He scanned the western horizon. "I sense heavy weather coming in. We're in for a bit of a blow."

His senses proved right. Next morning, they walked out to the headland, the wind bringing tears to their eyes and one look at the spray and froth being whipped off the white-caps to splatter high on the rocks told them they were stranded for the day. Padlor tried to reassure them, saying it would probably blow itself out and become calm enough for them to continue on the morrow, but that was hard to imagine as the wind flattened their clothing limb-tight and rattled it so forcefully behind, they had a struggle to stay upright.

Not only did they feel dispirited, but were soon ravenous. Their rations had been used up apart from a few peas and flour and so taking the previous night's mackerel scraps for bait, Erdi and Mardi walked into more sheltered terrain upstream, hoping to catch trout. They're a hard fish to catch when you're hungry.

While they sat on a log, dangling a line more in hope than expectation, Mardi said that by his calculations, the sun would darken in five days' time. That was when the moon would pass between the sun and their own world. It would happen about middle day. Erdi sensed the spirits listening. They should have knocked on the log before commencing the conversation. What if they were those dreaded malevolent spirits? He gave the gnarled bark a gentle knock, then another just for luck. His brother reasoned that considering the effect his prediction of the darkening moon had had on their own community, a similar prediction for the sun ought to have five times the impact on complete strangers. Maybe this could somehow be put to use in their attempt to rescue Vanya.

Erdi agreed, but couldn't see quite how. So much depended on coincidence, requiring them and Vanya to be in the right place at exactly the time the sun darkened. He didn't like to admit it, but sitting there hungry under a lowering sky, feeding diminishing bait to trout nibbling, but not biting, it all seemed too improbable.

"And why did you say your prediction would make more impact on strangers?" He asked, only just realising what Mardi had said.

"I don't know. It just seems that no matter how well you try to do something, strangers seem to appreciate it more than your own people. Take slingshot and storytelling for example. Our family simply expect it of you. Yet beating Gardarm on the Arrow Field made you a hero to folk you'd never even met before and each time you told our story on the Habren you had the villagers hanging on your every word."

"Steady on Mardi. Remember I had help from the headman, if that's the time you're talking about."

"Well it's true. Might as well tell you. This bad weather worries me though, Erdi."

He gazed at the western sky with a look of despair. Bank after bank of dark grey cloud continued to roll in relentlessly. Where they sat it was as dull as evening with not the slightest hint of the day brightening. "Erdi, I'm really scared for Vanya." His face was a picture of anguish. "If we're stuck here much longer, we'll miss the chance. Then I don't see how we can possibly rescue her." At that, Erdi's fishing line suddenly snapped taught and with its white belly flashing on the surface, a large struggling trout was hauled in.

He gave thanks to the spirits, moved further upstream and hooked another. They returned to camp with three in all held up in triumph. Wolf had foraged for shellfish. These went in the same pot as the peas, their trout were skewer roasted and when all was accompanied by scraps of bread baked from final bag shakings of flour it made for quite a delicious meal. They could have easily eaten the same amount again, but it had warmed their insides and was better than nothing. Amongst the stones washed down by the river, Erdi noticed a number perfect for using as slingshot. He gathered together a tidy pile for taking aboard. At least it was something positive to do whilst stuck there.

Next morning, catching the tide, they were finally able to shove off, their boat bucking and diving on a lively sea. The day's plan had been to try and push on to reach their final destination even if it took all their strength to do so. The spirits had other ideas. They were forced to take shelter about middle day having spent more time in the final stretch bailing than paddling. It was dangerous out there and the cold and wet had sapped their strength. Once in the lee of an island they could at last relax and paddle into the curved inlet, a quiet haven with two huts tucked into the embrace of the headland that reared up to defy the sea. Fishing folk emerged and stood watching the five strangers stagger off their boat, wet, hungry and dithering with cold. It wasn't the sort of day to be expecting visitors. Not the sort of day to be out on the water unless you had to. 'There again folk seemed in such a rush these days.'

They invited the newcomers in out of the cold and offered them a place by the fire. Their clothes were hung to dry and they were given warm blankets and food. Padlor offered them bronze in payment, but they waved this away saying there was plenty more food where that had come from. They slept all the warmer for hearing the rain beating on the roof and emerged next morning to a cool, but bright new day. They thanked their hosts and left on the morning tide.

By middle day they were at long last near their goal, hove-to waiting for the tide to lift them over a massive sandbar and upriver. They rode on the incoming waters, paddling their way past a cluster of houses on the southern shore of the wide sweeping estuary. There were boats hauled up on higher ground where the settlement stood, but eying the upstream shoreline, they could see the land gave way to low marshes and inlets. In the narrowing estuary they pulled alongside a simple wooden dock where numerous boats were moored. Quite a large community had become established at the point where the earliest opportunity to ford the river at low water and access to the sea at high water, coincided.

"We're here," said Padlor with a sigh and a smile.

A man on the dockside took their line and with the deft touch of experience, looped it round a mooring post. They made their way one at a time to minimise boat sway, stepping carefully atop the cargo before hauling themselves up the ladder on to the very threshold of famed Tinner country. Padlor led them between the houses. Old ropes lay rotting in tangled greening heaps, the new lay neatly coiled, fish traps hung in abundance and everywhere nets were draped for drying. The smell of decaying fish jabbed at the nostrils and the settlement gave the clear feel that industriousness took clear precedent over homeliness. They could sense the many eyes watching from dark interiors and the children that plucked up courage to peer from doorways didn't look the sort you'd encourage your own to play with. The air of poverty seemed strange to Erdi, having been regaled with tales of fabulous wealth and excesses down in Tinner country. It seemed that what the ferryman had told them back on the Gwy was in fact true.

On the far side of the village was a large hut fronting a horse coral. The man knew Padlor and welcomed them inside. It was obviously not his home. Ropes and harness hung everywhere and the place reeked of horse sweat. They were taken through to the back to view the two carts available and with Padlor being a fairly regular customer a deal for hiring horse and cart was not long in the striking. When it came to talk of hiring out three horses to complete strangers, however, there seemed to be a snag. He hadn't wanted to insult anyone, but it had to be seen from his point of view, what was to stop them hiring the horses and simply riding off with them? Padlor assured him his friends were to be trusted and gave his personal guarantee that the steeds would be returned. When Erdi produced three axe heads to secure the deal, an involuntary flicker of greed like a tiny snake strike lit the man's eyes. He took the deal. No person naive enough to offer three pristine ronds for just three day's hire would be likely horse thieves. With everything settled they went for some food.

"I take it you got those axeheads from up on the Habren?" surmised Wolf.

"I daresay," answered Erdi.

Padlor wondered what had been so funny.

The cart was collected and the boat unloaded, with two on board passing the goods up to waiting hands. These items were then offered up for Padlor to pack in his preferred order. With the bulk of the job done, Wolf drew Erdi's attention to a boat moored further along the wharf. Its bent-wood latticed frame was covered in hide and it had sufficient capacity to carry at least six men plus cargo. Wolf looked deep in thought, "That boat's from home," he said at last. "We ask Padlor to find out about it."

Now their own boat lay empty, Erdi had the chance to examine its construction. It was truly remarkable. The two oak planks forming the hull bottom had been trimmed to leave a small up-stand running the full length of each and half round hoops had also been adzed and bored to stand like short exposed tunnels, at intervals. Cross timbers through hoops and up-stands kept the hull rigid and wedges driven in forced the moss filled joints taut and watertight. A similar hoop and wedge technique held the side planks rigid and yew-wood bindings under the strain of wedges kept the whole structure as taught as a skin topped drum.

When Padlor asked for information on Wolf's behalf, regarding the hide boat, a local fisherman looking up from his net repairs, told him it had crossed before the recent turn in the weather and the wild mariners, the mere sight of whom had prompted mothers to lock up their daughters, were away with their copper for trading. The man had used the simple word, 'crossed' as if the formidable seas between this local haven and the distant shores of Erin were of little consequence. He also added, "They'll be no doubt dark into the drinking by now." Padlor didn't attempt a literal translation of this, but the gist was enough to bring a smile.

They accompanied the cart along the southern bank of the river, the preferred northern track being beyond reach on account of the incoming tide. Erdi asked Darew if he'd had much experience astride a horse. He answered with little enthusiasm saying, he could ride, but only as well as you'd expect from someone brought up in the marshes. This was considered good enough for what Erdi had in mind. Darew, although of course not native to the area, would have picked up a certain degree of knowledge regarding tracks and paths and any scrap of knowledge was a good deal better than the none he had. The most pressing need was to find a ford to the north bank that was not too far inland from where they'd docked and yet passable even at high tide. Mardi remained with Padlor on the cart and Darew mounted on Mardi's pony, led Erdi and Wolf to a narrow track he'd seen wayfarers occasionally emerge from. As hoped, it led to a way across the river provided the rider didn't mind wet feet. The far bank was too steep to contemplate driving a cart through. Erdi sampled the water. It was fresh. They were above the tidal point.

A trail leading from the river eventually bisected the track that Darew told them, connected Tredarn, the Tinner capital and Wade, the settlement they had just left. This was the route preferred when low water allowed. Their present trail led north over the moors and Darew told them, they had used it when trading up there in the past. A small stream running south through marshes immediately west, made any crossing towards the coast at this point almost impossible. The slavers would presumably be approaching from the northeast and their present trail curved conveniently in that direction.

They approached three houses strategically located where two paths crossed. Darew who knew a little of the local language asked if any riders had come that way recently. The answer was no. They took the track heading east. It bisected a well-used trail heading south, but they pressed on further east towards rising terrain where distant trees gave evidence of firm ground. Darew pointing, named two prominent tors on the northern horizon, but then declared he was not prepared to go any further. It would be dangerous, crazy in fact, to be out on the moors in the dark. So with the light fading and him getting decidedly edgy, they at last took a path south on the far side of what was in fact a tributary of Crooked River.

They trotted into Tredarn, half-moon glow from evening hearths lighting the track between the houses, to receive a severe reprimand from Padlor. Darew bore the brunt of his ire, being told, he should have had more sense than to be out on the moors that late in the day. One wrong turn could have had them lost and floundering in the marshes. Every year they claimed some poor soul. Erdi told him it was not his son's fault, but his own. In his desperation to get the lay of the land he'd lost track of time. He said their ponies were nimble, but would not be a match for the Tinner's mounts if it came to a race for safety. Knowledge of the territory would be everything.

Padlor was placated, but still muttered, his son should have known better and added, all would have ample time to familiarise themselves with the land further east when business took him that way two days hence. He winked and muttered to Erdi, "More of those wrapped goods. You know the sort. Those we dare not mention."

They were fed and put up for the night by Padlor's principal trading contact which was fortunate for the rest of the town sounded riotous.

Chapter Twenty-Five

The following morning Padlor went about the business that had brought him there and Darew agreed to accompany Erdi and his party as translator. As they explored the lower section of the town, Darew explained there were three likely places to enquire regarding news of slavers and women for sale. Entering the first of these, the proprietor could be seen, briskly moving and shoving things about, looking too busy to be bothering with the likes of them so early in the day. Darew's question stopped him mind you and from where she was perched a woman slid and sauntered expectantly towards them. Erdi sighed and asked Darew to rectify the situation, apologise for something obviously lost in translation and say they were enquiring about the possible arrival of slave women not seeking ladies of pleasure. "Tell him, one of the slaves happens to be my sister."

Things hadn't started well at all. The owner, other than flashing a glare of annoyance, continued as if they weren't there, busying himself clearing debris and wiping away evidence of the previous night's revelry. Only when Erdi dared ask for refreshment did he stop his activities. He slapped his cloth down as if hit by an insult, stood hands on hips and raised his eyebrows asking, 'Are you lot still here?' So you can imagine his look when Erdi then dared ask for barley water. They had come to a tough town. Tin-rich reveler's, late night squandering of new found riches probably kept this place going, not early morning sippers of barley water.

He eventually told them there had been rumours of slave girls being offered for sale, but in his line of work he heard rumours all the time. All he could definitely tell them was, and they could take it as fact, no slaves had yet arrived for sale, female or otherwise.

It seemed pointless asking the same question in the other two hostelries, in fact nerve racking, if run in a similar manner to the first, plus they'd only be drawing attention to themselves. In any case Erdi had discovered the main thing they needed to know, at last they were ahead of the slavers. Wolf however was keen to track down his countrymen and that nice man in the hostelry had said, they'd not be hard to find as they'd probably be heard before seen.

Erdi agreed this was of course a priority. He owed it to his good friend. Finding them gave Wolf his best of returning home, but first he requested time to think. He needed a place conducive to it, a place of calm, not one that evoked carnal pleasures and revelry. His mind felt numb and he was at a complete loss regarding what to do next. There had to be a way forward other than simply mounting up and confronting the slave convoy on its way south.

They wandered into the quiet upper part of town. A few suggestions were talked over as they walked, but all in turn were rejected as being either impossible or unrealistic.

A small defended citadel commanded the highest point of the Tinner capital and just visible beyond the palisade was the top of a dull green roof, the famed copper hall. Up on the Hafren they were desperate for the stuff and here they could afford the luxury of a complete roof fashioned from it. Even the high palisade gates had bronze adornments and the whole place gave the air of a world beyond reach. Whatever plan they came up with, it had to be enacted well away from this location.

They turned and took the short walk back downhill and Erdi remarked, he'd never been in a settlement this size before and how it felt strange not to be the centre of attention. Also, dogs didn't bark, obviously used to strangers or trained to blend in with town life. A few locals had begun to go about their business, those dwelling up-town looking prosperous and pleased with themselves, standing in marked contrast to the needy feel down amongst the hostelries. In fact, they met two actually begging.

Darew led them to the second eating house, in search of Wolf's compatriots. Waiting in the gloom was a man, red eyed and shaking. The proprietor went to hand him what appeared to be cider, but looking at the state of him, decided instead to hold the beaker for the man to slurp liquid from the brim, which in fact had such a remarkable calming effect, it enabled the imbiber to greedily guzzle the remainder of the mug unaided.

"Now then," the proprietor said to his new customers. He gave the pained look of a man hearing a loud slam whilst suffering from a thumping headache when Darew enquired after certain men from across the water. He told them that as far as he knew they were intent on catching the next morning's tide and hopefully wouldn't be back for at least a year. "Should give enough time for recovery," he added and he didn't look like he was joking. "You'll probably find them round at Cara's," he called out as they left.

As predicted earlier, they heard Cara's place long before reaching it. Roars, screeches of delight, laughter, a repeated refrain followed by da-di-da-di-da, indicating the singer had forgotten the next line, gave hint of the end of an all-night party. A reveler, heartily beckoned them to enter, almost flinging himself off balance in his enthusiasm to greet and wave them in. A few slumbering bodies lay curled up around the room oblivious to the racket. Four men remained standing, with difficulty, but technically still upright. They were tossing dice. The traditional method looked to have been long abandoned for they were taking in turns to aim for an ample cleavage. It was a puzzle as to what dice code they were following, but a direct hit into the fleshy fissure brought a roar and much shaking of the constrained bounty and a drop of the dice to the floor brought another. One competitor actually went down on one knee, pleading, beseeching the fulsome bosom to deliver the score required. Draped in the lap of the man stuck on the first line of his refrain, was the second of the escorts, blissfully waving a finger in accompaniment. Both girls had a certain allure, but neither looked the type you'd take home to meet your mother.

Amongst it all sailed Cara, furnishing drinks, up-righting stools and gathering empty drinking vessels.

The lively proceedings were brought to a sudden halt by Wolf, who slapping one of the men on the back, uttered a greeting that in all likelihood questioned the man's parentage and trading ethics. Of course, on hearing their mother tongue being spoken, they were momentarily stunned to silence, but then fell over themselves in the clamour to offer drink and cheer. Erdi was full of admiration for the man. What a test of will it must have been. Wolf declined offers of cider and beer and said he would gladly drink with them if and when they could land him on his home shore. He was told this was their last little celebration and they'd soon be leaving to sleep things off ready for cast-off in the morning.

Wolf replied solemnly; if that truly was the case, then it saddened him to inform them, he'd not be able to accompany them on the morrow. He was committed to fulfill the promise he'd made to these his good friends and until that had been honoured, he was bound to these shores. This had a sobering effect all round. They tried to plead and cajole, but still he wouldn't budge and in the end at their request, he gave a brief account of the saga: how he'd been delivered from slavery; the catastrophe of Vanya being taken; their journey up the Habren; the incident in the gorge; how the trail had led them here and finally he spread his arms and appealed to them, "You can't expect me to abandon such a noble quest having got this far."

The five wild rovers had a talk amongst themselves and returning, said they'd decided to put off departure until the following day. The leader of the five, knowing enough of the local language, explained to the two fun loving ladies why they'd be having to put up with them for yet one more day. With no doubt emotions heightened by alcohol and moved by the romance of the gesture, they hugged him, hugged Wolf, hugged everyone with tears in their eyes.

All turned to a figure darkening the entrance. It was the proprietor of the first hostelry. He beckoned Darew, imparted something of obvious import and left.

Darew passed on the news that the slave convoy had been sighted. It was, at the most, two days away.

At last they had the nugget of news they needed. Now they could plan in earnest. Yet Erdi was puzzled, "I'm amazed he took the trouble to come and tell us. It's the last thing you'd have expected considering his manner earlier."

"People can be strange," Wolf replied. "I've learnt over the years, you just never know."

Erdi was now keen to return and discuss the latest piece of news with Padlor, for perhaps he could be persuaded to set out a day early on his clandestine trip eastwards. There was not a lot to be gained from staying here in Tredarn, as they now had all the information needed and Wolf even had the offer of a boat home. Mardi agreed, but made an important point, their wild friends ought to be informed of the impending sun darkening. There was no telling how they might react and he was concerned, lest the magnitude of the event jeopardized Wolf's chances of returning home. If they viewed it as a bad omen, they could well postpone immediate departure or worse take fright, put to sea and leave him stranded.

With Mardi explaining, Wolf gave details of what was to be expected at full tide on the morning of departure. There were furrowed brows and worried looks, but Wolf assured them he had full trust in Mardi's explanation of the happening. It was something that occurred naturally and should not be taken as a harbinger of doom.

They had their doubts, but said they would take full advantage of the tide, putting to sea as planned, but then wait beyond the estuary mouth, remaining hove-to for one span of the sun. The length of a span was indicated by the gap between stretched thumb and forefinger with hand held skyward. Wolf had no clue as to how their near impossible mission was to be tackled, other than whatever they finally came up with would have to be done on the cusp of high tide, time of the sun's darkening. Therefore, the one span of the sun allowed to achieve this and still keep the appointment with his countrymen, would not be enough. It would take all of that just to negotiate the estuary. They settled on two and then a bit more for luck, but only if he and his friends joined them in the meal Cara was preparing.

Wolf asked what sort of meal and was told to wait and see as he wouldn't have tasted anything like it. It was a new wonder food.

When Cara brought in the pot for the contents to be ladled, they saw it did have pork mixed in with it, but basically it was what they called, beans. Apparently, they were easier to harvest than peas, were also bigger, but like peas could be dried and kept through winter. The men were taking sacks of the things home with them. They did warn of a serious side effect, however. "If you're after eating too many of them you'll not be in need of a paddle on board." A cheek was lifted to facilitate an indicative rasp, sending the two ladies into a fit of giggles.

The hoped-for success in the coming enterprise was toasted by their new friends. The beans, the girls and Cara had tumblers raised to them. The fact they'd turned copper into gold was toasted. "Copper to gold! Copper to gold!" was chanted and Erdi had the feeling they could be trapped in the hostelry for the rest of the day. He would have normally relished such a crazy, riotous piece of serendipity, but not today. His attempt to leave was blocked by a friendly but insistent embrace pressing him back down on to his seat and Wolf explained with an amused look, they'd soon be off, but the man still clinging on to Erdi had pleaded with him to stay a little longer in order to see Cara dance. It was something he and his rover friends had been promised and they wanted to share the experience.

"Cara dance?" said Erdi. "This is crazy. Come on Wolf we really have to go."

"It won't take long, Erdi. Try and humour them. After all they are taking me home."

"Spirits willing," added Erdi.

A big cheer went up as Cara, in full theatrical garb, made her grand entry and enthusiastic hands helped her up on to the dining board. First, she put on a sweet little innocent pose and in a faraway dreamy voice sang an introductory song, using her skirt as a suggestive prop. Her audience swayed back and forth in accompaniment.

> "The tide like fortune it comes and goes,
> Back and forth like a ladies' clothes.
> What d'you think sailor boys all chose,
> Low waters or the **high** tide?

As if slightly affronted by the loud cheer, Cara primly straightened the front of her skirt and waving an admonishing finger, like one would to naughty boys, continued.

> "The tide like fortune it comes and goes,
> Up and down like a ladies' clothes.
> What d'you think sailor boys all chose,
> Low waters or the **high** tide?"

The last line again brought a lusty cheer. The final verse was sung in a slow meaningful voice, with her skirt again adding zest, while fists bulging the lower bodice area at the end left no doubt as to the meaning.

"A sailor boy he taught me this,
My spring tide had left him thirsting.
But things led on from a tender kiss
And like the moon I'm full to bursting."

Words didn't really need translating. Whatever land men came from, whatever language they spoke the appeal was universal and they loved it, clapping and stamping approval. Even those that had been slumbering around the room had arisen as if from the dead. Mardi had a wide-eyed look of shock. They didn't get this sort of stuff back up on the Habren.

Then with a slightly lisping voice, theatrical emphasis and occasional clog rattling for punctuation, she came out with the following doggerel.

"I'm just a sthimple country girl come to town to earn my keep,
Daily grinding flour was not for me nor a lifetime watching sheep.
I was not in sthearch of riches, nor dreams of wild romance,
My only want was to keep myself and the gift I had was dance.
It was born in me, no need to learn, a thing I'll always treasure.
That plus knowing what most men want, cthertain things that give them pleasure.
Then one dark day my world fell in, there came a sthummons from the Lord;
I required his leave and blessing, couldn't dance on my own accord. (Rattle of clogs)

Stho. With each faltering step to the Lord's Grand Hall my hopes of future vanished,
It was sthaid the man was mighty vexed, like as not he'd have me banished.
Looking meek, contrite I gave the Lord, a sthideways look of charm,
My innocence stheemed to melt histh heart, I could feel his anger calm.
He sthaid one thing could sthave me now, he'd give me one more chance,
He'd heard tales of bringing joy to all, he'd like to sthee me dance.
He sthmiled and sthaid how wrong he'd been, 'Sweet thing like you can't sin,
Just lift my soul in raptures and I'll part your lips with tin.'
Stho, like a good little girl from the country, I was prepared to do as bid,
And with offer of freedom and a ring of tin, this is what I did."

The men watched entranced, as eying them with a knowing look, she slowly lifted her skirts, to sway teasingly, before rattling out a dance on the boarding in a rhythm that was so insistent it had them swinging their arms and clapping in time. For a woman past her prime she was light on her feet, showed no sign of fatigue and in fact maintained a provocative smile throughout. The dance ended with the flick of skirt, a bow and thunderous applause.

The pair of consorts familiar with the routine called out, "Did the dance please his lordship? Did he part your lips with tin?"

Cara grinned and with her tongue dropped a ring of tin into her hand. Showing it round to all she beamed and said clearly, now the impediment to her speech had been removed, "Yes!" Then raising her skirts once more, she triumphantly produced a second, sniffing it rapturously before holding it aloft between forefinger and thumb.

Erdi's groan of, "Ugh, I don't believe it," was drowned out by the roar of approval so loud, even Padlor said he had heard it and the two ladies present, even though they'd witnessed the act many times before, rocked with laughter.

Now at last Erdi was free to depart in the hope of persuading Padlor to alter his plans.

As they were leaving Mardi said to no-one in particular, "I thought women were meant to have hair down there."

"Not all men choose to retain their beards, Mardi," said Wolf chuckling to himself.

"Don't know what our mother would have thought of it all," added Erdi shaking his head. Had he really witnessed it, or had it been just a dream?

Meanwhile silently looking down, the ghostly daylight moon was indeed almost full to bursting. They returned to find Padlor had concluded his trading, exchanging the bulk of his wares for a manageable little stack of bronze. Erdi told him of the valuable gem of information they had come by and Padlor could now see the urgency this imposed on proceedings. He hadn't planned to move on so immediately, but after a few moments' consideration, said it shouldn't be a problem. Once he'd finished his meal and had exchanged bronze for gold, he'd be free to journey on to his final customer. Their host tried to cajole him into staying one more night as planned, but with Erdi's mission in mind and also mindful of the fact he still had forbidden cargo on his cart, right under the mighty Tun Mytern's nose, he hadn't needed much persuading to turn down the offer and go along with the plan to head east as soon as possible. By mid-afternoon they were on their way, bound for a large settlement on the southwestern edge of the moors.

Erdi was relieved to observe their route led them more northeasterly than due east, taking them on a course likely to intercept the slave column on its way south. What they would do then, he as yet had not the slightest notion, but spirits willing, they would at least be in the right place to do something.

Tall columns of smoke were evident long before the houses were visible. It was early evening with hardly a breath of wind and only when on high, as if reaching for the first dim stars, did the smoke spread to hang like a misty veil to the north. Their destination, when at last in view, resembled a random collection of upturned, smoke-seeping swallows nests scattered across the western slopes of a low tor. Even at that distance it was obvious there was no ringed earthwork protection or palisade. Padlor explained there was no need. Instead of threatening neighbours, these people were surrounded on three sides by sea and on the fourth by moors. They could lead their lives without the need to wall themselves in. Padlor remarked to Mardi, the headman could be someone he'd be keen to meet. He was the man who had smuggled Bastinas to safety all those years before, thus preserving the 'knowledge.' The knowledge of the people's metal, iron.

Villagers, alerted by dogs barking began to emerge and with Padlor being recognized, the headman was sent for. He strode forward to meet and greet, accompanied by his sons. While Padlor conducted his last deal of the trip, trading the remaining pelts and his wrapped secrets, Erdi suggested a tour of the community. The folk were silent, inquisitive, but not unfriendly and a small gathering of children stared unashamedly at the strangers while the less bold peered from behind their mother's skirts. Compared to those met previously, these felt more like Erdi's sort of people. There were obviously a few toothless smiles, a few frail, grey old souls, but generally an atmosphere of good health and contentment pervaded. There was no sign of the supposed abundance of tin having corrupted, in fact these people, although of a darker complexion, could well have fitted in back home.

The surrounding moorland seemed fairly featureless until Erdi, scanning the rising ground to the north with it's small stand of trees, sensed it had a familiar look. He asked Darew, "Is that the point where we finally headed south last night?"

Darew looking said, "Almost. We were actually a little further to the northwest." A map of the terrain was beginning to form in Erdi's mind.

After the evening meal the women melted away to leave their menfolk to discuss the usual weighty matters given serious consideration to at such times. Matters equal in immensity to their shadows cast by the firelight glow. Well that's the way they always viewed it and if the women were not privy to what went on, how were they to know any different?

The Teller flicked a concerned glance in the direction of the chieftain. When the man's stern glare melted into the hint of a smile, he counted his blessings and continued.

First as always, came cider, to lubricate the conversation. Padlor told of their journey, how stormy weather had held them up and Darew brought great mirth when describing their experiences in Cara's establishment earlier. The headman, Branok, who had merely smiled politely at the Cara anecdote, was keen to know how Bastinas was faring and had there been any trouble regarding the impact of the new metal? Padlor explained, the same as he'd explained the previous time and the time before that, that their remote location made it comparatively safe for Bastinas to carry out his magic, transforming red-brown rocks into weapons and tools. He had of late been sharing his skills with one of the village youths, Ardew and gradually the 'knowledge' would be spread far and wide. That was if enough had the courage to embrace the new way.

Erdi put the question for translation: how had it been possible for the wild rovers they'd met at Cara's, to exchange the base metal, copper for gold? Why wasn't gold the pinnacle? Why wasn't it prized as highly here as in other kingdoms?

Firstly, the headman bemoaned the influx of huge numbers of what they called 'incomers,' mainly young men, panning the waters for tin. They paid no heed to the rights of those born and bred there, virtually taking the very food from their mouths. It was more by accident than by design that these tin robbers amassed a side product of no use whatsoever in the smelting of bronze, gold. This was ultimately traded for copper in order to produce the metal craved for, the metal that exemplified power, bronze. The lust and greed for it had pushed tin and copper to unsustainable values. A crazy feeling pervaded their small world as if they were a society on the brink of disaster. Old values were being ignored and things seemed to be reeling out of control. Ancient wisdom no longer counted for anything and the formerly revered power of the spirit world was now treated by the incomers with complete disdain. Supposed pronouncements from that nether world, channeled through the Seer, still held sway over local folk, yet strangely those pronouncements always seemed to favour the ruling elite. Values such as respect and honesty, once considered essential to the fabric of society, were now viewed as a weakness by those striving for instant gratification in what they saw as their new modern world. The lucky few amongst the young incomers who'd blundered into overnight riches, had become the new role models and the old riches, held by the controlling minority was flaunted disgracefully. Tun Mytern had lost touch with his people and those expecting, in fact praying for a day of reckoning, watched in disbelief as the carnival of excess continued with seeming impunity. Amongst the ordinary people this utter veneration of bronze was often talked of as crazy, and yet with everyone else believing, an individual needed to be exceedingly brave to think differently? Wasn't it easier just to follow and have trust like the rest? 'How could the majority be so wrong?' So as tin became even scarcer and the value of bronze continued its inexorable climb, it created the strange phenomenon of tin and copper being treasured above gold.

At this point, Erdi leaning towards Padlor, asked him to suggest, discussion on the next subject would be better held between just the headman and themselves. Branok looked puzzled, but with Padlor's assurance that no offence had been intended, the village elders obeyed instructions to quietly rise and leave. The headman asked in a gently mocking tone, "Would the stranger mind and would it be in order for his eldest son, Cadan to remain?"

Erdi apologized, explaining that what was to be revealed would be best kept for now, between just the few of them and the headman and his son, listening intently, heard the saga explaining why these three strangers now sat at their hearth. Once the enormity of their problem had been fully absorbed, there followed an all-pervading silence. Almost a bar of doom on sound itself.

Finally, Branok asked had, any of them actually seen the slavers? On Erdi's description of them and their leader, he watched the headman's colour drain as Padlor translated.

"Gwyls!" he said with a look of horror. "We call them, 'The Wild!'"

With a look of panic, he told them, he would do all he could to avoid his people having contact with them, even to the point of temporarily abandoning the village as the slave column filed through.

He agreed with Erdi's assumption, that the girls were too valuable to be used as servants, shared out amongst the nobility. Being commodities of huge value, they would probably be offered for sale at auction. The incomers would likely go crazy for possession of them. Whatever Tun Mytern had invested in these girls, would probably be recouped tenfold. He anticipated a bidding frenzy.

Erdi then asked Padlor to mention the impending darkening of the sun, this revelation having been the main reason for the request to speak to the headman alone. Surprisingly Branok's mood lightened.

'Was this true? How did they know this?' If true, it was the one thing that could give hope. These men, these savages, had been the main protagonists involved in the burning of Magda. Who was Magda? Medicine woman to the people. Earth Mother who had dared to defy authority. It had happened two years previously and the people still held a deep loathing for those responsible. The good woman had warned, their sins of greed, gluttony and the many other excesses, invited a terrible retribution from the spirit world. This lone cry for sense and reason had been twisted to make the claim that, anyone not following the official view, derived from the ramblings of the only man supposedly in direct contact with the spirits, the Seer, must be against the spirits themselves and therefore in league with the evil ones. Tun Mytern's Seer, terrified by Sodron, the Gwyls leader, had had the roll of official accuser forced upon him and the poor innocent Magda had been sentenced to burn in order for her ashes to be flung into the cold, black wastes of the marshes.

However, the revered lady wasn't prepared to depart this world, without leaving Sodron a little something to remember her by. As they bent to light the pyre the brave woman's eyes had blazed like the heart of the fire that was about to consume her and she cast on Sodron the most solemn of curses. Onlookers said, his sadistic smile freezing to a grimace, took on a horrified look, as if serpents writhed inside him. She had called out, "By all the powers vested in me; from all the power raging through me from the old religion, I put a curse on you! The power from stone shall ensure your end!"

No-one really knew what she had meant, least of all Sodron, but the curse had left an impression as seering and fierce as the flames that engulfed its bestower. Despite his outward swagger, it was said, deep inside he was terrified. Erdi recalled the impact a stone from his slingshot had made the day the Tinners had come calling for beer and hospitality.

413

In Branok's view, Sodron would certainly not view the sun's darkening as a good omen. Any of natures' mysterious happenings would almost certainly be regarded as something to be feared by the man, who it was said, viewed each day as if it could be his last. He was haunted by the curse, secretly knowing it would eventually finish him. It was merely a matter of when.

Branok then described the likely route to be taken by the slave column. It would pass close to 'The Old Men of the Hill.' This was their name for the stone circle on the low tor immediately to the north.

A plan began to take shape in Erdi's mind.

The following morning, he suggested they ride and take a look at these Old Men on the Hill and Darew accompanied them as translator. Branok's son, Cadan rode on ahead to scout for first sighting of the slave column and Padlor remained behind in the village.

The stones were on fairly level ground and the circle was roughly 15 body lengths across. They were of various shapes and sizes, with some almost as tall as a man. Mardi whispered, he felt a very strong energy pulsating from the centre of the ancient shrine, convincing Erdi they were standing in the perfect place to attempt Vanya's rescue. Branok pointed to where he expected the slave column to appear from, saying that it would be forced to follow the high ground on account of the marshes directly west. Erdi asked Darew to describe where they had reached on their exploratory trip the night before last and Branok replied that if they had carried on directly east, they wouldn't be standing where they were now, but would have been lost in deep swamp. There was a way across, but only known to the locals. Branok led them down to a double boarded walkway hidden in the marsh grass. It was how they herded their sheep between pastures. To walk around using the shortest southern route took two whole spans of the sun and at least half a day if herding sheep. Now aware of the existence of the path, Erdi could pick out its route, made evident by the few supporting posts visible above reeds and tussocks. When asking why it didn't take the shortest direct line, he was told, it avoided what were described as 'the bottomless holes,' instead linking spongy sections where a lamb slipping from the boards wouldn't drown. In the most dangerous stretches willow hurdles guarded each side of the walkway.

"Would a horse manage it across?" Erdi asked.

"Try them," Branok invited. "If led quietly there shouldn't be a problem."

They dismounted and tentatively led their ponies on to the boarding, Willow withies secured the planks firmly to cross-rails that joined pairs of riven uprights driven deep into the bog. The horses were wary on the first crossing, but made the return trip like veterans.

They remounted and cantered over to a small wood of stunted oaks. This gave concealment and also a clear range of vision to the low ridge immediately north. To allay a nagging doubt, Erdi suggested viewing the surrounding country from the ridge crest.

The two conical hills seen previously on the northern horizon were welcome features in a fairly barren landscape. What he couldn't understand was, why had this route been chosen by the slavers in the first place? Why hadn't they come directly south using the safe firmer ground to the far west? This route across the moors didn't look any shorter and in fact seemed unnecessarily hazardous.

Darew translating, explained that Branok wasn't entirely certain, but felt the reason could possibly have been political. The territories to the northwest and northeast were controlled by under kings, subjects of Tun Mytern and although these in theory paid annual homage to the mighty man, recently there had been a serious falling out incited by the high-handed nature of the ruler. Perhaps there had been fear of the slaves being waylaid and held as hostages, forcing Tun Mytern to show a little more consideration to the wishes of his underlings. Also of course the slavers were feared and hated and would not be made welcome by either of the two rulers to the north. The trail across the moor ran directly between the territories of these aggrieved tribes and could be the reason why it had been preferred to the coastal route or the main trade route running down the centre of the peninsular.

Erdi prayed for this to be correct, not wanting to lay in wait only to find the column had taken one of the more practical trails. Darew allayed his fears saying, Branok had had it on good authority the slavers were heading towards them over the moor, he just hadn't been aware the dreaded Sodron was leading them.

They returned to the village, not a long journey and sought out a quiet place to formulate a plan for the following day. Everything of course depended on the information Cadan returned with. They needed him back soon for Padlor was anxious to return to his boat and without him or his son translating they were unable to discuss tactics and options with the headman. With the sun now having passed middle day Padlor had become decidedly edgy. He was keen to be off, hoping to return to Wade by way of the easier, more direct track following the north bank of Crooked River. Leaving now would allow passage for his cart over the ford at low water. He didn't relish having to go the long way round, or getting the timing wrong to be left stranded on that north bank with just the hard boards of the cart to sleep on.

The sound of rapidly approaching hooves came as a relief to everyone. Cadan dismounted, face flushed and looking slightly bothered, but then a smile creeping, indicated he'd been successful. By his reckoning the lead group, in fact the four feared Gwyls warriors, would be near about middle day on the morrow. That was if the slave girls didn't slow them. Then he cheerily added, "The way they're riding. they look in a bad way."

His flippancy annoyed Erdi who demanded to know, how many were in the lead group and how many of these had been

416

captives? Padlor translated what Cadan had surmised, explaining, the bulk of their supplies must have been used up for the pack horses of the lead group were now being used for riding. With them all now mounted the Gwyls had been able to pull ahead of the main column.

Cadan was a young lad reaching that cocky stage of maturity and was totally unaware he'd not really answered Erdi's question.

"How many slave girls were in the lead group?!"

"Four," he answered as if surprised to be asked again.

How could he be certain he'd seen the Gwyls?

Cadan's look in reply was enough. His cockiness faded. He'd seen them alright. With this information a plan could be devised.

Success or failure rested on two things, first Mardi had to be correct in his prediction regarding the sun's darkening and second Sodron, the Gwyls leader needed to be within the stone circle when it happened. Crucial to everything was Branok. Somehow, they had to persuade this man they hardly knew, to approach and guide the Gwyls to the Old Men on the Hill. Also, come what may, he had to be prevailed upon to co-ordinate their movements for arrival just prior to what was in fact the equivalent of high tide. Not much to ask really.

It was no surprise to find Branok wanting nothing to do with such a plan. His concern was for his own people and he didn't relish the merest glimpse of the Gwyls let alone going out to meet them. Why would they pay any heed to him anyway, he reasoned?

Here the Teller explained that for continuity of the tale, he would relate what each party eventually understood rather than go into endless detail of how it was translated for them to reach this understanding.

Erdi's whole being was coursing with the need for urgency, but resisting the impulse to give the headman a good shake,

417

somehow managed to remain calm enough to explain, "You can tempt them with the shorter route over the marshes."

"Granted it would save time on their way to Tredarn, but hardly enough when you consider the vast distance they've already covered."

"You can exaggerate the time saved. They're not to know any different," reasoned Erdi.

Padlor with his trading experience pointed out, "I suspect they're aiming to have those particular captives first on the market. First there gets best price."

"Yes, you're right," said Erdi enthusiastically, glad of Padlor's support, "They'll be keen to save all the time they can."

"But why should they have the slightest need to enter the stone circle, especially in view of Magda's curse?" Branok asked.

"Because that's where the food and beer will be," said Erdi.

"Now just a moment! You mean to say I not only ride out to meet these killers, but also take them food and beer. I'm sorry --------"

"You'll be guiding them away from your village," said Erdi. "Saving your people from possible rape and pillage."

"Nobody will be here to get raped."

"Vacate your houses? Not be there to welcome weary travelers? They'll feel spurned by their own people." Erdi warned, "They won't take kindly to that. You could find yourselves like others before you, returning to a burnt-out village."

"You call those animals my own people?"

"Like it or not they are. Three of them at least. The other I'm afraid to say is from my own tribe."

Branok was angry now, "What you're really saying is, you're asking me to commit suicide. They'll know they've been led into a trap."

Erdi talked this point over with Wolf and then said, "My friend here says, have no fear regarding that. By the time he's finished they'll be left in no doubt, your shock was as great as theirs."

The headman, as you can imagine, remained thoroughly unwilling and you could hardly blame him really. Erdi tried everything he knew to win the man's co-operation and as a last desperate ploy told him, "Without your help Vanya is as good as lost. Without you we might as well just give up." He looked him full in the eye, "Please, put it your people?"

"Why? It's not their risk it's mine?"

"But you'll be helping rid the land of this scourge."

Erdi, feeling he was losing their only chance, continued in earnest and Padlor translated. "Ask your people. They must have been willing to help Bastinas escape. You were brave enough to help him do that. Now Erdi beseeches you to help us rescue his sister."

Poor Branok. He left probably wishing he'd never offered the foreigners hospitality in the first place.

As they waited with no sign of a response, or any sign of life for that matter, Padlor became that tense and brittle, he could have punched the side of his cart in.

"Perhaps they've all gone to sleep in there," he said. "Look Erdi, I need to leave now, not soon, now or risk being stranded wrong side of the river by the tide."

Erdi, again somehow managing to appear like calmness personified, persuaded him to stay and help for just a little while longer. Without him and his son he had not the slightest clue what these villagers were saying. Everything seemed as finely balanced as the turn of tide itself.

At last people began to emerge and now the crucial nature of their brave headman's role in the scheme of things could be fully explained. He would obviously have already given a brief rendition of this, but it was vital they heard Erdi's version. Following it, there came a worrying silence and

Padlor, with fists clenched, tapped the ground impatiently with a foot.

After what seemed like an age one said, "I know it's a great deal to ask, Branok, but you will be leading those beasts away from the village." This brought encouraging nods and murmurs.

A woman's voice piped up, "And it might bring justice at last for poor Magda." The swell of agreement at this brought a glum look of resignation to Branok's face.

"Like as not you'll be saving the village," said another woman.

"You're a brave man, Branok," said a third.

"I'm proud of you," said his wife.

The cheer this brought trapped the poor fellow into the roll of reluctant hero and following Erdi's lead, they all broke out into warm applause.

Now the plan could be gone over in detail. Satisfied all had been made clear to Branok, including the exact angle of the sun at its expected darkening, Padlor was free to leave. He told them he would wait no more than a sun's span following high tide on the morrow. "Well maybe just a while longer." As he left, he shouted, "Be certain though, I'm not missing that tide!"

Things were fast approaching that crucial stage. Everything, as they say, was balanced on a knife-edge. With the spirits' blessing they could perform a miracle, or it could all go horribly wrong. Hadn't those Gwyls already had the devil's own luck?

Erdi and Wolf went into quiet discussion. The latter agreed they needed a support plan in the likely event of everything starting to lurch out of control. Too much depended on chance. Too much depended on predicting reactions. People rarely do exactly as expected. While they wrangled with the possibilities, to always return to the only realistic option open to them, Erdi busied himself constructing a rope halter and also coiled ready, a long length of twine for use as a horse lead. As Wolf honed his sword, the blade sang with menace and the word 'Habren' was chosen as the signal for the support plan to be swung into action.

All was explained to Mardi, who in turn told them, he also had an idea. He felt his appearance needed an added touch of authority. Offering no clue as to how this was to be achieved, he was gone, leaving Erdi and Wolf exchanging puzzled looks.

"We need look after him tomorrow, Erdi."

Erdi nodding grimly in reply, wondered, 'Will any of us come out of this alive?'

The following morning Branok was helped with loading a small light wicker cart with provisions. He looked pale and tried to disguise the fact his hands were shaking. He refused reward for the supplies saying such a thing could taint the spirit of the enterprise. Erdi didn't know quite how to thank the man and signed to him that he felt deeply humbled.

"Never mind that. Let's just get these things loaded!" No need for sign language or translation, his tone was enough.

To add to the unearthly feel of the morning Mardi appeared with face transformed. He tapped Erdi on the shoulder, who when turning, jumped at the sight of him. "Mardi! How have you done that?" He hardly recognized him.

It was a dull day to be to be starting out on the quest of a lifetime. It was cold, it was damp, with not the slightest ray of sunshine to give hope and remember, for their plan to work they needed a clear sky. Branok gave a crumb of comfort. Often when days started cloudy in those parts they tended to brighten with the incoming tide. He had used the same horizontal hand rocking motion that the headman on the Habren had used.

'Yes maybe,' thought Erdi, 'but not guaranteed.' He could feel the pressure mounting and the assembled villagers didn't help exactly, standing muttering, huddled together with looks of gloom as if witnessing the departure of condemned men.

On their way to the ancient stones, they saw no sign of the slavers and Erdi, who had ridden ahead to crest the north ridge, called out with relief they were still not in view. Their first hurdle had been cleared. To have the slavers there too early was in fact worse than having them arrive too late.

The horse was unhitched from the cart, which was left as an enticement in the middle of the circle. Having fitted bridle and riding blanket, Branok mounting with wearisome reluctance, pointed to the crucial angle of the sun's alignment to confirm he understood what everything depended on and cantered from view over the low north ridge.

They took turns as lookout. The morning seemed to drag interminably and Mardi said, if the slavers weren't in view soon, they'd need to rethink their plan. There were in fact only three options, direct attack, ambush from the clump of trees or Wolf's brave offer to stand and confront them on the causeway across the swamp. The first two options were dismissed by Wolf, saying he didn't mean to offend, but saw little future in pitting himself and two inexperienced young bloods fresh off the farm against trained killers. The final option stood more chance, but it came with a caution. Although only one of the Gwyls could offer arms at any one time, injury or death to the captives would be almost inevitable. They would either be used as shields or as hostages to guarantee safe passage over the marsh.

Wolf looked at Erdi and smiled. "Don't take offence my friend. You and Mardi have grown into men before my eyes, but you'd be no match for those killers. Not doing straight fighting anyway. Fortunately, the fact you don't look a threat could be an advantage, for they won't expect anything." He narrowed his eyes and twisted his sword like a skewer. "They let me get in close."

"Erdi, Wolf! The slavers are coming and I can see Vanya!"

He and Wolf rode up to the ridge, dismounted and lay flat in order to peer over the crest unseen. Branock was leading them over the moor. Erdi looking up to the sky, silently prayed for divine help. He pleaded with the spirits to send them success. Help them rescue Vanya and also prayed that the brave man enticing the killers towards them, would be given safe delivery home to his family.

The three rode off the ridge to wait, concealed in the small wood. It seemed hard to believe they were actually going ahead with the plan.

All eyed the north crest. "Come on!" urged Erdi. "Why are they taking so long?"

Mardi, constantly checking, gave concerned looks to the sky. The cloud had cleared sufficiently for the sun to beam down, but if the advancing column didn't appear soon, they'd lose their moment.

At last they came into view, but moving so slowly.

Mardi again looking skyward, sounded petrified, "Erdi the darkening is close I can feel it!"

Branok, glancing up at the sun's angle and at last seeming to sense, more speed was required, laughed and pointing to the cart, urged haste. Erdi could actually hear him now and acting the part, holding an imaginary skinful up to his lips, he reminded the Gywls, there was cool beer awaiting. They could quench their thirsts. Lured by such a prospect they kicked their mounts into a canter and the packhorses strung on lead ropes behind were jerked into doing likewise with their unwilling riders bobbling along and clinging on.

While the men greedily consumed refreshment, Branok as planned, re-hitched horse and cart. Miraculously things seemed to be falling into place. Mardi, again looking skyward, could feel all around being drawn into a state of suspension, like a deep breath before exhalation. Even the birds had fallen silent.

"Go now," he said. "Spirits be with you."

Erdi and Wolf breaking from cover, rode towards the standing stones. Instantly, the Gwyls dropped their mood of revelry and as one, four swords rang, flashing from scabbards.

"I have come to demand the return of my sister, Vanya," Erdi called.

On recognizing him, the Tinners looked visibly stunned, with Sodron in particular, staring wide-eyed as if at a ghost. His basic nature didn't fail, however, for he still managed to sneer an utterance for his right-hand man to translate. "You're free to buy her."

"We are not here to exchange bronze for her."

"Sodron says your friend's sword would buy a leg. We'll lop one off for you!" Their laughter sounded hollow, not masking entirely, their discomfiture at such an unexpected appearance.

"We have with us a Seer," said Erdi. "Here amid this revered ancient stone circle will be brought to fruition, the curse of Magda."

Erdi glared at the Gwyls leader, "Sodron! I'm talking to you!" His anger and hatred now overrode fear. "You do remember Magda, don't you? Today her curse will be fulfilled." Indicating the surrounding circle, he said menacingly, "The power from stone shall ensure your end!"

This utterance, brought an involuntary flash of alarm to Sodron's eyes and although glowering at Erdi, he looked stunned. How could a complete outlander know of the curse he was under?

"I almost smell his fear," Wolf muttered.

The man looked unnerved, to the point of remounting, but stood rivetted, at the sight of the vision that materialised from behind one of the largest monoliths. The mounted stranger, hair white, face ghastly and ashen, eyes ringed black, glared at him. His long cloak, adorned with a boar's tusk necklace flowed and when near centre circle, he crowned all with a Seer's hat. Tales of such venerated objects had been heard of when related in legend, but there right before Sodron was the actual, mysterious, revered sign of wizardry, bestowing its power to the mounted stranger. Sodron's terror was infectious, with all four freezing as if witnessing an apparition from the spirit world.

"Again, I demand the return of my sister, Vanya!" Erdi called out.

Sodron with the look of a cornered cur, snarled a stream of bile that poured, more in animal reflex than reasoned response. Translated it was slightly easier on the ears.

"My leader commands me to inform you, he fears no spirits, Seers or mad witches' curses, let alone demands made by one hardly old enough to leave his mother."

"His looks show different. He invites Magda's curse upon himself. Be in no doubt. The Seer has within him, mighty powers. Powers you have never known the like of. Power to cause the very sun itself to darken."

Their cries of derision rang with that same hollow sound as heard in loud empty boasts of bravery. In fact, all had that same fearful white eyed glint, betraying that wavering indecision between fight or flight. As yet there had been no threat of the former.

All waited. The moment was arriving. Mardi, raising his blackthorn wand, called to the heavens, "From all the power vested in me by the spirits, I am here before you to demand the safe return of Vanya, the girl enslaved. I harness sacred energy. Ancient magic from the stones. I call for the sun to darken. I call for the spirit of Magda to come forth. I call for her curse to surge through me;" he pointed his wand at Sodron and with eyes blazing growled, "surge through me directly to YOU!"

Then accompanying a slow raising of arms, a moody gloom began to pervade. Everything became strangely still and a dark curved shadow began to creep across the lower portion of the sun. The Gwyls warriors shrank in fear, each raising an arm as if something so inadequate would suffice to shield against such power and mystery raining down upon them.

Erdi beckoned Vanya to urge her horse forward. Her eyes looked hollow and dead. Her face was like those of her companions, gaunt and expressionless. Wolf slid from his horse. Erdi did likewise, walking calmly forward to pull the bridle and lead her pony across to join them. They were the only things to move in what resembled a dim scene of gloom frozen by witchcraft.

A spell broken by three riders galloping over the north ridge. As if snapped awake, one of the slavers drew Sodron's attention to the sun. The dark domed shape was edging away and the light was brightening. Looking directly at the sun, however, half darkened or otherwise, is never recommended. Wolf, taking advantage of their temporary blindness shouted, "Habren" and sliced with the speed of a snake. He grabbed Sodron dragging him backwards with a sword to his throat, while the recipient of the slice gazed back in disbelief and crumpled to the floor dead.

Mardi took immediate control of the horses. Erdi disarming Sodron shouted, "Either of you move and your leader is a dead man!" The one Gwyls to understand stayed the arm of the second and both remained rooted in a state of confusion. The three incoming riders, having been panicked by the sun's darkening and now seeing the most feared man in the kingdom with a sword glinting at his throat, reined in as if arriving at a cliff edge. Erdi, forcing Sodron's arms behind, bound them with the halter and by whipping the rope-end twice around his neck, around the halter itself and tying it off at his belt, had him incapacitated before he'd time to blink. The belated effort to free his arms made his eyes bulge. Thus trussed he was bundled on the cart and Wolf ordered the village headman to lead it from the stone circle. His sword swung for emphasis, hummed as it swiped Branok's hat off, prompting pace to immediately quicken down towards the marsh. It was needed. Out of sight beyond the ridge a dark thin line of humanity was relentlessly approaching.

One by one the horses were led onto the walkway. Mardi had control of his mount plus Wolf's on the extended lead, Erdi's was led by Branok, but on first sight of the marsh Vanya's pony took fright, braced its front legs and wouldn't move. Erdi tried to coax it, but finally it was a thwack from the flat of his blade that startled it to clatter on to the woodwork. Vanya led it to those awaiting, who if viewed from a distance, would have seemed to have been standing miraculously above their own reflections in the mire. Sodron, having been dragged from the cart, was pulled backwards, slow step by step, across the causeway, with Wolf's sword at his throat, while Erdi bringing up the rear, had shield held ready lest those gathered at the edge of the morass should release the arrows they had notched.

Halfway across, he sliced through the withies securing the boarding and heaved two planks as far as he could manage, into the marsh, then joined the others far side.

All mounted and Wolf raising his sword growled, "I think this man's tired of wiping his backside every morning!"

"No!" shouted Erdi.

Instead, frustrated by the order, Wolf booted the man full in the chest sending him backwards into the swamp. For good measure he hit Branock across the chest with the flat of his blade, sending the headman tumbling, falling theatrically as if his life depended on it. Which of course it did. As they galloped from range, Erdi turned to witness Sodron being dragged from the mire. He was black from head to toe and screamed instructions to his men across on the far side. Seeing their flight of arrows fall way short of the fleeing riders, his dance of frustration at that and the enraged struggle to free his arms caused a stumble into ever shorter backward steps and the inevitable splash was followed by a threshing of legs like those of a furious upturned beetle.

Further progress along the southerly trail was now at no more than a gentle canter governed by the pace of Vanya's pony. It was a worn-out beast of burden. Wolf still frustrated

427

by the reprieve of Sodron asked Erdi his motive. "You don't give a man like that second chance," he said. "Your decision will come back to haunt us."

Erdi explained, those pursuing would be forced around the marshes to collect their leader. If he'd have been killed and thus no further use to them, they could have taken the direct westerly track running south of the marshes and on their faster horses would almost certainly have cut them off.

As they angled across to the southwest, Erdi desperately searched the barren landscape for a feature he recognized. Still shaking inside, he attempted to reason with himself, almost reprimanding in an effort to stay calm. A rash move now could have them wallowing in a swamp. They slowed, to follow a stream running south. Far side was a small settlement. It was a relief to hear dogs barking and see people emerging to stare as their horses splashed across the water.

"Wade!" Erdi called out. They looked back dumbly. He shouted again with an enquiring finger pointing west, "Wade?"

Finally, one of the men understanding, indicated Wade to be to the southwest. However, urgent arm movements indicated, they should first go directly south. The trail joined another heading due west. He pointed to the southwest with a warning look and shake of finger---- go that way and you'll all be drowned. For emphasis, he again jabbed at the safe direction south and remembering the marshes seen on that exploratory trip with Darew, Erdi followed the advice.

The trail they eventually reached was the one Erdi recognized, the one from Tredarn, running due west along the northern bank of Crooked River towards Wade. His relief was palpable, but he now needed to remember the ford's location. The one Darew had shown him. Recognizing the landmarks, they crossed without difficulty and continued west towards the small port where hopefully the boat would still be waiting.

What a sight! There was Padlor waving at them, urging haste. Their mounts were kicked into one last effort and even the packhorse broke into a reluctant gallop. Vanya was helped aboard followed by Mardi and their belongings were caught as they were flung from the bank.

Erdi hearing a pounding of hooves, turned to see Sodron, like a demon arisen from the bog, plaits dancing as his horse thundered towards them, its hooves hardly touching the ground. His two henchmen savagely whipped their mounts in an effort to keep up.

"Get on boat," ordered Wolf. "Go! I do this." Erdi was shoved aboard and Wolf swung up on to his pony and drove the three loose horses before him. He had realized they'd all have been a sitting target.

Erdi helped Darew haul in the mooring ropes and Padlor and Mardi steered them into the main flow, but held station as best they could so not to completely abandon the heroic warrior risking his all for them.

The brave man, sword in hand, drove the horses full gallop at the advancing Gwylt warriors. The people of Wade first drawn by the thunder of hooves now ran for cover. In the confusion of horses careering and rearing, Wolf was magnificent. His blade stabbed and slashed and two bodies dropped to slump under the hooves. Then to Erdi's horror, above all the dust and clamour, as if pre-ordained, Sodron rode forward with sword flashing, ready to smite Wolf's brains apart. Everything inside screamed, "NO!!" Had his decision at the marshes brought about this? He swung his sling and summoning up all the power of the spirits and all the power of his ancestors, sent the stone winging to its target. Sodron stunned by the blow was unseated, tumbling backwards. Hauling himself to his knees, arm raised in defence and looking terrified at the sight of Wolf's sword held aloft, Sodron received Erdi's second shot, maybe guided by the spirit of Magda, by way of his nose that was smashed up into his brain. With a look of disbelief, he slumped to the floor dead. Wolf with sword still raised, looked down at the corpse and then at Erdi in amazement and wheeling his horse, rode at full gallop to where Padlor had steered the craft. Raising himself, all in one movement, he leapt from horseback, landing directly aboard amidst those clinging on in the madly rocking boat.

Arrows whined and fizzed into the water around them. More horsemen, pounding the riverbank, firing as they rode would soon have them at their mercy. Erdi and Wolf held covering shields while Mardi joined the two the boatmen furiously paddling to take them beyond range into the widening estuary. Now it was crucial to reach open water before their pursuers, boarding craft at the river mouth, positioned themselves to cut off their escape to the sea. Fortunately, wide inlets and marshland forced them onto the trail inland and as the desperate fugitives glanced southwards, silhouettes could be seen whipping their mounts across the skyline. Vanya sat in the prow of the boat unmoved and expressionless

Helped by the flow of the river and fast ebbing water they skimmed down the estuary to navigate around the emerging sandbar at the river mouth. At last, they felt a swell of relief as their boat heaved up over the waves and down into gullies. Riding the waters ahead was the awaiting black skinned craft with Wolf's cheering countrymen half standing to wave. There was little time or room for sentiment. With deft timing the two boats met, for helping hands to pull Wolf aboard. He held his sword out to Erdi.

"It's yours, Wolf. Goodbye my dear friend."

Outstretched fingers desperate for one last touch, met briefly on a wave crest before the boats were swept apart and a song drifted over the rolling waters.

"I hear sagas of love, tales of treasure men stole
And places of beauty over the sea,
But deep in my heart, deep in my soul
It's those misty blue mountains ever calling to me.

My home is calling, my home is calling,
Breaks my heart this farewell to thee,
Green pastures, blue mountains, wild winds of the west,
All these memories are calling to me."

The fact the words were in the tongue he had learnt whilst in captivity indicated he'd composed the song himself. Even Padlor had tears streaming.

Vanya, still worryingly quiet, sat looking distraught as a huge tear emerged to slowly roll down her cheek. "Wolfy's gone," was all she said.

The Teller told his audience he would conclude the tale the following evening. Exhausted, but satisfied, he left the stage.

Part 6

Chapter Twenty-Six

At last the tale was nearing completion. The Teller would gather up his reward and be on his way. Partly he envied those content with their stable way of existence, some never traveling beyond the next village, but for him, almost like a curse, he had always felt compelled to move ever onward. Another community, another saga told with elevated status from the platform, revered in the firelight, part of the people and yet apart from the people. There were those who looked up to him, some even envied him and yet without realising it they had the one thing he craved, contentment. He approached the looming edifice of the hall, knowing it would be packed. It almost bristled with expectation. Late arrivals were hurrying in through the entrance. He came to a halt on hearing one of those voices he dreaded, "Excuse me?"

The Teller turned and patiently awaited the question expecting it to be, 'How did everyone manage to understand one another at Cara's place?' He had used a little of what he called, teller's licence, to maintain the flow of the tale hoping no-one would notice.

Instead the man said, "I was just wondering. You mentioned something about Sarah's deputy, well that's what it sounded like and then never said any more about her. Forgive me for asking, but what has Sarah's deputy got to do with the story?"

I'm sorry. I should have explained. I think the word you're referring to is serendipity and it means something discovered by happy chance.

"Oh, so that's what it was. I'm sorry I asked, but.."

Please don't apologize. There are some words I really shouldn't use, silky, leviathan, machination, reunion, pre, tandem and flotilla for example, but when they're perfect for a particular line in the story the temptation gets the better of me. I had just hoped you would all understand the meanings, simply because of the context--------------- Sorry I'm doing it again. I hoped you would understand on account of what they describe and where they appear amongst the words that are recognizable.

"But how do **you** know them?"

The Teller smiled and gently jabbed his blackthorn wand skyward as an answer.

By now others had stopped to listen and another man plucked up courage to ask about a puzzling word.

"The other night you mentioned the word riparian and sorry to trouble you, but the wife didn't know what it meant."

Well didn't you tell her? *The teasing reply brought laughter.*

"Heavens no!" *said the woman who was obviously his wife.* "The only ripe airy 'un he knows to, is when he's ate too many beans." *Then turning to her husband, and giving an admonishing downward swipe with quite a prettily embroidered bag, she said,* "Yes you can look like that, but you know it's true!" *Sensing command of the little gathering she added,* "**and** the swine holds m'head under the covers!"

Really, *said the Teller as if utterly fascinated. He loved these people, but sometimes longed for company where conversation could skip and dance across numerous topics with breathtaking ease and where late-night talk could take* *you through to first dawn light, shocking with its speed of arrival.*

He hauled himself up on to the platform. There were things to be told that night he did not relish, but tell them he must for they were the truth handed down through time.

Padlor and his crew, having worked themselves safely out to sea, headed north with the southwesterly wind at their backs. The cargo had been successfully traded, the boat sat light on the water, Vanya had been rescued and yet they all felt heavy at heart. Erdi in particular missed his friend Wolf. It were as if part of his insides had been cut out, leaving him feeling sick and incomplete. It felt like a death, something he'd never recover from.

Padlor tried to lift the mood by shouting down the boat, "I told the trader in Wade his horses would be back. Bet he didn't expect them to arrive quite like that mind you. Came in like thunder! He might get to keep Vanya's nag as a bonus."

Every so often, trying not to look too worried, he gave a wary look behind. The enormity of what they had achieved would hardly be accepted without a serious attempt of retribution. The mighty Tun Mytern had his reputation to think of. Three incomers had slipped into the heart of his territory, wiped out the cream, the most feared unit in his fighting force and stolen one of the slave girls. Such an effrontery could not go unpunished. It was just as well this was his last trading trip down into Tun Mytern's kingdom.

As he mentally plotted their course to safety, he realised each inlet and cove they passed gave them a mounting advantage. Those pursuing would need to check every one, either by boat or by deploying mounted scouts. Although a boat crewed by a full complement of fighting men would travel at far greater speed than they could manage, the need to seek out their quarry would slow them. The first night's stop would be crucial. If they managed to come through that unscathed, they would hopefully be hard to catch.

437

They pulled into what had been their last port of call when traveling south. He could see the brothers had been completely drained by the rigours and stresses of the day and if pushed too hard would not be capable of enduring the long haul due on the morrow. The little cove was quietly tucked away and had a bonus, with luck they'd be offered a proper nights' rest in the fishermen's cottages. The tide was on the turn as they hauled the boat up onto the shingle. The stone anchor was dumped with a thud over the side and enough rope played out for her to ride high water.

They were welcomed and again offered food in the larger of the two huts. The lady within tried to tempt Vanya to at least eat something, offering tasty morsels, but with limited success.

"We've left them behind," Vanya whispered. Padlor acted as translator.

The kindly hostess asked, "Who have you left behind, my lovely?"

"My friends."

"But your friends are here, my lovely."

"I've left my friends and now Wolfy's gone."

The woman turned to Erdi with a silent question in her eyes. He took her to one side and had Padlor whisper enough details of recent events to explain Vanya's lack of appetite, but they all knew of course there was far more to it than that. He kept his deepest fears and inner rage locked inside. His sister Vanya was there in body, but her spirit was elsewhere. She was like an empty shell. It worried him, well in actual fact he was petrified. It was a condition he'd never witnessed before, as if some strange force had robbed him of his sister. 'Was the Vanya he knew and loved, lost forever?'

In the pre-dawn dismal shadows of next morning, they hauled in the boat, scrambled aboard and edged out into the chilly wide rolling waters. There was no sign of pursuing craft and they worked their way around the headland in the lee of a small offshore island. Padlor then steered them in a northeasterly direction. They paddled the day long, it felt never ending, rising and falling as if to the seabed anchored, with only the rollers making progress. Short rests were taken every two spans of the sun before grinding on through spray and dull waves, bent to the paddle over waves without end, paddling on 'til day became evening. They knew their lives depended on it. Arriving low tide in the mouth of a river estuary and hidden from open water by a low offshore island, they at last disembarked. Padlor's son, Darew had the task of hauling the boat inshore on the rising waters to drop anchor mid-tide. The pull of ebbing water during the night would have had enough drag to have caused their craft to founder had it been left to ride out in main estuary flow. They made no attempt to go upriver as they had done on their way south. That balmy day, swimming in the waters seemed like a lifetime ago. They dined on raw fish helped down by water. Lighting a fire was out of the question. All slept swaddled, worn out, on the beach.

Again it was mid-tide when they left. Their water skins had been refilled, but not their bellies. The brother's hands, rubbed raw the previous day, had rags tied around the palms in an attempt to alleviate the pain. It seemed to help, but once all became wet, blood oozed afresh and more raw fish as sustenance hardly lifted their spirits. Padlor and Darew of course had hands like leather from years of trading up and down the coast.

Erdi paddled on as if in a trance, repeating in his mind words to bolster each stroke, 'escape, freedom, Vanya, rescued, mother, Gwendolin, paddling home.' Padlor shouted encouragement, telling them he'd make sailors of them yet and admitted they were traveling further daily than would normally be attempted. Once they had rounded a prominent headland to steer due east, they had the full blow of the prevailing west wind to aid them. With light fast fading and the tide at full ebb they pulled into a small cove surrounded by high cliffs. They dropped anchor and hauled themselves ashore. The brothers found walking difficult partly from exhaustion and stiffness, but also because the ground seemed to be moving beneath them. Padlor laughed and explained it was a common when spending all day afloat. Their legs on the verge of buckling added a little humour to an otherwise grim situation.

Sheltered by rocks and cliffs they dared light a fire to have hot nourishment at last. While the fish was being gutted and washed Mardi replenished their water from the small stream that tumbled its way merrily down the curves and falls of a pretty valley. He scanned the skyline, but saw no sign of danger and returned to help scour pools for crabs and shellfish to add to the meal, mackerel once more. Erdi seized his gratefully, hands trembling from lack of sustenance.

They again slept in the open wrapped against the cool offshore breeze. Erdi suffered one of the worst nightmares he'd ever experienced. He dreamt he Wolf and Mardi were furiously paddling in pursuit of the Tinners holding Vanya captive, but each time they drew close the currents and winds drove their boat back forcing them into a never-ending pursuit. Each time close, but never close enough. He awoke soaked in sweat and with a stabbing pain in his gut. Finally sensing imminent disaster, he pulled himself into a half-bent posture and stumbled upstream to relieve himself. He was still sweating profusely, but the abrupt, noisy flight of whatever had been poisoning him brought immediate relief.

As he tidied himself, he heard horses approaching. Then muffled voices. Using the rocks as cover and pulling his leggings up as he ran, he arrived back unseen to where the crew still slumbered. He quietly roused each in turn, urging speed and silence. They ran as light as shadows down to the boat, a dark shape on a flat bay lit by a thin fractured wrinkle from the low moon. As they frantically hauled the craft in, hooves could be heard rattling across the stream bed. Crack of whip and guttural cries preceded clattering, splashing, cursing as the horses were driven across rock pools and shingle and

440

then lashed again to drum across sand. Erdi unceremoniously bundled his sister into the boat, more mindful of urgency than abrasions and bruises. The Vanya of old would have leapt aboard with the agility of a woodland sprite. Their night things followed, then came the mad scramble to get themselves afloat and out to sea. Vanya was terrified. Her worst nightmares were returning. She sat wide eyed, hunched in the prow tightly clutching her knees as if witnessing serpent devils wriggling after her. The horses were driven into the shallows and writhing, grasping fingers sought to take hold, desperate to wrench the boat back to shore. Two dismounted warriors waded, thrashing and stumbling in the fevered attempt to reach out and haul them in.

"Spear!" Erdi yelled. The weapon was passed to the stern and he continued its progress thrusting it deep into the nearest assailant. He watched the man fall, mouth still gaping wide in shock, hands clutching the javelin shaft, as he slid beneath the surface. Shields, now crucial to survival were hurried aft. Erdi stood and Mardi crouched, between them setting up a defensive wall, one shield atop the other, as the rest paddled furiously attempting to take them out of range. An arcing shower of arrows, whirring flight feathers whispering death through the darkness, thudded onto leather and splashed all about them like gannets diving for fish. Replies from Erdi's sling brought curses, a yelp of pain and a horse scream from the darkness. Hooves were heard heading fast back inland. The riders would now reveal the fugitives' whereabouts hailing down to those pursuing by sea.

They navigated way out from land across a vast expanse of bay and Padlor reassured them saying, even the fastest horses couldn't match their progress. The landward route was a great deal longer and horses would need resting. A rest? Everything in Erdi's body screamed for it, but still he paddled, still he encouraged Mardi, on seeing his brother almost spent. Once amongst the Lefels they'd be safe.

A long gloomy day of incessant paddling was fast turning to night as they sat waiting for the tide to turn, needing it to lift them up over the sandbar to safety amongst the reeds. They sat slumped with exhaustion, their hammering hearts, the only sound, apart from the sighing wind and occasional slap of water against the boat.

Padlor suddenly sat upright. Erdi had heard it too. Each time the breeze slackened the sound of a steady beat carried across the water. The rhythm of it drew closer as if some invisible monster was bearing down on them. The occasional dull drum of wood against wood confirmed their suspicions, they were being hunted. Erdi, straining to see into the blackness, detected a dark shape moving at speed. He wondered, 'had the spirits conspired to foil them when so close to safety? Would they be that cruel?' The menacing nemesis was fast approaching, crew bent together, working together, silent as ghouls; bow wave creaming as the pace increased. Was that craft of toiling demonic intent, from gloom emerging, surging towards them, aiming amidships, on course to ram them?

Padlor's look of fear, a dart of white in the darkness, stirred Erdi from his state of exhaustion. Terrified he shook Mardi, urging him into one last effort. Padlor called out, "Pull! Pull! Pull for you lives! Give all you've got! Get us over that sandbar!"

Even Vanya awoke from her trance, taking up the spare paddle to join them desperately spearing the boat towards the river mouth. If the tide was not up, they'd be stranded, run aground and marooned to be taken captive or slaughtered. Their boat, surging towards safety, suddenly stopped dead, throwing all forward body on body. Erdi and Darew leaping out, heaved while the rest paddled madly, re-floating the craft, now barely ahead of their pursuers.

Eight crew, working as one, silent, inhuman, were only four lengths behind. Skimming the water, bearing down at speed, they hit the sandbar and all aboard ended in a piling tumble of confusion and curses. This respite allowed sufficient time to advance beyond arrow range and Padlor, steering unerringly through the waterways and open pools, knew no stranger unguided would dare follow at that hour. They tied up on his home dock and stumbled ashore, shaking with trauma and fatigue.

The next morning the brothers were awoken early. It was not even light. Two flat-boats set out into the quiet misty marshes on a little mission. Their hunters were to be the hunted. If they had finally ventured into the Lefels they'd need to be taught a lesson. They were spotted, silently stalked and from close ambush, received spear and arrow, without sight of their adversaries let alone having chance to reply. The survivors escaped terrified, bloodied, but at least alive back over the sandbar and out to sea. These would now tell the tale of their close encounter with death and thus hopefully dissuade others from attempting similar. They would regale their comrades with an epic saga of bravery, fortitude and good fortune, but in truth, had Padlor ordered it, every last one would have been a corpse. Which unfortunately for them, is exactly what transpired.

Yes, they returned with a heroic tale to tell, but witnessed to their horror, Tun Mytern, with a face like stone, glaring down at them in a self-contained fury. He was in fact that incensed at their failure, he had them garroted in Tredarn market place.

Meanwhile back in the Lefels Erdi realized they had two choices. They could either ask Padlor to take them eastwards by boat to solid ground, where they could then trek northwestwards to the lower Habren, or wait until the need took him that way, trading for more charcoal from the forests lying west of the great river estuary. As the latter option gave Vanya time to recover from her ordeal, it was the one chosen. She was painfully thin and it still seemed as if her spirit lay trapped out there somewhere waiting to re-connect with her body. Mardi often sat with her, not asking questions, simply talking softly. He spoke of the family, Talia, Luda, her pony and reminded her of funny episodes that had happened during their lives. There seemed to be no light in her eyes or flicker of her old self, but she did appear to listen as his words attempted to gently penetrate. Occasionally a large tear would roll down her cheek and she would whisper, "We left my friends behind."

Erdi's attempt at reason, explaining it had not been possible to free the other girls and that her rescue had been a miracle in itself, received a black look from his brother. Then when he added, "It's reality Vanya, not some bedtime story," Mardi ushered him outside saying, time, not logic, was the best healer. His instincts told him she might return to something like normality once they had completed the circle. Once they were back where the river Gwy entered the Habren. Meanwhile it was best to let her mind heal on its own. Once, when Erdi losing patience, had marched towards where she sat, intent on demanding to know what had happened, what had they done to her on the journey south, Mardi had barred his way with such vehemence, Erdi had been quite stunned. He backed away angered, but once having had time to cool down, admitted his brother had been right and actually deserved respect for his handling of the problem. Let time heal. Meanwhile the brothers would help their new community, taking lessons from how they lived and coped with their strange surroundings, plus of course, they would do all they could to learn how to turn certain rocks into the new metal, iron.

They joined the turf cutting team, setting off with food each day towards the eastern fens. Using iron-tipped spades, fuel was cut and stacked to dry in small dark heaps and occasionally iron ore came to light. The brothers soon learnt what to look for. It was a particularly dull looking substance and if unaware of its potential it would have aroused no interest at all other than the fact some of the rocks made a rattling sound when shaken. It was loaded into baskets and carried back to the boat. Mardi of course, was keen to be done with turf and ore duties, eager to learn the next step in producing the new metal.

Padlor teasing him, said there'd be many more trips turf cutting before passage had been earned on his boat back to the Habren, but after a few days the brothers were told to go and help Bastinas. They learnt to roast and crush the ore, how to build a kiln and how to construct the efficient tall double-drum bellow and tube system that provided constant air flow and intensified the heat. The quantities of charcoal to ore soon became like second nature to Mardi and watching the glow on his face as the slag poured from the kiln base, Basty felt he was not teaching, but simply reminding the young man how the process worked. Together they hammered impurities from misshapen glowing blooms, dragged by tongs from the heart of the kiln and together they hammered, re-heated, folded, re-heated and hammered in a continuous process until gradually a metal bar emerged to be tossed, clanking on to the stack, ready for future use. When needed, these were re-heated in an open kiln, hammered and re-heated to white hot and hammered numerous times on the stone anvil, until between them, they had fashioned an axe head, spear point, ploughshare or any pick of various other artifacts. Erdi could manage the process, but his brother was the master. The skills he'd learnt when bronze smelting, somehow transferred to the new skills required for working wrought iron. Soon Bastinas was quite happy to allow him to operate unaided and was visibly impressed with the fine finish and invention the young man achieved in so short a time.

Mardi not only grew in girth of chest and muscle, his confidence grew to the same degree. It hadn't gone unnoticed. She was the same admirer as on the previous trip. Her name was Fynon. Her family was pleased with her choice of man and Mardi was welcomed like a guest of honour. He was still quite bashful, but they liked him all the better for it. Erdi of course had a warm love for his brother and would miss him

445

terribly if he decided to settle there in the Lefels, but he would put no pressure on him. When the time came, he would simply ask whether he wished to stay or return home to impart his new found knowledge to his own people. He would leave the decision up to him. Watching his brother's growing glow of happiness made him miss Gwendolin all the more. He tried to console himself with the thought they'd soon be journeying home and meanwhile, immersion in their new life in the fens helped alleviate the pain of love sick yearning for his lady and that aching emptiness now Wolf was no longer in their lives.

Some evenings Bastinas was invited to join them and with Padlor translating, the two young men listened in awe to tales of far-off foreign lands. It was hard to believe what they heard: the sheer multitude of people; the size of the armies; the baking heat of summer; the warmth of the strange sea that hardly rose or fell; the different animals and food. They were told of chickens, lions, domestic cats, rabbits, garlic cloves, onions, turnips, parsnips, oats, cabbage, spinach, lettuce, rocket plus other salad leaves, celery, walnuts, chestnuts, grapes, pears, mulberries, a multitude of sweet-smelling herbs and a splendid springtime flower, the daffodil. In comparison they seemed to have nothing. Not all was good mind you for there also existed deadly serpents and a disease spreading food thief, a rat. It all seemed so amazing they looked upon Bastinas not merely as someone from another land, but a man from another world as if he'd floated to earth from the sky. Listening to him opened an exciting window on to life, existing beyond their closed world.

Time moves on, however and after two whole moons Padlor announced the point had come to head north for more supplies before winter closing in made the journey too hazardous. Apart from that, the brothers needed to be at the Habren in time to catch a boat plying upriver before heavy autumn rains made the going impossible. Vanya had regained some of her womanly shape and even seemed to show glimpses of her old self, especially when in the company of a puppy. that for some reason followed her everywhere. Her name for him was Shadow, so that's who he became.

All was made ready for the journey. Mardi explained to Fynon and her family that it was his duty to see Vanya home safely, plus spread the new knowledge amongst his people. He promised a speedy return, spirits willing.

Even though the morning was cool and murky and as yet without sunlight, the whole village assembled to see them off. Many had tears in their eyes, not least Fynon and her family and all applauded when Vanya was handed Shadow as a gift. Bastinas also had a gift, solemnly handing Mardi a tiny package tied with thread. Inside was a needle with a central eye to allow it to be dangled horizontally from a length of twine.

Mardi held it aloft, mystified.

"Which way is it pointing, Mardi?"

He had learnt enough of the language to understand the question. "To the north, Basty."

"Try it again." Once again it swung to the north and then Bastinas holding the blade of his work-knife close, smiled on seeing Mardi's slight flinch of surprise, as the needle jerked to cling to it.

Bastinas explained how he'd stroked the needle with the magic stone from his homeland. Repeated stroking in the same direction had transferred some of the stone's magic. Mardi's needle would always point north and would always indicate the presence of iron. Thus, the most-simple of implements had been transformed into a thing of momentous importance.

Having timed departure to enable them to reach the sea well before low water, they skimmed out over the sandbar to the wide empty waters, no other boat in sight, neither friend or foe. The day would be long, but their hearts were light, with home beckoning at last.

The sun was low by the time they beached on the broad sands of the southern shore of the Habren estuary. Their last two spans of the sun had been tough paddling as the tide had turned against them.

They set out their things for the night and a fire was lit.

"Ooh, mackerel again," said Erdi rubbing his hands together.

Padlor's measured look, melted into a warm smile. He was going to miss the brothers.

The following day, the tide turning mid-morning helped ease their boat upstream and across the estuary, carrying them up to the small trading settlement on the west shore of the Gwy river at high water. Vanya looked around and something seemed to come alive in her face, "I think I know this place," she said almost in a whisper. The first positive utterance heard since her rescue. Erdi gave his brother a look and nodded acknowledgement, he had been right and also chose that moment to hand his sister a small gift.

"My lucky stones," she whispered in surprise and Erdi hugging her and offering a prayer to the spirits, dared hope they had delivered his sister back.

It was now past middle day and Padlor suggested food.
"Something other than mackerel," he said with a laugh. They made their way up to the clifftop hut overlooking the sharp bend in the river and were welcomed like a long-lost family. The headman was sent for; the ferryman was sent for and soon most of the village turned up to hear their story. Vanya didn't shrink from the attention and in fact had started to glow again.

Looking down from where they sat, the dock had more boats tied up than piglets suckling from a line of sows. Since the atrocity in the gorge many boats now traveled in convoy. Once sufficient numbers had assembled, they would either then voyage up the Gwy river or head north up the Habren for the final trip of the year.

Vanya's story had spread amongst the crews faster than a wind-blown grass fire and all wanted the celebrities aboard. Erdi felt spoilt for choice as to who they would travel with, but as departure was not until two days hence, they spent the time helping Padlor, loading his boat with charcoal and other supplies acquired from local traders in exchange for bronze. He was keen to move on all his holdings in the metal and in a way, felt guilty trading it at its inflated value, but if everyone still believed, what was he to do? The load was topped up with all the pelts and furs he could lay his hands on. People always needed warmth and winter was approaching.

It was a sad parting at first light on that final morning. They were all hunched, cloaked and hooded on the damp misty dock. Even the recent midday air had had that cool smell of autumn, impatient summer visitors had gathered in vociferous lines along the drying fishing nets and harvesting had been well underway. Padlor and his son waved as they disappeared from sight down towards the flat spread of dull silver, the Habren estuary. They needed to make fair headway west before the might of the tide turned against them. Erdi's convoy, departing two sun-spans later, would be lifted upstream by that same incoming power.

Chapter Twenty-Seven

Erdi felt drained of emotion. Those he had journeyed with, Garner, Padlor and above all Wolf, had stolen so much of his heart he felt he had nothing left to give his new crewmates as they journeyed up the Habren. It felt almost like a sickness. He helped paddle the craft, courteously answering questions, but had no joy left in his soul. Each time the convoy stopped for the night he was asked to relate more of what had happened on their adventure. Interruptions for translation and enquiries into detail he found tedious, just wanting to help in the day's labours, eat what was on offer and be left in peace to sleep. Yet each evening came payment time, with him required to sit and tell the tale by firelight.

In the gorge they were silenced by a grisly sight. Remains of the river pirates still hung rotting from the trees. Birds had been at work pecking to the bone, transforming last grimaces of agony into macabre, mocking grins. Some of the bodies had fallen for scavengers to rip and squabble over.

Finally, about a half day's travel on from the gorge, just prior to the huge loop in the river leading to Amwythig, the trading settlement on the Habren where their sword had been recovered, the three gave their crewmates hearty thanks and stepped ashore. It would be quicker now for them to cut across on foot to the ford of Hanner Bara fame.

There, they were ferried over the river and the owner of the facility, on recognizing them, refused any offer of reward for that or the food he served. He was astounded, they had actually managed to achieve what he'd thought impossible.

The feeling of being on home territory was not how Erdi had imagined. Everything seemed smaller somehow and snippets of news seemed of little consequence. 'How would they fit in again?'

Hanner Bara hadn't changed. She sidled up questioningly.

"He's not with us anymore," said Erdi. "He's returned to his homeland."

"Lucky the woman who claims him," she said. Hanner had heard of Vanya's plight, as had most and now realizing, the very girl in question was standing there before her, enfolded her in a tender embrace and led the way to a seat beneath the trees. As she spoke, Hanner occasionally took the young listener's hand, or softly touched her cheek. As the conversation continued their heads drew closer and to his amazement, Erdi could see, it was not one sided, Vanya's old spirit seemed to be returning.

Watching mystified he said, "Look at them talking. Whatever can they have in common?"

"Leave them be. It will do her good," his brother replied.

They finally reached home worn out, the day worn out and the dogs, they don't forget do they, welcoming them with tails wagging. Vanya's puppy began to yelp at the sight of them and drawn by the sound, Mara came to the door. With a shriek, she rushed forward hardly daring to believe her eyes and smothering her daughter in her arms, tears of joy streamed down her face.

There was of course great feasting and rejoicing in the family home, but beyond their compound the news was left to filter out in the most muted way possible. There were two reasons. First a stream of visitors, well-meaning or not, was the last thing Vanya needed on her way to recovery and also the truth of their story could not be told on account of Wolf's major part in it. The locals found it rather strange, Penda not calling for a general gathering in celebration, but there again, his had never been considered what you'd call a normal local family. In fact, some hardly considered them locals at all with

451

old Tollan, Vanya's grandfather, having originated from way out east somewhere. The swords and shields the brothers had carried home, were hidden, even though on that last section of the journey, they had felt no qualms at retaining their possession. Having to avoid warrior patrols between Habren and home had seemed as if nothing, mere child's play, compared with all they had been through.

Gradually Vanya began to appear like her old self. She found it comforting to be in Luda's company and was relieved no-one pestered asking, 'is anything the matter?' when sitting alone in the dark with her thoughts. Erdi once found her clutching an overhead branch, pallid and still as a lightning tree down by the stream with tears in her eyes. When he held her gently, she sobbed, convulsing uncontrollably. Mara said later, it was exactly what was needed.

Erdi, with family blessing, rode over Elsa's ridge to ask Gwendolin's father for his daughter's hand. The poor girl, visibly shaking, asked, "How do you know I even want to join with you?"

"Do you mean you don't?"

By way of answer, she flung herself into his arms.

The question of dowry was resolved thus. News had reached Prince Gardarm of the brothers' miracle rescue of Vanya along with a less palatable item of interest: his subjects held him directly responsible for events leading to her abduction. He demanded that the brothers appear before him, 'To be brought to account!' Instead, Penda and Dowid represented, saying the boys were no longer in the valley. This in fact was true, for after a quiet joining ceremony Erdi returned with Gwendolin to her family home. Mardi had gone with them and the food and shelter both received, was considered sufficient dowry.

Gardarm became extremely heated at the term, unknown whereabouts. 'How dare they take it upon themselves to talk to him like that!' He boiled himself into a fury, pronouncing, that anyone passing on the scurrilous rumour linking certain members of the noble family with the enslaving of four wenches from the valley, would be hunted down with vigour and severely punished. The mere fact that he, in such a powerful position, had felt a need to say that, rather than simply rise above the supposed slander, was proof enough as far as Penda and Dowid were concerned, the man was guilty.

With Mardi being safely over the far side of Elsa's ridge, he could now turn his hand to producing the new wonder metal. The word went about and a small number of young men filed to his door to take instructions in the art. All managed the basics, but very few possessed the skill needed to turn out tools and implements of fine quality.

One bright day Yanker came calling. Lady Rhosyn had expressed a wish to venture forth hawking. She was accompanied by her loyal maid in waiting and her trusted warrior guide, Yanker.

On their arrival, Erdi smiled to himself, thinking it hadn't taken his cousin long to charm his way into probably the most coveted post in the fortress. While Rhosyn was entertained by Gwendolin, the cousins talked together like old times. The three visitors of course swore never to reveal the brothers' whereabouts and just prior to leaving an odd thing happened. Lady Rhosyn on spotting a loose thread on Yanker's shirt reached forward, removed it and gave a gentle brush of the material to flatten it. She looked to Gwendolin slightly shocked when realising what she had done. The latter, mistress of tact, ingenuous of countenance, gave no hint of having surmised anything and instead, lightly scolded Erdi for not having had the thought to fetch Lady Rhosyn her horse.

The arrangement on the far side of Elsa's ridge could of course be only temporary. Someone always talks in the end. Gardarm given sight of the new metal, had proclaimed it a crime, punishable by death, for any caught owning implements made from iron let alone caught smelting the substance. Operations were moved to hidden valleys and deep into the woods and the brothers on Trader's advice moved into

Y-Dewis territory where they were welcomed and given protection. Thus the art of iron production spread west. Gwendolin was now with child and the Y-Dewis women seemed to love nothing better than making a fuss of her.

Chapter Twenty-Eight

The Teller paused briefly and took a drink.

Now we need to take the story forward. Erdi's son was well into his second year when one of the Bleddi warriors came through. He was a hulking brute of a man and Erdi thought it strange to see one of such imposing stature, appear so hesitant and nervous. He said he was journeying into Erdi's homeland to ask for the hand of a woman he'd spotted the day they'd been driven in battle, from the west gate of Gardarm's fortress. He described the lady in question and Erdi realised it could be none other than Luda. The warrior was desirous of Erdi's opinion regarding his chances before throwing caution to the wind and continuing further. One had to be bold in such matters, but there again no man wants to make a fool of himself. Erdi telling of her whereabouts, said as far as he knew, she was still unattached and gave the encouraging opinion that Luda, would in all likelihood view such an offer as a most prized gift from the spirits and readily accept. As it happened, she did just that and accompanied her champion up into Bleddi hill country glowing with gratitude at how life had turned out for her.

Meanwhile back in the valley, the old chieftain had journeyed on to the land of his ancestors and his passing was marked by a huge ceremony to which virtually all his former subjects attended, showing their last respects as his ashes from the funeral pyre were gathered and laid to rest in the revered and ancient royal burial mound. This left Lady Rhosyn a widow and her son, a prince too many.

Prince Aram had not been seen for many moons and rumours abounded as to his fate. The official story, that he'd ventured forth to procure a reliable source of tin had been dismissed out of hand. There had been no reports of him journeying down the Habren nor sight of him and his retinue on the Dwy and so people began to feel a sense of dread as Gardarm announced he would become an official guardian to the second in line to the throne, Rhosyn's son. He was that concerned for the boy's safety he had him watched night and day, secure in his own special place of confinement. A place not dissimilar to the one Erdi remembered so well. Then the horrifying rumour circulated, there was now no sign of the lad at all. It was at this point, on hearing a warning of impending incarceration and the menace of feet tramping towards them, that Yanker and the fair lady in his care, took flight. They sought protection in the Salter capital before eventually moving south to that prominent hill east of the Habren where he that now rules over all, resides. Lady Rhosyn had her jewelry, her handmaiden, her loyal protector, her life, but not her son. It was said she was almost sick unto death without him.

The bad weather that had blighted recent crops, far from being something to be dealt with until things improved, actually became normal and famine was talked of. The tribes in the western heights were becoming angry and restless. No amount of bronze sacrificed to the spirits made any difference and the spreading knowledge of the new metal began to make their reverence for the old seem pointless. At grand tribal gatherings there was talk of abandoning their homeland to settle in the fertile valleys to the east. Trouble was brewing.

Folk living in those supposed favoured valleys hardly considered life easy, as they also had to cope with the cold wet summers, but at least they were surviving. Not the family who had taken on slaves, however. The wet weather had inundated the recently reclaimed land and under the terms of the agreement, produce from their original holding was forfeited to pay the annual slave tithe. Under the pressure of this and dread of ridicule, the father had hung himself and the two eel-thief sons had fled south. The slaves wandered the valley taking any work they could in exchange for food and the smallholding down by the slow stream lay abandoned like a testament to greed and folly.

Way back in those ancient times, just as now there was a messaging system. If anyone's business took them near a main settlement, whether located atop a hill, deep in a valley or beside a river they would take it upon themselves to go out of their way to gather any news and do their best to relay it on to the intended recipient, trusting a helpful soul would reciprocate if or when it was their turn to be the beneficiary. The system helped keep people in contact with distant friends and relatives and also satisfied the curiosity of those who relished having access to other peoples' business. So just as there are those who love nothing better than to wallow and make a fuss over the illness or misfortune of a neighbour there were also those who seemed to somehow come by more than their fair share of news. Devotion to this pastime elevated them above mere gossips and attained them the collective title of 'carrion crows.'

The system served a good purpose, but of course was not recommended if you needed to pass on a secret. In fact, if desirous for a story to be spread far and wide, all that was needed was to whisper in the ear of a 'carrion crow.'

Apart from obvious lack of privacy the other drawback was reliance on the messenger to remember exactly what they had been told and to pass it on accurately. It wasn't at all uncommon for the content to be unwittingly altered as happened with the message, "Your wife will be glad to have you back again," being relayed down the line, to arrive as a bit of a stinger, "Your wife was glad to see the back of you!"

Anyway, the whole valley and the Y-Dewis knew that Mardi had a romantic connection way down in the south and that he would be heading that way as soon as he felt his duties had been completed. He was thrilled to hear that Fynon was still waiting for him, but unfortunately their messages reached other ears. Ears of those not moved by romantic notions.

The brothers had been warmly welcomed by the Y-Dewis people and were respected for their wisdom and abilities, rather than being judged by the fact that, not only were they no more than low born sons of a smallholder, they had at one point even spent all their daylight hours cleaning latrines. Erdi slid effortlessly into the chieftain's top circle as advisor and storyteller, plus they noted he was also a fair shot with the sling. As for Mardi, what had Gardarm been thinking of losing a man so skilled in metalwork and divination? Their respect verged on reverence. They clung to him like a gift from the spirits and always referred to him by his full name, Mardikun.

The esteem in which he was held had been all very well, but it did make trying to break away and keep the promise to his loyal Fynon, a touch difficult. Other opportunities were stealthily put his way in the hope of tempting him, but no, he was a one-woman man and Fynon was that woman. He was determined to journey south the following spring.

The time for the Autumn Fair was imminent. The brothers thought it wise not to venture forth for obvious reasons, but the Y-Dewis leaders attended as usual, needing to trade for the essential salt. They returned with a strange tale to tell. Everyone had been more than a little interested in the chance to see the boy prince, Rhosyn's son. Well, not to see him as such, but witness the fact he still lived. He had been an annual visitor even when only a babe in arms and now that rumour had it, he'd not been seen of late, his absence from the fair would be viewed with justifiable suspicion. Rather than have to concoct some lame excuse why he, Gardarm, the boy's protector was there without him, plus having to answer questions regarding the disappearance of his own brother and the prince's mother, he decided it made more sense to evade all questions and send the chief court advisor in his stead. Rival chieftains from both east and west had relished the chance of probing Gardarm for familial information, almost rubbing their hands with glee at the thought of witnessing his discomfiture, but their sense of deflation at having this denied was more than compensated for by what happened next.

Trader, having listened intently to Erdi's warning regarding the likely demise of bronze, now realised that not only could weapons and implements be made to a far higher standard from the new wrought iron, there was the added bonus, they were no longer beholden to their local chieftain for the raw materials. He thought it high time to devise a plan. His trading brain told him that when something went out of favour it didn't just taper off gradually, its appeal crashed almost overnight. He needed to do something with the bronze he'd amassed and quickly. He gathered a few worthies around him, Penda included and asked for their trust in allowing him to invest their small hoards along with his. Change was in the air. They had full faith in him and joined in his scheme.

At the fair the Salter chieftain asked as usual who would bid for his salt and instead of having to haggle with the only man with the wherewithal to take the whole consignment, he found on this occasion he was faced with two contenders, Gardarm's representative and a man known to all as Trader. He would let them fight it out. The bidding was brisk and there were gasps as the value of the salt soared beyond wildest dreams or for those in dire need of it, nightmares. It seemed the world had gone crazy. With an angry shake of head, Gardarm's man said he was no longer participating in such madness and Trader became, to everyone's surprise, holder of the salt.

The Y-Dewis chieftain when relating the tale to Erdi said, he knew Trader was his close friend and didn't wish to find fault with the man, but what happened next was baffling to the point of being wrongheaded. Trader refused all offers of bronze for the salt, saying only gold would procure it. The ordinary people, of course not having possession of such,

459

were incensed and virtually besieged the spot where the man traditionally carried out his business.

As regards possession of gold, apart from Gardarm, who of course wasn't present, the Y-Dewis chieftains were the only other holders and on doing their calculations it seemed Trader was willing to part with his salt for less than he'd given for it. They traded with what little gold they happened to have and topped up their full salt requirement with a handshake of trust. More gold would follow. These were men of their word.

Trader, on attempting to leave the fair, met with a problem, having been surrounded and noisily harangued by those in desperate need of what was sometimes referred to as white gold. Without it, how would they preserve enough meat to last them through winter? In attempting to placate, he was even beset by his own partners, the very men who had pledged their trust in him. They demanded their share of the salt immediately. Trader asking for calm, eventually managed to take them to one side and reason, it was time to keep their nerve, bide their time and above all, time to maintain trust in him, because he knew it didn't look like it, but things were actually going according to plan. Ten days is what he asked for. As a sign of good faith, he handed over the remainder of the bronze they held in common and told them to use it wisely, trading for pelts and furs only. He would hold back enough salt for their winter needs and the final details of their enterprise would be sorted out at the end of the tenth day. Penda felt the whole thing didn't make sense, but told the partners, he still had trust in the man's judgement and advised them to do as Trader had recommended.

This allayed fears somewhat and with their help parting the crowd, Trader went on his way, leading the small convoy of three carts, leaving behind a swelling sound, not dissimilar to bees quivering up the notion to swarm.

He returned home avoiding the fortress. A rider would have already told Gardarm the shocking news and Trader wanted any dealings done on his home ground, not on

Gardarm's. Also, it wouldn't do any harm to give time for the man to cool down. He didn't envy the court representative's task explaining why he'd let the salt go. Trader imagining the scenario, chuckled to himself.

To open negotiations an official, not the one who'd lost the salt I hasten to add, was sent accompanied by an armed guard for the oxcart carrying the bronze. Trader instantly dismissed the offer, telling the man, the deal was gold or nothing, hadn't they been listening and how dare they insult him with fake axe heads! They were the new poorly fashioned imports, good for nothing other than for trading. Whoever had smelted the things had skimped on tin and hadn't even taken the trouble to smooth the rough edges left over from casting.

Trader stressed that he would accept gold for his salt and nothing less would do. The amount of salt for trading was weighed and the amount of gold required in that trade was clearly stated. Again, it was obvious the man was letting the salt go for less than he'd given for it. Prince Gardarm was reluctant to part with gold, but the man was clearly a fool and ought to be taken advantage of.

The representative returned with the gold, the deal was done and Gardarm let it be known, with the salt now being in his possession, it was there for trading. As the bronze poured in, Gardarm visibly gloated at the amount of profit and the people thought Trader must have not only lost his touch, but also his senses. His partners growled amongst themselves, but still waited.

On the sixth day Trader whispered something of import into the ear of a 'carrion crow'. The man was told it was confidential and to keep it secret. Soon the whole valley knew, as from that moment on, Trader would no longer be taking bronze in any form for his goods. He would trade, animals, food, furs, pelts, grain, beer and anything else of the like, but not bronze.

It was Grik the fish who shone a shaft of light on Trader's latest mode of operation. He was doing his rounds again and on listening to general derision regarding the man's dealings, pronounced, Trader's manouvering to be the smartest business move he'd ever encountered. With the vision of an outsider he said, "It's brilliant! Don't you see? You don't need bronze anymore." He was like the spark that burnt the forest down. "You have iron right there beneath your feet."

That's all it took. A sense of panic set in. Those trading their goods up at the fort declined the bronze offered, but would take anything in its stead. Gardarm could see his world collapsing around him. He needed to take drastic steps and quickly. A proclamation was sent around the territory stating, refusal of royal bronze was an offence punishable by imprisonment. Supplies to the fort instantly dried up. What was the point in trading worthy items for something that would soon be worthless? Meanwhile it was obvious, the value of silver, amber and of course gold, was about to soar. These were commodities that could be easily transported and if needs be, hidden. They would retain their worth come rain, feast or famine. With the new metal just lying there ready to be picked up, bronze was no longer needed and sacrifice of it certainly hadn't helped the weather. It was still cold and wet.

On the tenth day Trader's partners had a little meeting to divide their spoils. It wasn't the actual business of allotting the correct shares that took the time, it was the feasting and drinking afterwards. Celebrating to a degree commensurate with the success of their venture, kept them up the whole night through to the following morning.

The Teller paused and looked at his audience. You might be thinking, how was it all happening so quickly? Almost breathtaking speed. But you have to understand, Trader had been right. What had bound their society together for countless generations was now collapsing like a dam breaking. Bronze tools were still used of course, but that's all they now were. Useful tools. Bronze was no longer an inflated form of currency.

Gardarm's next move was not to trade, but to levy what he needed from his subjects. He sent troops to help themselves. As before, it was argued the people needed protecting and those protecting, needed feeding. The people were robbed to the point of starvation. A finely balanced system was teetering on the point of collapse. The only thing that prevented outright rebellion was fear. Gardarm bought his warriors' loyalty with privileges and bronze, but even they were beginning to wonder whether their once prized hoards were becoming worth no more than a pile of useful utensils on a flooded market.

King Gardarm, as he had started to call himself, became ever more desperate and erratic, his panic surging all the more, once realising he was now entirely alone. He had no one to turn to. He had become isolated. Where was Aram when he needed him? Why wasn't he there? Why had he left him to battle alone? Aram should be there helping in the valiant attempt to maintain the structure of the revered system. How could it be collapsing? Something that had been so long established couldn't just collapse! He paced the great hall and raged to the heavens. What had been his bastion of power was fast turning into a trap.

"Why am I so alone? Find Aram for me!" Courtiers eying him in fearful silence, realised the man was going mad before their very eyes. If he didn't now know what he'd had done with his poor gentle brother then he was capable of anything.

As his demons closed in around him, Gardarm's face began to take on a haunted look. "It's not me to blame," he ranted. "Why do they haunt **me**? Why are their faces driving me mad?"

They gave him no rest. Servants feared for their lives as he wildly slashed his sword in a crazy fevered attempt to exorcise. But try as he might the devils remained. If he drove them from one place, they simply rose up in another. They knew they could bide their time. Taunt him when he least expected. One even leered from the surface of his beer, laughing as the mug was flung down in horror. Why could no-one else see them? He demanded the Seer come banish them.

The man arrived, horrified to witness Gardarm shaking as if taken by fever. He did his best to hurriedly concoct some form of incantation, but of course it did no good and no matter what else Gardarm tried, his demons could not be driven away. If he fled one place in an attempt to escape, they seemed to anticipate, arriving before him to rear up and taunt him at the next. They leered, mocking, knowing soon he'd need sleep. Then they'd have free reign to torment as he thrashed back and forth through the night. He grew to hate his bed, eying it as a vehicle of torture, waiting to take him on yet another fevered journey through darkness.

In the waking hours his brain raced, plagued with helplessness and confusion. Belief needed to be restored. Bronze had been revered almost to the point of worship. The knowledge of it had come from the spirits. It was therefore considered, once fashioned into worthy items, to be the ultimate embodiment of gratitude when gifted back to those spirits. Gardarm was in deep wild-eyed torment, as inside his head, bringing searing stabs of pain, an intense battle raged. He had been the main upholder of the belief. The belief in bronze. He had been avid in his commitment to the spirits. So why had those same spirits now turned against him? Why was the weather like constant winter? The incessant rain blew in from the southwest. Knowledge of this new metal had also emerged from the southwest. The spirits were offended, insulted by this new abomination, iron. Rid the kingdom of iron and everything would return to normal. The soaking deluge driven in on the south wind would cease immediately. 'That's it! Get rid of the iron!'

I know it sounds crazy, but the man was driven to the edge of madness seeing his world crashing about him.

His warriors were sent out on a campaign of terror. People in fear of their lives informed on neighbours, houses were burnt, stores were raided, starvation loomed and finally two men were dragged in for having produced the banned metal for distribution. The poor wretches were paraded through the villages, nooses round their necks. The Seer proclaimed to all, 'The spirits had been offended by the people spurning them. The spirits themselves had gifted them the magic of bronze. Gifted the chosen ones, the secret of its fabrication. Return to bronze and fair weather would return along with it.' The two men were hanged down by the Arrow Field.

Only Elsa had dared speak out in their defence. The rest of the tribe had been shocked, confused and petrified. They attempted to cling on through the coldest months, but many old, infirm and new born didn't make it through to spring. The frosts were almost over by the time old Tollan lost his fight with fever and some dreadful thing that had gurgled in his lungs. The news reached the brothers who immediately prepared for the journey to pay their last respects. Mardi packed extra. for he wasn't postponing it any longer, he intended to travel south. He felt a sense of elation. Fynon would be waiting for him. Their journey had to be done in secrecy and at night.

They took refuge at Trader's, on the morning of the funeral and under cover of dusk, set out again, to arrive home as Tollan's pyre was blazing. They received quiet greetings and warm embraces. There were some tears, but it was more a celebration of the man's life than time for sadness. Penda's words of tribute gave thanks to the fact that without Tollan and grandma Vana the rest of the family would not have been standing there in tribute. The prevailing mood was like a gathering to see a loved one off on a pleasant journey. Tollan had had a good life and his soul was now being guided by the spirits to a better place. He would be joining his ancestors. Food and drink, was of course on offer and Mardi ate quickly. He could not risk a prolonged stay. He was given extra provisions for his journey.and at last would be heading south, to the place where he'd felt most alive. Back to Fynon.

Suddenly, from out of the darkness, the man posted as lookout ran towards them, panic on his face. He shouted for Mardi to flee for his life. Close behind, a small troop of soldiers, with the Seer at their head, cantered into the firelight.

To the horror of all Mardi was seized. "By order of King Gardarm we take this man into custody. His collaboration with evil; his secret concoction of a banned substance has brought disaster to the land." Out from the trees, more warriors urging their ponies into the light, confirmed the compound had been surrounded from the very start. The Seer, with a sickening look of triumph, swung his mount round to leave and Mardi was manhandled astride a horse to be led away, hands tied and a noose dangling from his neck. Screams of protest and cries of rage made no impression on the bristling array of spears.

Everyone was there for the execution. The portion of the Arrow Field nearest the Hanging Tree was packed, but nobody believed it would really happen. Surely they couldn't go through with it. At the last moment, all thought he would be reprieved. It had just been a show of strength to frighten all into compliance. Doubts began to creep in, however, when Elsa, in a piteous state, was hauled before Gardarm. They had hunted her down and some brute had left an angry weal across the side of her face. The self-proclaimed king gloated as warriors, with unseemly relish, ripped the clothes from her body. The crowd gasped, then groaned, hardly believing what they were witnessing. The poor woman was beaten and forced to crouch inside a wooden cage. Her once beautiful auburn hair now hung lank and grey. She was hauled up to the branches and as the small pen began to slowly rotate, many groaned and sank to their knees, unable to believe what they were witnessing.

The Seer's voice rang out. "You see before you the caged witch known to all as Elsa. If she is so powerful, why does she not free herself? If the spirits she consorts with are so powerful, why don't they help her fly to freedom. Spreading his arms, he called out mockingly, "Fly Elsa, fly!" A smug, sickening smile accompanied, "Need I say more?" Then in a lofty tone he sneered, "She ought to consider herself fortunate, for up there she will be benefited with the most advantageous of views," before adding with menace, "To witness the fate of the malignant one. The one who has consorted with evil and brought the wrath of the spirits down upon us! Brought cold and starvation to the people! Has lured the gullible into dangerous new ways! Insulted the spirits with this new abomination, iron! We sacrifice this man in the cause of good! To show that evil has been beaten, his body will be taken from here on the morrow and cast into the cold black waters. That witch, trapped like a bird, will be dragged there to join him!"

The women screamed and Mara made a frantic effort to reach her son. The crowd was beaten back and Mardi called out over his shoulder as he was bundled towards the hanging tree, "Erdi, save me from those waters! Don't let them --------" The rope was slung over a branch and Mardi was hoisted aloft, his writhing legs receiving spear jabs.

"Dance! I want to see you dance!" The owner of the spear wore an eyepatch.

The crowd, with hands to faces in horror, couldn't believe what they were witnessing. Penda, launching himself forward in a last desperate effort to save his son, was beaten to the floor.

"Hang him alongside his son!" ordered Gardarm.

An almighty screaming above the roar of protest caused him to pause. "Out of the kindness of my heart I let this man go free." But be warned. "Any attempt to encroach on this most holy of sites; any attempt to come near before that witch's evil has been drowned from her body, will meet the same fate as the condemned." He turned to his troops, "Now disperse them!"

The crowd was forced back. Erdi, having realised his lone effort would not have saved his brother, had climbed unnoticed into the branches of a nearby tree. He waited, holding back his grief, anger and hatred, keeping it burning inside like a furnace. As the day wore on and the last of the multitude had been driven off, the warriors also began to drift away back up to the fort. Finally in the twilight only two remained on duty, squatting, talking and laughing quietly up on raised banking. The subject of their jesting was Elsa, but I'll spare you the details.

Erdi slipping from his lair, crept to where his brother hung slumped from neck down. The tail end of the noose had been tied off to a nearby sapling. Erdi lowered his brother, still limp, gently to the grass. An angry cry rang out from the top of the hillock.

Erdi felt no fear, only rage. "Come meet the future," he coaxed offering his dagger. It was iron. "That's no answer to this!" roared the warrior hurtling downhill, his bronze sword raised.

Erdi whirling his sling, said through gritted teeth, "But this is!" His erstwhile friend, spread-eagled by the impact, tumbled and slid headfirst to arrive Erdi's feet. His good eye blinked open, thus enabling Blade to witness the only sharp thing to ever enter his brain.

Erdi looked up. There had been a second guard. He spotted him scrambling up over the bank. There was a whirr of sling and a stone pinged off the top of man's scalp. Erdi, light of foot, topped the bank and caught the man scrambling away like a crippled dog and a blade, that had been beaten and quenched to hardened steel, opened the man's throat through to the spinal column.

Elsa's cage was lowered and on crawling free, her attempt to stand brought a gasp of pain. Erdi, preventing her from falling, supported until the worst of her crippling stiffness had passed. He stripped Mardi of his clothes for her to dress. The poor woman was dithering with cold and his brother had no further use for wool and leather. He managed to lift the corpse across his shoulders and they set out towards his home. Mardi was not to be cast into the cold black waters. Elsa with face once so bronzed, but now pale as iced milk, pushed on ahead doing her best to clear a way, pulling back branches to aid his progress.

Avoidance of the main path and the weight of Erdi's burden made the going painfully slow. Darkness had descended when the demented cries of hunting dogs reached them. Fearful glances exchanged, conveyed there would be no chance now.

They reached the stream the brothers had played in as children. The old willow, the Easy Tree, that even an infant could climb, was still there. The yelping and belling of the dogs echoed through the woods, the spine-tingling sound closing in upon them. Harsh urging shouts from the warriors and their horses' pounding hooves sent ice through the veins.

Erdi looked about in desperation, "We'll go upstream. Lose the scent. I'll help you up into that willow."

Elsa followed and beneath the tree, she clung grimly to Mardi's corpse, while Erdi, avoiding leaving any telltale scent on the bank, pulled himself directly from the stream, up into the branches. He reached down and hauled up his brother's corpse.

"Now you, Elsa."

Looking up and with eyes brimming, Elsa turned, crossed the shallow pool and stumbled off through the trees. The hounds arrived, wheeling, searching, eager for scent. One slavering brute frantically weaving back and forth near the willow, was too intent nosing the ground to look up. The scanty willow branches were still not in leaf and even at night, such a born hunter would have recognized the profile of a figure hunched low in hiding. A cracked-bell howl of triumph excited the pack into a yelping frenzy, fighting for places in loping pursuit of the fleeing woman. The warriors thundered through and without breaking stride, crashed on amongst the trees in a fevered blood lust. Erdi with his brother's body cradled in his lap fought back the memory of their first time there as children. Their vow to always return. He clenched his teeth in the effort to shut out the memory of his young brother's entreaty. "Can we always return to the Easy Tree? Promise? Even when we're grown up?" If he had allowed such memories to flood his brain, all strength would have dissolved into uncontrollable grief. Mardi was lowered with the care he would have taken had he been still alive. He followed jumping lightly to ground. He'd not gone far when the sound of screaming and cacophony of growling, ripping and barking reached his ears. He froze in horror, but somehow had to force himself to continue forward, on through the living nightmare. He stumbled towards home, bearing his brother, not as he'd proudly carried him all those years before, but prone across his shoulders.

He managed to resist the compulsion to roar his grief to the heavens, the intense effort to fight it back, working on all but his eyes. Everything seemed to swim and hardly able to see his way forward, he beseeched, muttering through clenched teeth, as if his brother still lived, "Hold on. Hold on, I'll get you out of here Mardi. No tears. No tears, Mardi. Tears later."

Winter had passed and fuel was scarce, but what they had was loaded into the playhouse and Mardi's enshrouded corpse was laid across it. The little hut had been where those astonishing visions of their world's interrelation with sun and moon had first sprung into his brain. It seemed a fitting place. Mara was brought a stool. Standing on it she lovingly tucked her son in, combed his hair and softly placed a kiss on his cheek as if bidding her boy goodnight. Penda gently led her away. "Let him go now, Mara. The soldiers will be here."

Low hanging branches crackled and sparked as tongues of flame from the inferno leapt taking Mardi's spirit skyward. Those in the small gathering held each other in grief, tears streaming as they watched the pyre collapse and engulf the dark shape of Mardi's body.

Erdi couldn't risk staying. He had ensured his brother's remains had been saved from desecration. His spirit saved from an eternity in the cold dark waters. He needed to be clear of the valley before morning and so mounting Vanya's pony, leant down to hug his mother and Vanya one last time. Holding back the tears he said, "Take care of Mardi's spirit. Lay him gently to rest."

Both nodded, incapable of speech.

"And say a prayer for poor brave Elsa? She gave her life for me."

Penda, as ever a comfort said, "With those hounds? She wouldn't have lasted long."

Erdi groaning inside, exchanged a look with his mother, words not needed. Each knew what the other was thinking. He pulled away sadly from those arms outstretched with such longing. He was given wishes of luck and good fortune by all. He vowed to return. He vowed to all and the listening spirits, his brother's murder would be avenged.

When the soldiers came calling all they found was a small community, an innocuous pile of smouldering ashes and an angry silence. Questions were eventually answered, but with a glowering defiance and no regard to honesty. These people had nothing to lose now and that made them strangely threatening. The commanding officer, as if he himself had been moved by events and converted to some burgeoning new form of religion, felt a compulsion to confess, explaining to blank faces, "We thought we were pursuing two people, your son, by some miracle brought back to life and Elsa. In the end it was just the one the dogs caught. Somehow Elsa and your son had become one." Although receiving puzzled looks of disbelief, he continued, "What have we done? Two people, two spirits becoming one. What have we done?" With shake of head, he led the soldiers away.

When the ashes had cooled, Mardi's charred bones were gathered, broken and placed in a funeral beaker. A special place had been made for him up in the ancient cairn. Reverently interred with him were his blackthorn wand, boar's tusk necklace and magic needle.

Some in the Teller's audience had tears in their eyes. I'm sorry, *he said*, but this is how it happened. I know I made the telling almost irreverently brief, but believe me, relating the tragedy of Mardi and Elsa is never easy. No matter how often I tell the tale I always feel a dread as this part, looming like a black cloud, awaits. I know the legend of Elsa and Mardikun persists to this day. I've often heard the haunting ballad; watched the scenes acted out; two souls joined by tragedy, but what I'm telling you now, I know it's sad, but this is what really happened.

I'll now take you forward a little in time. When Erdi returned to the Y-Dewis with his terrible tale to tell, the tribal leaders were incited to great anger and insisted on immediate vengeance. Erdi, although also boiling inside with hatred, suggested caution and careful planning. They needed to amass food, extra weapons, clothing and siege ladders. On his instruction a huge iron cone was fashioned. It would be heated and beaten, to clench when cooled on to the sharpened end of a felled trunk and used to batter down the fortress gate. They would not fail to gain entry as had the Bleddi warriors.

The force set out from their western fastness, accompanied by women, children and all their livestock. Not just a mission of retribution, but a full-scale invasion. Progress was slow, but determined. With their families camped safely in the borderlands the attacking force swept on towards the fort. Many local men joined them. Servants, women, children, artisans and their families, against Gardarm's orders, had all fled the bastion. He was alone with his Seer, his holy men, his garrison and his demons.

The ensuing battle was intense, fearful to behold and decisive. The main gate, with flanking guard towers ablaze and structure unable to withstand the iron-clad battering, flew open. The Y-Dewis, with Erdi at their head swarmed inside slaughtering all, whether resisting, surrendering or fleeing. No quarter was given. Defenders were hunted down like animals. Gardarm was dragged from where hidden in the Great Hall.

The age of bronze was to be given a fitting end. The Seer was ordered to officiate; call for the spirits to witness; bless the flames; bless the very instrument of retribution. His master was stripped and dragged over to the trunk that had smashed the gate open. Bent over its girth, he was carefully strapped in place, for his backside to receive the red-hot blade of his late father's gigantic bronze sword, offered up for a fitting.

There arose a few hoots of involuntarily laughter from the audience.

Down in the valley, the close-gathered throng, looked at each other aghast. They realized something extraordinary must have happened, for not even a stuck pig screamed like that. Many had covered their ears. The Seer was then ordered to go forth, descend and throw himself on their mercy. Looking down from the smashed and burning east gateway, his wispy white hair blowing in the breeze, the Seer, petrified at the sight of his own people silently awaiting, beseeched, pleaded for leave to remain. Jabbing spear points forced him down from the hilltop. Erdi had had plans for him and Gardarm to swing from the same branch they had hung his poor brother from, but events had spiraled way beyond his control and the Seer was swallowed up by the very people, that had so long been held in his power. To quote Penda, 'He wouldn't have lasted long.'

The Teller looking down at his audience, smiled and said, So, my Lord and you most wonderful people, you have been very patient - that concludes my tale. The knowledge of iron had arrived. The knowledge brought to his people by Mardi.

The Y-Dewis were welcomed as settlers and rulers. Erdi continued as trusted court advisor. His cousin Yanker took on a similar roll in that prominent fortress to the east that now rules over all. And if you scratch into the ancestry of the leader there, you'll discover a certain amount of Yanker's input. He and his lady, Rhosyn were blessed with children.

Their beautiful daughter, Bryda married the chieftain's eldest son and when the old ruler died, she found herself queen to the new lord above all. The start of a dynasty.

Oh and Vanya. What happened to Vanya you ask? If I'm honored by an invitation to return one day, I'll relate more of Vanya's story. *The Teller waited for the cheers to subside.* But to suffice for now, she married her prince and that most respected of lords sitting below me now is their direct descendent.

The room burst into a thunderous applause.

The chieftain standing in acknowledgement, raised the massive pendent he wore. It was a finely napped handaxe in a gold surround.

The Teller bowed to his host, trying not to reveal how stunned he had been on seeing the relic he had described, materialise right there before him. When all had calmed, he cleared his throat and continued.

So we return to aged Erdicun at Vanya's funeral. He led the sad procession up to the place prepared in the ancient cairn. Vanya's urn, bedecked by her amber pendant was gently laid within. Other items, beads of colored glass and earrings of gold were added before finally, Erdi placed amidst all, two small perfectly round white pebbles. Each had a tiny face incised. Vanya's lucky stones.

He said sadly, "Goodbye, Vanya. Please look after Mardi until I get there."

Old Erdicun turned and walked away from the grave his eyes shining with tears.

The following morning the whole community gathered for the Teller's departure; leaving to wend his way to yet another gathering; welcomed there with a tale to tell; crafting words; endlessly attempting to paint pictures in people's minds. His horse was absolutely laden with gifts the people had insisted he take, undeterred by his protestations, he'd already been amply rewarded by the chieftain.

He was followed by old and young, filing in silence, down to the lower gateway. They felt dejected seeing him go. The general mood was not only brought on by respect and a genuine love for the man, but also by the sadness at the realisation he would no longer be there to endow that sense of feeling special. Now it would be back to the daily grind with little to look forward to. They found it hard to imagine he would make another tribe glow the way he had them. He of course had his trade to ply, but surely now it would be in an indifferent manner, not connecting with other communities and plucking at emotions as he had with theirs. The thought of him putting heart and soul into doing so, almost engendered a sense of betrayal.

All peered at the figure slowly heading into the distance, wanting to be sure he actually rode from sight. Some had speculated he might just vanish off the track right there before their eyes, spirited away to somehow catch tales from dim history and gather more strange words out of time with their world.

All watched in silence as the Teller drifted out of their lives.

Rough Sketch Maps For The Tale Related By The Teller

From all the clues handed down from the story as related by the Teller I've managed to produce these very rough sketch maps. Although the topography in the late bronze age would have been completely different, I have still managed to give a rough approximation to the rivers, coastal route and the main hill forts and other settlements. It was exciting to find corroboration from archeological finds.

The river Hafren was obviously the bronze age precursor for the Welsh, river Hafren, or river Severn in English, meaning the Gwy must be the Wye, Dwy the river Dee and Nwy the Vyrnwy. This would put the main hill fort, central to the story, at Old Oswestry and the capital of, 'he that ruled over all' in the iron age, would have crowned what is now called The Wrekin. The Salter capital is where Beeston Castle now so splendidly sits and the Feasting Site would have nestled in a river loop somewhere in the region of Bangor on Dee.

Central to everything is of course Erdi's hamlet. From all the clues in the story this must have been at what is now Whittington Castle. I'll let you fill in the other locations. Only if the wish takes you of course.

The first sketch map shows Erdi's home territory, the second shows the route taken in section four, the third, that taken in section five and the fourth shows the southern portion of the Tinner realm. Tredarn of course must be modern day Bodmin, Crooked River, the Camel and The Old Men on the Hill, the Trippet stone circle.

The Author.

Rough Sketch Map For First Three Sections Of The Story

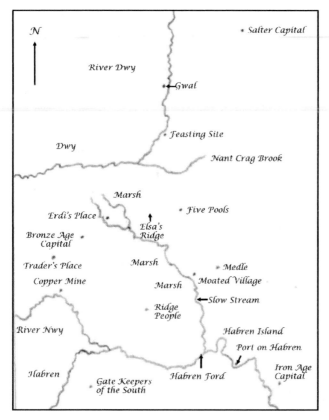

Sketch Map for Sections 1, 2 & 3

Rough Sketch Map For Fourth Section Of Story

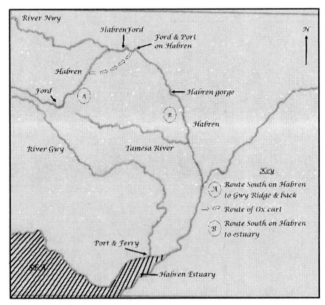

Sketch of map showing route taken in Section 4

Rough Sketch Map For Fifth Section Of Story

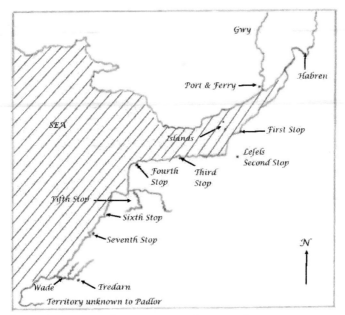

Gwy

Habren

Port & Ferry ⟶

SEA

Islands

⟵ First Stop

Lefels
Second Stop

Fourth
Stop

Third
Stop

Fifth Stop ⟶

Sixth Stop

Seventh Stop

N

Wade   Tredarn

Territory unknown to Padlor

Sketch Map showing route taken in Section 5

Rough sketch map showing southern portion of the Tinner Realm

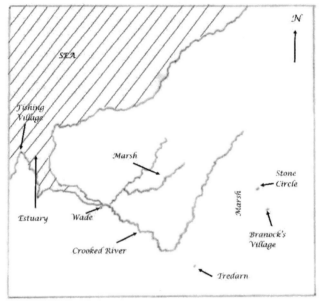

Sketch Map of Tinner Realm